THE BALLAD OF CURLY OSWALD

THE BALLAD OF CURLY OSWALD

By Curly Oswald

IndieBooks

The Ballad of Curly Oswald
By Curly Oswald

ISBN: 978-1-908041-29-6
ISBN: 978-1-908041-30-2 (ebook)

Published by IndieBooks Limited
4 Staple Inn, London WC1V 7QH

www.indiebooks.co.uk

Set in Minion Pro 12/14

Printed by TJ International, Padstow, Cornwall

For all my friends and family, wherever they may be.

With many thanks to Charlotte Knott for her valuable input.

INTRODUCTION

HI. I'M CURLY Oswald.

That's something I don't get to say these days, but lately I've been feeling a need to assert my true identity – after having spent almost all my adult life as someone else.

The thing is, officially I don't exist. I never have done and presumably never will do. I've had to rely on a kind of ghostly doppelgänger to get me through administrative situations, one who doesn't share either my real name or my nature – or my sex, for that matter. And to whom I'm eternally grateful, for a multitude of reasons.

To begin with this alter ego was just a name, a useful and necessary mask; gradually, however, it became easier to use it not only on official documents but in my private life as well, though I still asked friends and lovers to call me 'Curly', maintaining it was a nickname I'd always been known by. But now it seems that the mask has almost entirely taken over and has even acquired a character of its own – one which is very unlike and perhaps unworthy of the remarkable person who originally bequeathed it to me.

Until a few weeks ago none of this bothered me; I didn't think about it and wasn't even really aware of it. The transformation has been slow, unnoticeable to someone such as myself who isn't normally given to dwelling on the past. The present supplies more than enough to occupy the mind.

At least it did: but not any more. Not since my circumstances were turned upside-down by two events. The first was quite trivial, yet led directly to the second, a personal cataclysm which was to hurl me back like a boomerang into my intrinsic Curly-ness. The boomerang analogy is quite apt, in fact.

*

I was at a cocktail party, networking. I've become good at this, having developed a talent for discreet showing-off, gently smiling my most 'charming and mysterious smile' – (I quote my hostess) – which somehow manages to persuade both men and women that I possess talents and knowledge which are essential to their wellbeing and can be found in no-one but myself.

The party was in Monaco, on a yacht. Like its owner, this yacht is large and ostentatious. The owner's wife is considerably smaller than her husband but has an even greater desire to dazzle, very obvious this evening as she came tripping towards me in a shimmer of jewels and haute couture. She was followed by a glittering-eyed blonde who I thought I recognised from somewhere – an ex top model? Some other kind of former media celebrity? Both women had complexions like gleaming stretched plastic and perfect pearl-white teeth, reminding me that I should get my own fixed, now that I could easily afford it. I just never seemed to have the time.

'Here he is!' cried Mrs Kalashnikov – (obviously not her real name, but it will do for present purposes). 'Our genius!'

I'm used to these people. They have more money than they know what to do with but they can never have enough flattery – which has to be deferential without ever descending into servility. The women like to be flirted with, but in a 'alas-I-know-it-can-never-be' fashion which doesn't get you, or them, into trouble with their menfolk. On the contrary, it makes the latter feel even more enviable; not only are they far, far richer than you, they've also got the luscious female goodies that you can only dream about. They're not to know that my dreams do not include their Barbie dolls. As compensation for what they see as my inferior status they will graciously open their wallets in return for services rendered.

I readied myself to flirt. 'Mrs K!' I exclaimed, taking her outstretched hand and bending over it in a restrained but meaningful way, as if only enormous self-control prevented me from smothering it with kisses. 'Do you know that you are looking particularly gorgeous tonight?'

She acknowledged the compliment with a little sideways nod and one of her characteristic grunts. I released her hand and turned to her companion. 'And so are you, Madame, if you will allow me to say so.'

I was rewarded with a blink, a flash of brilliant turquoise, a surprising colour which I assumed was provided by tinted contact lenses.

'Jo-Ella has a *very* wonderful villa on the Cap d'Antibes,' said Mrs Kalashnikov, speaking as if this fact was the entire justification of her friend's existence. 'But...' She gestured helplessly. 'You tell him, *chérie*.'

Jo-Ella sighed despairingly. 'Yes – it is wonderful – I had it all redone just a few months ago – but it just isn't *right*. When I'm there I feel so – well... kind of – *restricted* – you know?' She had a soft, blurry American accent and spoke so quietly it was hard to hear her against the party chatter all around. Suddenly she tossed her head and the silk waterfall of her hair glistened like a shampoo ad. Perhaps that was where I'd seen her before.

'And then I saw *all this* –' she swept a hand vaguely but dramatically around her – 'and I knew right away it was the style I needed. So I just had to meet you. I need someone who can empower my inner visions... I'm sure you understand.'

I leaned a little closer – not too close, just enough to show that I did indeed understand. 'You think I might be able to rebalance your home?'

She touched the arm of her hostess. 'Tammy tells me you're fantastic with *feng shui*.'

'I have had the privilege of studying with one of the great traditional Chinese masters.'

'That's *sooo* cool... when could you start?'

'Well, I'm committed to a couple of other projects at the moment so I wouldn't be free to begin the real work for a couple of months.... would you be willing to wait that long?' I looked searchingly into her contact lenses. It was just possible to make out the edges.

'I guess so – I have to be in Geneva soon – how about October?'

'Yes, quite possibly... autumn is a very propitious time for transformation. But of course I'll have to make a preliminary visit so I can absorb the aura of the place. I need to know if the basic structure is correctly aligned.'

'You mean it might have to be turned around or something?'

'Not necessarily. Sometimes it's just a question of moving a door or a few windows. Or knocking down a wall or two. It sounds to me as if you have a problem of negative energy build-up, so it'll be essential to clear all the blocked pathways of the vital forces. Then we can concentrate on the rest – colours, fixtures, plants – all the elements which will optimise a healthy and positive energy flow.' I handed her my card. 'I could probably look in next week – if that would be convenient for you, of course.'

'Oh, *sure*. I'll call you tomorrow.' She gave me the kind of look that convinced me that she would.

Mrs Kalashnikov beamed. 'You see? I knew. I always know.' She gripped Jo-Ella's elbow. 'Now come my darling, I must introduce you to the Prince...'

As they disappeared into the crowd I found myself involuntarily looking behind me, as you do when someone unknown is staring hard at you. I saw straight away that I was being pierced by a glare of beady intensity, aimed at me by a slim woman with long dark hair who was sitting on a bar stool only a few feet away. She was wearing quite a simple black outfit and at first I took her for one of the stewardesses, until I noticed her scarlet high-heeled sandals – not really standard footwear for a stewardess. She also had some hefty diamonds attached to her ears. If she hadn't looked so overtly hostile I would have found her attractive.

'Good evening,' I said pleasantly, in an effort to deflect her animosity. Perhaps she had mistaken me for someone else.

'Christ, what are you?' she spat. 'Why do you act like a smart-arse bourgeois Pom?'

'Probably because that's what I am,' I replied amiably. Although I'm not used to verbal attacks by fellow-guests at my clients' social gatherings, there didn't seem to be any point in returning fire. She was almost certainly drunk. She also sounded Australian – and I'm a sucker for an Australian accent.

'Well, you don't look like one,' she said shortly.

'Looks can be deceptive.'

Her eyes narrowed. 'I can see through people, you know.'

'That must be handy.'

'You don't really believe all that crap you were spouting just now.'

'Sorry?'

'Oh, for Christ's sake. That *feng shui* bullshit.'

What the hell did it have to do with her? 'I find it can be very helpful to certain people,' I answered, as silkily as possible.

'Helpful! These people don't need help. They need a kick up the backside.' She took a big gulp of champagne and held out her glass to the Filipino steward behind the bar, who refilled it impassively.

'And yet you accept their hospitality.' Now I was beginning to want to fight back. 'Or are you just here for the booze?'

'Very funny, Mr Pom.' She leaned her elbow on the edge of the bar counter and it slipped off. She seemed to deflate a little. 'I'm here as a fancy accessory to my husband. That bogan over there that's chatting up the tart in the purple mini-skirt and the two-metre platforms.'

'You mean Terry Evans?' I know him slightly, in his professional capacity. He's the broker who sold the Kalashnikovs the yacht, and who in fact recommended me to them.

'I didn't realise -'

'He was married. Yeah, it's easy not to notice. I hardly notice it myself half the time.'

There wasn't a lot I could say to that, but it went some way to explain her anger.

'But that isn't why I'm having a go at *you*,' she said, rather unnervingly. 'It's not some kind of displaced hatred thing. Terry's got bugger all to do with it. I just thought when I saw you, there's a person who looks like I could have some kind of normal contact with, and then it turns out you suck as much as the rest of them. Because you've decided to play their game.'

'Listen, I'm just an interior designer. I'm not going to bite the hand that feeds me.' She'd got me on the defensive now. Shit.

'So you're responsible for this Disneyland kitsch, I suppose.' She jerked her head towards the stars twinkling in the ceiling, and waggled a foot contemptuously at the transparent pedestals of the bar stools, filled with liquid in which lighted bubbles changed colour as they rose upwards. 'And the trashy artwork,' she added. She was referring to the *trompe d'oeil* panels along the walls of the saloon, illusory niches overflowing with flowers and dimpled nymphs. Philippe, the artist I'd hired to paint them, had done a really good job there.

'I'm responsible for realising the fantasies of the people who pay me to do so,' I replied, trying to inject humour into my voice but aware that I just sounded pompous.

'You mean like a whore.'

'No, like a professional.'

'That's what I said.' She slammed down her glass and walked off unsteadily.

I saw her wobble and almost fall, but I didn't even think of going to her aid; gallantry had deserted me. I was alarmed and annoyed that I'd let a few drunken insults disturb my usual cool. Why hadn't I been able to stay 'zen', as the French say? Did I really have such a swollen and fragile ego?

In an attempt to restore the party spirit I drank three glasses of champagne in quick succession, but they didn't seem to have any effect. So I left.

Out on the quay the air seemed oppressively hot after the yacht's air-conditioned interior. I started up my trendily retro Vespa scooter without putting on my crash helmet: I needed the wind in my hair. Tough luck if I was stopped – I'd just have to pay the fine.

I set off in the direction of Villefranche. At any rate I thought I did, until I realised a few minutes later that I'd taken a wrong turning. Fucking Monaco – nothing but swooping Grand Prix bends and tunnels and ridiculous one-way systems. At night it's like being in a golden high-rise maze. Infuriated, I doubled back and accelerated sharply.

I have no memory at all of what took place next.

*

When I woke up, three days later, I thought I was dead. Everything was white and unfamiliar – the walls, the clothes of the man and woman peering down at me. Could they be angels or were they simply other dead people? Then I tried to move and a shaft of red-hot agony zipped through me. Clearly I must still be alive, because as far as I knew you weren't supposed to feel pain after you died – but what had happened? I couldn't make sense of what they told me: I was in hospital, I'd had an accident. What accident?

I was aware that these people were speaking sometimes in French, sometimes in English with a French accent, but I couldn't work out why. They wanted me to tell them my name. Then I realised I couldn't remember what it was.

This obviously worried them – but not half as much as it worried me. Amnesia is no fun at all. I was lucky – it only lasted for a few hours, during which I plunged around helplessly inside my head searching for a past and an identity which had loosed their moorings and vanished without trace. I think I became almost delirious with horror, and with pain too, as I couldn't stop twitching my head in my abortive efforts at recall. Eventually someone gave me an injection and I sank into exhausted semi-consciousness.

It was while I was in this state that a faint greenish light began to suffuse my brain – very slowly, as if on a dimmer switch. Then objects started to come into focus. Trees… a bonfire… a caravan…. YES! I knew this place. And I knew my name.

'Curly Oswald,' I murmured. It hurt to speak, but I felt suddenly ecstatic. 'My name is Curly Oswald.'

There must have been someone close enough to catch my words, because all of a sudden there was a flurry of voices and activity which brought several medical staff to my bedside, asking me to repeat what I'd just said. When I did, they frowned. 'But can't you tell us your *real* name?' asked one of them softly.

I was bewildered. Why didn't they believe me? 'I'm Curly Oswald,' I insisted. 'Ask the others, they'll tell you.'

'Others?'

'Ashley, Zoë... anyone. Stella, Jelly Bean, Rick –'

I stopped short as another layer of memory flipped into place, and I remembered the truth about Curly Oswald: my non-existence. And I was able to pronounce the name that my assembled audience was hoping to hear. Everyone smiled. But my euphoria had faded: instead I felt oddly desolate.

The feeling wouldn't go away. It had nothing to do with the fact that very soon I was able to grasp the full extent of my injuries, and understood that it would be many months before I could start earning a living again – by which time I'd be virtually broke, if not in debt, as I'd never bothered to take out private medical insurance. Strangely enough, all that didn't worry me. It was something else.

That night I dreamed I was lying on the grass, in warm sunshine. Abruptly, a large shadow blotted out the light. 'Get back to where you once belonged,' said a female voice. It had an Australian accent. 'That's just a song,' I said. 'It's a fact,' said Ashley, for the voice had changed and it was he who was speaking now. 'You're a traitor. Write it down.' I felt I was sinking back into amnesia, and woke in panic.

So that's what I'm going to do – write it down. That's to say, record the past, a past I've not so much denied as completely neglected, so much so that for some years now I've allowed myself to drift through life without truly being at the helm. That's why my second self has smothered Curly Oswald. I don't mean I want to go back to using that name – in any case, I don't see how I could, apart from in these pages. But it's Curly who should be driving the boat.

*

I want to write as well as I can, in honour of the dead as well as the living, all those who were part of that rather curious bubble of space-time in which I spent the early part of my life – a sort of anthropological backwater of the late twentieth century. It was by no means completely cut off from Outside, as we called the rest of the world, but it was not at all what Outsiders considered normal. In fact many of them saw it as dangerous, a menace to civilised society.

It's true that most members of our community would have liked to bring about social change, but not in any threatening kind of way – more through being a shining example that sooner or later everyone else would want to follow. An over-optimistic aim, but one which was based on good intentions.

I shall change the names of the places and most of the people – including, for obvious reasons, the one I now use myself. But to everyone who helped to make me what I am – or rather, what I'm not – I want to say what I should have said at the time: thank you. And I hope you're still grooving along.

1. WATER BABY

I WAS BORN in a pond, in southern English woodland, on a fine evening during the summer of 1969.

'When's *my* birthday?' I asked, present aged three at Elvira's ninth birthday party. I remembered my own last party, but not the date it had been attached to.

'First of August,' said Gogo promptly, who could see that I needed a magic day to call my own, just like any other Western child. So August the first it became, even though later on I grew to understand that no-one was at all sure about this. An unusual lapse for such a zodiac-minded group of folk, but understandable when you bear in mind that for much of the year most of them had no idea of the date – apart from Electricity Bill, who needed to be on time for his work engagements, and his partner Ginnie, our astrological expert and calculator of horoscopes. At the time of my birth they were still away visiting a guru in India. They'd planned to be back for the event, but my mother, notoriously unreliable, had miscalculated when it would be by several weeks. I'll never even know whether my arrival in the pond took place before or after Mankind's Great Leap on to the Moon – an event which had been largely disregarded by our community, dismissed as imperialist American propaganda.

'Well, he's obviously a Leo,' said everyone. 'Aquarius rising, probably.'

At any rate, I must have arrived before the end of August, because I was taken as a tiny infant to the Isle of Wight Festival, strapped to my mother's bosom in a beaded leather papoose made by her companion, Erryk. For once – no doubt with Erryk's help – she'd managed to get her dates right, convinced that the vibrations of the Festival would be good for my emerging consciousness. Whether they were or not I can't say, but apparently I remained calm throughout – perhaps reduced to a semi-comatose state by the marijuana smoke drifting among the crowds. I didn't even complain when Bob Dylan arrived on stage late and obviously grumpy. 'Oh man, they've fucked his head,' Erryk would often say sadly. 'The managers, the System...'

But back to the pond.

It was warm, limpid green and dappled with sunshine. Water boatmen darted lightly over the surface and tiny fish nibbled at my mother's ankles. Despite a sprinkling of algae around the edges the water wasn't stagnant, as it was fed by a small stream which trickled down from a spring higher up in the woods. This spring, shaded by holly and ash, was considered sacred by our community and was known as the Mother's Spring, in honour of Mother Earth. We called the pond Galadriel's Pool, and the little watercourse which flowed out of it and down to the river, Galadriel's Hair. There was some tenuous connection here to the River Ganges, believed by the Hindus to flow from the hair of Shiva; not a very apt connection perhaps, but it added to the holy ambience of the place, and it's not hard to understand why my mother had chosen to give birth here. 'My waters mingled with the Mother's,' she would say. 'It was the perfect welcome for you.'

Being young and fit, and having had a problem-free pregnancy, she felt no need whatsoever to go up to the House and call the nearest medical services when her contractions began. Instead, she stuck to her plans for a Natural Birthing Ceremony. She simply abandoned the wispy watercolour she was attempting to paint, and rolled and smoked another joint. Then she removed her clothes and staggered off to find her two best friends, Marjoram and Tiger Lily, who were to be my Fairy Godmothers. Supporting my mother between them they made their way down to the pool. Others, including Erryk, had offered their help, but having consulted various oracles she had decided that this simple female trinity would provide the most powerful and appropriate combination of forces to assist her. The oracles had – correctly as it turned out – predicted a boy, and my mother believed that only a carefully balanced concentration of femininity would be capable of zapping the more undesirable of my male tendencies. These the three of them would somehow vaporise and disperse with the aid of suitable incantations.

Marjoram, although she had never completed her nurse's training, had at least some rudimentary knowledge of midwifery, and came armed with a kettle and a camping-gas burner, an African carved wooden bowl, many cloths of handwoven Indian silk, and a pair of silver sugar tongs 'just in case.' She also brought along a bottle of one of her herbal concoctions for my mother to sip when the pain became intense. Tiger Lily was less practical but provided spiritual sustenance by improvising tunes on a bamboo flute – the reason, perhaps, why this type of music has always had an unsettling effect on me.

Not that my birth was a difficult one. My mother's labour lasted through the afternoon and into the early evening, but several joints later, as the sun was beginning to set, she gave a great shriek – 'a Cosmic Cry,' said Erryk, who had heard it from the caravans, as indeed had everyone else – and there I was, a pinko-beige tadpole wriggling in the shallows. The sugar tongs proved quite unnecessary.

'You slid out like a fish,' said my mother, who had been keen to name me Minnow.

'Too slippery,' objected Marjoram. She was deeply into medicinal plants and thought I should be called Borage, one of the ingredients in her bottle of Birthing Juice. 'So he'll be rooted in the Earth, and grow up to be a Healer. And it sounds so masculine – in the positive sense of the word. *Borage*. It's got something strong and noble about it.'

But my mother disliked the fact that Borage rhymed with porridge, something which reminded her of her allegedly unhappy childhood, and in any case she didn't want any pressure put on me to become a healer or anything else. If there was one thing she was adamant about – (in general she was too vague – or stoned? – to be adamant) – it was that I should have the freedom to express myself in any way I chose. I don't know whether she would have been ecstatic had I channelled my freedom of choice into, say, accountancy or mainstream politics. As it happened, by the time I began seriously to consider my adult future, she was no longer around.

In fact, the question of my name was settled very quickly. Once Marjoram had neatly bitten off the umbilical cord and I had been cleaned up and dried off, with all traces of blood, mud and algae wiped away, it became clear that I had a surprising amount of blond curls on my head. 'Oh, he's so *curly*,' said my mother, leaning back exhausted against the trunk of an ash, myself already clamped firmly to a nipple, while Tiger Lily played on and Marjoram rolled another joint.

Tiger Lily gave a joyful tootle and waved her flute in the air. 'Curly!' she exclaimed. '*That's* his name.'

'Curly, groovy,' murmured my mother.

'Well, it's cool for now,' said Marjoram. 'You can always change it later, when the curls fall out. Hairy babies go bald after a week or two.'

'That'll still be OK, ' said Tiger Lily, 'Curly's what we call bald people in Australia.'

'Anyway, once his aura's a bit stronger it'll transmit his *real* name to you,' added Marjoram. 'His *Inner* name.'

But the curls stuck, and so did the name. 'That's because your aura was already so, so, powerful, it gave us your true name right away,' Tiger Lily told me.

For the last part of the ceremony, Marjoram scooped up the afterbirth from the bank and slipped it into the wooden bowl along with the umbilical cord. She and Tiger Lily helped my mother to sit up, me still at her breast, and together they chanted the Anti-Negative-Maleness spells over myself and the bowl and sprinkled both with pond water and wildflower petals. When I was a few years older I used to beg them to repeat the spells to me, as I thought secretly that if I recited them backwards I would become fiercer and stronger. But they never would tell me, maybe because they guessed my motives. 'Secret women's business,' said Tiger Lily, quoting an expression of the Australian Aborigines from whom she claimed descendance.

Finally, setting me carefully down on one of Marjoram's pieces of Indian silk, my mother cast the contents of the bowl into the pond, as a sacrifice of thanks to the Earth Mother and a tasty snack for the fish.

Her two friends helped her to her feet. Up till this point she had been naked except for a silver Egyptian ankh hung round her neck on a leather thong, but now Tiger Lily pulled from her kaftan pocket – (at the front, like a kangaroo's pouch, in honour of her putative Australian bloodlines) – a filmy green garment which she placed over my mother's head. 'You are a mother. You are of this Earth.'

Marjoram lifted me into my mother's arms and the four of us set off slowly in the dusk up the slope to the caravan, where Erryk had prepared large quantities of his nutritious root soup. Everyone had gathered in a circle around the caravan steps. Incense smouldered, candles flickered, the first stars twinkled. As my mother walked towards them she sang softly the lullaby she was to sing to me all through my infancy: *'Curly Wurly, Curly Wurly Curly, Wurly Curly Wurly he sa-a-ang. Here comes the Curly Wurly man, still singing songs... of lo-o-ove ...'* It was her version of a number by Donovan, *Hurdy Gurdy Man,* said to be about a drug dealer. The only clear recollection I have of my mother's voice is of her singing this song, monotonous and hypnotic.

*

Her own moniker was Wing, or at any rate this was the name she had chosen for herself even before she moved to Lothlorien, as our little colony was called. Erryk had never known her as anything else. Years later when I was sorting through her things, I discovered one of her old fairy-tale books tucked away under a bunk in the caravan, the flyleaf bearing a signature in a child's handwriting: *'Brenda Oswald.'* Of course the book could have belonged originally to her sister, or even an aunt, but I rather like the idea of my mother having been christened Brenda. It betrays, to my mind, a pleasingly ninety-fifties petit bourgeois origin. Unlike her, I have no quarrel with the petite bourgeoisie, even if I don't want to join their club. After all, they're the hobbits of our time, leading industrious if unadventurous lives in clean and tidy bijou residences. (This, of course, is just a fantasy about what I never had. I'm well aware that in reality those twee semis can harbour wild eccentricities, angst, even evil, just like anywhere else. And who knows what Wing was escaping from? She never went into much detail about her past. 'I only came alive when I moved here,' she would say. 'All that went before is just a horrible mist...' And then she would change the subject).

It may well have been my maternal grandparents who bequeathed to me a genetic predilection for tidiness. I like to be able to find things easily and I appreciate a certain visual order, in contrast to Wing who was utterly chaotic – the gene skipped a generation. Already at the age of five or so I would go around the caravan folding up scattered clothes and stacking dirty plates in neat piles, much to her alarm. 'It's so they look smaller,' I protested.

Although, along with petit bourgeois convention, she had discarded 'Brenda' (or whatever), she had hung on to 'Oswald' – only she had modified it to 'Os Wald'. She claimed that the name had deep connections with the Earth, as Os means 'bone' in French, and Wald 'forest' in German. Her new initials also had a strong appeal, and she embroidered, stamped and painted them all over the place: W.O.W.

'Wow!' exclaimed everybody when they looked at the big flowery curves which decorated the bright blue door of our caravan. Literally flowery, as she had painted pink roses on the two ends of each W and daisy petals all round the O.

Soon after my seventh birthday it struck me that my own initials would be C.O.W. Appalled, I complained to Marjoram. 'I don't want to be a cow. Cows are girls.'

'But cows are sacred,' she replied. 'Didn't Arjuna tell you that? It's really cool to be a cow.'

'Arjuna was an arsehole.' I hadn't cared for Arjuna at all.

Marjoram frowned slightly. 'Maybe. . . Some of what he said made sense, though. Still, if you really don't like Os Wald, why not just be Oswald, all in one word?'

Relieved, I announced my decision to Erryk. He looked worried. 'C.O.? That stands for Commanding Officer. Too much like the army.

Wing wouldn't like the sound of that.'

But I did. And Wing wasn't there. So the next time Erryk went off to sell his wares I overpainted her initials on the door with fighter planes and tanks. 'How do you *know* about those things?' he asked despairingly when he carne back that evening. He wasn't aware that the twins, Rain and Shine, had a children's encyclopedia which contained pictures of these fabulous objects.

As a concession to Erryk, and because I was after all essentially a hippie child, I had also painted a big C.O. with the C as the moon and the O as the sun, and underneath I added E.G., Erryk's own initials, carefully coloured brown inside a large pale green egg. I wondered why Wing had never thought to add his to her own. After all, he lived there too.

When I pointed out these additions to Erryk he smiled sadly. 'Very nice, Curly. But that isn't how you spell egg, you know. Never mind.'

It was around the same time that I stopped wanting to hear about that aquatic summer afternoon – the Birth Idyll, as Erryk called it. He had obviously been expounding on the subject one day when I strolled out of the woods, hoping for a snack, and found him in conversation with a friend of his, an Outsider, who had dropped by for a visit. She was a plump girl who smiled too much, or so it seemed to me. Perhaps she had designs on Erryk and was trying to insinuate herself into Lothlorien as his new companion. If that was the case, my subsequent behaviour may have helped to change her mind.

'So is this *him?*' she gushed, reaching out in my direction. 'Your little dwelling-mate?'

Dwelling-mate! This term was new to me, and sounded totally soppy. I scowled and drew away, repelled also by her hands in their greenish-grey lace gloves. Mouldy, I thought. Rotting leaves.

Erryk gave one of his melancholy smiles and pulled on his soft, draggly beard. 'Yes, this is Curly. Curly the Water Baby. He of the Birth Idyll.'

The stranger gave a gasp – of pleasure or amazement, I couldn't tell and certainly didn't care. She opened her arms as if to engulf me. 'And are you going to be my little friend too, Water Baby?'

A flash of anger shot through me like a bolt of red lightning. Itwas the first time I had consciously experienced such rage. 'I'm *not* a baby!' I screamed. 'Idyll, widdle, tiddle, PIDDLE!!' So saying, I spat loudly on the ground, as I had often seen Ash do, and stormed back into the woods. I don't remember ever seeing that girl again.

Quite apart from the instant dislike I took to her, I was indeed far from being a baby any more, and no longer wanted that phase of my life discussed in public. Although later on in life I began to appreciate it again, I was, as I realised on that day, sick and tired of hearing about my amphibious entry into the world. But until then I had thoroughly enjoyed hearing the story – from any of the major participants, each of whom had their own distinctive style of telling it.

Marjoram's account was probably the most down-to-earth. She had herself given birth the year before, to the twins, and she was perhaps a little envious of Wing's back-to-nature experience.

'Of course your mother was lucky,' she would say. 'In my case there were complications.'

'But couldn't you have done something with your herbs?' By now Marjoram's herbs had the reputation of being practically all-powerful.

'Rain and Shine had a different karma,' she said matter-of-factly. 'They had to go through all that hospital shit before they could come out the other side. Which they did, thanks to the afterbirth rites.'

She had insisted on bringing back this item from the hospital in a Moroccan earthenware jar which she had specially prepared and blessed – (herbally) – for the purpose. The afterbirth had then been buried by herself and Gogo, the father of the twins, in the clearing close to the Pool, and crab-apple seeds planted on top. Aptly enough, two of these pushed up shoots to the surface and appeared to be growing well. The twins themselves, after a sickly start, began to be healthy babies soon after these shoots appeared. They were non-identical, a girl and a boy, and they didn't look much like either of their parents. 'Flower fairies of the apple blossom,' said Wing.

Marjoram herself was a tall, large-boned girl. She had a round, flattish face framed with short wavy brown hair – ('too much bother to grow it') – and uncommonly small but sweet features: narrow dark-blue eyes which twinkled as if shot with slivers of sapphire, a cherubic mouth, and a little snub nose set between rosy cheeks. Her manner was generally brisk and jolly – she would have made a good matron had she stayed in conventional medicine.

Tiger Lily was a completely different kettle of fish. Dark and voluptuous, she was always a bit grubby and dishevelled, though somehow that only added to her appeal. Her fingernails, for instance, were chipped and dirty, (unlike Wing's which she constantly filed and cleaned), but the dirt was mainly oil paint and smelt gorgeous. The rest of her exuded an intoxicating blend of patchouli, sandalwood and musk. She had a great mass of dark springy ringlets, dusty but streaked with gold, and they fell across her big brown eyes and full, sensual mouth... Yes, of course, I was mad about her.

She gave off an aura of lazy, amused sexiness which I found irresistible even as an infant, and I would gravitate instinctively towards her rather than to Wing. She let me rub perfumed oils on to her neck and arms, and cradled me in her lap while she told me stories. Hundreds of them. She was a born storyteller. According to her, at the moment of my birth: 'the Rainbow Serpent flashed his tail in the depths of the Pool... I saw it with my own eyes, Curly.' Maybe she really was partly Aborigine, or perhaps that was just a myth she'd woven around herself. It didn't matter. She was certainly Australian, and used some thrilling Australian expressions.

'Christ, I'm so hungry I could eat the arse out of a low-flying duck,' was one of my all-time favourites, and when I was around four or five I would beg her to repeat it over and over, while I rolled on the ground almost sick with giggles.

'Don't keep saying that, it's cruel to ducks,' protested Wing, but Tiger Lily just laughed. 'Bloody hell, Wing, get over it. It's a joke.'

Wing... my biological mother, certainly, but not my emotional one. Marjoram and Tiger Lily shared that role, and they were maternal in their attitude towards her as well. She was only eighteen when I was born, several years younger than they were, and she looked even younger still. I suppose her fairy-like appearance, along with liberal doses of dope and magic mushrooms, really had convinced her that elfin blood flowed in her veins. That's how she'd chosen to play her life, at any rate. Ethereal.

She was slight, with that translucent skin which looks almost blotchy in places. I used to trace with my finger the patterns of faintly indigo veins which showed each side of her pale grey eyes, and around the rims of her ears. These I found particularly fascinating, as they were rather large for her size and stuck out quite markedly, poking through her long fine white-blond hair. 'Elf ears,' said Erryk, who, as I realised later, was very much in love with her.

She was already pregnant when he discovered her at a Christmas market in Hampshire, shivering by his stall in a tatty Afghan coat and grey mittens. She told him she had left her parents and was living in a squat: he offered to take her with him to Lothlorien and she agreed. It was probably the name of the place that swung it for her, as she never seemed more than mildly fond of Erryk, though she never showed any antagonism towards him either. Previously he'd just been plain Eric but she changed the spelling to make it more elvish and of course he didn't object, being the kindest, gentlest of men and a natural-born hippie.

His soft brown hair, (the colour of beech leaves in winter, said Wing), fell copiously around his long, rather doggy face and large, mournful dark eyes. But behind the mist of melancholy which hung permanently round him, he was remarkably practical – just as well, as Wing was hopeless. And he was a model father-figure to me, at least during my earliest years.

Who was my 'real' father? I haven't got a clue. He must have had very curly hair and presumably darkish skin, as mine is a light tan colour with a few freckles, and my eyes are brown – 'medium sherry', Zoë used to say. I've inherited my mother's ears, but nothing else as far as I can see. My hair grew considerably less blond as I grew older, reaching a shade which Tiger Lily flatteringly termed 'bronze'. The curls became if anything tighter.

'Your dad? Some wandering minstrel, I expect,' said Jack much later, when I started to wonder a little. When I was small the question never even crossed my mind. Us children felt we belonged to more or less everybody, although naturally we each felt closer to certain adults than to others.

'*You are a child... of the Universe,*' sang Erryk as he strummed on his guitar, and that seemed good enough for me – as it did for all of us in Lothlorien.

2. *WELCOME TO ELFLAND*

I'M AWARE THAT all this perhaps sounds too good to be true, but in fact that wasn't the case. Not all the members of our community spent every waking moment of their lives drifting around in a drugged fog of loving peacefulness – though a few certainly tried to, Wing being one of them. In reality, life in Lothlorien contained plenty of action, not all of it welcome: there were practical difficulties and clashes with Outside, besides sporadic conflicts and jealousies amongst ourselves. And there was the occasional tragedy. But it was only the great dramas that really affected us children, such as the havoc wreaked by Arjuna, the kidnapping of Chipolata, the Invasion, and the terrible story of Neat Pete.

In spite of the ups and downs, our little world held together pretty well, at least during the years when I was living there; at that time it was still possible to believe, providing you didn't live Outside, that the Age of Aquarius was just around the comer. One of the binding forces was the powerful conviction held by all its members that a simple, 'natural' life of sharing, caring and soft drugs was the only way to go. Material excess was out, inner discovery and home-grown were in. The setting helped, of course.

It's time I enlarged on the origins of Lothlorien – or 'Elfland' as we sometimes called it, as in the bark of a huge beech at the edge of the settlement someone – (Ashley, I think, though he always claimed they were there before he arrived) – had carved the words *WELCOME TO ELFLAND*. Zoë had suggested the name *Lothlorien* and everybody found this highly appropriate, Lothlorien being one of the places where the elves lived in *The Lord of the Rings*, a book that all self-respecting hippies regarded rather as a Mormon might regard the Bible. We were so steeped in it that as a small child I believed it was factual history, and keenly awaited the Second Coming – or would it be the Third? – of Gandalf the Magician.

Back then in the 1960s, when peace and love and equality were all the rage, there were a few rich and privileged individuals who began to have twinges of guilt about being the beneficiaries of inherited wealth. It wasn't the first epidemic of this type of unease; in the thirties certain well-off aristocrats has chosen to throw in their lot – and their cash – with communism and various other left-wing causes. This time around they leaned less towards pure politics; they wanted to be like the hippies and renounce materialism in favour of sex, drugs and rock'n'roll, with a touch of the the Mystic East thrown in for good measure. Thus they, too, could explore the Inner Self and get rid of their hang-ups. Those who felt themselves culpably fortunate tried to assuage their guilt by mixing with the truly cool, hoping that the latter's authenticity would rub off on to them. So they frequented their hang-outs, paid their restaurant bills, and learned the joys of cannabis, LSD and magic mushrooms.

Such a person was the man who we all referred to as Our Lord – although I don't think he really had an official title.

'Our Lord my arsehole,' Ashley was fond of remarking on his bad days.

'What's wrong with him?' I once asked idly. I wasn't that interested in Our Lord. In those days, I wasn't aware quite how much we all owed him. He was just a rather amorphous and diffident figure to be seen from time to time hovering in the vicinity of Bill and Ginnie's caravan, long-haired yet somehow clearly not one of us.

'Bloke with a load of bread he didn't earn,' said Ash in reply to my question, pushing back his matted reddish locks and glaring at me with bloodshot blue eyes.

'Did he steal it?'

'His great-grand-dad did. From his downtrodden workers. So he could buy himself that sodding great useless house and send his kiddiwinks to public school. Turn 'em into toffee-nosed bastards who could carry on screwing the underprivileged. It's all about Class, Curly, and Class is a dirty word. Don't you forget that.' Ash favoured a kind of woolly communism, especially when he was particularly stoned or hung-over.

'Still, it's nice of him to have us here.'

Ash snorted. 'Nice! It's us that's nice, more like. Makes him feel all cuddly, having fairies at the bottom of his garden.'

'Cuddly?' 'Fucking smug.'

'Electricity Bill likes him.'

'Course he does. Bill's always out for the main chance.'

It was rare to hear Electricity Bill spoken of so cynically. But Ash had known him far longer than anyone else had, ever since they were at school together – before the force of Bill's personality had reached full strength, presumably. So he didn't view Bill quite as the rest of us did.

As for me, I knew from an early age that Bill was the Leader of the Pack. He gave off waves of chilly charisma as if he was surrounded by a powerful electric field. This made his nickname especially appropriate, though in fact it stemmed from his trade as an electrician. Not any old electrician either.

'Screwed his way into telly,' was Ash's version of the early part of Bill's career. 'When he was eighteen him and his boss were working on this bird's house. Rewiring. She had some fancy job for the Beeb, so Bill decides to hop into her knickers. Next thing, he lands himself a job with this TV lighting crew.'

There was a good deal in this account that I found mysterious at the time, but I accepted it all as part of the Superior Being that was Bill.

He no longer worked in television. While at the BBC he had rubbed shoulders with a number of rock bands, who were no doubt impressed as much by his aloof and peculiar aura as by his talent and imagination. Thanks to these new connections he rose fairly quickly to the more exalted position of freelance lighting director, much in demand for festivals and touring gigs. Now he was mixing with the rich and famous, though all the time retaining his legendary cool – that impression he gave of being effortlessly at the cutting edge of life while at the same time inhabiting a zone way, way above anything so trivial as fashion. He didn't even have long hair – he didn't need it. He had Style.

Inevitably, he came into contact with Our Lord, then like Bill in his late twenties. He had recently inherited his old man's estate, but was desperate to distance himself from his degenerate ancestors and identify instead with the Counterculture. Bill spoke to him about his desire to establish an Alternative Community – and as luck would have it, Our Lord had the perfect place for one, a derelict campsite in the woods in a far corner of his grounds. His father had set it up soon after the Second World War as a philanthropic gesture towards his factory employees. The idea was to give them a chance to spend their hols being reinvigorated physically and mentally in the healthy air of the countryside, although in practice things didn't turn out quite as planned. A few of the workers became so reinvigorated that they trashed a couple of the caravans; another was burnt to the ground. The toilets became blocked with unsavoury objects; the septic tank overflowed; pets were brought along and then abandoned in the woods. After a few years the site was closed down.

However, the shower block remained, and this Our Lord undertook to have entirely overhauled. He had a big washing machine put in, and an immersion heater with a tank heavily insulated in thick white padding.

Bill took charge of the electrics; he wired up the new installations, repaired and extended the original ones, and ran a cable to each of the seven spacious new caravans that Our Lord purchased for the site. They were custom-built, not touring caravans but the static variety – mobile homes, really, but we always called them caravans. 'We are, existentially, travellers,' Bill liked to say. 'Journeyers on the Spiritual Path, if not on the material highways of this world.' (He himself, because of the nature of his work, did a lot of travelling on real roads as well, in his old but extremely classy and well-maintained Triumph Spitfire; in fact most Lothlorien-dwellers had some kind of vehicle for their forays Outside, parked on a gravelled patch at the edge of the settlement).

And so it came to pass, in the autumn of 1966, that Lothlorien was born, complete with light, heat and running water. Our Lord paid all the bills. It must have cost a bomb, but hopefully made his conscience feel very warm and cosy – as we ourselves were, even in winter.

Our caravans had a central living space with a kitchen area incorporated, a smaller room at either end, and a little washroom with a basin and mirror. A pipe brought water to each caravan from the shower block, but our major ablutions were conducted in the latter. Bill didn't believe in chemical loos, so in all weathers we trekked over to the shower block, though a chamber pot was kept in each caravan for emergencies. When much later I first lived in a house, an indoor bathroom and loo seemed extraordinary luxuries.

Rather than being arranged in a straight row, the caravans were dotted about irregularly in clearings among the trees, close enough for neighbourliness but still giving everyone a degree of privacy. Each little clearing had its own particular atmosphere. And at the heart of the settlement was the Fireplace, surrounded by log benches and often used for communal cook-ins, also when Bill called a Meeting.

We even had our own telephone – a fat red payphone installed in one of Our Lord's outhouses, connected to a square black answering machine. On most days someone, usually Bill, would go up to check for messages. He had paid for the phone to be put in as it was essential for his work, but of course it was useful for everyone to have easy contact with Outside from time to time – apart from Wing, who had no desire to ring anybody. (When I was about five Bill also got himself a pager; if she heard it bleeping she would cover her ears and wail).

'What have you got all these mod cons for?' a female visitor once asked – Rick's proto-yuppie sister, if I remember rightly. 'Isn't that cheating? I thought you were supposed to give up all that sort of stuff if you wanted to live the simple life. Why don't you just have log fires and wash in the river?'

'It is not our aim to destroy these woods either by burning them for fuel or by polluting the watercourses,' replied Bill quietly. 'And to live simply does not imply dirt and discomfort. We are here to follow the Sufic wisdom of being *in* the world but not *of* it.' That shut her up. I don't recall her visiting us again.

Her brother Rick was a musician, who along with his girlfriend Zoë and daughter Elvira formed part of the original core of the settlement. He had the distinction of being much the tallest person in Lothlorien, and he also had the longest hair, fairish but rather stringy, like the rest of him. Normally he kept it tied back in a ponytail, but sometimes when he played guitar in the evenings he liked to let it loose; as he threw his head from side to side his glasses flew off and his hair swung like strands of fine raffia – one of my earliest memories. Other members in at the beginning – all the men less hairy than Rick but still much hairier than the women – were likewise friends of Bill's: Marjoram and Gogo, Sean and Stella, Ashley, and of course Bill's companion Ginnie. There had been one other couple, who hadn't apparently fitted in as hoped, and who disappeared after less than a year. They were replaced by Neat Pete, exceptional in that he was introduced not by Electricity Bill but by Our Lord.

Theoretically, Our Lord himself was going to occupy the seventh caravan, but somehow that never quite worked out. Perhaps he missed the space and comforts he was used to, perhaps his time was too much taken up elsewhere – he had a house in London, for instance, and probably all kinds of business activities he didn't care to talk about. Or maybe he just didn't really feel at ease in the midst of a bunch of ravening hippies – and least not enough to embrace their way of life wholeheartedly. It's also possible that he was afraid of us getting to know him too well. With hindsight, I imagine that there were perhaps aspects of himself he preferred to keep private.

The spare caravan didn't stay empty for long, as after a few months Marjoram met Erryk – then Eric – at a Christmas fair in Middington where they both had stalls, she selling herbal remedies and he his leather bags, belts, chokers and so on. She felt right away, and quite correctly, that he would be a desirable element to add to Lothlorien, which he took to like a duck to water – after, of course, being vetted by Bill and Ginnie. He brought a girlfriend with him, as I discovered with some surprise when I was around five or six.

'Look Stell, isn't that one of Trish's headbands that Curly's wearing?'

observed Zoë one day. Like nearly everyone else, I had quite a collection of headbands. I stuck feathers in them to become a Red Indian, (even in Elfland that politically incorrect name was still used in those days), or leaves and twigs as camouflage when I was on Patrol in the woods with the other children. We would regularly tour the boundaries of our domaine, on the lookout for Orcs and other marauding Outsiders: on one occasion they were real, though that story comes much later. This particular headband was made from string and wooden beads. I'd come across it not long before in an old shoebox filled with odds and ends under Erryk's work table in the caravan.

'Who's Trish?' I asked.

'Oh, she used to live with Erryk,' said Zoë. 'Before Wing. Long ago, when he first got here. We used to call her Miss Macramé.'

'Why?'

'That's what she did all the time. Macramé.'

'What's that?'

'Knots in string, like your headband. With beads. Erryk used to sell them on the markets with his own stuff.'

'We all wore them to start with, to be friendly,' said Stella. 'But they were ever so itchy. Mine gave me a rash. I think she used the wrong kind of string.'

'And that's when Pete started to lose his hair. The beads rubbed it off at the sides. At least that's what he said.'

I took the headband off at once. It didn't make me itch at all, but I certainly didn't want my curls to start falling out.

I mentioned the matter to Erryk.

'Trish... oh yes, Trish...' He frowned slightly, as if it was an effort to dredge up her memory. 'Yes, I sold quite a few of those headbands. I don't think it'll do any harm to your hair. Pete was losing his anyway.'

I checked with Pete. He was definitely thinning at the temples, though his thick black ponytail was always groomed and shiny.

'Alas,' he said, fixing me with his dark eyes, as round as bright buttons. 'The recession of my fabled locks is as unstoppable as the ebbing spring tide. Whatever I said about the headband was purely in jest.'

Nevertheless I wasn't prepared to run the risk, so I put it back in the shoebox.

'What happened to Trish?' I asked Erryk.

He sighed. 'She wasn't... she didn't really... she couldn't...' He shook his head. This was an unsatisfactory answer, but Erryk often had a bit of trouble forming thoughts into words. So I asked Marjoram instead.

'Trish! Wow, I haven't thought about her for years. She always looked as though we were going to eat her. She was terribly shy, poor thing. We did try to make her feel at home. Erryk was sweet to her, of course, but she couldn't really handle the rest of us. She stuck it out for about a year and a half and then she split.' Marjoram laughed. 'Maybe the last straw for her was when Tiger Lily arrived.'

'Why?'

'Well Curly, imagine you're a fragile little plant with a weak root system, and suddenly this huge vigorous flower – well, tiger lily of course – starts pushing up next to you. You couldn't survive.' Marjoram's analogies were always drawn from the plant world. It was probably Tiger Lily's name that predisposed Marjoram towards her right from the start.

*

It was a sunny afternoon in May '68. At the weekends parts of the House and gardens were open to the public, so the main gates were open too. Through them drove a combi painted all over with bright psychedelic designs. In it were four young Australians, touring around the UK after a winter spent working in the bars of Earl's Court. That day they were tripping on acid.

They didn't have any idea where they were, as the signboard at the entrance had made no sense to them – although, as Tiger Lily said later, she clearly remembered having spotted it: 'It was sort of shimmering. I just knew we had to go in.' So they sailed unheeding past the Lodge, home of Janet the Great, Our Lord's housekeeper, who sold the admission tickets. Although a bulky woman, she could move remarkably fast when she wanted to, and I can imagine her running outside with stridently indignant cries – but she wasn't quick enough to catch the offending vehicle as it disappeared round a curve in the drive.

Halfway to the House the combi broke down. After a while the Aussies got out and began to wander aimlessly, communing with the wildflowers and the insects. Tiger Lily, more adventurous than her mates, followed the flight of a butterfly as it took off from a stalk of cow parsley and fluttered up the drive. Rounding another bend, she came upon the House displayed in all its Georgian glory. (It wasn't, in fact, exceptionally glorious. 'But when you're tripping – man, it looks like a fucking fairytale,' said Tiger Lily. 'Especially if you're from Toowoomba.')

She continued making her way towards this vision. The weedy gravel beneath her feet began to metamorphose: 'I saw these yellow bricks.

Quivering. I realised I was Dorothy on my way to meet the Wizard of Oz. And you know, Curly, that's another name for Australia. Oz. That's when I was kind of *flooded* with this sense of Cosmic Rightness. And then I saw the Sign.'

A few hundred yards before the drive reached the House a track led off to the left, winding along the side of the Sheepfield and down to our woods. Across this track a padlocked chain hung between two trees. From it dangled a small wooden panel painted with the word 'PRIVATE' – a prosaic little message, quite unequivocal to someone in a normal state of mind.

'It *glowed*, man. I didn't read the letters, I just sensed the Inner Meaning. It was calling to me.'

So she slipped under the chain and ran down the track – quite a long way, almost half a mile. She'd been wearing a long dress that day, she told me, and it was a miracle she didn't fall – 'But I was flying, darling.'

The first person Tiger Lily saw as she approached the caravans was Sean, doing his press-ups in the long grass. Sweating and out of breath, she paused in wonder.

Sean and his girlfriend Stella were known as the Blond Bombshells. Stella was originally from Scotland, but had moved down to London after leaving school to pursue her dream of becoming a fashion model. She'd had a certain amount of success, and still went off from time to time to do a bit of modelling – 'Just twin-sets in catalogues for old ladies, love. Nothing high fashion' – and she had to maintain her professional image of girl-next-door, fair, willowy and wholesome. So she could often be found in the shower block carefully retouching her roots with the help of Zoë, who was a hairdresser and stylist by trade. On the other hand, Sean's thick, honey-coloured mane was natural, and he was immensely proud of it. Indeed, he was immensely proud of his whole body.

I don't recall him ever being employed in any kind of gainful occupation, except intermittently by Our Lord as what would today be called a Personal Trainer. Stella's occasional modelling jobs must have been their main source of income. But I do have vivid memories of the jungle displays he sometimes put on for us children, when he would swing from branches and toss us bananas, all the while howling like Tarzan. At the end he would throw back his lustrous flowing locks, beat his chest and laugh wildly, like the Celtic super-hero he imagined himself to be.

'Curly, you're going to *love* being a man,' he said to me once, flexing his biceps. 'It's such a fucking groovy thing to be.' At the time I didn't doubt him.

He exercised regularly, outside if the weather was fine. 'Thinks he's Mr Universe,' Ash would mutter rather sourly. He himself was on the short and stocky side, and although his skills and creativity were far superior to Sean's, he no doubt envied the latter's physique.

On the day Tiger Lily turned up Sean had started his work-out much later than usual, as he and Rick had been up until the early hours of the morning, smoking and jamming; Sean had recently got hold of a set of bongo drums and liked to accompany Rick's guitar with what he termed 'primordial rhythms'. When Tiger Lily took in the sight of him pumping rhythmically up and down, golden hair flashing in the sunshine, it was clear to her that she was in the presence of a fertility god. She fell instantly in lust – 'though in a totally *spiritual* kind of way, because I was tripping. I couldn't have *done* anything about it.'

Awe-struck, she stepped closer.

'Let me worship you,' she said. (This must be true, as both she herself and Sean remembered these words. They were teased about this for years – although not in front of Stella).

He paused in mid push-up. 'Hey man, where did you spring from?'

Sean, facing away from their caravan, hadn't noticed Stella standing in the open doorway. Tiger Lily was too far gone at this stage to notice anything but Sean.

'I've come from far away, to be with you,' she replied.

'FUCK OFF, BITCH!' screamed Stella. It was a primal response to a serious threat. She would have seen straight away that her own style of clean, rather bland prettiness was no match for Tiger Lily's far more exotic sexual charms.

Sean jumped up in alarm, but Tiger Lily just smiled beatifically, having a similar reaction to Stella's outburst as she had had to the word 'PRIVATE'. Then she fainted into Sean's arms, her crimson dress billowing around her.

'Let go of that woman!' Stella shouted.

'How can I? She might hurt herself,' answered Sean.

By this time Marjoram and Ginnie had appeared on the scene, having heard Stella's outburst. Ginnie extracted Tiger Lily from Sean's strong grasp and led her, now semi-conscious again, towards her own caravan. She sat her on the steps and then fetched a blanket and a cushion from inside so that Tiger Lily could lie down in the shade. Tiger Lily beamed foggily. 'Wow, this is such a cool trip.'

Marjoram, realising that she was dehydrated, brought her a large glass of water mixed with chamomile syrup. Tiger Lily gulped it down and drifted into a deep sleep.

She awoke some hours later to find herself in warm blue twilight, surrounded by a small circle of strangers – but clearly the right kind of strangers. To her left Ginnie was performing her evening meditation. With eyes closed and legs neatly folded in the lotus position, she was immaculate, as always: a high priestess in a pale orange silk kaftan, a stick of incense burning in front of her. Marjoram knelt on Tiger Lily's other side, patting her temples with a herbal compress. Erryk had brought along his guitar, and softly played and sang the type of folk music he felt was appropriate for coming down from a trip. Sean crouched on his muscly haunches, well displayed in tattered denim shorts, and smiled quietly to himself. 'Like the fucking Cheshire Cat,' grumbled Ashley. He himself, already smitten, just stared. Gogo bounced around dispensing glasses of homemade blackberry wine, a favourite evening tipple in Lothlorien. Rick was loading up his bong.

Absent, understandably, was Stella, also Zoë, who was providing her with sisterly support. Trish of the headbands was never even mentioned as part of this story. Perhaps her root system had taken one look at Tiger Lily and already withered away. Neat Pete was away on one of his mysterious business jaunts, Bill off doing an electrical job somewhere.

Tiger Lily looked around. 'Bloody hell, I've died and gone back to the Dreamtime,' she said. Then something occurred to her. 'Christ! Where are the others? What's happened to the combi?'

In fact, these had already been taken care of with remarkable efficiency by Our Lord, luckily in residence at the House that weekend. Alerted by Janet the Great, who had rung from the Lodge to let him know about the unauthorised intrusion of the combi, he had taken his jeep and gone down with a couple of friends to see what was happening. No strangers themselves to acid, it didn't take them long to assess the situation. They rounded up Tiger Lily's mates, put them back in the combi and towed it up to the House. Our Lord felt the Aussies could become paranoid if taken indoors, so his friends escorted them to a private part of the garden and encouraged them to have a rest – supervised, in case the trip turned bad or they started doing anything funny with the rare plants in the shrubbery. A garage mechanic was called out to examine the combi.

One of the Aussies, surfacing into normality, began to wonder where Tiger Lily might be. Our Lord, who up till then hadn't been aware there was a fourth member of the party, guessed quite correctly where they should look for her.

'Gary!' exclaimed Tiger Lily. 'Jesus, man, where were you?'

'Haven't a clue. Nice place though. This bloke's been really good.' He clapped Our Lord on the shoulder. 'He's going to take us somewhere we can jump on a train.'

'Train? We've got the combi.'

'Combi's buggered. Cost a bloody fortune to repair – not worth it.' Tiger Lily's face lit up. 'Then I'll live in it.'

'Where?'

'Right here, Gary. I've found my spiritual home. You guys just carry on without me.'

Everyone was a bit put out by this announcement. However, such was Tiger Lily's depth of conviction that somehow, coupled with the force of her charm, it carried the day. If Bill had been there things might have turned out differently. But Ginnie, in Bill's absence accepted as the head of the community, was for some reason particularly taken with Tiger Lily. She probably thought, too, that an extra woman would help to redress the male/female balance of Lothlorien, then at a level of seven men to five women. So whatever Bill's reservations may have been when he got back a week or so later, Ginnie must have talked him round.

By that time Tiger Lily's presence was a *fait accompli*. The combi had been towed down to the woods and she had arranged the interior to her liking – largely thanks to Ashley and his carpentry skills. He ripped out the seats and made a folding bed with storage space underneath, a table with shelves above it where she could paint and store her materials, and even a small kitchen arrangement with a cupboard and an old electric hotplate he salvaged from somewhere. At first she couldn't use it as she didn't have any elecricity, but Bill soon fixed that. It was all a little cramped, but very cosy and colourful once she had draped her Balinese sarongs around and stuck some of her artwork on the walls.

It didn't take her long to learn the ways of the community, and she proved to be a dab hand at chicken care. 'I know all about chooks,' she said. 'I can communicate with them on the spiritual plane.' The rate of egg production allegedly soared in Elfland's chicken coop.

Although there was some initial concern about how she was going to survive on a material level, she rapidly put everyone's minds at rest. 'I can tell fortunes. I've got Tarot cards with me. And I'll sell my paintings. I'll go along to the markets with Erryk.'

That may have been what finished off the mysterious Trish – not that there was ever the smallest hint of any hanky-panky between Tiger Lily and Erryk. It was Sean she had her eye on, though she was prepared to bide her time. She never made any advances towards him, befriended Stella as far as possible, and in general was on her best behaviour. Was Ashley rewarded for all his devoted kindness? Yes, occasionally: she thought it was only fair. Tiger Lily had a great sense of fairness.

In her own mind there had never been the slightest question of her not staying in Lothlorien. 'Couldn't have shifted me with a bloody bulldozer, mate.'

3. THE COMMANDMENTS

THEY DIDN'T DESCEND from the sky on tablets of stone, but there was a set of unwritten rules in Lothlorien that everyone adhered to more or less unfailingly. They had been laid down by Bill at the beginning, and agreed upon by everyone else – any dissenters wouldn't have been allowed to join the community.

Financial viability was one of these rules. There was to be absolutely no reliance on the State, no claiming of the dole. Dependence on Our Lord, on the other hand, obviously didn't count. For us he was a bit like the sun, I suppose – dispensing endless free energy. And water, of course. But all other needs had to be met by the efforts of the members of the community, which meant for most people participating to some extent in the economy of Outside, although no-one had what you could call a regular job. This tied in well enough with the 'in-the-world-but-not-of-it' philosophy propounded by Bill. As he himself continued to work periodically in the world of rock concerts and festivals, he was by far the most financially viable of everyone. His Spitfire was certainly the smoothest car in Lothlorien.

Gogo was one of the few who didn't earn money Outside; he was too busy and useful within the Community. As an ex-schoolteacher, he gave lessons to us children, and was also in charge of Gandalf's Garden, often referred to as Gogo's Garden or simply the Garden, a plot of land on the edge of the woods which produced not only most of our marijuana but a good deal of our vegetables too, slugs and rabbits permitting.

The rabbits were kept pretty well at bay by the various cats, which were loosely attached to the House but often came down to the woods to visit us and hunt. The slugs, on the other hand, were an ongoing problem. Slug pellets were out of the question, so Wing elected to go round the Garden each evening and perform her own method of slug-control. When they emerged at dusk and began to slither up the stalks, she would gather them up with a spoon into a bowl and take them down to the far side of the river, with a few lettuce or cabbage leaves as a kind of starter pack for their new life. Caterpillars and snails received the same treatment. As soon as I could walk I usually went along too, first with my own little spoon but later on picking off the slugs with my fingers to show how macho I was.

I remember one particularly wet spring when we simply couldn't keep up with the slug reproduction rate, and Gogo was becoming frantic. He fetched cinders and ash from the boilers up at the House and sprinkled them around the base of each plant, but the rain soon dispersed them enough for the slugs to find a way through.

'Fuck it, Wing, I'm going to put out some beer.'

'That's murder!' said Wing, shocked and pained.

'No – I'm giving them a choice. I'm not forcing them to drink. But if they do, at least they'll die pissed and happy.'

'How do you know?' I asked. 'Maybe drinking makes them really sad. Like Ash.'

'I don't know, Curly. I'm making what's called an *educated guess*. And hey man, who are we growing these veggies *for?* Us or them?'

As a concession to Wing, he agreed to leave a small row of cabbage plants beer-free, and for the next few weeks, while the rainy period lasted, she de-slugged these as usual, hoping that the majority would still prefer a tasty cabbage leaf to the lure of alcohol. In the meantime, I made a tour of the twenty or so yoghourt pots that Gogo had sunk into the earth, emptying their contents and refilling them with beer. Each was protected by a slightly larger plastic pot, upturned and with an opening cut into it, allowing the slugs to get in but protecting the beer from dilution by the rain. They looked liked miniature igloos. I enjoyed lifting off the roof of each one and examining the slugs floating beneath, usually around ten of them, all sizes. Sad or happy? I couldn't tell. Gogo used to assure me he could see them smiling.

Gogo had been christened Gordon, a name far too solid and heavy-sounding for such a wiry power-pack. He was shorter and lighter in build than Marjoram, with dark curly hair – (though not quite as curly as my own). When he first dropped out he grew an Afro, but once he moved to Lothlorien he found it kept filling up with leaves and bits of twig, so he got Zoë to cut it short. To compensate for his shorn locks he grew a moustache and goatee beard instead, which gave him a look halfway between an imp and a pirate. He was as optimistic as he was energetic. 'In twenty years everyone will be living this way,' he often said. The logistics of this didn't bother him.

'You mean the whole population will be splattered all over what remains of the British countryside, and probably engaging in tribal wars,' remarked Neat Pete.

'No man, it'll all work out. You'll see.'

However unrealistic his hopes, Gogo's vegetables were a triumph, which was just as well, since vegetarianism was another of our rules – although what you chose to eat Outside was your own affair. Ashley in particular was partial to a burger and chips in town from time to time. That good old hippie cliché, the lentil stew, was one of our staples, and I remember those stews as being delicious. They were enriched with plenty of onions and other veggies, plus herbs from Marjoram's part of the Garden along with those she picked in the wild. And they were loaded with garlic, as were all our savoury dishes; this was perhaps one of the reasons why Outsiders frequently took a step back when confronted with an Elfland-dweller. We weren't aware of it ourselves; we all must have reeked of it, cancelling each other out, so to speak. 'Nature's best preventive medicine,' said Marjoram. It was indeed rare for any of us to fall ill, even with a cold. We felt smugly healthy compared to the snuffling Outsiders we came across during the winter.

Besides Gogo's cultivated garlic, in springtime and early summer we used to gather a couple of wild varieties which thrived in the soggy spots down by the river and next to Galadriel's Pool. There was the really smelly kind and another, rarer species with long thin leaves and flowers almost like white bluebells. This last was a favourite of mine and I liked to pull up the delicate little bulbs and crunch them raw. 'Don't take them all,' Gogo would say. 'We don't want them to disappear.'

Just last year, to my amazement, I spotted some of these plants growing thickly on a shady bank by the roadside, not far from where I was staying but in a far posher neighbourhood. It's not possible, I thought, there's not enough rain... Then I realised that they didn't need rain, being amply watered by the run-off from the well-irrigated private garden just above. I stopped my scooter to check: they were virtually identical to the plants I'd known as a child – droopy white flowers, curious three-sided stems. But did I pick any? No. I didn't even touch them. I drew back as if from something magic and dangerous. I couldn't tell you why, exactly. Perhaps I was afraid of being infected with too great a nostalgia for a past I put behind me long ago. Now, of course, I'm wallowing in it – but my view of the world has been radically transformed since my accident.

There was a multitude of other edible plants that we gathered in the woods: blackberries, hazelnuts and sweet chestnuts in the autumn, and the tiny triangular beechnuts that Shine and Jelly Bean used to peel and nibble. Layla didn't like getting her nails dirty, and us boys couldn't be bothered with the beechnuts – they were too fiddly; we preferred hunting for mushrooms . From an early age we were taught by Marjoram to identify which were edible and which poisonous, and she also made us familiar with all kinds of different greens – yarrow, nettle tops, wild mustard and species of vegetables once cultivated but later forgotten. Even ground elder. For gardeners who find this a pest, my advice is: cook it. It's tasty. My own preference was for a plant called Good King Henry, because I liked the name. There was another called Fat Hen. When he was still too young to really understand what he was saying, Rain used to twist the stalks to break them, yelling 'I'm wringing their necks! I'm wringing their necks!' We both found this hilarious. I remember one day when Wing heard him and got terribly upset. Rain was so alarmed by her torrents of tears that from then on he left those plants alone.

Erryk was something of an expert on roots, wild carrot and parsnip among them, and he even roasted and ground dandelion roots as an alternative to coffee. For those who craved caffeine, Rick and Zoë in particular, real coffee was included on the list for the shopping trips to the supermarket in Middington. It was generally Ash who volunteered to go on these expeditions in his old pick-up truck, giving himself a chance to enjoy not only a dose of meaty fast food but also a couple of pints in the pub where he fancied the barmaid.

He never brought any beer back with him, as all alcohol consumed within the community had to be brewed by ourselves – another rule. Gogo made wine from flowers and berries, and he and Erryk made beer and liqueurs from various roots. 'Cat piss,' said Ash. He and Rick brewed their own beer from kits they bought in town, which Bill tolerated though it was clear he considered it a form of cheating.

It was probably because Ashley's friendship with Bill went so far back into the mists of time that he got away with a far more flagrant transgression of the rules: he had a dog. Dogs were Not Allowed. Dogs consumed large quantities of meat; they barked; they worried sheep. Our Lord had about a dozen of these, kept more as pets than anything else. He seemed to be very attached to them, and on fine days, when he was in residence at the House, we often saw him enjoying a bucolic moment under the oak-tree in the Sheepfield. That was their principal territory, although they also had the run of the grounds and served as useful and decorative lawn-mowers. Sometimes they wandered down to the Garden. They pushed their black noses through the wire fence and gazed thoughtfully at the vegetables, with a canny, knowing look in their yellow eyes. Everyone liked the sheep, and none of us wanted to see them worried, or indeed stressed in any way. So the No Dogs rule made perfect sense.

And then one rainy evening – I was just six and remember it well – Ashley came back from an excursion to Middington, opened the passenger door of his pick-up, and lifted out a small hairy object. He was quivering with rage.

'Abandoned,' he spat. 'Some stupid sodding fucker left him tied up to a telegraph post. And the rope was long enough for him to wander on to the road. He was just lying there. He'd given up hope. It's a wonder he hadn't got run over.'

The animal, very wet, stayed put in Ashley's arms, shivering but otherwise immobile. It wasn't instantly recognisable as a dog.

'Oh the poor, poor little thing,' cried Wing, dropping her bowl and spoon on the ground – (the two of us were about to do the slug run).

'Don't just stand there snivelling, woman. Help me dry him off. I'll take him inside.'

While Wing ran off to get some towels, I followed Ash up the steps into his caravan. 'Pass us that rug, Curly, there's a good lad. Now fold it up a bit and put it on the workbench… that's the ticket. We'll put him here for now.' He lowered the animal tenderly on to the blanket.

Wing came back with a towel, my special red and blue striped one that I normally wouldn't let her use, though for once I didn't mind. Ash began to rub the creature vigorously. It put up no resistance.

'It's a dog! ' I exclaimed.

'Well done, Curly,' said Ash grimly. 'Now, would *you* have left it to die in the middle of nowhere? Would you?'

'No,' I said.

'Of course you wouldn't. Only some cretinous imbecilic fuck-wit would do a thing like that. I hope he rots in hell. Or *she*', he added, looking darkly at Wing. 'Let's not discriminate.'

'What does that mean?' I asked.

'It means that women aren't any better than men,' replied Ash shortly.

'How can you *say* such a thing?' protested Wing, close to tears. 'A woman would *never* …'

Ash tickled the dog under its chin. 'Safe home now, old son.'

'But you can't *keep* it,' said Wing.

'Oh? What am I supposed to do then? Take him up to Janet's and tip him in the bin?' (The rubbish bins, where once a week we deposited our non-organic waste, were behind the Lodge, just inside the main gates.)

'Well, perhaps Janet…'

'He's staying *here,*' said Ash. 'Comprendo? Dig? Here. With me.'

'You could take... Isn't there an RSPCA in Middington?'

'No there sodding isn't. And even if there was, I'm not giving any other idiots the chance to get their hands on him.'

'But Bill... And what about Our Lord?' 'Bugger the pair of them.'

We were used to Ash's fits of stroppiness – but this came close to blasphemy. We remained silent.

The dog staggered to its feet. Ash patted it fondly.

'He wont cause any trouble,' he said. 'You can tell he's a hippie dog. Look at him.'

We looked. I'd seen dogs Outside, of course, and plenty of pictures in books, so I could tell that this was an unusual specimen. He was long and low, with stumpy legs and a coat of mottled white and brown curls, especially thick on his floppy ears and the top of his head. But his muzzle, thin and pointed, was as smooth and polished as a conker. So was his tail.

'It must be a kind of dachshund,' said Wing.

'Kind of bastard, more like. He's a miniature sausage-poodle-Basset, I'd say.'

'He's nice,' I said sincerely. I think I felt a kinship because of the curliness.

'You can pat him too, if you want.'

Tentatively, I reached out my hand. This was the first time in my life I'd actually touched a dog. The ones in Middington tended to bark at us. This dog didn't. He wagged his tail and rolled his eyes. We bonded.

'Would he like a hot water bottle do you think?' I asked.

'Good idea. You run off and make him one. Not too hot – just fill it up from the tap.'

At the door of the caravan I paused. 'What are you going to call him?'

'Why not 'Gimli'?' suggested Wing, this being the name of the heroic dwarf in *The Lord of the Rings.*

'No,' said Ash. 'He's not that sort of shape. I think I'll call him Chipolata.' And Chipolata stayed. Amazingly, Bill gave his permission, encouraged by Ginnie.

'I told them we were brothers in a previous life,' Ashley explained. 'Ginnie likes all that kind of stuff.'

'Is it true?'

'Don't see why not. That's what it feels like.'

Chip, as he was usually known, had such a docile nature that no-one could really object to him, even Our Lord. He certainly wasn't a sheep-worrier, and the nearest he came to a bark was a feeble yap if someone trod on him by mistake. He stuck close to Ash, who fed him dog-biscuits and vegetables. Sometimes one of the cats would nick a few of his biscuits, but this upset Ash more than Chip, who had quite a friendly rapport with the cats.

There were about four or five of these, working cats whose job was to keep down the rodents at the House. As I've said, they quite often came down to Lothlorien, especially when the weather was wet and cold; although they were semi-wild they appreciated a nap in a warm caravan. The most sociable of them was a female tabby which was particularly attached to Ginnie, who called her Parvati. Apart from the odd saucer of milk we didn't give them anything to eat – we had nothing they would have fancied. They were fed intermittently up at the House by Our Lord's mysterious mama.

This woman was a shadowy, reclusive figure, divorced from her husband but brought back to the House after his death by Our Lord. We knew of her existence, as Zoë went up to do her hair from time to time, but Elvira was the only one of us kids who'd actually seen her, having once accompanied her mother on a hairdressing sortie.

The only one, that is, until an early autumn day when she and I were out gathering wild salad greens along the side of the Sheepfield. Layla, her younger sister, had tagged along. She would have been about five at the time, myself just six, and Elvira a sophisticated eleven, already showing signs of her future persona.

'Fucking rabbit food,' she said, ripping at the leaves.

'Fucking rabbit food,' repeated Layla sweetly.

Elvira scowled. Layla wasn't as cutely naive as she appeared at first sight.

Suddenly we became conscious of a disturbance not far away. Over the brow of the hill appeared a woman with dishevelled grey hair, running down the track towards our woods. She was not alone. Just behind her pounded Janet the Great, the housekeeper, trying to catch up.

'Stop! You can't go there!' she shouted.

'Shit, it's Momma Lord,' said Elvira. 'Looks like she needs a shampoo and set.'

'You mean Our Lord's mother?' I asked, impressed by her rather witch-like appearance.

'Yeah. She's neurotic.'

'New-rottic,' said Layla, rolling the unfamiliar word round her mouth.

'Full of hang-ups,' I told her, proud of my superior vocabulary.

'Zoë says all rich people are full of hang-ups,' said Elvira. 'But *I* won't be, not when *I'm* rich. I'll just be bloody happy.'

By now Janet had succeeded in grabbing Momma Lord's arm. They stopped, each gesticulating with her free hand. A heated argument was clearly in progress, although they were too far away for us to hear what they were saying. After a minute or two, Momma Lord seemed to give up. She went limp, and almost collapsed on the ground. Janet caught her, turned her round, and propelled her back up the track.

'Fat cow,' said Elvira. We weren't keen on Janet, and she was even less keen on us.

Myself and the other children had virtually no contact with her, but if we did happen to cross her path up by the Lodge she always gave us a look that was far from friendly.

We reported what we'd seen to Zoë.

'Poor woman,' she said. 'She's always saying she'd like to come and meet everyone, but Our Lord tells her she mustn't. He's afraid we'd turn her on, I suppose.'

'What's wrong with that?' asked Elvira.

'He thinks she might become paranoid. Freak out completely. Personally I think it would do her the world of good. Give her head a bit of a spring-clean. All she does is sit and watch telly all day.'

Now this was truly shocking. Within Lothlorien, 'television' was an even dirtier word than 'dog'. Radio was allowed, as it didn't stop you doing other things while you were listening, but TV was a total no-no. And yet not only Bill but quite a few of the others had made a living from it in the past: Zoë as a stylist, Rick as a musician and Ginnie who had been some kind of junior production assistant. Stella hadn't worked directly in the business, but as a model had appeared in several TV commercials, including an ad for deodorant in which she'd met Sean, (who himself did a bit of modelling at the time), flaunting his seductively silky and odour-free armpits.

In fact, it was all this inside experience of the medium which had finally turned them right off it, and everyone else was quite content to go without too.

'It's the most dangerous drug of all,' Gogo told us.

'It numbs the spirit,' said Ginnie.

'Fucks up your brain cells,' said Rick.

'Keeps the masses quiet,' said Ash.

And so on.

So the children of Elfland grew up without its contaminating influence. We didn't miss it, because we'd never known it – except for Elvira, who had vague pre-Lothlorien memories of being plonked in front of a flickering black-and-white box when Rick and Zoë wanted some peace and quiet.

Gogo once took us younger ones for an educational peek through the windows of the Lodge, so we would learn to recognise the monster. He must have picked a moment when he could be pretty sure of catching a programme of no interest whatsoever to small children – no animals, no cartoons, not even sport or dancing girls. Just talking heads in suits. I remember finding the coloured light quite alluring, but certainly not the picture itself. Janet and her husband Greg were sitting stolidly in front of the set on a brown and orange striped settee, munching crisps.

'You see?' murmured Gogo. *'Couch potatoes.'* I thought he meant the crisps. In any event, we found this glimpse of telly-watching less than tempting. From then on, if ever we should pass a shop Outside with television sets in the window – which wasn't very often, as there wasn't one in Middington – we would all make rude noises and look the other way. At the risk of sounding like a totally boring old fart, I think our elders were probably right to keep it out of our lives. There was so much else to do in Lothlorien.

We had plenty of musical evenings, usually round the Fireplace – (the fire made from dead branches only, of course). Erryk played reasonably well on his acoustic guitar, though Rick was by far the most accomplished musician. On his electric guitar, a black Stratocaster, he would perform some extraordinary solo riffs when he was in the mood. 'He must be connected somehow to the spirit of Jimi Hendrix,' said Zoë; of course she was biased. Sean had a pair of bongo drums, Tiger Lily her Balinese flute, and Ginnie a collection of exotic little percussion instruments. Us kids liked to invent our own; Rain, for instance, made himself a pair of maracas out of a couple of old tennis balls he filled with tacks. Not the most musical of the bunch, I still enjoyed bashing glass jars with bits of stick. Erryk showed me how to vary the note by filling the jars with different volumes of water.

We all sang, too. Stella had a particularly good soprano voice, clear and strong – our very own Joan Baez. Erryk knew the lyrics to all Bob Dylan's songs, and composed his own Dylanesque numbers – including *The Ballad of Curly Oswald* written when I was still a toddler. *'Born of fire, into water,'* it began, *'of the wingéd elven daughter...'* I don't think I need go any further.

And we had story-telling evenings as well: here Tiger Lily was the star, though once again everyone joined in. The stories were by no means always fictional or mythical. Often they dealt with real life, events from

Lothlorien's past – (my birth, for instance) – or weird, amusing, sometimes distressing encounters with Outsiders. These true-life stories were part of the glue which held Lothlorien together, an ever-growing oral history which belonged only to ourselves, the Elves' Inheritors. That was what Sean called us. In those halcyon days men could get away with expressions like that.

These entertainments came at the close of days packed with activity for us children. There were games in the woods, of course – when we had the time. As soon as we were old enough, we were encouraged to take on simple responsibilities such as collecting the eggs and helping in the Garden. The best was the laundry run, when we did a round of the caravans to pick up dirty washing for the machine in the shower-block. The vehicle we used for this, which we either pushed or rode in, was a shopping trolley from the supermarket in Middington. It could become a car, a tank, a dragon... anything.

Then there were lessons, although lessons isn't really the right word to use as it sounds too schooly. All the adults were happy to teach us their various skills if we showed an interest, but our principal instructor was Gogo. But no timetables were involved, no curriculum. 'School,' he would say, 'is simply society's method of conditioning kids to believe that for most of the week, for most of your life, you'll have to be in a place where you don't want to be, doing something you don't want to do.' He just taught what he felt like teaching at any given moment. This unpredictability was half the fun.

Quite often he would take us for a trip Outside. 'Come on kids,' he called one warm spring evening. 'Jump in the car. We're off to the seaside to learn all about tides and the moon.'

I looked up. 'There isn't a moon.'

'There will be, you'll see.'

'What about supper?' I asked a little anxiously.

'We're taking it with us.'

'Will the ice-cream place be open?' We loved going to the seaside. The nearest resort was less than an hour's drive away.

'No Curly, it's closed at night. Anyway, we're going somewhere much wilder than usual. But you know what? We're going to look for driftwood and build a fire and then we're going to bake some spuds and toast some of Marj's homemade marshmallows. I've got a whole big bag. And we're going to gather seaweed and make jelly with it tomorrow.'

'And some more marshmallows?' I asked. Marjoram used seaweed to make her marshmallows, gelatine being out of the question as it came from animals.

'Quite possibly. Now listen to this, kids – if we're really lucky tonight we might even see *phosphorescence*.'

We did, too. I'll never forget that evening: the full moon rising like a golden peach, the swish of pebbles dragged back and forth on the beach by the waves, the scent and sizzle of the marshmallows that we stuck on skewers and held over the embers of the fire. And the tiny sparkles of brilliance drifting around the rocks – only a few, but enough to reduce even Rain and me to silence by their magic. 'They're sea-fairies,' whispered Layla, and for once we had to agree with her.

The next day we wrote an account of our outing, as we always did – in my case lavishly illustrated as I loved to draw and was good at it. All of us could read and write by the age of five – because we wanted to. Books were a big part of our lives. Everyone had books, but the most interesting, to us, were Ginnie's, as she had hung on to all her childhood classics, and Gogo's, because he had picture-books about more or less everything. He also took us on regular forays to the library in Middington. I remember its fabulous smell – and the way in which parents often pushed their children away from us. '*Gypsies*,' was a whisper we heard more than once. 'We are not,' Shine would reply loudly and loftily. 'We are the *Elves' Inheritors*.' But that didn't seem to help much.

Perhaps the most varied collection of literature, and the one which finally absorbed me the most, was Jack's. I realise that up till now I've only once mentioned Jack in passing, and Loose not at all – the two people who were to be absolutely pivotal in my life as I started to grow up. Even now they still stir up a powerful and ambivalent cocktail of memories.

But they didn't arrive until the autumn of '76. Arjuna and all his mischief-making happened first.

4. *GREETINGS FROM THE UPPER REALM*

IT WAS A normal day...

That afternoon I'd gone over to Ashley's caravan, as I enjoyed watching him work, and I relished the smell of sawdust. When he was in a good humour he would lend me a few tools and show me how to use them on pieces of scrap wood. My first creation was a T-joint. I was extremely proud of this and went around showing it to everyone. 'Wow man, Curly's made his first joint!' said Sean, and fell about laughing at his own joke. Personally I didn't find it all that funny. I understood the pun perfectly well, but felt that Sean wasn't taking my handiwork very seriously.

'What else do you expect from someone who's so far up his own arse?' said Ash. I nodded sagely, in what I hoped was a knowing, grown-up manner. Later on I asked Marjoram just what Ash had meant.

'He means that Sean's in love with himself,' she explained.

'But isn't he in love with Stella?'

'Well, *she's* certainly in love with *him*. And Sean likes being looked after, so I suppose it's an arrangement that suits them both. Anyway, he's harmless enough -- and he makes us laugh, doesn't he?

This was true. Even Ash guffawed when Sean did his Tarzan act in the trees or strutted about with a home-made spear à la Conan the Barbarian. In spite of all his grumpy comments he wasn't really ill-disposed towards Sean. Ash's grumpiness was just part of his protective clothing, the psychological equivalent of his long and cruddy sheepskin coat.

He often sang while he worked – although 'droned' would perhaps be a better word. '*We-yall-live in a hippie colon-ee, hippie colon-ee, hippie colon-ee...*'

'It's not a hippie colony! It's a yellow submarine!' I would shout, annoyed at his bastardisation of one of my favourite songs.

'Same difference,' Ash always replied.

I liked it better when he sang one of his own compositions.

'I sleep in a tree like a chimpanzee,
'And I don't give a fuck if I'm covered in muck
'And I don't give a toss if I'm covered in moss
'Cos I'm never alone like a rolling stone...'

He did sleep in a tree. When he moved to Lothlorien he had chosen to gut most of his caravan, so that he could convert it into a carpentry workshop. Then, in a large and solid beech-tree nearby, he had constructed a bedroom for himself using bits of old timber salvaged from the House. He frequently did wood-working jobs for Our Lord - the repair of a staircase, for instance, or the creation of a new set of panels for the dining-room; he was a skilled joiner as well as carpenter. As Sean did, he had a perfectly amicable relationship with Our Lord, despite his sometimes disparaging remarks about him. His real hatred was reserved for Janet the Great. Their simmering mutual loathing was to flare up a few years later in an explosion which would almost tear apart the fabric of our little universe.

His magic domaine in the tree, constructed around the trunk and furnished with various fittings taken from the caravan, seemed to me like a masterpiece of architecture; Ash had been inspired by a book showing photographs of hippie tree-dwellings in the forests of California. Access was by a ladder, probably not as high as it appeared then, but still, I reckon, about fifteen feet off the ground. At night, having climbed to the top with Chipolata under one arm, he would hoist up the ladder and hang it on a couple of hooks fixed to the trunk of the tree, well out of anyone's reach.

'Protection from marauding females,' he said.

In fact these weren't much in evidence. In any case, when he did rnanage to score Outside he seldom brought his conquest to Lothlorien, but relied instead on the back of his pick-up, which he could convert into what he called a nookie parlour. He kept a stash of blankets and covers behind the seats in the front for this purpose, and had even fashioned a set of folding upright supports which he could quickly erect around the bed of the truck, and which, with a large bedspread thrown over, served as a temporary canopy. Within Lothlorien he would sometimes deploy the system so that I and the other children could play inside the fringed, musty gloom created by the bedcover – a perfect nomad's tent or bandit's hideout. I have a feeling it was used much more often in this way than as the enticing love-nest Ash intended it to be. His man-of-the-woods image was just a touch too wild and shaggy for the local girls. He had more luck when he went further afield, to a rock festival for example, or on a tool-buying expedition to Chandleford, which was a town considerably larger than Middington.

What made him really happy were the rare evenings when Tiger Lily scrambled up the ladder after him. 'He needs keeping warm sometimes,' she told me. I knew there must be more to it than this, as Ash had a perfectly efficient electric heater in his treehouse, hooked up to a long cable. He also had a big pile of sleeping bags.

'It's a shame you can't get together with Ashley more often,' I once overheard Wing saying to her. 'You put him in such a good mood.'

Tiger Lily laughed heartily. 'Jesus, man, I came to Europe for a bit of finesse,' she said. 'Not to get groped by a bloke like Ashley. He's got about as much sophistication as a cold meat pie.'

'But he has a heart of gold,' said Wing. 'And he's so good with his hands.'

'Not with me he isn't,' retorted Tiger Lily. 'And that bloody dog won't stop poking his nose in everywhere. Wants to be part of the action.'

She wasn't speaking unkindly, but I felt sorry for Ashley. Still, in the words of his song, he was never truly alone – at least not once Chipolata had entered the picture.

He acquired a wicker basket for Chip, a kind of garden trug with a sturdy handle, which he lined with old sweaters. Chip was content to stay in his basket providing it was positioned close to his master, which it normally was since Ash took him everywhere, including up to the House when he had a job to do there. No-one minded about this except Janet the Great.

Although in principal she disapproved of Lothlorien and all its inhabitants, she was obliged to tolerate us because of Our Lord. The one she tolerated most, in fact I think she had something of a crush on him, was Bill – not only because of his electro-magnetic quality but because he was the least hippie-like in appearance, had reasonably short hair, and was unfailingly courteous towards her. Zoë and Sean were also fairly frequent visitors to the House, and although they must have looked – (to her) – extremely peculiar, they were nonetheless civil, smiling, and appeared well washed, so she couldn't actively object to them. The rest of us seldom saw her – apart from Ashley. He had taken against her right from the start. 'Like my Aunt Tessie,' he said. 'Stupid, fat and bigoted.' Janet's opinion of him can't have been any more favourable. With his unkempt hair and disregard for all niceties of dress, Ash gave an impression of being dirty even when he wasn't, and his charm level was never very high either. But he wasn't openly rude to her. Not, that is, until the day when she first spotted Chip.

Ashley was replacing some rotten skirting boards in Our Lord's bedroom; Our Lord himself was away in London. Janet passed by the open door with a stack of clean laundry. She caught sight of the basket, and more particularly its contents, and stopped short in horror.

'What in Heaven's name is that?'

'That's Chipolata,' replied Ash, affably enough. 'Say hallo to Janet, old son.' Chip wagged his tail.

'You know perfectly well you're not allowed to have dogs! Get him off the premises immediately or I'll call up London.'

'Go ahead. You'll find he's had official clearance, so to speak. He's a nice little chap, wouldn't hurt a fly.' Ash lifted Chip out of his basket and gave him a gentle push. 'Go to Janet. Show her what a friendly dog you are. Jump up and give her a lick.'

Janet recoiled so swiftly that she dropped the pile of laundry. Chip waddled over and sat on it, dribbling slightly.

For a moment Janet was too shocked to speak. Red-faced and open-mouthed, ('like a stranded puffer-fish,' gloated Ashley later), it was at this moment that her eyes strayed to the basket.

'And where did you get that basket?' she managed to gasp.

'Found it in the drive,' replied Ash, thoroughly enjoying himself. 'Under a tree. Seemed a shame to let it get rained on.'

'I've been looking for that for weeks! That's my log basket!'

'Well, it's my Chip basket now. Finders keepers. You wouldn't want it back, anyway. Too smelly – take a sniff.'

Provoked beyond endurance, Janet swooped down and tugged fiercely at the laundry, causing Chip to roll off it in alarm. Holding the pile at arm's length, presumably to avoid all contact with germ-laden dog-drool, she charged away down the corridor.

Ash related this story with glee that evening, as we sat round the Fireplace. While everyone laughed, and Rain and I tried to do Janet-in-a-rage imitations, Bill remained unsmiling. He cleared his throat, a sign he was about to Pronounce.

'In the interests of us all,' he said finally – (when he began with these words we always knew that the Pronouncement would be a serious one) – 'it seems to me essential that you attempt to make peace with Janet. And buy her a new basket.'

Which is just what Ash did. He tied a big pink bow round it and left it in the porch of the Lodge, with a red rose and a note inside: *To Janet, with love and licks from Chipolata.*

Sadly, this peace-making gesture met with little success, in spite of the fact that from then on he was always excessively pleasant to her whenever their paths chanced to cross. 'Hey there Janet!' he would call. 'You're looking well today. Everything OK? Enjoying life, are you?' But she never replied. For years, right up until the day of their final showdown, she never spoke to him at all.

Today Chip was as usual nestled in the ill-gotten basket, on the top step of Ash's caravan. Ash had brought his workbench out on to the grass as he preferred to work in the open air if possible, even on a chilly March day such as this. Always more mindful of his pet's comfort than his own, he had thoughtfully placed a blow-heater just inside the caravan's open door and angled it towards Chip, whose ears stirred in the warm air current.

Ash's hands were partially covered by a pair of rainbow-coloured mittens that Wing had knitted for him, but even so he stopped work from time to time and blew noisily on his fingertips. The sun was bright but there was a keen wind which reddened his nose and made it run.

'Spring,' Neat Pete would declaim, 'is just winter with daffodils. And we're supposed to be *joyful*! My God, I'm not surprised it's the most popular season for suicides.'

I sat down on the steps and stroked Chip. 'What are you doing?' I asked Ash.

'Just drilling and screwing.' Ash gave a mighty sniff. 'Ha! I should be so lucky.'

While I was pondering this I noticed a figure in a long white gown walking slowly towards us, apparently deep in thought.

'Here comes Ginnie,' I observed.

Ash looked up and grunted. 'Yup. The First Lady herself.'

'What's she wearing that dress for? She's had it on for the last two days.'

'Search me. Ask her. Probably some new yoga thing.'

My puzzlement was well-founded: white clothes are not very practical as woodland wear, and within Lothlorien no-one wore white or indeed any pale, unpatterned fabric, apart from Pete, who spent less time exposed to nature than the rest of us. Ginnie's garments, though always elegant, were generally dark.

Her orange and yellow kaftans were the exception, but those she wore only when she was meditating. Morning and evening she would spread out her woven straw meditation mat, either in the doorway of her caravan, or more often outside on the ground if it was dry. Cold weather didn't bother her. 'Physical discomfort is only in the mind,' she said. 'It can be mastered through spiritual discipline. You should see what the Holy Men in India can put up with.'

Whether spiritually disciplined or just unusually thick-skinned, she didn't appear to suffer any pangs of chilliness, even in winter. I have a clear image of Ginnie, like a bright flower on her mat, surrounded by glittering frost. Not a shiver, not a goose-bump, disturbed her tranquillity. At these times she would meditate alone, as no-one else was holy enough to sit still outside in the freezing cold. On more clement days she would usually be joined by some of the others.

After twenty minutes or so of immobility, Ginnie would rise from the lotus position in one slow, fluid movement; the rest would follow, a bit less gracefully. Then it was time for yoga. Ginnie changed into a leotard and conducted a half-hour session for all who cared to join in. I enjoyed a good number of the yoga positions, especially the Cobra, but like the other children I soon got bored by the slowness and stillness of it all.

Doubtless it was this daily routine which gave Ginnie her superior poise and equanimity, but I have a feeling that these were reinforced by a certain inner glow of self-satisfaction at being so fabulously in control of her body.

Now she approached Ash and myself with careful, measured steps, somehow managing to avoid all the puddles which sparkled along the muddy path. Ash put down his tools and we both automatically stood to attention. Ginnie stopped in front of us, put her palms together in an attitude of prayer, and inclined her head forward.

'Namasté,' she said gravely.

This was new. We stared.

'What?' I said.

'Namasté,' she repeated. 'It's an ancient Sanskrit greeting. It means that the divine essence in me salutes the divine essence in you.'

Though Bill and Ginnie had been to India and done the whole ashram/guru number, they hadn't up till now adopted much of the ritual paraphernalia which went with it, apart from the yoga and meditation – which they'd already been doing anyway, long before their trip. 'We went to learn, not to copy,' said Bill. 'In Lothlorien we have to find our own way to higher consciousness. Our aim is to apply the principles without slavishly following the practices.'

Yet here was Ginnie all of a sudden performing a mini oriental rite. It struck me that her strange white robe, gleaming in the sunshine with a silky sheen, could be linked to this new behaviour.

'Why have you got on that white thing?' I enquired.

Ginnie smiled at me, in her most gracious, I-am-favouring-you-with-my-smile kind of way. 'That's what I've come to tell you about.'

I should stress that Ginnie was invariably kind and charming to everyone, especially children . Her kindness was, I'm sure, quite genuine. Yet I never felt close to her. When we had our communal hug-ins she was the only person I wasn't all that keen to hug. We were all, of course, first-class huggers, and not just of each other, but of the trees, rocks, even the sheep. (The sheep didn't mind – they were used to it). We could even do abstract hugging: 'Oh, I'm in love with this moment,' someone might say. 'Let's *hug* the moment.'

Bill was the least demonstrative hugger, but his hugs, though brisker than most, were a manly, straightforward sign of approval that I was glad to receive. On these occasions he turned the electric barrier off. I don't think he was fundamentally a cold person; just someone who took himself, and life in general, terribly, terribly, seriously.

And his sense of humour was almost non-existent. All of which kept people at a distance but only strengthened his aura of authority.

But Ginnie... I can't really explain my reticence towards her. Physically, she was appealing, with an even-featured, unassuming prettiness which went well with Bill's more strikingly pointy good looks. She had a shining cap of chestnut hair similar to his own; you could have taken them for brother and sister. And like Bill, Ginnie didn't have much sense of humour either, now I come to think of it.

She looked steadily at Ash and me with her clear grey eyes.

'I have some wonderful news,' she said.

'You've won the Pools,' said Ash.

'Oh Ashley, how *can* you... No, it's far, far better than that. Something on another plane altogether.' She paused to make sure she had our full attention. 'This evening we shall be receiving a visitor - from India. Someone quite extraordinary. We're incredibly lucky that he's agreed to come here. It's for him I'm wearing white, you see – to prepare myself psychically. It's a symbol of Spirit Incorruptible .'

You could somehow tell that this was an expression she had only recently learned.

She noticed the way Ash was looking at her. 'That's not *me,* of course,' she went on with just a touch of confusion. 'I mean, I'm not there *myself,* not yet. I've still got miles to go before my spirit is incorruptible ... but that's what all of us here are aiming for, isn't it?'

Silence for a moment while Ash scratched his chin. Bits of sawdust showered down from his beard.

'So what's he into then, this bloke?' he said finally. 'Is he some sort of guru?'

'I suppose you could say that... though you can't really put a *label* on him. He's beyond that kind of thing.'

'Blimey,' said Ash. 'Sounds like he dropped from the sky.'

Ginnie gave a quiet little laugh. 'Perhaps he has – in a way.'

'What's his name?' I asked.

Ginnie's face lit up with a soft radiance. 'Arjuna,' she said reverently.

This was exciting. 'Like in the Bag story? Is he a warrior prince?' I was referring to the Bhagavad Gita, or rather a version of it in a book of Ginnie's entitled 'Hindu Myths Made Easy' or something of that nature.

'No Curly, he's not a warrior. He's the most peaceful person you could hope to meet. A spreader of happiness.' I had a fleeting vision of Erryk spreading butter and Marmite on his home-baked bread, as he often did for my breakfast.

'When you're in his presence,' Ginnie went on, 'You feel... well, your mind starts to *tingle*. You'll see."

My disappointment at this new Arjuna's lack of military prowess was now tempered by curiosity; what would happen when my mind began to tingle?

'Is he going to stay the night?' I asked.

'We hope he'll be staying *many* nights, Curly.'

'Where? In the Sheikh's Palace?'

'No, Bill and I are going to move in there. Arjuna must sleep in our caravan.'

The Sheikh's Palace was one of those tent affairs that could be attached to the back of a caravan to provide some extra covered space. Bill put it up as a guest-room for visiting friends or family who were going to stay a night or two but hadn't brought a tent of their own. It didn't matter whether the guests were his own, Ginnie's, or anyone else's: Stella's mother Fiona, for instance, came down from Scotland to visit at least once a year, being the one parent who actually enjoyed being in Lothlorien. Although Sean and Stella had a spare bedroom it was clogged up with Sean's weight-lifting gear and exercise bike, and anyway Fiona preferred to have a bit of privacy. I think it was she who had coined the name 'Sheikh's Palace', partly because of the Berber carpet and fabrics that Ginnie would spread on the groundsheet and camp beds, but also because when the wind was high the whole structure did shake. It had never fallen down, however.

Bill and Ginnie never slept there themselves; the fact that they were going to do so now was a big surprise. Their caravan was somehow more private than anyone else's, although everyone was invariably made welcome there during the day – unless Ginnie was meditating or Bill was Thinking. Occasionally someone might lie down on the settee for a stoned nap, but they would always be gently helped outside when Bill or Ginnie considered it was bedtime. The settee could be expanded into a perfectly good bunk, but this was always kept free in case Jelly Bean wanted to sleep there. (I'm coming to Jelly Bean.) As in all the caravans, apart from Ash's, there was a bedroom at each end, one smaller than the other; Bill used the small one as his office, and the other, where they slept, was the only bedroom that I'd never seen inside. 'It's the Inner Sanctum,' said Rick. 'The nerve-centre of Lothlorien.' I'd always longed for a glimpse of this sacred precinct, and envied Arjuna's favoured status.

'Bloody hell,' said Ash, as surprised as I was.

'Yes, I know it must seem a bit odd... but he really is amazingly special. You'll understand when you meet him.'

'Can't fucking wait.'

'Oh, and Ashley – I do think we should all make an effort not to swear in front of him. It would be an insult to – to his purity.'

'Well in that case I'd better stay out of sight.' Ash jerked his head towards his dog. 'He doesn't mind me swearing – do you Chippo? And he's as pure as the driven snow.'

Ginnie ignored this. She had, after all, known Ash for a long time.

'Bill's gone to London to pick him up. They should be here around seven, but it's better if we don't make any fuss when they arrive. Arjuna will probably want to rest for a while after the journey, and clean up a bit. Let's try and keep the showers free so he won't feel crowded. Then I thought it would be a really cool thing if everybody could get together outside our caravan around nine-thirty so he can greet us all.'

This was clearly a set of orders.

'Do the others know?' I asked. 'I can go and tell them, if you like.'

'No, it's OK, I've been round to see everyone.'

'Did you find all the kids?'

'Yes... except...' Ginnie's face took on a familiar expression of faint worry tinged with helplessness, which could only mean one thing. 'Do either of you know where my daughter is?"

Which brings me, at last, to Jelly Bean.

Jelly Bean: the sole phenomenon capable of upsetting Ginnie's equilibrium, a force of nature falling well outside the range of her and Bill's powers of control, even though it was they who had brought her into being. Her conception had come about not long after my own birth.

This latter event had provoked such a fit of broodiness in Stella, Zoë and Ginnie that they all decided to go off the Pill, with the aim of creating Cosmic Aquarian Triplets. Zoë fell pregnant immediately – (unfair in a way, since she already had Elvira) – followed a couple of months later by Ginnie. Sean and Stella, much to the latter's frustration, didn't seem able to come up with the goods.

Even in the womb Jelly Bean was exceptionally turbulent. She didn't just kick, she stamped her feet and threw herself around as much as she could in the limited space available. 'You could actually see her pounding her fists on Ginnie's belly,' said Tiger Lily. 'She was just raring to go.'

According to legend, it was during a summer thunderstorm that she burst upon the world, almost four weeks before she was due. Ginnie, who had hoped to have a natural birth like Wing, was rushed to Chandleford hospital, Bill driving the Spitfire like a maniac through the winding country lanes. They arrived in the nick of time. The baby was swiftly placed in an incubator.

In those days parents weren't allowed much hands-on contact with premature babies – the reason, Ginnie believed, why she and her daughter had never really bonded. 'She seems so... disturbed,' she would say. 'Her previous incarnation must have been terribly violent. That's why she chose to be born in Lothlorien this time round. In an environment of peace and harmony.'

But peace and harmony never seemed to be particularly high on Jelly Bean's list of priorities. I don't think she ever tried to cause trouble out of malice: she was just innately wild. If she'd had a former life, it was as the Cat who Walked by Himself. As an infant, she would never simply lie and gurgle when awake, as Layla did – she screamed until she was picked up and taken for a walk. Once she could crawl she was away on her own. Bill and Ginnie – indeed everybody – tried to keep an eye on her, but Jelly Bean would just pretend to take a nap, wait until no-one was looking, then trundle off on all fours like a baby all-terrain vehicle, slithering down caravan steps and over any obstacle in her path, advancing unstoppably through puddles, bushes, even Galadriel's Pool – where she must, luckily, have stuck to the shallow side. 'The Mother protected her,' said Wing, who on that occasion had caught sight of her sploshing up the bank and carried her back, dripping and screaming, to a distraught Ginnie. Anyone who spotted her roaming about would always bring her home, yelling and covered in mud but undamaged apart from a few scratches. Although it was against Lothlorien principles to put children in cages, Ginnie in desperation asked Ash to make her a large play-pen. Jelly Bean shook the bars and shrieked like a banshee, so the play-pen was broken up and recycled as a wigwam for the twins and myself.

As soon as she learned to walk her field of operations widened considerably, although at suppertime the smell of cooking usually tempted her back into the fold. But not always: Ginnie would sometimes find her asleep under a caravan, or in the chicken coop – (she had quickly worked out how to open the gate in the fence). Once, worriedly searching the woods by torchlight, with Tiger Lily as moral support, Ginnie discovered her curled peacefully inside a hollow oak-tree next to Parvati, the tabby cat from the House.

'You see?' said Tiger Lily. 'Wing's right. The spirits look after her.'

'We can't just *leave* her there, though.'

'Whyever not? It's a warm night. Look at her – she's happy as a pig in shit. You shouldn't fuss about her so much, it's just her karma. If she wants to go walkabout, you'll never be able to stop her. None of us could stop her.'

Ginnie had to concede the truth of this. 'But am I doing something wrong?' she asked.

'Of course you're not, petal,' said Tiger Lily. 'You should be glad she's so independent. It's a blessing, believe you me. When civilisation collapses she'll cope heaps better than any of us.'

It was not, of course, her parents who had given Jelly Bean her name. Soon after her birth everyone drove over in turn to Chandleford hospital to visit Ginnie and take a peek through the glass at the new arrival. Zoë, Marjoram and Wing went together, taking Elvira with them. Elvira, who for her first six years had been an only child, was only too pleased at any opportunity to put some distance between herself and Layla. She'd never been a baby-minded little girl: she scorned the company of all us younger children until we were old enough to understand what she was saying, so she could show off her knowledge of the world.

'That's Emily,' said Ginnie, exhausted but happy, gesturing proudly towards the incubator. 'Look how perfect she is!'

The women cooed and clucked and admired the baby's tiny toenails.

'She looks like a half-chewed jelly bean,' said Elvira.

Zoë repeated this back in Lothlorien and everyone – (though perhaps not Bill) - thought it was a very amusing and typically Elvira remark.

Rain and Shine, then aged two, started to chant: 'Jelly Bean, Jelly Bean, we want Jelly Bean!' and repeated this at regular intervals throughout the following few weeks, rising to a grand crescendo when mother and child finally arrived back in Lothlorien. Ginnie tried vainly to call her Emily, but people would just say, 'Who? Oh – you mean Jelly Bean.' In the end she gave up. Besides, Jelly Bean herself never answered to the name of Emily, so Ginnie was obliged to address her as everyone else did. In conversation with others she simply referred to her as 'my daughter.'

Ash and I didn't, of course, have the faintest idea where said daughter was now. 'Maybe with Sean?' I said.

'No, he hasn't seen her today.'

Jelly Bean had recently become fixated on Sean, because he had taught her how to climb trees and swing from ropes like he did. She frequently insisted on cuddling up with him at night, which must have been rather hard on Stella. Earlier on she'd been especially attached to Tiger Lily and the combi, and spent a lot of time in there splashing paint around before falling asleep on Tiger Lily's giant bean-bag. On some evenings she burrowed into my own bunk, forcing me to sleep on the floor, as I found her too alarming to have as a bedfellow. Bill and Ginnie, keen for her to feel more at home in their own caravan, tried to entice her with cosy nests of cushions and soft toys. Most of the toys ended up being given to Layla.

'Oh well...' Ginnie gave a sigh. 'I just hope she'll turn up in time. I do think it's important for her to – to be blessed along with the rest of us.'

But as nine-thirty approached there was still no sign of her.

Most of us had obediently adhered to Ginnie's instructions, disappearing tactfully indoors when we heard the Spitfire corning down the track. But with Layla and the twins I sneaked over to a vantage point next to the Garden where we hoped to get a quick clandestine glimpse of our visitor. We discussed his alleged mind-tingling skills.

'Perhaps he's got a magic wand,' said Layla.

'Don't be daft,' said Shine. At seven she was already a practical and rather bossy girl, with a keen interest in science. 'He might have a magnet in each hand or something. So he can make an electric current and give your brain a little shock.'

'I don't want a little shock!'

'Don't be such a baby. It won't hurt you.'

'If you're scared, just don't go near him,' I advised.

Rain, quieter than his sister and more of a fantasist, considered this. 'I don't think it'll make any difference how close you are. He probably uses *telepathic powers.* '

Gogo, overhearing us through his open window, came out to shoo us away.

Later on, assembled on blankets spread on the grass in front of Bill and Ginnie's caravan, the adults smoked and chatted quietly. The twins,

Layla and I had been allowed to sit at the front providing we didn't make too much noise. Elvira, feigning a lack of interest in the whole affair, chose to remain at the edge of the group. Pete, too, sat slightly apart, his spliff as usual wedged in a long ivory holder. Thickets of candles in glass jars had been placed all around, and cast flickering light into the surrounding trees. Shadows moved within the Sheikh's Palace; soon Ginnie came out to join us, followed by Bill himself, dressed like her in a long white robe. He had never before affected much hippie gear apart from the plain Indian cotton shirts he wore with his understated flares, so to see him clothed like this now only added to the solemnity and the strangeness of the occasion. The caravan door was open, the interior illuminated by still more candles. A faint sound of tabla music drifted out, and a strong scent of patchouli incense. The wind had dropped but the air was still chilly, though no-one seemed to be worried by the cold. The suspense was palpable: it shimmered all around us.

Someone – maybe it was Ginnie – began a spontaneous 'Om.....' and straightaway everybody else joined in. (Omming, like hugging, was a communal activity that we all enjoyed). Soon the night was vibrating with a richly-textured harmony of oms, growing in intensity – and then suddenly dying away as a shadow darkened the light in the doorway.

On the top step appeared a slight figure, robed in white, a golden band round his long dark hair. A soft sigh, a gasp of wonder, went up from the women. Then total silence fell. I was sure I could feel my mind tingling.

The figure raised his hands together – first above his head, then against his forehead, and finally at chest level.

'Namasté,' he said.

'Namasté,' we all murmured in response, Bill and Ginnie perfectly imitating his gestures.

Arjuna's gaze swept over the group and his face lit up with a wide angelic smile. He opened his arms as if to embrace us all.

'I bring you greetings,' he said. 'From the Upper Realm.'

It was at this moment that a crazed, unearthly whooping rang out from high in the tall poplar tree behind the caravan. Everyone looked up. The leaves were quivering wildly. Among them it was just possible to make out a dark furry creature which appeared to be shaking the branches.

'Shit a bleeding brick,' muttered Ashley audibly.

It was Jelly Bean in her gorilla suit.

5. *CONSCIOUSNESS ARISING*

'THAT GUY IS is so fucking far out... he's *galactic*.'

'Mind-blowing.'

'Totally out of sight, man. He's changed my whole perception.'

Comments like these flowed freely around Lothlorien for the first few weeks following Arjuna's arrival. Almost everyone had fallen into a kind of collective trance, respectfully saluting each other with bows and namastés all day long. Even Ashley, even Elvira made the effort. The whole atmosphere was charged with radiance as Lothlorien moved a rung up the spiritual ladder.

'He's just so... THERE,' said Wing to Pete one day. 'I think you mean *here,* dear.'

She and I were drinking tea – my own heavily laced with condensed milk – in Pete's caravan. I liked Pete's caravan. The prevailing tidiness and lack of clutter made it seem much bigger than our own. 'Can't we be neat too?' I once asked Wing. 'No, Curly,' she said. 'There's three of us and only one of him.' I knew this was only part of the truth.

It was very soothing, being chez Pete, and not only because of the neatness. There was also the awe-inspiring experience of drinking tea from a china cup and saucer with gold rims and patterns of violets, rather than out of a clumpy earthenware mug. And then there was his music. No Dylan, Hendrix or Frank Zappa, no bongo drums or bamboo flute: instead, cascades of Bach, Mozart, Gregorian chants, or opera. Today it was the turn of a compilation of arias sung by Maria Callas.

Her voice soared and swooped, drowning the patter of the April rain on the caravan roof. Even at that age – six and two-thirds – I could recognise the extreme emotion in her voice. It induced in me a pleasant melancholia.

'Ah, Maria, Maria,' sighed Pete, as he often did, 'you suffer for us all.'

'She ought to meet Arjuna,' said Wing. 'He'd be able to help her.'

Pete raised an eyebrow. 'I doubt it. I can't imagine she'd take to him in a very big way.'

'Why not? How could anyone resist his – his – *goodness?* He loves *everybody.*'

'Then I'd better watch out, hadn't I?' murmured Pete, but Wing was lost in contemplation of her tea and didn't seem to hear.

Pete, I knew, had never been entirely captivated by Arjuna, and although I enjoyed all the excitement and activity attendant on his presence amongst us, I had a few reservations of my own as well. I somehow couldn't swallow all this loving everybody business. How could you love, for instance, Janet the Great? Ivan the Terrible? Attila the Hun? Or, worst of all, the *Black Riders?*

'But he does,' said Wing. 'And we should, too.' I wasn't convinced.

What I did find remarkable about Arjuna was his power over Jelly Bean, established at the time of their first memorable encounter.

He had, of course, looked up along with the rest of us and quickly spotted the simian apparition in the poplar tree. But he didn't react with the appalled embarrassment of the Lothlorien adults. Far from it. He simply began to laugh, quite softly, but with obvious delight. Wing later compared the sound of his laugh to the tinkling of temple bells. To me it always sounded as if he were crying.

At any rate, he laughed and laughed, and raised his arms skyward. 'We are doubly, triply blessed!' he exclaimed at last. 'It is Hanuman!'

'No, it's Jelly Bean!' yelled Layla.

'Shut up, silly,' I hissed. 'He means Hanuman the Monkey God.' Layla wasn't really into the Bhagavad Gita.

'But she's not a monkey, she's a gorilla!' 'Maybe he needs glasses. Now be quiet.'

'Do come down, sweetheart...' Ginnie sounded a little desperate. 'Arjuna so wants to meet you.'

Jelly Bean appeared unmoved by this plea.

'I have monkey nuts!' cried Arjuna suddenly. 'Especially for you!' He turned to reach inside the caravan, and as if by magic produced a bowl of peanuts in their shells. 'Do you think you can crack them?' he called sweetly.

This was an inspired move on his part, and added weight to Rain's theory of his telepathic powers: Jelly Bean was a nut-fiend. The previous autumn, like a squirrel, she had made little hoards of hazelnuts and beechnuts all over the woods, under stones and in holes in trees, sometimes adding a few walnuts or brazils lifted from the greengrocer in Middington – (when Ginnie found out she stopped taking her daughter shopping with her). Even now, at the beginning of spring, she would sometimes come across one of these hidden stocks that she'd forgotten about. To her credit, she usually shared them with the twins, Layla and me. Often they were a bit mouldy.

At the irresistible temptation of a new kind of nut – raw unshelled peanuts not being a readily available commodity in our part of the country – Jelly Bean swung into action. First a long length of rope came tumbling down from the tree. The upper end, we realised, was tied round the branch she was standing on. 'That's one of Sean's,' whispered Shine. 'He was up there the other day, remember?'

Jelly Bean began to slither down the rope – no mean feat for a five-year-old, but then she wasn't exactly an ordinary five-year-old. I can't say we held our breath, because by now everyone was used to her acrobatic skills. Descending hand over hand, her ankles firmly crossed around the rope as Sean had taught her, she made a successful landing to one side of the caravan and then scrambled round to the front steps. She pushed back the head of the gorilla outfit so it bobbed like a macabre hood behind her cropped hair.

It was uncanny, the extent to which she resembled a miniature Ginnie – but with a much sharper and more feral expression. Sometimes we called her Mini Ginnie, though not to her face as the name made her growl and spit. But apparently she didn't mind being addressed as Hanuman, because she approached Arjuna with what passed, in her case, for a smile. As usual, she came straight to the point.

'Nuts,' she said.

'Help yourself,' said Arjuna munificently, holding out the bowl towards her. She tipped as many as she could hold into one hand, conveniently larger than usual because of the glove section of the gorilla costume, which was nicely finished off with black plastic fingernails.

It was Stella who had bought it for her, while up in London for a couple of days' modelling. She'd spotted it in the window of a charity shop.

'And you know, it looked so divine, after all those boring pastel twinsets I'd been wearing all day,' she told us. 'So I went in and asked if they had a couple of bigger ones, because I thought maybe Sean and me... They didn't though, but then I remembered Jelly Bean and all her jungle games, and I knew it would be perfect for her.'

Jelly Bean was of the same opinion. She was already wearing it for much of the time before Arjuna's arrival, and all the time, as far as I can remember, after it. While not becoming his abject slave, she nonetheless followed him around a lot, showing off with cartwheels and other stunts which always made him laugh. And she often ran small errands for him, for which she was rewarded with more peanuts. He was amazingly generous with these, not only towards Jelly Bean but the rest of us as well; fragments of peanut shell could soon be seen scattered around everywhere. 'Manna from Heaven,' said Pete. Arjuna himself ate a good deal of them – where did they all come from? Had he brought them with him?

Wing had picked up a piece of broken shell – probably out of my hair – and was idly drawing circles with it in the surface of her tea. Usually she did this with her fingernail. I found the habit quite annoying.

'Drink up, sweetheart,' said Pete, looking out of the window. 'Tiger Lily's coming to fetch you. You don't want to be late for Temple Time, now do you?'

'Oh –' Wing stopped stirring, gulped her tea and stood up.

I opened the door just as Tiger Lily reached the caravan steps. She was wearing her flowered plastic mac, and from the sides of the hood long wet curls spilled out in a way I found particularly enchanting. We namasté-d.

'Namasté, Soul-friend,' said Wing. She stepped outside and put up the lacy white parasol she used as an umbrella, adopting what I thought of as her holy look. 'I'm ready.'

'Hey, Pete!' called Tiger Lily. 'You wanna pose for me later on?'

'In the nude? I'm not sure that's such a good idea.'

'No, you can keep your clothes on. I might put some eye-liner on you though.' 'How delightful. To what do I owe this honour?'

'I'm doing these Egyptian-style paintings, you know? And you've got the right sort of profile.'

'Of course, darling. Nefertiti is my middle name.'

'Plus, you're the only person who sits naturally in that sideways kind of way.' 'Just a trick I learned when I was posing for all those tomb friezes.'

'Probably where we first met. I was already an artist back then.'

'Oh yes, Ancient Egypt!' said Wing. 'I'm sure we *all* knew each other.'

'What was I?' I asked. I liked the idea of living in Ancient Egypt.

'Tutankhamun, most likely,' said Tiger Lily. 'You've got the eyes, at any rate.'

Wing plucked at her arm. 'We mustn't be late...'

'That's right, my lovelies,' said Pete. 'Run along and open your minds to the Infinite.'

'Aren't you coming?' asked Wing.

Pete peered out at the rain. 'Not today. I'd rather stay here with Maria.'

'But think of your karma!'

'I was thinking of my shoes, actually. I'm just not in the mood to go traipsing through mud and wet grass – much as I admire Arjuna's talents as a showman.'

Wing frowned. 'You mean shaman.'

'No darling, *showman.* Or magician, if you like. One who brings you illusion in the form of truth.'

'Oh, but *everything* is illusion,' said Wing earnestly. 'That's what he's always telling us, isn't it.'

'Exactly, my poppet. Just hang on to that.'

*

Temple Time: our new daily ritual, performed every afternoon at five in the equally new Temple of Consciousness Arising. This was the name bestowed by Arjuna on the small and rather dilapidated marquee which Our Lord, eternally obliging, had loaned to Lothlorien to prevent us from getting wet as our consciousness arose.

For the first few days following his arrival Arjuna had conducted a teaching session every afternoon from the steps of Bill and Ginnie's caravan, with the rest of us clustered on the ground outside in suitably respectful cross-legged positions. On the fourth day a heavy shower passed overhead.

'The rain is Nature's own champagne!' said Arjuna, and smilingly retreated a few paces backwards into the shelter of the caravan doorway. This raised a laugh, at least from those prescient enough to bring an umbrella. Everyone else grinned weakly and got drenched; we were, at this stage, far too much in awe of Arjuna to move.

'What does a little rain matter?' said Ginnie afterwards, when a certain amount of damp grumbling took place. 'We should *all* bring our umbrellas in future.'

'We can't concentrate if it's pissing with rain,' said Ashley. 'Even with an umbrella, it's still dripping all round you. Too fucking distracting.'

'And bear in mind,' said Rick, squeezing the water from his ponytail, now even lanker and stringier than usual, 'we're not as spiritually advanced as you are, Ginnie.' He wiped his glasses with his long thin musician's fingers.

'I think they are right,' said Bill gravely.

So he took Arjuna up to the House and introduced him to Our Lord, who was much taken with our exotic guest and agreed to lend us one of the little marquees he kept stored in the stables for use on the rare occasions when he threw a party in the gardens.

There was a tree-free patch of grass next to the shower block which Bill decided would be the best place to erect it. As the ground sloped slightly, Rick, Erryk and Gogo – with a bit of help from Rain and myself – dug a trench along the higher section for drainage purposes, and Ash lined the sides with planks to keep the soil in place. Wing cut up an Indian scarf so that she and the other women could stitch pieces on to the canvas to patch the holes and cover up the manky bits.

Arjuna oversaw the operations with his usual benign calm. 'And now we will bless this holy place with love,' he said once the work was complete. 'Everyone must bring a treasured object and place it on the altar.' The altar was an old table, also from the House, that Ginnie had covered with a lace tablecloth.

I thought long and hard about this, not being over-eager to part with any of my treasured objects. Rummaging through my toy box I found a Dinky Toy fire engine with two wheels missing. I decided this would count, because I *had* treasured it, at least when it had all its wheels; so I duly plonked it among the other offered goodies. They made up an eclectic assortment, ranging from a bronze, multi-limbed statuette of Shiva – (Ginnie's) – to a pot of dried herbs which Marjoram had prepared at full moon to ward against evil vapours. Erryk, I remember, provided the sheet music of *Mr Tambourine Man,* rolled up and tied with a leather thong. Wing added one of her own works, a little mat of white crocheted cotton in the form of a heart. She had made it specially.

'Gracious, such a symbol of pure love,' remarked Pete. His own contribution was one of his small framed photos of Judy Garland.

I'm aware that up till now I must have given the impression that my mother was nothing but a rather woolly-minded and impractical waif, but in fact that was only half the picture. What she lacked in day-to-day organisational skills she made up for in the handicrafts department. On her old black sewing machine – (I loved its gold lettering and twirly patterns) – she fashioned drifty but very well-finished pieces of clothing; most of us had at least one Wing-made item in our wardrobe. She was good at knitting and crochet too, and we wore her tank-tops with pride. She also made bedcovers and ponchos – it was fun to watch the evolution of a single crocheted square into a multi-cellular psychedelic entity. On my own poncho she embroidered my name in red below the neckline, upside-down, though of course it was the right way up if I was wearing it and looked down at my chest. 'It's so you never forget who you are,' she told me. At the time I didn't think this was likely, but now I know otherwise. I wish I knew what happened to that poncho.

Erryk used to display Wing's creations at the markets, hanging them from a rail along one side of his stall, and they sold very well. Occasionally she would go with him, at least when she needed to shop for yarn or fabric, but in general she didn't much like going Outside. She only really felt safe within Lothlorien.

Now that Arjuna was among us she began to take more interest in cooking: previously she had left that side of things to Erryk, who was an imaginative cook, always ready to try out new combinations of plants, whether wild, from the Garden, or brought in from Outside. In the main his recipes were much appreciated. I particularly enjoyed his aubergine and garlic paté with ginger and crushed peanuts. On the other hand, his radish and raisin risotto cooked in homemade root beer, although alliterative, was less successful. Wing rarely contributed to these efforts, though I do have a clear memory of her scattering a salad with wild rose petals she had gathered from the hedgerows round the Sheepfield. They looked like pale pink snow, and I hoped they would be sweet, like ice-cream, but they weren't.

Communal cook-ins around the Fireplace had always taken place quite regularly, but Arjuna's presence stimulated the women to organise more of these than usual. Ginnie pored over Indian cookbooks and went to Chandleford to look for extra spices.

'Currying favour,' said Pete. I thought this was a very clever pun once he explained it to me. Pete enjoyed cooking too, in a rather theatrical way. 'To the magic cauldron!' he would cry, rising to stir the mixture in the big saucepan set over the fire. He taught us kids lines from the witches in Macbeth, which we recited with enthusiasm. 'Eye of newt!' shouted Layla as she threw in a few sultanas.

Zoë used to shudder at this. 'You shouldn't quote from that play,' she said. 'Ask any actor. It brings terrible bad luck.' But we didn't believe her, and neither did Pete.

The wonders of Arjuna were often discussed on these occasions.

'He's just so beautiful, he radiates.' Stella said a lot of this kind of thing.

'He's got gorgeous eyes,' mused Marjoram. 'Hypnotic.'

'They're simply a reflection of his *inner* beauty,' said Ginnie piously – even a little sharply.

'Yes of course, it's his *essence* that's beautiful,' agreed Zoë. 'That's what we're talking about, isn't it?'

'Is it?' murmured Tiger Lily.

Wing tended to keep quiet during these conversations.

'Do *you* think he's beautiful?' I asked her one evening after dinner. We were all seated round the fire – all, that is, except Arjuna himself, who always had his meals taken to him in Bill and Ginnie's caravan.

Wing was busy crocheting and didn't look up, although her crochet hook paused in mid twiddle. 'The most beautiful thing about him,' she said after a moment, 'is that he's here, in Lothlorien, with us. He could be anywhere, and yet he's chosen *us*.'

'Krishna descends on Middle Earth,' commented Pete.

'Oh man, that's such a cool way of putting it,' said Erryk.

*

The weeks slipped by... Arjuna seemed to be more and more settled into Lothlorien. He generally got up later than the rest of us, and spent a long time in the shower block, emerging squeaky clean and beaming, always in white robe and golden headband. Anyone he passed on the way back to his quarters would be greeted with a namasté and a gentle pat on the head. It was funny to see him patting Rick, the latter being well over six feet tall while Arjuna was on the short side and had to reach up on tiptoe. 'Bend, bend!' he would say, laughing his tinkly laugh, so Rick, always a little stooped, would incline his head still further in order to get the full benefit of the saintly pat.

'It's freaky, it's kind of like these amazing riffs are piercing my skull – I mean I can actually *sense* them, you know? And he makes me feel almost... *friendly* towards the world. That's so weird.' Rick was known for his caustic views on more or less everything. When I was small I found him rather alarming. The first time I saw him coming back from a gig on his motorbike, guitar case strapped vertically on to his back, loud curses issuing from beneath his helmet – (it was raining and he was very wet) – I screamed because I thought he was some kind of Orc.

'He's still working out some bad karma,' Zoë would say when he was in a particularly foul mood. 'But his heart's in the right place.'

Rick's musical creativity had certainly exploded back into life in recent weeks, after one of the long depressive periods which often overcame him during the winter. Was it Arjuna's powers or the lengthening days of spring which had caused this new flowering of his talent?

Zoë had no doubts about the matter. 'Arjuna's taught him how to tap into his Source,' she sighed contentedly. 'He's in touch with his true Buddha Nature. It makes him so much easier to live with. He's almost *nice*.'

'And noisier,' added Elvira, but with uncharacteristic mildness.

Lately, like her father, she had begun to seem softer and better-tempered – though she still chewed gum, a habit that I found inexplicable. Why chew something you couldn't eat? And if you swallowed it by mistake it got stuck inside you and blocked up your intestines, according to Wing. Apart from the chewing-gum, however, Elvira's manner and appearance were definitely changing. She became strangely polite. Her clothes were neater and cleaner.

She had her mother's plumpness and freckles but not her cherubic face – (Layla had inherited that, without the freckles). Instead she had Rick's prominent nose, and short-sighted blue-grey eyes behind little round gold-framed specs. And like him, she was rather tall and ungainly. But she had Zoë's hair, gingerish and frizzy.

'That's why I became a stylist,' Zoë would say. 'At least I can get some vicarious hair satisfaction, even if my own hair's shit.' She attached wonderful coloured beads to the ends in the hope that the weight would straighten it a bit, and hid the rest beneath a wide headband or a long silk scarf. In pre-Arjuna days her daughter had scorned such artifice and let her hair fly wild and free, but now she took to tying it back with ribbons and sometimes stuck wildflowers in it. She even insisted on being the one to take Arjuna's meals to him in Bill and Ginnie's caravan. No-one objected, as this new-style Elvira was so much more pleasant than the old version.

Before his lunch Arjuna supposedly spent an hour or two in meditation; his lengthy morning ablutions were, we were told, a preparation for this plunge into the Absolute. During the afternoon he reclined on the settee in the caravan, nibbling his monkey nuts and receiving individual visits from members of the community, until the moment for Temple Time arrived. After that was over he liked to go for a walk in the woods, often with Jelly Bean tagging along, his gorilla-suited court jester. If it was raining they played draughts. He taught her poker too, and how to lay bets with nuts. She transmitted this interesting new knowledge to the twins, Layla and myself, and it became our new craze. Layla, to our extreme irritation, turned out to be the most skilful player.

Gogo expressed his doubts about the suitability of children becoming obsessed with gambling, but Arjuna put his mind at rest. 'They are learning the ways of the gods, how Vishnu can give and yet Kali take away. These lessons they are absorbing on a karmic level.'

During the first weeks of his stay he would be available after dinner for anyone who wanted to visit him for a final bedtime blessing. Then he would retire 'to study and contemplate.' But soon he took to spending his evenings up at the House; Our Lord had recently got back after a short absence and had supposedly expressed an interest in discovering his Inner Light.

'He has a pure soul,' I heard Arjuna say to Bill one day. 'But it is obscured by too much worldliness.'

'In what way?'

Arjuna sighed deeply. 'He is too attached to the material plane.'

'He is nevertheless an exceptionally generous man,' said Bill. 'Without him we wouldn't be here. And neither would you.' I think he was beginning by now to feel the strain of sleeping on a camp bed in the Sheikh's Palace. In addition, he had been waiting for quite some time to have access to the shower block, which Arjuna had been occupying for longer than usual that morning. 'Please excuse me, Arjuna, I have to –'

Arjuna placed a gently restraining hand on Bill's arm. 'Yes yes yes... but now you must suspend your bodily functions for just one precious moment, like I have taught you... This is so important and perhaps you have some influence. You see, he could be giving so much more. That wonderful house, for example – it could become an ashram, a beacon of enlightenment for the whole of the country!'

'With him running it, I suppose,' said Ash, when I reported this exchange to him. 'And thousands of fucking disciples disturbing our peace and quiet.'

That struck me as a very bad idea.

A little later we became aware that although Our Lord had gone back to London, (or to some island in the sun – he was apparently partial to these), Arjuna was continuing to head up towards the House after his evening meal. As he set off along the path, pacing slowly with eyes downcast, no-one felt it right to approach him. 'It's a walking meditation,' said Ginnie. 'He probably just goes round the Sheepfield.'

This meditation could sometimes go on until midnight, according to Jelly Bean, who was often out and about in the woods waiting for him to come back.

'Maybe he goes up to the Lodge to see Janet,' suggested Layla.

This didn't seem very likely.

'Or Our Lord's mum,' said Shine.

'I'd better go and see,' said Jelly Bean.

Her news, when she brought it to us next day, was disturbing. 'Shine's right. He's with the mum. I climbed up a drainpipe and I saw. They watch TV and she gives him sweets. Rolos.'

Rolos! Television! How could a holy person be involved in such profanities? 'Should we tell the others?' asked Rain anxiously.

'Not yet,' I said. 'I'll go and ask him about it. There must be an explanation.' So that afternoon I set off to see him during Visiting Time, something none of us children had done so far, as it seemed to us to be for adults only. I hoped to catch Arjuna on his own, but looking in through the open doorway of the caravan I could see no sign of him, although there were two unfinished cups of tea on the floor, and the end of a joint still smouldering in an ashtray.

I noticed that Ginnie's precious ornaments and photographs had all been removed from their usual places and were jumbled together on a high shelf, in order to make way for Arjuna's belongings – toiletries, magazines, records. There were new stains on the lace mats, and peanut shells were everywhere . The door to Bill's office was ajar; peeping inside I could see suitcases and bags piled haphazardly, and a number of hessian sacks with red and blue writing stamped on the outside. Presumably Bill had been obliged to move his desk and typewriter into the Sheikh's palace.

I peered more closely at the writing on the sacks. *'PATEL & SONS...'* I read, followed by some words I didn't recognise, then *'finest foods from India.'* I cautiously touched the hessian. Beneath it the contents felt smallish and knobbly. Unshelled peanuts!

Suddenly, from the direction of the bedroom, a soft murmuring became audible.

Approaching the door I saw that although it was pushed to it wasn't completely shut. Should I knock? It might be wrong to disturb him. On the other hand, I was longing to get a glimpse of the Inner Sanctum. Maybe if I just checked what he was doing... praying? Silently I opened the door a few inches.

Arjuna was seated with his back to me, at a small dressing table against the wall opposite the door. Behind him stood Zoë. She appeared to be massaging his neck.

'Oh yes – oh *yes* ... down a little bit...' said Arjuna. I didn't know whether to interrupt or not.

'And now –' he stirred and raised his head, and I could see from his reflection in the mirror in front of him that his face glowed with a beaming smile. Then he caught sight of me.

'Why, Curly!' he exclaimed. 'What a wonderful surprise!' His beam widened but he didn't turn round.

Zoë, however, swivelled to face me with the speed of lightning. Her face was bright pink. 'For Christ's sake, Curly! Can't you knock?'

'No no, his presence is a great blessing,' said Arjuna. 'Come in, come in.' He turned towards me and opened his arms. I advanced gingerly into the room.

'As you can see, Zoë has been attending to my unruly locks.' He giggled.

It was true that her cutting scissors lay on the dressing table next to Arjuna's headband, and the floor around his chair was strewn with tiny snippets of black hair.

'Oh yes,' I said, 'a haircut and a neck rub.' This was in fact one of her specialities. So why did she look so embarrassed?

'I'll be off now,' she said briskly. Picking up her scissors she swept out without so much as a glance in my direction. Odd.

Arjuna himself was totally unperturbed. 'So Curly, what can I do for you?'

I didn't answer him straightaway, as I was too busy taking in my surroundings. I'd been expecting an Aladdin's cave of wonders, so I was surprised and a little disappointed by the room's comparative plainness.

The ceiling was draped with lengths of white filmy material, gathered up in the middle to give a tent effect. They were held in place along the tops of the walls by means of dark wooden battens carved with simple flowers – I thought I recognised the hand of Ashley here. The walls were painted terra cotta; one was decorated with a line of Indian miniatures, and opposite them hung a long white panel with a few black squiggles on it, which Ginnie later explained to me was a Japanese scroll bearing a Zen Buddhist text.

When anyone talked about this kind of thing they spoke in a tone of voice that indicated the sanctity of the subject, which we never thought of questioning – at least, not until we were considerably older. We grew up imagining that the Buddha, together with various Nordic, Oriental and Egyptian deities, all lived just around the corner out of sight, in a soft feathery cloud which kept them permanently invisible. They were able to move around individually by detaching themselves from the main cloud in order to wander abroad in smaller, personalised clouds, but they always went back to the big candyfloss land to sleep. It must have been Layla who was responsible for the fluffiness of this imagery.

I was aware that Arjuna was waiting for me to speak, but I wasn't quite ready yet. Although I couldn't have put it into so many words at the time, I was conscious of an obscure rivalry which had recently sprung up between the two of us, and I wanted to score a point or two.

So I kept silent and looked around at the furniture – though apart from the dressing table and chair where Arjuna was sitting there wasn't a lot to look at, and most of it was white: a wardrobe in the far corner, a chest of drawers on one side of the bed and a set of shelves on the other. On one shelf a small Buddha sat between a miniature vase of daisies, a burning incense cone, and a candle flickering in a holder shaped like a lotus bud. This was the most minimal shrine I'd seen – every caravan had one, even Pete's. I'm not sure Ashley's really counted, as he said it was the panel where he hung his tools, but he did have a tiny Buddha pendant that Wing had given him, dangling on a thong among the saws and chisels. Ours was crammed with all kinds of stuff: pebbles, shells, beads, bones, dead beetles, flowers both dead and crocheted, and the remains of old incense sticks, which I liked to try and pick out without moving anything else – a hippie version of Spillikins that Erryk had taught me.

The bed itself had a dark red cover, rather rumpled, and on it lay a pile of cushions in pale neutral tones, glinting with a few discreet gold threads. Over the window hung the same deep red fabric; this was never drawn back, so it wasn't even possible to peek into the bedroom from outside.

Perhaps this closed curtain was the reason why I found the place curiously oppressive, even though it was quite brightly lit by a lamp on the dressing table. There was also a light suspended on a chain from the centre of the tent-like ceiling, with a bulb inside a metal shade set with many small panes of coloured glass. These cast rainbow-hued lozenges around the room, which I liked. I also liked the feel of the Persian carpets under my feet – (we never wore shoes in warm weather) – although there were quite a few peanut shells scattered about on them. I wondered what Ginnie, who was as neat as Pete, would think about those.

'I think you have lost your tongue, little one,' chided Arjuna sweetly.

I didn't like the sound of that 'little one'. 'Just looking,' I said rather coldly. 'I've never been in here before.'

'So that is why you came to see me? Only to have a look around?'

There didn't seem to be any point in beating about the bush. 'No, I want to know why you go and watch television with Our Lord's mother.'

Arjuna dissolved into laughter. 'You have been spying on me!'

'No... yes.' I didn't want to incriminate Jelly Bean.

'Oh Curly,' said Arjuna, still shaking with mirth, 'do you think it is wrong for me to watch TV?'

'Of course it is. Television's bad.'

'For you, perhaps, but not for me. I am incorruptible. Do you know what that means?'

'It means that nothing can make you dirty.' That, at least, was Wing's definition. 'Well well well, what a lot of words you know, Curly. So perhaps you can understand that all seekers after Truth must at the beginning be approached on their own ground. Their first steps on the Path must be taken on familiar territory – otherwise they will fall by the wayside.'

He was talking like he did during Temple Time. Wing had told me that it didn't matter if we didn't understand everything, because simply being close to him made us better people. 'You absorb the darshan,' she explained. 'It's as if you're drinking a really delicious fruit juice. Imagine it like that.' I tried, but failed.

'You eat her Rolos,' I said to Arjuna accusingly.

'Of course I do! They are the offerings of a Seeker. I cannot refuse them. I must joyfully accept all offerings, however humble. Even a broken fire engine, Curly.'

What a nasty little dig.

'That wasn't an offering to *you,*' I retorted. 'It was a Treasured Object for the Temple.'

Arjuna leaned towards me. 'I *am* the Temple, Curly.' He stared at me without moving a muscle, and all of a sudden I understood what Marjoram had meant when she said his eyes were hypnotic – cloudy green, with a yellowish ring around the pupil, they were now fixed unblinkingly on mine. I began to feel a bit dizzy.

He leaned a little closer. 'I am *God,* Curly.'

For a second or two I believed him. But then he blinked his long dark lashes and laughed again, and the spell was broken. 'Now run along and play. And may the force of Brahma guide you.'

As I left I was assailed by the first headache of my life, and had to go and lie down in Tiger Lily's combi.

All in all it had been an unsatisfactory interview.

6. *KARMIC STRESSES*

THE WAIL OF Wing: one of my least favourite sounds.

'What's going *on*? What's the matter with everybody?'

'Hang loose, little elf,' murmured Erryk as he stirred the soup. 'It's just a – just a...' He reached out with his free hand to stroke her hair. Wing moaned and ran out of the caravan.

Erryk and I looked at one another but found nothing to say. His melancholy seemed thicker and deeper these days. It hung around him like a grey felt cloak. I wanted to cheer him up, but couldn't think how.

Perhaps Wing's wail was justified, for something was most definitely amiss in Elfland. The happy fizz and sparkle present in the air during the early days of Arjuna had gradually been displaced by a darker kind of electricity, one that even Bill was powerless to fix. He himself, never very talkative, became more silent than ever. Ash stopped singing while he worked, and took to muttering under his breath for long periods, broken by the occasional explosive outburst.

'Sodding mantras! Fucking useless ...' Then he'd throw down his tools and stomp off into the woods with Chip trotting worriedly behind him.

Rick and Sean, normally good jamming partners, began to criticise each other's music, which caused Sean to beat his bongos extra hard to work off his frustration, while Rick's compositions became blacker and wilder. This got on everyone's nerves. Pete turned up the volume of his classical music and shut the door of his caravan. We could see the walls vibrating during the really loud bits.

Gogo and Marjoram neglected the Garden.

Shine was disgusted. 'It's full of weeds!' she exclaimed to Rain and myself. 'Come on, you guys, we'll have to do something about it. Go and get Elvira. We'll have a weed-in .'

'What about Layla and Jelly Bean?'

'Waste of time. Layla can't tell a weed from a lettuce and the Bean doesn't give a toss.'

Jelly Bean no longer danced attendance on Arjuna, or helped him during Temple Time by sprinkling the rest of us with holy water from his silver bowl and distributing monkey nuts. One warm and stuffy afternoon, not long after the discovery of his TV evenings, she had without warning leapt up on to the altar and scattered all the treasured objects on the ground.

'Rolos!' she shrieked.

Arjuna, as always, beamed. I was beginning to find that beam more and more irritating. 'This is very, very positive. She is working through her karmic stresses,' he told us. 'But I think it would be better if she did so *outside* the Temple. Run along now, little monkey.'

Thus banished, she had never returned. She took off her gorilla suit and left it hanging high in a tree opposite Bill and Ginnie's caravan, where it swung lopsidedly, a grinning ghoul. She appeared less frequently at mealtimes; Ginnie would leave out plates of food for her, but she didn't always eat it. From time to time we saw her nicking an egg from the chicken house, or foraging in the overgrown Garden for a carrot or a potato, which she crunched up raw. But as Shine observed, she couldn't give a toss about the weeds.

'Oh shit,' said Marjoram, when she spotted the four of us diligently at work among the veggies. The twins and I hoed and raked; Elvira trailed behind us, slowly picking up the weeds and dropping them into a basket. Her new niceness had recently morphed into an oddly trancelike state.

'We should never have let it get like that.' Marjoram sounded plaintive, almost Wing-like. 'But Gogo's been so busy...'

Doing what? Mainly, it seemed, driving into Chandleford every second day to buy various little luxuries for Arjuna which weren't available in Middington, such as special soaps and shampoos, cones of patchouli incense, and gooey sweets from the Indian shop. I would have liked to try those, but he never offered. In Gogo's absence, Marjoram had been giving us more lessons herself, but we could tell that her heart wasn't in it.

'You can't clear the whole damn Garden on your own!' she said now.

'Yes we can,' said Rain doggedly. All of us were fed up with the adults at the moment, and preferred to keep away from them as far as possible.

'Rubbish. You 'll be here all night. It's our fault, anyway, not yours.' Marjoram was beginning to sound more like her usual self. 'I'll go and round up the girls and we'll finish it off in no time at all.' She strode briskly away.

'Oh well, at least we've had an effect,' said Shine.

Marjoram came back with Zoë, Stella and Tiger Lily.

'Ginnie's with Arjuna,' she said shortly. 'I don't know why – she knows it's supposed to be time for his foot massage.' She had concocted a special herbal ointment that she used for this purpose.

'You couldn't weed if you were massaging,' I pointed out. Marjoram gave me a Look.

'And where's Wing?' asked Elvira.

'Out of her head in Galadriel's Pool. She says he told her that her Inner Light needed rebirthing.'

'Loada bullshit,' said Tiger Lily, yanking vigorously on a stalk of giant hogweed. Her disenchantment with Arjuna had been growing for some time. Early on she had painted a portrait of him which I much admired, in which his fingers and toes extended into branching leaves and flowers; not long ago, however, she had added blood-red blobs which dripped from the top of the picture into his mouth, previously smiling but now changed to a gaping hole. 'Why?' I'd asked her. 'Because he's bloody well bleeding us dry. At least that's what I think – let's hope I'm wrong. But the Tarot says I'm right.'

She was now the target of three beady-eyed glares.

'Arjuna *never* speaks bullshit,' said Stella. 'If we can't always – uh – *resonate* with his teachings, that's only because we're still so far below his karmic realm. But if we follow him he'll show us how to get there. We have to learn how to *receive*.'

'I really, really know I'm receiving when I go to trim his hair,' said Zoë dreamily. She shot me a quick glance. 'I can feel the darshan flowing up my scissors and through my hands...'

'Yeah, his hair's definitely been looking a bit strange lately,' said Tiger Lily.

'...and then into all my chakras,' continued Zoë, ignoring her.

'I get all that just from being near him,' said Stella. 'I don't have to *touch* him.'

'I can't help it,' said Zoë. 'He's just so – so –'

'Magnetic,' said Marjoram. 'Let's face it, girls, he does give off a pretty strong sexual vibe.'

'Don't talk crap!' said Stella. 'It's a *spiritual* force.'

'What's wrong with being sexy as well as spiritual?'

'We shouldn't think of him on such a – *human* level. He's an avatar.'

'So avatars are bum pinchers, are they?' said Tiger Lily.

A moment of stupefied silence. Rain and I giggled.

'What are you trying to say?' cried Zoë.

'I'm saying that he pinched my bum.'

'Don't be ridiculous,' said Stella. Her cheeks were red. 'You imagined it. He'd never, ever stoop so low.'

'What, you mean to arse level? Sorry mate, he did. Quite a few times. That's why I steer clear of him now.'

'Then it was a lesson,' said Marjoram firmly. 'A *metaphor* . To show you that you're far too attached to the earthly plane.'

'And koalas fly,' said Tiger Lily.

'You were probably asking for it,' said Stella. 'You know he treats everyone in the way they deserve.'

'I wasn't doing any asking, mate. He's not my type. I prefer blonds.' She looked steadily at Stella for a moment or two, then turned her gaze beyond the fence, where Sean had appeared. He was plucking handfuls of grass and presenting them with extravagant gallantry to a couple of the sheep who had wandered down to see what we were up to.

It was Elvira who cut off the unfortunate drift of this conversation. 'He pinches my bum too,' she said nonchalantly. She spat her chewing gum into the feathery carrot fronds. 'And as a matter of fact –' She stopped short as she registered the general shock and horror.

'Of course he doesn't!' screamed Zoë. 'Stop pretending you're a grown-up, Elvira. You're twelve years old, for Christ's sake.'

'Twelve and a half,' said Elvira coolly. 'And I am grown-up. You said so yourself – remember? When I had my first period back in February. Welcome to the club, you're a woman now – that's what you said.'

'Fuck,' said Zoë.

The rest of the weed-in continued in silence.

*

'Quick QUICK! He's changed colour!' Layla raced from caravan to caravan, battering on any doors which weren't open. It was early morning and not everyone was either awake or in a particularly good mood.

Erryk, Wing and I were having breakfast outside, but not exactly together, as the sections of tree-trunk which we used as seats had been migrating further and further apart. My mother and Erryk weren't talking much these days, and I found the pair of them increasingly boring. So I was pleased by this noisy diversion created by Layla.

She grabbed my arm and pulled me in the direction of the Temple. As we approached I could hear Indian music playing softly within. Some of the others were already gathered outside it; the rest drifted up in a rather bleary fashion, but soon opened their eyes wider when they beheld the unusual sight before them.

In front of the Temple a wide ring of wildflowers had been laid out on the grass – harebells, ragwort and hemp-agrimony. (Marjoram had long ago taught us the names of all the wildflowers). In the middle of this circle Arjuna was dancing – or perhaps twirling would be a better word. Between the thumb and forefinger of each hand he delicately held a stick of burning incense – and he was clothed in brilliant, shiny green.

Green!! After so many weeks of nothing but snowy whiteness! As the initial shock wore off a bit I realised where I'd seen that green before: in our caravan, folded up under Wing's sewing table. It was a piece of material she'd bought quite recently, during a rare trip Outside with Erryk to one of the markets.

'That kaftan – Wing made it!' I whispered to Layla.

The fabric shimmered in the sunshine as Arjuna tripped round and round with graceful little steps, his eyes cast heavenward. But he noticed soon enough when everyone was finally present and correct. He did a last pirouette and then stood stock still to face us. He coughed softly, whereupon the music stopped and Ginnie came tiptoeing out through the flap in the marquee known as the Temple Gateway. So she was in on the act.

Without speaking, Arjuna raised his arms and then lowered them, indicating that we should sit down. We sat. He gazed slowly round to make sure we really were all there. We were – he must have picked a day when he knew that no-one would be away Outside, whether in London, at a market or anywhere else. I even spotted Jelly Bean peering out of a nearby elm tree. (There were still some left back then).

'Watch out for the searchlights,' said Tiger Lily under her breath, as Arjuna swept his penetrating stare over the assembly. Layla and I, seated between her and Pete, ducked our heads.

His inspection complete, Arjuna finally began to declaim.

'To all travellers on the Path, to all seekers after Truth, I say: Greetings! This is a very, very special day of celebration. And why is it so special? Because today... I bring you glad tidings of great joy!'

Pete leaned over us and spoke quietly to Tiger Lily. 'Haven't I heard those words somewhere before?'

'Now why do you think I am wearing this marvellous green robe which has been so beautifully made for me?' Arjuna shot a dazzling smile at Wing. 'Hm? I know you are surprised but I think you cannot guess. So I will tell you! It is because green is for GROWING! And that is what *you* are doing – you are growing! Look at these flowers on the ground – blue, yellow, pink, all different... but what do they have in common? They all have a *stalk*, and that stalk is green, and it is growing. Just like all of you!'

'Those flowers aren't growing, they're dying,' murmured Tiger Lily. 'Waste of good butterfly food.'

Arjuna wagged his finger playfully in her direction. 'I know you are saying nasty things. Do you think I have not been noticing how all of you are becoming so *bitchy* lately? And how some of you have been neglecting Temple Time? Of course I notice – I see *everything*. And I rejoice! Because all this means that you are growing. So you are having *growing pains*. You know what are all these bitchy feelings and sayings? No? I will tell you. They are your spiritual impurities which at last are rising to the .surface.'

Looking around, I could see the rapt attention on almost everybody's face. As far as I was concerned he was just spouting his usual mumbo jumbo.

'You see, even if you are not realising it, you have been absorbing the vapours of the Upper Realm that I have been breathing into you through psychic channels. It is not possible for you to avoid these vapours. And slowly, slowly, they are replacing every cell in your body. So your body is using all of its functions to cast out the old cells. They are coming out of *every single orifice.*'

This was more interesting. Layla scratched the infected mosquito bite on her arm and squeezed out the pus. '1.ook!' she called to Arjuna. 'They're coming out of a hole in my skin!'

'Yes, yes, yes! See how the child understands. She is pushing out unhealthy cells. But they are coming out of *all* your holes! When you perspire, they are oozing from your pores. When you go to the toilet, they are being *evacuated.* And this is making me very, very joyful. Even when you speak your nasty words, these are just your impurities which you are casting into the wind. And when you sneeze, you are *blowing* them away – shoo, shoo, shoo!' He flapped his arms vigorously and his kaftan shimmered in the brightening sunlight.

By this time Layla and I were spluttering and choking. I saw that the twins were in the same state.

'Look at the children, how they are laughing,' said Arjuna happily. 'This is so healthy. It is one of the very best ways of cleansing your body. Now you *all* must laugh – like this – ha ha hal Ho ho ho!'

'Ha ha hal Ho ho ho!' the adults chorused obediently. The next moment they collapsed into fits of real giggles.

All the stresses of the past few weeks suddenly evaporated and the air seemed softer and sunnier – it really did. This phenomenon was much talked of afterwards.

'Our collective relief was made manifest in the atoms of the air,' said Bill.

'It was proof of his holiness,' said Stella.

'Trick of the light,' said Tiger Lily.

At any rate, this abrupt change in the atmosphere gave rise to a major outbreak of hugs and kisses. In the midst of all this cheeriness arose a double, harmonised Om – Gogo and Marjoram. Seconds later we were all engulfed in a rising tide of omming.

*

So the magic was back – more or less. Attendance at Temple Time went up again, though Pete and Tiger Lily still stayed away, and so did I, despite Wing's pleadings. Although I was pleased that everyone seemed so much happier and more relaxed, I couldn't get rid of the feeling that Arjuna had been here far too long.

'Is he going to stay for *ever?*' I asked Tiger Lily. I was watching her paint, as I often did; she had set up her easel on the grass a few yards behind the combi and was putting the finishing touches to her portrait of Pete. He was sitting neatly sideways, as requested, between the open back doors.

Tiger Lily frowned as she dipped her brush in a bowl of water and wiped it on a rag. 'Seems like that's what he's aiming for.'

'Can you blame him?' said Pete. 'Free board and lodging in a delightful rural setting, complete with attentive servants and a harem of female adorers – it's a dream situation.'

'I just can't understand why they're still so bloody spellbound.'

'Well dear, he does have more than his fair share of charisma. My God, if I had that much, *I'd* start a cult. And he has a lovely line in rhetoric.'

'What's rhetoric?'

'Rhetoric, Curly, is the art of speaking so persuasively that you can make people believe what you're saying. It's full of things like dramatic pauses and repetition and all the other tricks which stir up the emotions of your listeners.' Pete could be a wonderful talking dictionary.

'You never fell for all that though, did you?' said Tiger Lily. 'No, dearest flower, I'm far too steeped in cynicism.'

'What's –'

'No Curly, one word a day is enough. You can ask me tomorrow.'

'But didn't you fancy him a bit at the beginning?' asked Tiger Lily.

'Good God no! I like them butch, not in evening dress.'

I knew Neat Pete was gay, of course. Marjoram had already given us a short lesson on homosexuality. 'A gay man falls for other men. A gay woman falls for other women. Some people think that's wrong, but only because they're ignorant. In fact homosexuality occurs quite frequently and naturally throughout the animal kingdom.'

When, as a small child, you have something explained to you in such a clear and simple way, you accept it without question. My only concern was that Pete seemed to be so permanently alone.

'Why don't you ever bring back a nice man to live with you?' I asked him once. He'd just got back from a short stay in London. 'There must be loads of them up there.'

'Oh Curly, they are legion. But I'm not easy to live with, you know. I'm probably better off on my own.'

'What a pity Ashley isn't gay. Then you could – '

'*No,* we most emphatically could *not*.'

It seemed a shame.

'I've always been faintly surprised,' he said now to Tiger Lily, 'at the suddenness of your own disillusionment with our sainted guru.'

'Oh, once he started groping me I went off him pretty quick. I thought it was kind of accidental at first, but then I realised it wasn't. I tried to tell the girls but they reckoned it was my fault. I read the cards the other day and he came up as the Devil.'

The fascinating subject of the bum-pinching seemed to have become taboo since the episode in the Garden. I'd broached the subject with Elvira and been told to bugger off. Zoë and Marjoram had been politer but no more helpful – unusual in Lothlorien, where the policy was that Children Must Always Be Told The Truth. However, following her revelation, Elvira no longer took Arjuna's meals to him, as Zoë had insisted on taking over waitress duty herself.

'Fuck you,' said Elvira. She sulked and reverted to her former stroppiness, which I found quite comforting in a way, as the new version had begun to seem artificial and wimpish. Zoë was dismayed at first, but after Arjuna's memorable Green Speech, as it came to be known, she put a braver face on it. 'Growing pains!' she said brightly, each time that Elvira swore at her.

Us younger children got a lot of mileage out of that speech. 'Whoops! There goes a Spiritual Impurity!' Shine would say, burping energetically after a meal.

'Here's a bigger one!' said Rain, letting off a loud fart. The adults smiled indulgently while we fell about laughing.

But I still felt that Arjuna had long outstayed his welcome.

'I think he wants to take over the House,' I told Pete and Tiger Lily, recalling his words to Bill outside the shower block. 'He said he wants to make it into an ash-something.'

'Ram,' said Tiger Lily. 'Holy shit.'

Pete pursed his lips. 'I very much doubt if *Our Lord*' – he always put a peculiar emphasis on the words – 'would agree to that.'

'But maybe he's persuaded the mother,' I said. 'With rhetoric.'

'Well I can tell you one thing,' said Tiger Lily grimly. 'If he sticks around much longer, I'm out of here.'

From that moment on I became utterly determined to get rid of Arjuna as soon as possible.

*

Once dinner was over, and after the slug pick-up with Wing – (the Garden was once again being properly cared for) – I decided to go for a solitary walk to consider what I was going to do. 'I'll see to those,' I said, taking the slug bowl from Wing's hand. 'I need to be alone to think some things through.' This was a favourite saying of Bill's, and was always respected.

Wing smiled and patted me vaguely. 'Make sure you put them somewhere nice.' Dusk was beginning to seep into the woods as I made my way down to Galadriel's Pool. The water held all the light from the evening sky, silky turquoise streaked with pink. But was it deep enough to drown in? Did Arjuna know how to swim? Would it be best to drug him first – and what with? And who could I trust to help me? I couldn't drag him all the way here on my own.

It soon became clear that the Pool was not the way to go. Even if he did drown here, he would subsequently float to the the surface like Ophelia in that picture book of Ginnie's, which would cause a lot of fuss. I imagined everyone looking down weepily at the corpse as it drifted in the shallows, eyes open but sightless, hair streaming like thin black eels, green robe streaked with paler green slime... (Arjuna had stuck to his new colour; Wing must have bought enough material to make him several of those kaftans. Almost every day I spotted her washing one of them, or stroking it as she hung it out to dry).

No, there could be no such theatrical display. He had to simply *disappear.*

I carried on down to the river and jumped on the stepping stones to the far side, where I searched for a welcoming patch of mud on which to tip the slugs. There weren't a lot of them, or much mud either; it had been a hot dry summer up till now. I examined the river as I crossed back over it. It wasn't very deep, especially not at the moment. If you threw a body in you couldn't expect it to be carried far before it got stuck between some rocks. I decided to abandon the water option altogether.

Then a new idea struck me like a sudden beam of sunlight: poison!

I gazed at the tall clumps of hemlock water dropwort along the river bank. A handful of chopped roots mixed in with his curry – that should do the trick. Unless, of course, he was rushed to hospital and had his stomach pumped. (I knew about that sort of thing because Marjoram had told us about the time when she had accidentally poisoned herself as a child). They'd find the poison and realise it must have been put there, which would cause even more fuss. Worst of all, Arjuna would probably survive.

Now mushrooms, on the other hand… But I hadn't spotted any yet. From the general look of the woods I could see that it must be getting close to my birthday, a time when, during rainy summers, quite a few mushrooms were already in evidence. I knew that several species of these were potential killers; the trouble was that it hadn't rained properly for ages. Still, that meant that it must do so soon.

Feeling more optimistic, I took a path which led to a comer of the woods where the tallest beeches grew and where I hoped the earth might still be a bit damp. But it was bone dry and entirely fungi-free. A little further on, right by the wall of the estate, a few broken stone columns poked up like fingers through a mitten of ivy which spread over the surrounding piles of rubble. These were the remains of an ancient chapel, overhung on one side by three big yew trees . It was a pleasingly creepy place, where we liked to frighten ourselves by playing at ghosts or vampires, so it seemed an appropriate spot for me to work out the details of my plan.

I sat down on a heap of stones and ran through the poisonous mushrooms likely to pop up first. Beechwood sickeners: they had a strong taste of pepper, Gogo had told us, so they might be too easily detectable, even in a curry. Earthballs, with their spooky purplish-black interiors, would be far too obvious. That left the deathcap: not only the most common of the three, but also the most lethal. Gogo had said that there was *no known cure*. Thousands of people had died from eating them, because when they were fresh they tasted quite nice. And by the time you started to feel ill, it was too late to do anything about it. Even having your stomach pumped out wouldn't work.

A couple of those, cut up and added to Arjuna's evening meal, should be more than enough. They wouldn't make him actually *vanish*, which was what I wanted most of all, but at least his death would be certain and have the extra benefit of being plausibly accidental. He liked to walk in the woods before dinner; what could be more natural than to take a few nibbles at a harmless-looking mushroom? We children were always nibbling at things, which is why we'd been taught about all the woodland poisons as soon as we were able to understand. But Arjuna was from India, and thus unfamiliar with English fungal lore.

All that was needed now was some decent rainfall – preferably just after my birthday. I didn't want the demise of Arjuna to distract from the preparation of my cake – or the other treats which went with it. Our birthday teas were thrilling occasions, thanks to communal planning by all the adults. Ginnie and Marjoram might do the baking, for example, then Stella the icing, Zoë and Stella the decoration. Wing liked making candles, and Ashley often constructed an interesting wooden cake-stand. Tiger Lily painted fabulous cards, Rick, Erryk and Sean all composed new variations of 'Happy Birthday', Pete made up funny poems, Bill made a speech... It was essential that nothing should get in the way of all this excitement.

So it would be at the age of seven that I was to become a murderer. It was a solemn thought. I confess it sent a powerful shiver of pleasure running through me. How could a child growing up surrounded by strictly pacifist ideals, who knew quite well that killing was wrong, harbour such deadly intentions? Because I believed I was in danger of losing the person closest to my heart: in such circumstances your finest principles fly out of the window like a speeding bullet.

My toxic musings were interrupted by a low cry. I jumped and turned towards it.

The light was failing fast now, but in the thick darkness beneath the yews it was possible to make out a large pale amorphous shape. It was moving. My nerves, already on edge, began to jangle like alarm bells. Was it a real ghost? For a moment I was transfixed with fear.

Another little cry – followed by a soft 'Yes... yes!' in a voice that I knew well. At the edge of the billowing white sheet – for that's what it must have been – I glimpsed part of a blonde head which even in the gathering gloom I recognised as Stella's. Behind it, draped over a low branch, hung a swathe of dimly gleaming green fabric.

I knew what they were doing, of course. Nookie. Silently I stole away.

*

Once, when I was about four, I'd woken in the middle of the night after a dream of food and decided to have a root around to see what I could find to eat. As I was peering into the chilly but fascinating depths of the fridge, I became aware of strange cries coming from Wing and Erryk's bedroom – very similar to those I'd just heard beneath the yew-trees. Alarmed, I opened the door to see what was going on. What I saw seemed totally inexplicable – Wing kneeling astride Erryk on the bed, swaying and moaning.

'Legolas!' she called softly. 'Take me to Rivendell!'

Perhaps she was dreaming – or did she think *I* was Legolas, the elf hero in *The Lord of the Rings*? No – her head was thrown back and she couldn't have seen me. But Erryk had. He put a finger to his lips. 'It's OK, Curly,' he mouthed. 'Go back to bed.' So I did, reassured but very puzzled.

The following day I asked him what they'd been doing.

'We were *making love,*' he said gravely. 'It's... a thing adults do.'

'Why?'

'Because… well, it's a wonderful thing.'

'What's Legolas got to do with it?'

'Nothing, it's just… Wing – she's an elf…'

This was a typical Erryk-style explanation, so I went to Marjoram for further enlightenment. She gathered all of us children together, (apart from Elvira, who knew everything already), and gave us what I'm sure was an excellent and fully comprehensive lesson about sex. I remember that it sounded pretty weird, and that afterwards Layla and I decided to give it a go. We didn't have much success.

'You're too young,' said Tiger Lily when I told her. 'No point trying to do that till you're older.'

'How much older?'

'Oh – maybe fourteen, fifteen.' 'And then can I do it with you?'

Tiger Lily roared with laughter. 'Better ask me nearer the time.'

As it happened, we forgot most of the details so conscientiously described by Marjoram, and had to find them out for ourselves a good deal later on. But we did know plenty of the terms used to describe the principal activity, as we often heard them in the adults' conversation. 'Making love' sounded silly, 'screwing' too much like woodwork. 'Having a fuck' and 'fucking' didn't feel quite right as the words were used in so many other contexts. 'Nookie', Ashley's word, was the one we liked best. We knew that a lot of it went on, although it didn't occupy our minds very much. But somehow I was sure Stella shouldn't be doing it with Arjuna.

*

'He loved it!' said Zoë, as she set Arjuna's empty plate on the ground.

We were sitting around the Fireplace, digesting a particularly delicious summer pudding that Marjoram had made with fresh raspberries from the Garden. As I think about that evening I can almost smell those raspberries, and hear the breathy notes of Tiger Lily's bamboo flute as they drifted into the still night air. As usual, although I loved to hear her play, the music gave me an odd feeling of disquiet.

'Where's Bill?' asked Layla suddenly.

'What you wanna know for, nosy?' said Elvira.

'I need to ask him if Ashley can build me a Wendy House.' Bill had to grant planning permission for any new structure within Lothlorien.

'He's at a gig, sweetheart,' said Zoë. 'He went with Rick, remember? It's a new festival.'

'When will he be back?'

'Tomorrow night or the day after.' Ginnie smiled very sweetly. 'I'm sure he'll say yes to your Wendy house, darling.'

'And I want a BENDY house!' shouted Jelly Bean, appearing unexpectedly from the shadows beyond the firelight and the candles. 'Bendy like a helter skelter.'

'That might be a bit harder to make, my poppet,' said Ginnie. Jelly Bean melted back into the darkness.

I woke in the night to the chug of Rick's motorbike; it was a dark green Royal Enfield which made a lovely noise rather like a tractor. It slowed and stopped. The door of Rick's caravan opened and then shut with a bang; he must be in a bad mood, I thought. A few minutes later Bill's Spitfire came zooming down the track at top speed. It skidded to a halt and the car door slammed violently. Another bad mood. And why were they here, anyway? Ginnie had said they wouldn't be back for a day or two. Later we leaned that the festival had been completely washed out by a massive freak thunderstorm, together with all the sound and lighting systems. But at the time all I knew was that Bill was in a truly foul temper.

'Ginnie! Where the hell are you?' He was inside the Sheikh's Palace now, shaking the poles and punching the canvas walls. Next I heard him charge up the steps to their caravan. 'Open this fucking door!' He started to pound on it. The wood splintered.

Then followed a great deal of confused shouting. I could just make out: 'And you can fuck off out of here!' (Bill) and 'Nooooo...' (Ginnie) before the voices were drowned by a crash – as the Sheikh's Palace, weakened by Bill's assault, fell down.

'Get in the car!' Bill was still yelling, Ginnie sobbing hysterically. The Spitfire accelerated up the track, tyres squealing.

*

A terrible stunned silence hung over Lothlorien next morning. It was as if we had all been paralysed by a shock wave. Finally some of us did begin to stir and venture outside, but nobody spoke. We moved liked zombies, afraid to look each other in the eye.

Wing was still in bed, curled up motionless and invisible under the covers. Erryk began wordlessly to gather his market gear together. Only once he had put it all in his car and driven off did I realise that he had forgotten to prepare any breakfast. I took a yoghourt from the fridge and poured myself a glass of orange juice. Then I cut a couple of slices of Erryk's homemade bread and stuck them in the toaster. Once they were done I buttered them with care and spread Marmite on one and honey on the other, in rather bigger quantities than Erryk was apt to use. This all made me feel very grown-up, and I resolved always to get my own breakfast from now on. I took it outside and sat on the steps. No-one else seemed to be around.

There was a rustle at my feet and Jelly Bean emerged from under the caravan, where she had apparently been nesting.

'I saw!' she exclaimed. 'Bill broke the door – come and look.'

I put down my plate and followed her cautiously to the disaster area.

It was a troubling sight. The Sheikh's Palace lay in a huge crumpled heap; the caravan door swung crookedly open on one hinge, the other torn out of the frame. The dark red bedcover I had seen inside had been roughly pinned up over the opening. As we stared, this makeshift curtain was pushed to one side and Arjuna came out. He had a towel over one arm and was carrying his sponge-bag. Jelly Bean darted off like a bird but I stood my ground. He smiled and waved at me nonchalantly, as if nothing at all was out of order. Nonetheless I was sure I spotted an evil glint in his eye. As he disappeared in the direction of the shower block I had a sudden crazy impulse. I looked around to make sure that no-one was watching – then I leapt up the steps and into the caravan.

It was a mess: books, papers and clothes were strewn everywhere. On top of the general junk heaped on the table I caught sight of a passport – I knew what it was because Ginnie had shown me hers and Bill's not long before, and explained what they were used for. I picked it up. It was identical to theirs, dark blue with the golden lion and unicorn embossed on the front, which I liked a lot. Today's passports are far less handsome. Only the name at the top was unfamiliar: MR. S. PATEL. Inside this was expanded to MR. SUNIL PATEL. But the photograph inside was of someone I knew only too well – a younger, short-haired version, but definitely Arjuna.

I didn't understand everything on the page opposite the photo, but I knew that the most important stuff about the person was contained in the words written in capital letters, by hand. Did I have enough time? Yes – if I was quick. On the settee I found a biro and a packet of envelopes. On one of these I copied out the handwritten bits: RETAILER – KAMPALA, UGANDA – 14.4.41 – (I was struck by this symmetry) – GREAT BRITAIN – 5ft 7ins – DARK BROWN – HAZEL – SCAR BEHIND LEFT EAR. Underneath I added the name, then put the passport back where I'd found it. I kept that envelope for years, just in case – of what? I'm not quite sure.

I hurried back to remains of my breakfast and thought hard about my discovery. Arjuna wasn't Arjuna at all, that much was obvious. And he didn't have an Indian passport. The word 'retailer' was a bit of a mystery, but it didn't sound very holy. Should I tell everybody about my new information? Perhaps it wasn't necessary. Bill had been very, very angry last night – perhaps Arjuna was going to leave! But – was it really Arjuna who Bill had told to fuck off, or was it Ginnie? Or both of them? Or even someone else who'd been in there as well? Of course if Arjuna did leave I wouldn't need to kill him, which might not be such a bad thing after all... Suddenly everything seemed far, far too complicated. I ran off to find the twins.

By an unspoken understanding we took ourselves off to play on the far side of the Sheepfield, in order to keep well away from the morbid atmosphere within Lothlorien. Layla ran after us, carrying her Sindy doll; despite the best efforts of her parents, she adhered obstinately to gender stereotypes.

'Don't leave us here! Sindy's frightened!' she screamed, and for once we didn't tease her. We didn't even talk about Arjuna or the events of the night before – hoping, I think, that by the time we returned everything would have somehow magically sorted itself out.

When we began to feel hungry, Rain shared a few raisins he found in one of his pockets, and the rest of us scratched around for edible leaves under the hedgerows, but as lunches go it wasn't very filling, so after a while we ventured back to the caravans.

'We've got some leftover summer pudding,' said Shine. 'And walnut bake. We can eat it in the woods. What have you got, Curly?'

'Bread – cheese – apples – maybe some other things.' I went off to have a look.

I found Wing kneeling on the floor, surrounded by even more mess than that in Arjuna's living quarters. She was obviously having a major rummage, which usually meant she'd lost something important. The settee cushions were thrown to one side so she could get at the stuff stored under the seat, and through the open doors I saw that the drawers under the beds were pulled out and their contents spread all over the place – my own belongings too, I was annoyed to see.

'What are you looking for?' I asked crossly.

'Oh – Curly! You made me jump.' Wing stood up and turned towards me. Her face was red and streaming with tears. She came over and hugged me with unusual force and then, between little sobs, she began to sing in a croaky voice: '*Curly Wurly, Curly Wurly Curly, Wurly Curly Wurly he sa-a-ang...* ' I hadn't heard her sing that for years. She began to run her fingers through my curls, almost pulling them, and I could feel her desperate unhappiness overflowing on to me. I broke away to the fridge, grabbed what food I could find, and dashed outside again to the sanity of the twins and the woods.

Late in the afternoon I heard Erryk's car approaching. With any luck Wing would have calmed down by now and things might be back to normal. As I drew near to our caravan I heard a jubilant cry from the treetops: 'He's gone! He's gone!' Jelly Bean, as usual, knew more than the rest of us.

So my most cherished hope had been realised: Arjuna had disappeared.

And so, it transpired, had Wing.

7. EQUINOX

TODAY I HAD a surprise visitor.

It was just after 'lunch', that's to say my midday dose of baby food which still seems to be all my ruptured digestive system can cope with. As the last of it slipped blandly down my gullet I had a sudden intense longing for one of the garlic-rich stews of my childhood: Erryk's roots, Gogo's veggies, Marjoram's marjoram... I could even taste it in my mouth. Not surprising, I suppose, as my mind is sloshing around so deeply in the past at the moment.

This hallucination of the taste-buds was interrupted by a light tap on the door of my ward. In walked a woman I didn't immediately recognise, as she was wearing sunglasses and a wide-brimmed straw hat. When she took them off it still took me a few seconds to register who she was. I blinked in astonishment.

'Mrs Evans!'

'Just Jeannette to you, thanks.' She dumped a plastic bag on the bedside table. 'Brought you some grapes.'

'Why? I mean – that's very kind, but I don't think I can eat them at the moment.'

'Tough. Give them to your favourite nurse.' She looked hard at me. 'So what the hell hit you?'

'The wall of a tunnel, so I'm told.'

'Like Princess Di.'

'Not quite. I'm still here.'

'You nearly weren't though, were you.'

'That's what they say.' I stared at her. Her long black hair gleamed and she was wearing bright red lipstick. 'How did you know?'

'Word gets around,' she said laconically.

No doubt her husband, Terry the yacht broker, would have heard about my accident. But I still couldn't work out why she'd come to see me.

'I came to apologise.' I remembered her peculiar knack of apparently replying to my unspoken thoughts.

'What for?'

'I shouldn't have insulted you like that. At the party.'

'It really didn't matter, you know,' I said faintly.

'Yes it did. I'd had a few too many. I'm not normally quite so rude.'

'Forget it. I had too much to drink myself.'

'You didn't look that pissed to me.'

'Well I wasn't then, not when we were having – that conversation.' I was beginning to weary of this one, too.

'When I was slagging you off, you mean.' She pulled a few grapes out of the bag. 'I know I upset people sometimes. Especially men with egos. You probably drank too much because of me, and that's why you crashed.'

'Your own egotism does you credit.' I watched the movements of her shiny red lips as she popped the grapes one by one into her mouth.

'Christ, don't you ever stop acting like a wanker?' She looked at me with disgust as she chewed.

'Oh, fuck off.'

I'd spoken without thinking, out of an intense tiredness. To my astonishment she smiled. 'That's more like it.' She moved to the door and then turned back. 'You look quite cute with all those bandages round your head. Still got all your hair?'

'My head had to be shaved.'

'Have to call you Curly then, won't I?'

I experienced a brief electric shock. It must have registered on my face, because she laughed. 'That's what we call bald people in Australia.'

'I know,' I said coldly. Of course I knew. Tiger Lily had told me.

'Never mind, it'll grow back.' She flashed me another brilliant scarlet smile. 'Catch ya later.'

A phrase which could have come straight out of Tiger Lily's mouth – spoken by a woman who couldn't be more different. The door closed behind her and I drifted into a troubled doze.

*

'Oh no – not *Death* – ' The colourless girl with haunted eyes drew back in her chair.

Tiger Lily leaned forward and touched her arm reassuringly. 'Death can be a really really positive card. It's a symbol of transformation. And look where it is – right in the centre here. You're in the process of eliminating a very negative force from your life.'

Alarm spread over the girl's face. 'Does that mean he's going to leave me?'

'No, darling. It means *you* are going to leave *him*. You're going to learn to answer back and assert yourself.'

The girl drooped. 'But we're booked to go on holiday tomorrow. To Torremolinos.'

Torremolinos. It sounded deeply exotic, a violent land where jungles seethed with monsters and armoured warriors. I resolved to look it up in the atlas when we got back to Lothlorien that evening. Of course I wasn't to know then that our homecoming that day would be taken up with a far more intense distraction.

'*Go* then,' said Tiger Lily firmly. 'You can dump him once you're over there. It's the Equinox – that's a great time for change. Have a rave. Find someone else. Should be easy enough if you catch yourself a nice tan. You need a bit of sunshine.'

'I know… I've been so depressed lately I've hardly been outside except to go to work.'

'Oh yes, let's look at your work… The cards are showing me some kind of healing… and money changing hands…'

'Yes!' The girl looked amazed and pleased. 'I'm assistant manageress at Boots.'

'If you can manage Boots you oughta be able to manage yourself. And it looks like you should be studying some kind of alternative therapy so you can set up on your own. Forget working for other people. See this card? The Hanged Man? It means you're ready to turn everything upside-down.'

'Well, we have got stock-taking next week…'

'We're not talking about the shop here, sweetheart. We're talking about *you*. Here's the card to visualise whenever you start feeling unsure of yourself. The Empress. She's your future – a strong, free woman.' Tiger Lily turned to the corner of the booth where I was sitting on a little red stool. 'Pass me the sacred cloth, Curly.'

I handed her the scarf, dark blue chiffon spangled with bits of glitter. She unfolded it and laid it gently over the spread of cards on the table. 'That's all I can tell you for now. The cards have spoken. Come and see me again when you get back from your trip.'

'Oh, I will – and thank you.' The girl gave a brave little smile. 'And I will try and –' She rose and picked up her things from the floor.

'Remember – trust in the cards and you can't go wrong.'

I opened the flap in the booth with a little bow.

'Is this your son?' It was a familiar question posed by Tiger Lily's customers.

She gave her usual answer, smiling mysteriously. 'Yes and no. He was a gift from the Elves. He's a changeling child.' I gave an elvish wink, which always seemed to disconcert the clients a bit. Then I quickly flashed my tongue out and back in again, like a lizard catching an insect. Tiger Lily had taught me this trick and it generally put a stop to any more time-wasting enquiries.

'Wow... amazing...' The girl hurried out, fumbling with her umbrella as she left the shelter of the covered marketplace and headed into the soft September drizzle.

'Saw her in Boots this morning,' said Tiger Lily. 'When I went to get Ginnie's pills. '

'Did she see you?'

'Nah. I had my hood up. In this business you gotta keep your eyes open without being too conspicuous.' She reassembled the cards and wrapped the scarf around them. 'Any likely customers out there at the moment?'

'Maybe...' A small group of people stood under a couple of umbrellas not far off, giggling and looking in our direction. A young man was pointing at the sign and laughing.

The sign was a blackboard decorated round the edges with shooting stars. In the centre was written in bright mauve letters: *'TAROT READINGS'* and underneath, in white handwriting: *'Tiger Lily, world-renowned Australian Seer, blends Ancient Aboriginal Wisdom with the Eternal Tarot to enlighten your Path. £5 for Major Arcana only, £7.50 for Major and Minor.'*

It was propped against one corner of the booth, a simple tent which Ashley had recently made using poles and pieces of tarpaulin salvaged from the wreckage of the Sheikh's Palace. For years Tiger Lily had just had a couple of screens to set up around her folding table and chairs, but this new arrangement looked more imposing and had allowed her to raise her prices. She had painted the outside of the tarpaulin deep violet, a colour which sometimes came off on people's hands if it was out in the rain. Inside she pinned up oriental patterned fabrics, some of her paintings, and various charms and amulets. My favourite of these was a tiny silver dragon which I called Smaug. Light came through a gauze-covered opening behind her chair and also from a night-light in a purple glass bowl on the table, which cast flickering reflections in the depths of her big dark eyes.

Lately she had started to use me as an assistant at her Tarot-reading sessions in the various market towns she went to with Erryk. I dressed in a short sparkly black robe over yellow satin baggy trousers – part of Wing's remaining stock of handmade creations – and a turban stuck with a jewelled brooch. (When I finally get out of this place I quite fancy dressing like that again, if only to see whether I'd still be taken seriously. I doubt it).

Tiger Lily herself always wore a flowing gown of some sort, and loads of twinkling costume jewellery she'd picked up for next to nothing at bric-à-brac stalls. 'Gotta get the image right,' she said. I thought she looked totally stunning. She had a large supply of long chiffon scarves in dramatic colours and she would drape one of these over her hair – sometimes over her entire face, if she felt like adding extra mystery value. My turban would be made from another; I was allowed to choose which one I wanted on the day and then Tiger Lily would wind it carefully round my curls.

A fancy-dress excursion like this was always an enormous treat – but only one of the many which were being showered on me at the moment. My birthday party, some weeks before, had been exceptionally sumptious. Everyone – apart from Erryk who was sunk in catatonic misery – was being more than usually nice to me. Of course I enjoyed all this attention, but it really wasn't necessary; Wing's departure hadn't, I must confess, affected me very much at all. Arjuna had gone too, therefore Tiger Lily had stayed, and that was what mattered.

Anyway, Wing would be coming back. She'd left me a note: *'Darling Curly Wurly, you know I love you, but I have to go and find myself.'* I didn't imagine that this could take very long, though I didn't have a clue what it meant. It was just a typical Wing-ish statement.

'Do you think she's gone to India?' I asked Erryk, just to try and get him to talk. He stared at me sorrowfully but said nothing. Although I couldn't care less about Wing's search I was extremely concerned about Erryk's condition – we all were. He hardly spoke at all. He continued with his leatherwork and his market-day routines, but in a dead-eyed, Zombie-like fashion. As if in a dream, he would carefully pack what was left of Wing's crocheted and hand-sewn wares into his car along with his own, and then display them reverently on his stall. Money from their sale he put into a special leather pouch that he had embossed with the picture of a wing.

Car-trips with him to the markets could be alarming, as his attention was now liable to veer far from the road. 'For Christ's sake, don't kill us all, even if you are feeling suicidal,' Tiger Lily snapped one day as he swerved vaguely into the path of an oncoming tractor. That seemed to shock him out of his trance for a while, though it didn't make him much chattier.

A series of strange girls turned up at the caravan to visit him. 'He meets them at the markets and they follow him home,' said Tiger Lily. 'They think he needs mothering.' But Erryk's utter lack of interest eventually turned even the most persistent of them away, though my own bad manners often helped to speed up their departure. They all seemed pretty stupid to me.

In the evenings he spent hours strumming sad Dylan numbers, *Forever Young* in particular. *'May your hands always be nimble, may your feet always be swift...'* he would croak softly, his eyes oozing with tears. 'Don't think Twice' was another song he returned to again and again. When he got to: *'I once loved a woman, a child I am told...'* he would break off with a soft groan and throw his guitar down on to the settee. I soon became tired of this, especially as he often forgot to cook. In spite of all my efforts to cheer him up nothing seemed to work. A pall of despair hung over our caravan, and I found myself spending more and more time away from it. I was still small enough to be quite comfortable curled up on a bean bag, so I frequently slept either with the twins or in Tiger Lily's combi, providing she didn't have one of her periodic visitors – (more on those shortly). Sometimes Ashley made room for me up in his tree-house, next to Chipolata's basket. I loved the sway and creak of the branches and the closeness of all the woodland night noises, but Chip licked and dribbled too much for the experience to be truly relaxing.

Erryk wasn't the only one to remain dumb on the question of Wing's whereabouts.

No-one seemed to want to talk about her – I suppose because she was now too much connected with Arjuna, who had become virtually Unmentionable, as if he had never existed, had never been part of Lothlorien. With hindsight, I can see that this was probably the best way to get things back on track.

Very soon after his disappearance and the tumultuous night which had preceded it, Bill had called everyone together for an Emergency Meeting.

'The collective karma of Lothlorien has been severely tested,' he said. 'Some of us have been found wanting.' Ginnie sat motionless as he spoke, eyes cast down.

'Wanting what?' asked Layla. Zoë shushed her into silence. She too seemed unusually subdued.

'From now on we will do everything possible to learn from this experience and put it behind us. That is the only way in which we will be able to re-establish the peace, and above all *mutual trust*, essential to our communal living. Otherwise it cannot continue. Is that clear?'

Sean exhaled a long cloud of smoke from his spliff. 'Hea-*VY*,' he breathed. Stella gave him a sharp prod.

So a veil of silence was cast around the subject of Arjuna. If someone did occasionally drop his name into the conversation it was as if they were speaking of no-one more important than a casual visitor. As if by magic, the Temple vanished. Ashley cleared away the remains of the Sheikh's Palace and repaired the door of Bill and Ginnie's caravan; they moved back into it as if nothing had happened.

But the twins, Layla and myself did sometimes hold clandestine discussions about Arjuna-Time, as we called it.

'I think Wing went to Rivendell,' said Layla. 'To live with the other elves.'

'Don't be silly, Layla. Rivendell isn't a real place.' Shine had come to this realisation earlier than the rest of us. 'She must've gone off to India with Arjuna.'

'But why?' I asked. 'I know she liked him, but not as much as Stella did. Or Ginnie. They did nookie for him. Wing just did sewing.'

'I think she liked him *more*,' said Rain thoughtfully. 'Sewing takes longer than nookie.'

'Stella probably did it because she wants a baby,' said Shine. 'You know how she goes all gooey when she sees babies Outside. Sean can't make one.'

'Are you sure?'

'Well, if he could, he'd have done it by now, wouldn't he?'

'Zoë did nookie too,' said Layla.

'How do you know?' I wasn't entirely surprised.

'I heard the noises. When I went to fetch her one day. In Bill and Ginnie's caravan.'

'Why didn't you tell us?'

'Zoë made me promise not to. She said it would bring bad luck.'

'And what about Marjoram? She used to do his foot massages.'

We couldn't make up our minds about Marjoram.

'Do you think Elvira did?' asked Shine.

'She can't have,' said Rain. 'You have to be older.'

'She's tall enough though, isn't she,' I said.

'Ask her, Layla,' said Shine.

'I don't speak to her. She's horrible. *You* ask her.'

'Don't be daft.'

Elvira had become even more bad-tempered recently. She dyed her hair and her clothes black and slouched about like a moody stick-insect. Quite often she hitched a ride into Middington or even Chandleford and stayed away until nightfall.

One day she came back with a safety-pin through her ear.

'What's that for? Is part of your ear falling off?' I inquired.

Elvira scowled. 'It's *punk*, knobhead.'

Rick and Zoë had tried without success to put a stop to her solitary outings. 'I just wish she'd *talk* to me,' sighed Zoë. 'She's not even thirteen, for God's sake. *Anything* could happen to her.'

'Not looking like that,' said Pete. 'She'd scare the knickers off the most seasoned psychopath. I'm surprised anybody stops to give her a lift.'

In fact, as we soon found out, she had somehow struck up a friendship with two brothers whose parents owned quite a smart-looking house only a mile or so from Lothlorien. Their father had a building firm in Chandleford, according to Bill. He had been the first to see her there, getting out of a large car with the two boys. Much to Elvira's embarrassment and disgust, he had approached the car to ask a few questions. As usual, Bill's charisma produced results, and the boys' father had assured him that the 'young people' were just going through a phase that they would soon grow out of, but in the meantime he preferred to drive them in and out of town himself rather than risk them attempting to hitchhike.

'Or they might try using public transport, even worse,' remarked Ashley.

Zoë was very relieved to hear about the builder's sons. 'At least they're from a nice family.'

Rick gave her a funny look. 'So now you think capitalist entrepreneurs are *nice*.'

'Well, you work for them, don't you? What do you suppose record companies are?'

Only earlier today Tiger Lily and I had spotted Elvira in the market, lounging with her two new friends and a couple of girls, all of them dressed in black and draped in chains. One of the girls had cropped green hair and the other had a crimson spike sticking up on the top of her head. I thought they looked like aliens.

'It's just the new fashion,' explained Tiger Lily. 'They think hippies are past it.'

Old-fashioned or not, her Tarot readings remained as popular as ever. All kinds of people seemed desperate to know their destiny: housewives, teenagers, students, sales reps – even the Middington butcher, though he wasn't too happy when Tiger Lily told him that the cards advised a change of career.

The group of gigglers I'd seen a few moments before had drawn nearer now. We could hear them whispering just outside the booth.

'Go on Ollie, I dare you,' said a girl's voice.

'I'm not spending a fiver just to be told I'm brilliant and gorgeous and bound to pass my exams. I know all that already.' I guessed that the speaker was the young man I'd seen pointing at the blackboard.

'We'll pay, won't we chaps? It can be your birthday present. What else can we give the man who has everything?'

'I can think of a few things…'

'Oh, just shut up and get in there,' said another girl's voice.

Tiger Lily looked at me. 'Do your stuff, Curly.'

I opened the flap again and stepped outside.

One of the girls caught sight of me. 'Look! Isn't that absolutely the sweetest thing you ever saw! What's your name? Are you the fortune-teller's little boy?'

I ignored her and directed a piercing stare at our prospective customer. He reddened slightly and gave a rather uncomfortable laugh. 'Good lord. It's the Genie of the Lamp.'

The other male in the group tittered. 'What have you been rubbing, old man?'

Ignoring him too, I beckoned imperiously. I really enjoyed doing this little act. 'Come. You have been summoned by the cards.' I spoke in what I thought was an appropriately mysterious tone.

'You *see*? No wriggling out of this one,' said girl number two. They all pushed their companion towards me. Half laughing, half protesting, he tumbled past me and through the flap.

'Greetings,' said Tiger Lily softly. 'Sit down and take a minute to let go.'

The young man remained standing. As his eyes adjusted to the relative gloom he stared first at his surroundings – the hangings, the pictures, the charms, the candle – before focussing on Tiger Lily herself. She was gazing at him unblinkingly with one of her most compelling expressions.

'Well, you certainly look the part,' he said. 'Not that I've ever been to a fortune-teller before.'

'I'm not a fortune-teller. I'm just a channel for the cards. They've been picking up your vibrations – that's how I knew they wanted to speak to you.'

'OK then – so what have they got to tell me?'

'Nothing, until you pay them. What's free is never valued.'

'Oh, you mean I've got to cross your palm with silver and all that jazz.'

'A five pound note'll do the trick, mate. Unless you want a reading from both Arcanas. That's two pounds fifty extra.'

'I'm sure one will be ample...' He took out his wallet and handed her the money. 'Actually, my friends are paying for this. It's a birthday present'.

'You've got good friends then. You're a lucky bloke.'

'You really are Australian, aren't you? Did you grow up in a humpy in the Outback – that's what they're called, isn't it? A friend of mine's been there.'

'I come from a place called Whoop Whoop,' said Tiger Lily. 'Ever heard of it? No, I didn't think you woulda done. Now stop playing funny buggers and get your arse on that chair.'

Startled, the young man sat down.

She unwrapped the cards and passed them to him. 'Shuffle. They need to feel all your energies. Now give them back to me.'

While she laid out the cards in silence, I examined him more closely. I could see he was the type that Tiger Lily might invite back to Lothlorien – blond, square-jawed, blue-eyed, quite tall. She was in the habit of picking up male customers occasionally, if they took her fancy. Clearly infatuated, they always jumped at the chance to spend some time with her in Lothlorien. Bill tolerated these intrusions into the community because she never let them stay for long; a week was her absolute maximum, then she would push them out without a second thought, even though they sometimes begged to stay. 'Combi's too small,' she told us. 'Anyway, I don't need the distraction. I've got other things to do. They can just hang on to me as a fabulous memory.'

As no doubt they did.

'Wear 'em out, kick 'em out,' said Pete.

'You got it, mate,' replied Tiger Lily.

This one, however, seemed warier than most. And as the reading progressed his flippancy faded and he became more and more uneasy. He kept glancing towards the side of the booth as if he as was worried his friends might be listening.

'Take a squiz outside, Curly,' said Tiger Lily. 'If his mates are hanging around you can tell them to piss off.'

I looked, and saw they were having a drink at a stall some way off.

'Good,' she said. 'Now listen. See this card? The Moon? That's telling me you're deluding yourself. And other people as well. Because the impression you're trying to give has got nothing to do with what you really are. And look here – the Tower. Disaster. You're going to destroy yourself if you carry on like this.'

'Like what?'

'I don't have to tell you that. You know already. But here's the Star – if you change your path it'll guide you. There's no need to be scared.'

'No, there isn't, because I'm afraid you're talking nonsense.'

'It's not me that's talking, darling. The cards are reflecting your own subconscious. It's telling you to break out of your conditioning and have the courage to be yourself.' I was struck by her forcefulness. Usually she was gentler with her clientèle, but then she seldom met with such resistance.

'Look, I didn't *choose* to come in here, you know. I only came –'

'Because your friends pushed you into it for a laugh. But in fact they did you a favour. Oh and by the way, you're a student, I suppose? What are you studying – law or something?'

It was an inspired guess. The young man opened his mouth like a fish and then shut it again.

'And you hate it, don't you. Better switch to something arty. Try drama school. You should do well there, specially with a name like Oliver. Sounds a bit like Laurence Olivier, doesn't it? That's a good omen.'

There was a moment of total silence.

'How did you know my name?' he said finally.

'It just came to me, sweetheart.' Her voice was kinder now.

'My parents would go absolutely beserk if I left university. And if they knew that I…' Oliver was speaking very quietly.

'Well, you gotta choice to make. Either you please them and suffer, or you go out there and get yourself a life. Be true to your nature. They'll forgive you once they see you're happy. So will your mates.'

Oliver stood up abruptly. 'They'll be waiting for me.'

'So's the future, petal.'

When he'd gone Tiger Lily put her face in her hands. 'Christ! He's a total fucked-up mess. I tell you, it's exhausting being a bloody agony aunt.'

'What was the matter with him?'

'Just about everything.'

'I thought you were going to ask him to come back and visit.'

'No way! He's gay as a wombat on acid – I could see as soon as he came in. Nothing wrong with that, except he can't admit it.'

'He might have got on well with Pete.'

'Pete would scare him shitless.' She sighed. 'I've had enough for today, Curly. Go and see if Erryk's ready to pack up.'

*

I've been thinking: how could I possibly remember all these conversations in such detail? I was just a kid. Although I believe there's a theory that everything we live through gets stored away in the furthest recesses of our brains, even if most of it is usually beyond recall.

All I know is that everything I'm writing down comes bubbling up as if from a deep well of memory, like perfectly formed scenes from a technicolour movie. Could this be a result of the drugs they're stuffing into me? Whatever – it's all entirely true to the spirit and the people of Lothlorien. That particular Tarot afternoon seems especially clear and sparkling – probably because of what happened shortly after it.

We had driven back from Chandleford and were bumping down the track past the Sheepfield. The rain had stopped and sunshine twinkled in the puddles; I was about to take off my fancy outfit so I could get out and splash around in them, when suddenly Jelly Bean darted out from behind a tree. She'd been waiting for us, and looked quite damp.

Erryk slowed the car. She leapt on to the bonnet and banged on the windscreen in excitement.

'A campervan! A campervan! With a big pig and a spider monkey!' Jelly Bean loved pigs, and had for ages been wanting one as a pet. And spider monkeys were among the creatures she most wanted to emulate. So no wonder she was excited.

'Quick quick! They're having a party!' She scrambled on to the roof-rack of the station-wagon. 'Drive!'

As we resumed our progress towards the woods we could see wisps of smoke rising from the outdoor fireplace. I breathed in deeply – a delicious scent of goodies wafted towards us. While Erryk parked the car I raced over to see what was happening.

Marjoram was crouched by the embers of the fire, toasting a batch of her Herb Bundles. (Herbs, oats, egg, grated cheese, rolled in breadcrumbs – a gourmet snack). Everyone else was sitting in a semi-circle passing round bottles of Gogo's home-made wine. They faced towards the campervan.

This wondrous vehicle was standing a little way back from the fireplace, and seemed to me already very much at home. Like Tiger Lily's combi it had a big VW logo on the front, but it was longer, shinier, and much, much newer. And instead of having fading psychedelic patterns painted all over the outside it had a crisp two-tone colour scheme: the lower part was orange, the upper section white. Best of all was the pop-up tent protruding from the top – I'd seen these in lay-bys Outside and had always wanted to climb in and have a look. Gogo had explained to us that there was an extra bed up there. A striped awning, also orange and white, shaded the space next to the side door, and underneath it were a picnic table and two chairs. Each chair was occupied by an unknown person.

I ran towards them. The figure on the left, dressed in dungarees and a bit stout around the middle, stood up and saluted me smartly. This was a most delightful greeting; I was going through a phase of wanting to join the army. I looked into a pink face with an upturned and indeed rather porcine nose, small sharp eyes set close together, all topped with short fair bristly hair. So this must be Jelly Bean's pig – disappointingly human but nonetheless appealing, especially as I couldn't tell if it was a man or a woman.

The saluting hand was lowered and held out towards me. 'You must be Curly. My name's Jack.' The handshake was firm, the voice quiet. Male or female? I still wasn't sure.

'And that's Loose.' Jack nodded towards the other person, who was most definitely a girl, albeit an unusual one. She was not so much sitting in her chair as wound round it; her thin brown arms and legs, emerging from a tight black T-shirt and cut-off jeans, seemed to be twined everywhere, contorted into impossible angles. Even if she wasn't a real spider monkey she looked just as exotic. Her head was small and round, like a hazelnut, and sticking out from each side of it was a bunch of straight black hair tied with fluorescent green ribbon. I wanted to pull them. She had a wide mouth, which now opened and let out a cackle of manic laughter as she unfolded herself. She got up and planted a smacking kiss on each of my cheeks.

'I am *enchanted* to meet you. I think we will be *marvellous* friends.'

She didn't sound like anyone else I knew. I was hooked immediately.

8. *NEW BLOOD AND NON-EXISTENCE*

'YOU'RE NOT A hippie though, are you,' said Shine.

'No,' said Jack. 'I'm too old to be a hippie. But I've got nothing against them. Otherwise I wouldn't be here.'

'How old are you then?' I asked. It was hard to judge; apart from a couple of deep vertical furrows between the eyebrows, Jack's face looked smooth and soft.

'Forty-eight next birthday. Old enough to be your grandmother.'

Forty years older than me! That was truly ancient. Even Bill and Ashley weren't much more than thirty-six or seven. (Sean, the oldest member of our community, was a few years their senior, but he didn't look it).

'You can be *all* our grandmothers!' said Layla. It was quite true that there was a definite lack of grandparents in Lothlorien. They certainly didn't visit, at any rate. I knew that Rain and Shine had at least three of them, none of whom approved of our lifestyle. Gogo and Marjoram went to see them from time to time, but the twins were always reluctant to go too. 'They're very boring and they think we're rude,' said Shine. Rick and Zoë never mentioned their parents and neither did Bill and Ginnie, so probably they were even more disapproving.

Jack considered Layla's remark carefully. 'That would be an honour and a privilege,' she said, and she smiled. 'I never expected to become a grandmother.'

Although none of us had been sure at first, we had all guessed pretty quickly that Jack was in fact a woman. Nevertheless, we'd double-checked with Marjoram.

'Yes, of course she is,' she said. 'Jack and Loose are lesbians – gay women. You remember what that means, don't you?' We did. Marjoram also told us that Jack was a writer, which was exciting, and that Loose was French, which explained the way she spoke and was even more exciting, as we hadn't met anyone from France before. We'd been befriended by a Dutch family during one of our visits to the seaside, and occasionally an

American tourist in Chandleford would strike up conversation with us – (presumably taking us for quaint local colour) – but that was the extent of our contact with people from overseas.

Today, the morning after the campervan's arrival, we had gone along for an in-depth exploratory chat. It was already pretty clear that Jack and Loose were to become permanent fixtures in Lothlorien, and we wanted to be sure of their suitability.

'We don't want any more Arjunas,' said Rain. 'He seemed nice too, at the beginning.' But we soon came to realise that there was nothing remotely Arjuna-like about either of them.

That morning as we approached the van we saw Jack sitting alone at the table outside. She had a cigarette in her mouth, and a huge electric typewriter in front of her. Bill had already fixed them up with a cable the day before; its trail was visible from the fresh earth stamped down above the narrow trench he had dug for it. Like all our cables, it ran underground from the shower block. In the early days of the colony the wires had simply been strung through the trees, until the day the fuses blew and Ginnie discovered the charred body of an over-inquisitive and electrocuted squirrel beneath a neatly chewed wire. So while Ginnie buried the squirrel with due ritual, Bill, Rick and Ashley buried the cables. The ends which emerged to be plugged into each caravan were protected by steel casing, unpalatable to rodents.

We were thrilled by the sight of the typewriter. Bill had one, but it wasn't so big and impressive – and this one had a metal ball in the middle with letters on it – the so-called golf ball, as we learned later. And he typed slowly with two fingers, looking at the keyboard, whereas Jack's hands danced rapidly over it even though her gaze remained concentrated on a sheet of paper to one side.

Jelly Bean went up to it and gave it a tap. 'What are you writing?'

Shine pulled her away. 'Bean!' she hissed. 'At least be polite. Say 'Good morning' like a proper person.'

'Good morning,' we all chorused.

Jack had stopped typing. She put out her cigarette and leaned back in her chair. 'Heigh-ho. Here comes the inquisition committee.'

'What does that mean?' asked Rain suspiciously.

'It means you're going to ask me a lot of questions, if I'm not mistaken.'

'That's right,' said Shine. She was a straightforward girl. 'First of all, why did you come here?'

Jack blinked. 'As a matter of fact, we came for some hassle-free peace and quiet. Though all of a sudden I'm not so sure we came to the right place.'

'How did you know about Lothlorien?' I asked. 'Are you somebody's friend?'

'Well, I've known Ash since he was a kid, though we didn't have much to do with each other. Has he ever told you about his Aunt Tessie?'

'The horrible fat aunt who hates everybody?'

Jack laughed. 'That's the one. She's my mother's next-door neighbour. They're thick as thieves. I heard them talking about Ashley during one of my misguided visits to the parental home.'

'What were they saying?'

'Oh, that he was living a depraved existence with a bunch of hippies in the woods, that kind of thing. I thought it might be our kind of place. So I asked Tess for Ashley's parents' number, and they told me how I could get in touch with Ash, and I phoned him, and he got me to speak to Bill, and so we came down here to have a look. We liked what we saw, and no-one seemed to object to us, so here we are.' She paused. 'Is that enough explanation for you?'

For me it was, because I trusted Ash completely. And once it had been established that Jack was to be our grandmother I felt sure she must be a good thing, because we had read about grandmothers in books and they seemed to be generally cosy creatures.

But now I wanted to know more about Loose. 'Is *she* a hippie?' I asked. It was impossible to tell.

'Loose? Not really, she's just Loose. You can't put a label on her. She's unique.'

'Where is she? Is she inside? Can we talk to her too?'

'She's off exploring. You'll have plenty of time to talk to her later.'

'Does she climb trees?' asked Jelly Bean.

'Oh yes. And once she's up there she starts singing.'

'Like a bird?'

'Like herself. You'll hear her soon enough.'

Rain frowned. 'I suppose French singing sounds different. What happens if you want to sing together?'

'I can't sing to save my life. And I can't climb a tree either. Maybe that's why we're a couple – opposites attract, so they say. It's certainly true in our case.'

'Is it nice being lesbians?' inquired Layla.

'"Nice" doesn't really come into it. You are what you are, that's all, and you have to make the best of it, whatever the rest of the world may think. If you find someone to love who loves you back, then you're lucky.'

'I'm lesbians with my Sindy doll,' said Layla. 'We love each other very much.'

Jelly Bean made a loud retching noise. I sympathised – Layla could really go much too far sometimes.

'Don't take any notice of her,' said Shine. 'She doesn't know what she's talking about half the time.'

*

Jack wrote her first drafts in longhand, on paper. And that's what I'm doing now, using a large notebook and a biro. As in nearly all French notebooks – and school exercise books too – the pages are covered with a grid of small squares. The idea behind this rather irritating format is supposedly to encourage neat, regular handwriting, but from looking at the handwriting of the French people I know, I'd say the system doesn't work. Not that it matters these days, when everyone writes electronically most of the time.

Once I'd decided to start writing, and was physically capable of doing so, I'd asked Marco, my business partner, to bring me pens and notebooks into the hospital. He was horrified. 'No no no! I will bring you an iPad.' My own had been crushed in the accident, although, astonishingly, my mobile phone had been thrown clear and survived. But I'd turned it off, and asked Marco to see to the tedious business of getting in touch with my professional and social contacts. I don't want my recent existence contaminating my past – the latter is much more important to me at the moment. And I can only capture the spirit of that past using its own materials – certainly not an iPad. So that means writing as I did back then, and like Jack did.

Everyone in Lothlorien was rather in awe of Jack's status as a writer, including Bill. He and Ginnie had spotted us crowded round Jack that first morning, and called us away.

'You children must *not* interrupt Jack when she's working,' he said.

'Is she writing stories?' I asked.

'No, she's a very serious non-fiction author.'

'She deals with *women's issues*,' said Ginnie, and there was something in her tone of voice which suggested that this was too deep a subject to be discussed further. Probably she hadn't read any of Jack's work; although she'd kept all the books from her childhood, I don't remember Ginnie reading anything other than books and magazines on subjects which she felt concerned her directly, that's to say astrology, yoga, and spirituality in general. And occasionally interior decorating.

Zoë, however, had previously come across several of Jack's articles.

'She's even had stuff published in the States,' she said. 'And she's written a book as well.'

'She's *incredibly* relevant,' said Stella.

So what were these mysterious but incredibly relevant women's issues? We decided to go back to Jack for elucidation – though not, of course, while she was still sitting at the typewriter. Instead we went to help Gogo in the Garden, but an hour or so later we saw Jack pull a cover over the magic machine and get up from her chair, so we approached for a further round of questions.

'Well… I don't think you'd find it very interesting,' said Jack. 'Without going into all the boring details, I suppose you could say that I'm trying to persuade people that the world would be a better place if everyone realised that women were as important as men.'

'I thought they were *more* important,' said Shine. Only a few days earlier, Rain and I had been rather alarmed when Gogo had explained to us how the human race could survive and breed perfectly well even if all the men on Earth were wiped out, providing they'd left the women with some frozen sperm.

At this point Jelly Bean began to jump up and down. 'Listen listen!'

Bursts of erratic sound were coming from the direction of the Sheepfield, which was hidden by the trees which rose behind the campervan. Jack smiled. 'There comes my own important woman.'

We hurried over to a gap where we could see what was going on. Loose was running down the slope; her arms swung like windmills and every few seconds she threw back her head and let out huge musical whooping noises. The sheep were running with her, but we couldn't tell if they were enjoying the spectacle or trying to flee from it.

Loose swerved past the Garden fence and into the woods, arriving breathless and ecstatic at the campervan. She flung her arms round Jack's neck.

'This place is so – so… I am *overwhellummed*. Isn't that a wonderful word? O-ver-whell-ummed. I learned it last week.'

We were rather overwhelmed ourselves. In wonder, we watched as Loose twined herself into another impossible-looking position in the chair next to Jack. 'Look!' she cried. 'The yellow one is coming!'

She pointed over at Sean, who was sauntering towards us, spliff in hand. 'Hey, what's with the freaky singing, man?' (Sean was the only inhabitant of Lothlorien who seemed permanently stuck in the phraseology of the '60s).

'I sing because I am happy!' said Loose. 'It just comes out – whoosh, like that.'

'Unreal. Totally instinctive.'

'Like a monkey,' observed Jelly Bean with satisfaction.

'We are all monkeys!' said Loose. Jelly Bean clapped her hands in delight.

Loose turned to Jack and tweaked her nose. 'But maybe this one is not so monkey. More… *sanglier*.'

'She means wild boar.' Jack seemed perfectly content with this description.

'Wy-eld bo,' said Loose, and screeched with laughter. 'But sanglier is better. I love sangliers – they are so savage. And so good to eat.' She licked Jack's cheek, and Jack reddened with pleasure.

'Out of sight,' murmured Sean. 'You and me ought to get together, lady. Jam a little. Your voice and my bongos – real jungle music.' He sucked deeply on his joint. 'Loose and the Wild Man – I can see the album cover.'

'Is Loose a French name?' asked Rain.

She guffawed again. 'No! It's what the English call me because they can't pronounce my real name.'

'What is it?'

'Lucette.'

'Loosette, that's easy,' I said.

'*No* – you don't say the "u" right. Look: you make your mouth like a tiny "o". Then you say "ee" through it. Lu-cette.'

'Lu-cette!' we trilled, like a line of little birds.

'Bravo! You want to learn French?'

We nodded enthusiastically.

'I will teach you something useful – *j'ai faim*. Repeat.' We repeated. 'It means "I am hungry". And now I am *very* hungry, so I think we must have lunch.'

That was our first French lesson. Many more were to follow.

*

The dynamic of Lothlorien had definitely shifted. Although the Arjuna period had been swept under the carpet, there had no doubt been unresolved and unexpressed tensions lingering in the air. These were blown away by the major distraction provided by the arrival of Jack and Loose, and everyone – with the exception of Erryk – seemed bouncier. New ideas and projects started to pop up, particularly among the women.

Stella, for instance, decided to learn how to make jewellery, and began to take lessons at Chandleford Tech. 'I can't be a model for ever,' she said.

'I don't want to be one of those grinning old dears in the stair-lift ads.' She wasn't in the least bit jealous of Sean's obsession with Loose's voice, because Loose was a lesbian. I remember evenings when Stella would sing in her crystalline soprano accompanied by Loose's strange, deep contralto harmonies, while Rick improvised some stunning riffs and of course Sean banged happily on his bongos. Even Erryk sometimes strummed along.

In spite of her respectful attitude towards Jack, Ginnie was the only person who seemed rather ill at ease with both her and Loose – especially Loose, who I think she found a bit alarming. This was understandable – Loose was better at yoga. She must have been at least partially double-jointed. During Ginnie's classes she achieved the most complicated positions with a facility bordering on the miraculous, even some that Ginnie herself had a bit of trouble with. Worse still – while she did so she disturbed the usual pristine silence of these sessions with snatches of song and the occasional gleeful yell.

'Maybe you could… try to be quieter,' suggested Ginnie diffidently.

'Why? My body is expressing its *joy*. Yoga must be full of *joyfulness*, you say so yourself.'

So Ginnie let the matter slide; she could see that the rest of us were attending the classes more often and more assiduously these days because we liked to watch Loose's rubbery contortions. But not long afterwards she launched herself into new territory, somewhere she knew Loose wouldn't follow – because study and reading were involved, two things Loose didn't do much of. (This seemed strange to me at first. 'I told you opposites attract,' said Jack, when I asked her about it one day). So what *did* she do? She took photographs – I'll come back to those later.

Ginnie's new field of research was aromatherapy. Here she was well ahead of her time, as it would be several years before its perfumed tendrils were to wind themselves into mainstream consciousness. To begin with, she enlisted Marjoram's help to make some aromatic oils using dried rosemary and lavender from the Garden, plus cinnamon sticks and citrus peel, all steeped in Baby Oil. But when, during a visit to friends in London, she heard about someone there who had started to make the oils and sell them by mail order, she decided that was the way to go. She was never really into hands-on fabrication if she could avoid it.

'It's all very well for you – you've got a *private income*,' said Ashley. He spoke as if it were a disease or serious disability.

'Yes, I do I have a small amount of money,' replied Ginnie equably. 'And I intend to use it for the benefit of others. Besides, the oils I'm buying are much more varied and high quality than any we could make here. I've got a wonderful calming recipe which induces spiritual balance – would you like me to blend some for you?'

Marjoram, inspired by the remaining homemade oils, was now busy developing a new range of herbal beauty products. These included a hair conditioner which really did give us all fabulously soft and shiny hair. It went down a storm with Zoë's new private clients; much to Elvira's disgust, Zoë had found these through contacting the mother of her elder daughter's new friends down the road. If Stella was available she would drive Zoë to these rendezvous and collect her later on; if not, Marjoram or Erryk would oblige. Zoë refused to let Rick take her. 'It gives the wrong impression, a class hair stylist arriving on a motorbike,' she said. She had a new look as well – she'd cut her hair. Out went the beads, headbands and scarves; in came the ginger astrakhan cap effect, her hair now so short that it hardly looked frizzy at all.

But it was Elvira who struck out the most radically. A few weeks before the Winter Solstice – (yes, of *course* we did that instead of Christmas) – she announced in the middle of a communal cake-making ceremony that she wanted to go to school.

'Boarding school?' asked Layla hopefully.

'Course not, crud-face. Middington Comprehensive.'

A collective shudder rippled through the cake-makers.

'WHY, for fuck's sake?' shouted Rick. We'd hardly ever seen him so upset – even in his blackest moments he wasn't usually as angry as he was now.

'Sweetie, you'll never get a better education than the one you're getting here,' pleaded Zoë. 'You can always go and take some exams later, if you really want to.'

'Stuff my education,' said Elvira. 'I'm sick of all my mates thinking I'm a weirdo.' She seemed to have quite a number of mates Outside nowadays, acquired presumably through the builder's two sons.

'What does she *expect*,' lamented Zoë. 'She *looks* like a weirdo.'

'No darling, that's the way they all look these days,' said Tiger Lily. 'You've seen them. She's just rebelling against her background. It's normal. Healthy. You did it too, remember?'

'Yes, but I had something real to rebel against. It's Paradise in here compared to where I grew up. And I was *fifteen* when I rebelled. She's *twelve*.'

'That's right, go on, talk like I'm not here.' Elvira chucked a handful of raisins into the cake-mix and stirred viciously. 'And you seem to be forgetting that I'm thirteen at the end of the month.'

'You gotta admit that the kids here grow up a lot quicker than they do Outside,' said Tiger Lily.

I suppose we did, no doubt because we'd always been treated as small adults, never excluded from the adult world or talked down to. We'd often been struck by the fact that the children we came across Outside all seemed so… well, childish.

'And educationally speaking, you're almost certainly more advanced than the other kids your age,' said Gogo.

'She may be now, because you're such a fucking brilliant teacher,' said Rick. 'If she goes to that school it'll be downhill all the way.'

On account of Elvira's advanced age compared to the rest of us, and because she and Layla bitched each other continuously when they were together, Gogo had got into the habit of giving her lessons on her own. During these one-to-one sessions she became, so we were told, almost polite. We'd heard Gogo telling her parents that she had above average intelligence too, which struck us as impossible. 'He just said that to be nice to Rick and Zoë,' said Shine. Elvira's favourite subject was history, so Layla often suggested historical ways of getting rid of her: the gallows, the guillotine, boiling oil...

Now, smarting at being called crud-face, she began to chant: *'Roses are red, violets are blue, God made me pretty, what happened to you?'* Heaven knows where she'd picked that up. Perhaps from some kids in the Middington library.

'If I need any more crap from you I'll squeeze your head,' said Elvira. 'Why don't you just piss off and stop breathing?'

'Let's cool it, guys,' said Gogo. 'Elvira – I think perhaps we should respect your wishes. You obviously need to spend more time with your peers.'

'*Thank* you, Gogo,' said Elvira. 'Though what I really need is to spend more time with some normal people.'

*

Elvira had Bill's blessing also – he must have been sick of seeing her mooching aimlessly around, completely out of tune with everyone else. So Rick and Zoë agreed to arrange an interview for her at the school in Middington. Gogo drove them into town, because he wanted to be there in case any awkward questions were raised about the style of Elvira's education up till now. In any case, both parents insisted on being present, and there wasn't room for all of them on Rick's motorbike.

'When she was small I used to take her in a rucksack,' said Zoë wistfully. 'She used to poke her head out like a little dog. She loved it. We trained her to duck if the fuzz were around. Then when she got too heavy and I was afraid the straps would break, Rick carried it on his chest, balanced on the tank.' I wish I'd been alive at the time to witness this spectacle. Layla, on the other hand, was not a natural biker and wouldn't have been seen dead inside a backpack. Even as a baby she'd made that very clear.

On their return from Middington Elvira looked triumphantly smug. After a lengthy interrogation the headmistress had pronounced her academic level more than adequate, and she was enrolled to start school at the beginning of the new term in January, providing she took the safety pin out of her ear.

'But how are you going to *get* there?' Now that Elvira's school attendance was a fait accompli, Zoë could see a host of practical problems looming up. 'I can't see Rick dragging himself out of bed at the crack of dawn every day to take you in on the bike. And anyway, what if he's away working?'

'I don't need him,' said Elvira. 'Or any of you. You think I want to be seen getting dropped off by a *hippie*? I'll go in with the boys – their dad says he'll pick me up at the Lodge. With his *enormous luxury car*.'

'Oh, so you'd got all that planned out already, had you? Before you even knew you'd be accepted?'

'Yes, of course. Do you think I'm daft or something? And by the way,' she went on, 'know what I want for Christmas? Yes, I did say CHRISTMAS, you clapped-out has-beens. I want a pair of contact lenses. Rick might still be stuck in John Lennon land but I'm not.'

But her tone was relatively affable. And henceforth, now that her wish to go to school had been granted, she became a whole lot nicer – though in a condescending kind of way.

'You'll feel like I do, when you're older, ' she told me. 'You won't want to stay locked up in a time-warp for the rest of your life.'

'But I like it here, Elvira.'

'Liz.'

'What?'

'LIZ. L. I. Z. That's what you can all start calling me from now on.'

'Why?'

'Because it's my *name*, stupid. E-*liz*-abeth. If it's good enough for the sodding Queen then it's good enough for me.'

'But what do you mean, it's your name? Your name's Elvira.'

'That's only what they started calling me when they moved here to fucking fairyland. My *real* name is *Elizabeth Sarah Maxwell*. That's what it says on my birth certificate.'

'Birth certificate?'

'Oh, for Christ's sake, Curly. The bit of paper you get when you're born. Everybody's got one. Ask Erryk, he must have yours. You've probably got a real name, too. No-one's *seriously* called Curly – that's just a nickname.'

Intensely disturbed, I marched off to our caravan. Erryk was working at his bench, stamping patterns on to bits of leather. Beside him were a half-eaten apple and an unfortunately empty packet of chocolate biscuits. These days I usually had my meals with the twins, as Erryk had become so unreliable as a food-provider.

'What's my name?' I demanded loudly.

He looked very surprised, as well he might. 'Oh – Curly – is something the matter?'

'Yes! I want to know what my real name is.'

'Well – it's Curly, of course. Curly Os Wald. No – you stuck it together, didn't you. Curly Oswald.'

'But what's on my birth certificate?'

'Birth... oh. I don't think... no, I'm pretty sure...'

'Where is it?'

'You haven't... we didn't... you haven't got one.'

'Why not? Did Wing take it with her?' Erryk flinched; I knew it hurt him to hear her name, but these were exceptional circumstances and I had to get at the truth.

'No... no. She never – got one made for you. I think... she wanted you to be free.'

'Free from what?'

'Oh, the System, you know...'

The System. I had never quite grasped what this was, but I'd heard it spoken of often enough to know that it lay somewhere in the realms of Outside and was basically Evil incarnate, as bad as the eye of Sauron in his tower. If Elvira's birth certificate was part of the System it was probably the cause of her dodgy temperament. And she must have been wrong when she said that everybody had one.

'So Rain and Shine and Layla and the Bean – they haven't got one either?'

'I don't... yes – yes, they must have. They were born in hospital, Outside. You get registered sort of – automatically. Parents have to – well, the mother, anyway...'

It was clear that I was never going to get to the root of the matter with Erryk. I decided to ask Jack. She was bound to have the most extensive knowledge of the System and Outside, having spent more time there than anyone else. And she was my Grandmother.

Inside the campervan she and Loose were enjoying an early-evening aperitif of Gogo's raspberry liqueur. A cassette tape was playing one of their favourite songs and Loose was singing along – quietly, for once. I liked that song a lot, and had already memorised some of the words: *'Avec ma gueule de métèque, de Juif errant, de pâtre grec, et mes cheveux aux quatre vents…'* It's years since I heard that song, but just thinking about it now brings tears to my eyes.

'This song is about an old man and a young girl,' Loose had explained to me. 'He loves her.'

'And does she love him?'

'Oh *yes*,' said Loose, and ran her hand over Jack's head. Jack sniffed.

I didn't really like to disturb this evening's happy domestic scene, but I had to. Nevertheless I waited until the end of the song. Jack joined in for the last few lines, speaking rather than singing: *'Et nous ferons de chaque jour, toute une éternité d'amour, que nous vivrons à en mourir…'* They looked deep into each other's eyes. Even at that age I was touched.

However: 'I've got something very important to talk to you about,' I blurted out.

Jack reached for the bottle of liqueur. 'You look as if you could do with a drink.' She poured a few drops into a glass and filled it up with fizzy water from her beautiful red soda siphon.

I took a good swig followed by a deep breath. 'I haven't got a birth certificate.'

To her credit, Jack didn't laugh. 'Well now, how do you know you haven't got one?'

I explained. 'So that means I haven't got a real name, either.'

'Ah. There you're wrong. Your real name is what you're known by. Take me – I was christened Jacqueline. But I haven't used that name since I was eighteen. I got my first bank account in the name of Jack, and then all my other official junk as well. Then I was able to get the name on my passport changed. So I'm really and truly Jack.'

'And I'm really Curly Oswald?'

'Of course you are.'

It was a huge relief.

'You might well need a birth certificate when you're older – but only if you decide to become part of the system. But I expect that can be sorted out easily enough when the time comes. I'm sure Bill will help you. And so will I, if necessary.'

'I don't think I'll ever want to be part of the System.'

'I don't blame you. At any rate, for now you can just enjoy the fact that it doesn't know you exist.' She picked up her glass. 'Let's drink to that.'

9. *SOLSTICE, SCHOOL AND SOCIAL WORK*

I REMEMBER THAT December as being mostly cold, wet and muddy; this could be because Rain and I spent a good deal of time trawling for the elusive aquatic reptile which lurked – or so we hoped, ever since Gogo's recent lesson on dinosaurs and the Loch Ness monster – in the depths of Galadriel's Pool. The trouble was that these depths weren't particularly deep, even in times of heavy rainfall.

'They're really slippery, these things,' said Rain. 'It just keeps sliding out of the net.' We were dragging the bottom of the pond with a large shrimping net that we normally used either at the seaside or for catching tiny fish in the river – (we always threw them back, of course). Even though all we brought up from the pond was weeds and slime, we were convinced we'd touched the monster at least twice.

'It's probably got a hidden underwater tunnel leading to its lair,' I said.

Rain agreed. 'It pulls stones and stuff over the entrance, so we can't detect it. There might be a whole *nest* of them in there.'

But we soon forgot about the monster in the excitement of the preparations for the Solstice. They were centred mainly on food. Presents were reserved for birthdays, Father Christmas being an invention of the capitalist consumer society Outside. And the Christian Nativity story, although charming, was simply one of many interpretations of older, more authentic traditions concerning the Rebirth of the Sun.

We did put up decorations, however: holly, ivy and mistletoe and yew were permitted inside the caravans, as they were ancient pagan symbols. Outside we hung strings of coloured bulbs among the trees, which we left in place for two weeks before the Solstice itself and two weeks after it; these were also acceptable, as bringers of Light into the Darkness. They transformed the chilly gloom of the damp and leafless woods and lifted everyone's spirits. 'What shallow creatures we are,' sighed Pete. 'Hang up a few fairy lights and instantly we all feel *merry*.'

This particular year's festivities were particularly memorable, thanks to Gogo's new creation: an earth oven hollowed out in the ground next to the Fireplace. While I was helping him to line it with old bits of hessian I caught sight of the words *'PATEL & SONS'* on one of them, and realised that it must be the remains of one of Arjuna's peanut sacks. Gogo turned it over when he saw me looking at it. 'Dead and buried,' he said, smiling. I had an unexpected vision of Wing curled in the wet soil. It must have shown on my face, because Gogo squeezed my arm. 'Just speaking metaphorically,' he said with a grin. 'You know what a metaphor is, don't you?' I nodded silently.

Our first cake-making ceremony of the season had been planned in order to give this oven a trial run. Ashley and Gogo had pulled out dry branches stored under the caravans and built up a good blaze in the Fireplace above some specially selected large stones from the river; while these heated in the fiercely glowing embers, us children, supervised by Marjoram, busied ourselves with stirring the cake ingredients together. In the middle of much happy spoon-licking Elvira dropped her bombshell announcement about school, which suspended proceedings for a while, but by the time that had been dealt with the mixture was ready and the stones were hot enough to be lifted out of the fire and placed in the oven. Shine solemnly poured the richly-textured gloop into a greased biscuit tin, and put the lid on tightly. Gogo deposited it on top of the stones. We covered it with thick wodges of leaf-mould interspersed with a little earth, and Jelly Bean jumped on top and shouted: *'Bake, cake, don't break, be a treat for us to eat.'* Then we left it to its own devices until the following morning.

The disinterment was exciting, like digging up treasure. We scrabbled at the muddy blackened leaves and were surprised at how untouchably hot the tin still was. Its contents turned out to be reasonably satisfactory, if a little heavy; so on the eve of the Solstice itself we prepared a bigger, better version with a lot of extra baking powder. Jelly Bean stomped even harder on the buried cake-tin and added a few decibels to her cake-chant.

As usual, it was Ginnie who presided over the next day's rites, waking us all well before dawn by ringing a little bronze bell outside everyone's door until she heard the mutterings of disturbed slumber. We all had to have a quick shower because, as Ginnie unfailingly told us each year, 'The sun must be welcomed in a state of purity and cleanliness.' The twins, Jelly Bean and myself all had a shower together in order to be the first outside, leaving Layla to wash her Sindy doll in one of the hand-basins. Elvira – (I couldn't get used to the idea of her as Liz) – was the last to get up; we heard her yawning loudly and swearing as she bumped into a tree on her way to the shower block.

Ginnie, already cleansed and purified long before the rest of us were awake, was waiting by the Fireplace, bathed in the glow of the fairy lights. She was raking over the red-hot embers of the previous nights's fire, which she had stoked up the evening before so it would stay alight to encourage the sun to come back. We were longing to dig up the new cake ourselves, but knew quite well that she, as High Priestess of the Solstice, would be doing the honours this time around. Once everybody was assembled she put on a pair of thick green rubber gloves and removed the earth and gently steaming leaves from the top of the oven with the aid of a trowel. Then she changed into oven gloves.

'My God, this woman has accessories for every possible occasion!' said Pete.

Choosing to ignore both this remark and the faint sniggers which followed it, Ginnie lifted the tin, opened it, and turned the cake out on to one of her brass Moroccan platters, freshly polished and glinting with reflected colours from the strings of lights. We gazed on it with awe. The risen golden dome, evenly knobbled with fruit and nuts, showed clearly that the improved recipe had been a big success. It looked even better than the conventionally cooked Solstice cakes we'd made in previous years.

'It's *so* symbolic,' breathed Stella.

As its wonderful scent reached our nostrils even the chronically bored Elvira looked a touch perkier, though we all knew that the actual tasting would have to wait for a while. Ginnie picked up an ivory-handled knife, her best one with its silver blade etched with twiddly patterns. ('This belonged to my Great Aunt Rose,' she'd told me once, and I'd wondered if this aunt had been as large as Janet the Great). As we watched in suspense she slowly cut a slice from the cake. It looked perfect. She placed it on a smaller brass plate and stood upright. Holding the plate in both hands she turned and began to walk out of the woods, Bill lighting the way with a flaming branch from the fire. Falling into place behind the two of them, we began the procession up to the sun-summoning site, a spot high enough on the Sheepfield to give a clear view over to the south-east. Everyone was commenting on how warm it had become – we hadn't needed to bundle up in the usual layers of sweaters and jackets.

Sunbeams, however, were absent – hardly a surprise, as it was rare that we actually saw the sun at dawn on the Solstice, or indeed during any part of the day. A dim blueish glow behind the clouds on the horizon indicated that it was nonetheless still there. Facing towards it, Ginnie raised the plate of cake above her head and began the Incantation, addressing a whole host of ancient Sun gods – just to be on the safe side, I suppose.

'Helios, Inti, Amun Ra,
'Lugh and Mithras, Surya,
'Sol Invictus, shine on us!'

Then we all repeated the chant in unison. It had, you may notice, a very similar metre to the one composed by Jelly Bean for the baking of the cake; no doubt she'd been unconsciously influenced by her mother.

'O Sun, sustainer of this Earth, accept our offering!' cried Ginnie.

'Accept it and return!' we all yelled in response.

Scoff if you will, but this little hillside ritual really did have a solemn and sacred feel to it, rarely matched by anything I've experienced in places of worship I've visited since – I actually get a shiver thinking about it now. Even Jack, who'd taken part out of politeness I think, admitted later that she'd found it quite moving. Loose chanted the loudest of us all.

Finally Ginnie divided up the offered cake so that we all got a taste; not much, but enough to send us hurrying back to Lothlorien to share out the rest for breakfast, sitting round the Fireplace where Bill built up the fire to honour the Sun and served us his special Solstice spiced hot chocolate.

The remainder of the day was devoted mainly to the consumption of other goodies, plus the occasional snooze or musical interlude. *Here Comes the Sun* and *Let the Sun Shine In* were bedtime favourites, sung softly, as by then we were all pretty zonked or simply bloated with food. As always, everybody had made the effort to prepare something special: cheese fondu (Ginnie); spud'n'onion bake (Ash); savoury pancakes (Zoë); toffee apples (Bill); lemon meringue pie (Stella). Marjoram and Gogo stuffed a big pumpkin with rice and herbs, and Pete made his Date Surprises – 'because there's nothing more delicious than a surprising date.' Interestingly, all forms of curry were missing from the menu this year, but we had the new delights of Loose's cream-filled profiteroles and Jack's caramelised parsnip brochettes. Erryk had pulled himself together sufficiently to concoct an excellent bean and barley soup. Even Sean, with Rick's help, had managed to come up with a batch of chocolate nut clusters – dope-free for us kids but heavily laced with chopped marijuana heads for the adults. That year Elvira ate some of the latter and I must say they had a very cheering effect on her. It was odd to see her reduced to fits of giggles.

She didn't get her contact lenses, though. For those she had to wait until her birthday, but that was less than two weeks later, shortly before her first day at the Comprehensive. Zoë had taken her to the optician in

Middington immediately after her interview at the school, but the objects of desire weren't to be ready for collection until early in the New Year.

'Everything shuts down for so *long* Outside,' said Zoë. We were all, or at least most of us, having a communal dish-washing session in the shower block on the day after our Solstice feast.

'So the people of this great nation can stuff themselves senseless with meat and booze for a whole fucking week and then spend almost as long eliminating it all,' said Rick. 'While wallowing in mountains of useless consumer goods.'

'Like your new stereo,' said Elvira. 'Not that I'm criticising. I'm going to have *loads* of consumer goods in a few years' time. Even if it means getting hitched to some disgusting rich old lecher when I'm sixteen.'

Zoë groaned softly.

'Yeah,' continued Elvira, encouraged by this sign of parental despair, 'he can buy me all the presents I want and we'll have a *real Christmas*. You know – a *holiday*. When you have *fun*. Not like in this dump.'

The concept of holidays versus work was one I didn't understand at the time; it didn't really exist in Lothlorien, and it ran counter to Bill's philosophy. With tea-towel in hand – (he believed males should participate in domestic duties, at least if they weren't doing something more important) – he now paused in his wiping to deliver the relevant passage of this philosophy, one we already knew well.

'"Fun", as you call it, can be found wherever we are, whatever we're doing. Every Life Activity is equally valuable and enjoyable if performed with a maximum of attention to, and appreciation of, that activity.' Ginnie nodded gravely as she stacked up dishes with meticulous care. As I've said before, they didn't have much sense of humour.

Even Elvira didn't dare answer back to Bill. She just closed her eyes and dropped a plate on the floor.

She closed them even more once the contact lenses were finally fitted, at any rate for the first few days, blinking continuously in the effort to get used to them before the school term began. The fitting took place on her birthday, which she chose not to celebrate in usual Lothlorien style – ('that's for kids, I'm a teenager') – but instead at McDonald's in Chandleford, newly opened a few weeks earlier and already a top destination for the terminally trendy. Ashley was the only person willing to take her there, her friends from up the road being away on a trip somewhere warm.

'She pretended she wasn't with me,' he said. 'Still, the burgers were pretty good.'

'Please, spare us the details,' said Pete.

The lenses did make Elvira look different – her eyes seemed larger, if more watery. She looked happier, too. But the effect was rather spoilt by the dissolving black eye make-up which tended to run down and streak the thick whitish gloop she had recently taken to wearing on her face.

'Yukky yuk, freaky muck,' said Layla. But Elvira had by now risen so far above our sphere that she didn't react.

The first day she set off for school turned out to be something of an anticlimax. She didn't look too extreme – she was dressed in jeans, black lace-up boots and an old bomber jacket of Rick's, pretty standard gear in fact for most of the Middington adolescents. Her face was free of the heavy white make-up though her eyes were still ringed with as much black as she thought she could get away with. She'd taken out the safety pin. Most of us, adults and children, had gathered by the track leading out of Lothlorien for a solemn send-off. For the adults, I now realise, it must have been very hard to witness this defining moment of Elvira's defection from the community, but they all made an effort to be supportive and encouraging.

'Good luck, old thing,' said Rick roughly. Zoë tried to hug her but Elvira drew away.

'We all wish you well, El…*izabeth*,' said Bill.

'And we hope you will learn all that you need for the advancement of your spirit,' added Ginnie rather gnomically.

Expressionless, Elvira just gave a slight nod and mounted her new trail bike. This had been a birthday present from everybody, to serve as her transport as far as her friends' house, where she would leave it for the day and then be driven to school with the two boys in their father's car. She wobbled off up the track past the Sheepfield, standing on the pedals to push herself up the slope. As she reached the brow of the hill she sat down on the saddle, gave a vague wave without looking back, and disappeared.

'Hurray!' yelled Layla. Zoë burst into tears.

Henceforth, Elvira became something of a half-presence in Lothlorien, almost a wraith. She came back to the woods each evening but hardly communicated with anyone. Some time before she had refused to go on sharing the same bedroom as Layla, so she now slept either on the settee in the main part of Rick and Zoë's caravan or more often in Pete's spare bedroom, where she could concentrate better on her homework. 'I hardly know she's there,' he said. 'And it makes me feel so up-to-the-minute, sharing with a punk.' During the weekends she was usually elsewhere. 'Fine, fine,' she said if she was asked how things were going. She seemed perfectly calm and content in her aloof isolation. Her opinion of herself as a superior being, apart from the rest of us, was now firmly established.

'She's like a sort of mutant,' I said.

'She always was,' said Shine.

*

It was probably Elvira's entry into the educational mainstream which gave rise to the memorable incident which took place a few months later.

We had a new game by then, inspired by the Greek myths that Gogo had recently been teaching us. It was called Trojan Horse, and involved the shopping trolley. I've already mentioned that us kids used this to collect laundry from the caravans and take it to the washing machine in the shower block. These days, instead of putting it straight into the machine, we pulled most of it out so that Jelly Bean and Layla could climb into the trolley, where they crouched down together while the twins and I piled the laundry back in on top of them. We squashed it down well so as to completely hide the girls, before backing ourselves and the trolley into one of the shower cubicles. Then we closed the door and waited for the next visitor to the block. The adults had soon cottoned on to the following stage of the game, and in general played along very satisfactorily – though Ashley could sometimes get a little grumpy if he was hungover.

On this particular morning things turned out a bit unexpectedly. We hadn't been waiting long when we heard two sets of footsteps approaching on the gravel outside, accompanied by Gogo's voice. At this point we always got rather over-excited, so we weren't paying attention to what he was saying.

'Can we take on *both* of them?' whispered Rain anxiously.

'Course we can,' replied Shine, as bold as ever.

Rain needn't have worried, because just then we heard one person stop, while the other began to make their way inside.

'CHARGE!' we roared, hurtling out of the cubicle. Layla and Jelly Bean jumped up from their soft and slightly smelly hiding-place, screeching as loud as they could and pulling ghastly faces. They leapt out of the trolley and hurled themselves upon the person – (at first I thought it was Erryk, confusingly beardless and in a red anorak that I didn't recognise) – who found himself tackled to the floor with five children holding him firmly down in the middle of jumbled heaps of laundry.

'Trojan Horse!' yelled Jelly Bean, sitting astride his chest and waving one hand triumphantly in the air.

'The Greeks win!' I shouted. 'We demand Helen or your life!'

Then I saw that it wasn't Erryk – it was a complete stranger.

We must all have realised this at more or less the same time, because an abrupt silence fell. I think we were, for a few seconds, paralysed with shock. Then Gogo came running in.

'Kids! For Christ's sake! Get off him!'

Scrambling to our feet, we instinctively backed up against the wall in a line, as if we were facing a firing squad. We stared at our victim, who was struggling to stand up, his face almost as red as his anorak. His state of appalled shock was obviously even greater than our own. He stared back at us.

It was evident that he was very much an Outsider. I remember that under the anorak, which had fallen open, he was wearing a mustard-coloured cardigan and peculiar greenish neckwear – not a tie, more of a cravat, I suppose. He looked rather younger than the Lothlorien adults. His hair was of a similar brown to Erryk's, though shorter; he pulled a thin black comb from a trouser pocket and tidied it into a sort of bowl-shape, the front rim of which fell in a neat straight line above his eyebrows. Again like Erryk, he had a floppy moustache, grown perhaps as a sign that he was rather daring and different. But it couldn't disguise that typical Outsider look: smooth pasty face, opaque and worried eyes. (Opaque? Well, that was my impression. Outsiders frequently appeared to us as masked, non-transparent – 'covered in mist', as Shine used to say. And now I come to think of it, a great many people still seem to me like that – but I'm so used to it I've stopped noticing. Or perhaps I've become masked myself).

Of course our visitor had every reason to look worried, having just been attacked by a band of savage feral children, for that's how we must have appeared. Gogo picked up the big clipboard which had fallen to the floor and handed it to him. 'I really must apol...'

He was cut short by Shine. Taking the initiative, as she so often did, she stepped smartly forward. 'It's not Gogo's fault. We are all extremely sorry. We were playing Trojan Horse and we thought you were one of us. If you are hurt Marjoram will make you some special medicine and Ginnie will do some aromatherapy for you.'

We all nodded earnestly. 'And Zoë can give you a nice massage,' said Layla.

The stranger gave us a very odd look. 'Trojan Horse...' he muttered.

'Yes, you know, when the Greek soldiers built...' began Rain.

'Look – there's no point hanging around in here,' said Gogo wearily. 'This isn't really the place... Just stick that laundry in the machine first, will you?'

We rushed to do his bidding and them followed him outside.

'The man's still in there!' said Jelly Bean. 'Shall I get him?'

'No, Bean, for goodness sake leave him in peace to have his pee. That's what he was hoping to do before you all jumped on him.'

Several of the others had assembled on the log seats by the Fireplace: Bill and Ginnie, Marjoram, Jack and Loose, Zoë. Pete was watching the proceedings from the steps of his caravan some distance away. After a few minutes our victim came out of the shower block and walked over to join us. He had obviously regained his composure – he was brandishing his clipboard at shoulder height as if it was a weapon, and looked quite jaunty.

'Well well well, that was quite a welcome,' he said cheerily. Bill raised his eyebrows.

'They were playing Trojan Horse,' explained Gogo. Ginnie gave a little groan.

'All over now, all forgotten, eh kids? Time to attend to the matter in hand.'

'Who are you?' asked Jelly Bean loudly, voicing what we all wanted to know.

Gogo took a deep breath. 'Yes. I must introduce you. This is Mr Elsworthy, children, and he's...'

'Just call me Malcolm.'

'.. a social worker from the County Council.'

Naturally, that didn't mean a thing to us, though from the watchful expressions on the faces of the adults we could tell that Malcolm represented some form of threat.

'He wants to know if you're getting a good education.'

Bill coughed. 'You must be aware, Malcolm, that the whole question of home education within our community was gone into in some detail at the time of its founding, and was judged to be completely satisfactory.'

'Yes indeed, but that was before my time. I'm something of a new boy here, ha ha, and it's essential that I get up-to-the-minute information on any – um – problem areas.'

'I see. Well, I think we can quite easily demonstrate that we are certainly not one of your so-called "problem areas". Quite the reverse, in fact. Gogo – Gordon – is a first-class educator.'

'No doubt. But as laid out in the 1944 Education Act, each child should be educated according to their individual aptitude or ability, either at school or elsewhere, and that's what I'm here to verify. No offence, Gordon.'

Gogo looked grim but said nothing.

'First I just need to check exactly how many children are being schooled within your – um – commune.' Malcolm looked down at his clipboard. 'Elizabeth Sarah Maxwell, thirteen years – I believe she does go to school now.'

'Yes, unfortunately,' said Zoë.

Malcolm frowned. 'So may I ask why you took the decision to send her there?'

'We didn't decide. She wanted to go. It's just a teenage revolt. She'll soon realise that she was learning much more here.'

'Hmm... now then – Rain and Shine... is that correct?'

'*Yes,*' said Marjoram. 'Totally correct.'

'OK, OK. Just a bit unusual, that's all... So. Rain and Shine Collins, eight years.... Twins?'

'That's us,' said Shine. 'And we know a *lot*.'

'Well, that's what I'm here to find out, isn't it?' Malcolm's tone was jocular but contained a hint of menace. He consulted the clipboard again. 'Layla Marianne Maxwell, six years.'

'ME!' said Layla. 'And I know just as much as them, and so does Sindy!'

'Sindy?'

'My doll,' said Layla. 'She's my best friend. And she's much cleverer than my stupid sister who goes to that stupid school.' She smiled winsomely.

Malcolm cleared his throat. 'So that just leaves Emily Jane Bennett-Howe, also six years.'

Silence. Then: 'Oh – I suppose you mean the Bean,' said Shine. 'Our daughter,' said Ginnie at the same moment. 'But I'm afraid she doesn't answer to –'

'My name is *Jelly Bean*,' said Jelly Bean, fixing Malcolm with a glassy stare.

'That's a rather strange name, isn't it?'

'Not as strange as Malcolm,' said Jelly Bean.

But Malcolm ignored her and now fixed his attention on me. 'And who might this young gentleman be?'

I was about to tell him, when Loose jumped up and swooped to my side. She put her arms around me protectively. 'Zees eez Pierre. 'E eez my nephew from Paree and 'e 'as been *vairy* ill. 'E eez 'ere to 'ave 'oliday to get better.'

What was going on? Loose's English was pretty fluent and she didn't normally speak with that exaggerated French accent. The others looked a bit surprised too, apart from Jack. While Malcolm was gazing at me she rose quietly and murmured something first to Bill and then to Gogo, who both nodded and whispered briefly to Ginnie, Marjoram and Zoë. I still didn't understand, but I realised that Loose must have a good reason for this game, so I was happy to go along with it. I gave Malcolm a shy little grin, but he now seemed rather more preoccupied with Loose.

She fluttered her eyelashes at him and gave me a gentle prod. 'Dis bonjour au monsieur, Pierre.'

'Bonjour,' I said.

'Convalescing, eh?' Malcolm looked doubtfully at me. I must have appeared a picture of radiant good health.

'That's right,' said Jack. 'He had pneumonia. The country air's done him the world of good.'

'It's wonderful to see him looking so much better,' said Zoë brightly.

'So how long is your holiday going to go on for, Master Pierre?'

I looked towards Loose for guidance. ''E doesn't speak Eenglish vairy well,' she said.

'Oh? No parler anglais?'

'Leetle beet,' I said bashfully, and coughed several times in what I hoped was a realistic way.

'That's funny. I could have sworn I heard you shouting in English back there – ' Malcolm pointed over his shoulder towards the shower block.

'That was me,' said Rain.

Malcolm still looked unconvinced. He gave a heavy sigh. 'All right, all right. Let's get down to business.' He tapped the clipboard, his talisman. 'Now then you lot, can you tell me what you're learning about at the moment? Apart from the Trojan War, ha ha.'

'Medusa!' Jelly Bean twirled her fingers in her hair so that it stood up in short spikes. 'She had snakes on her head!'

'Did she now.'

'She could turn you to stone.' She stuck out her tongue and glared.

'That's enough, Jelly Bean,' said Gogo. 'We all know you like the Greek myths, but why doesn't someone explain to Malcolm what else we've been studying lately?'

'Sperms!' said Layla. In fact it was ages since we'd had the lesson on this subject, but in recent weeks Layla had returned to it enthusiastically, as she wanted to find a way to get her Sindy doll pregnant. Although in many ways far more savvy than she chose to appear, she was still seized from time to time by some totally irrational obsessions.

'Did you know, Malcolm,' she went on, 'if you put your sperms in the freezer you can still make babies even if you're dead?'

Malcolm flushed and turned to Gogo. 'Do you really think this is the sort of thing you should be teaching children of this age?'

'Of course. I'm preparing them for the future. Sperm banks are going to become more and more necessary – seed banks of all kinds, in fact, if we continue to destroy so many natural plant and animal species.'

Such prescience. Sometimes Gogo got it absolutely right.

'Well, that's all very fine and dandy, but what about the basics? The three Rs?'

'Three whats?' asked Jelly Bean.

'Reading, Writing and Arithmetic. Ever heard of those?'

'That's not three Rs, that's R, W, A,' Rain pointed out.

'Oh, so you do know some spelling then.' Malcom sounded surprised, if a touch sarcastic.

'That's because we read and write all the time,' said Shine. 'Even the Bean's good at writing.'

'The B… Ah, yes.'

'*Me,*' said Jelly Bean severely. 'And I can do maths as well.'

'OK then – what's seven times nine?'

'Sixty three, of course. What's fourteen times seventeen?'

Malcolm appeared nonplussed.

'I can tell you, if you don't know,' said Jelly Bean. She waggled her fingers as she concentrated on her calculation. 'Two hundred and thirty eight! It's easy. Gogo showed us how to do teen-times quickly.'

'We're doing fractions and decimals at the moment, though,' said Rain. 'And imaginary numbers like the square root of minus one. They're fun.'

'I like Jommetry better,' said Layla. 'You can make a square into lots of little triangles, did you know? You can do it with matches. And soon we're going to do Algie Bra!' She shook with giggles.

By now Malcolm was reduced to silence.

'I think you've made your point, children,' said Gogo. 'Now – why don't you go and get your essay books to show Malcolm?'

With an instinctive desire to show off too, I began to run after the others. Loose grabbed me and pulled me back. 'Ne cours pas, chéri. You must not run. Remember your leetle lungs.' I remembered, and coughed vigorously. Loose turned to Malcolm with a radiant smile. 'Do you 'ave cheeldren?'

'Um – no.'

'One day you will make beautiful cheeldren.'

Malcolm reddened. Once again he seemed at a loss for words. 'I – I've never met a French hippie before,' he said eventually. This seemed an odd answer to Loose's observation, until it occurred to me that he would have liked to make these beautiful children with her. She lowered her eyes prettily. 'In France I am not 'eepie. I am *baba cool*.'

'What – like a rum baba?' Malcolm was looking very chirpy all of a sudden.

'I think Pierre needs a dose of his cough medicine,' said Jack.

'Yes, yes, I will geev it to him. Viens, chéri.' Loose led me away to the campervan.

We collapsed inside, trying to smother our laughter. Then her manner changed and she became very serious. 'Curly, I told him all this because you are not in the System. The System doesn't know that you were born. Maybe it won't matter if it finds out later when you are a grown-up, but I think that today it would make too much hassle for everybody. Especially for you. Malcolm could even take you away, because you don't have parents.'

'But I have all of you!'

'Of *course* you do. But people like Malcolm – they see these things differently.'

I was silent for a moment, as I took in the potential horror that Loose had just saved me from. Then I burst into tears. Loose hugged me tightly. 'You mustn't worry, Curly. You will always be safe with us.'

When I started to recover I asked her why she'd put on that funny French voice.

'Because ordinary Englishmen, they *love* that accent. They think it's so sexy. I thought Malcolm needed to be – *distracted*. So he would think more about me than about you.'

I was speechless with gratitude.

Loose took my hand. 'Come on – let's go back and see what is happening.'

During our absence Malcolm had inspected a number of essays, all illustrated: Rain's on the dinosaurs, Shine's on the fjords of Norway, Jelly Bean's on the winter habits of woodland fauna. Now Layla was insisting on reading one of hers aloud. 'I wrote it yesterday. It's history and it's very interesting.'

'I don't suppose I can stop her, can I,' said Malcolm, smiling pleasantly at Loose.

'No, you can't,' said Layla.

Her essay, read out in her sing-song reciting voice, went something like this: '*Once upon a time there was a queen in England called Bo-dis-seer who painted herself blue and was a brave warrior. Later on there were some other queens but the most powerful was called Elizabeth the First. She was not a warrior but even strong men were afraid of her. One of them put his cloak over some mud so she could walk on it without getting her shoes dirty. But she wore too much make-up to cover up her spotty skin and no-one knew the make-up had poison in it so she died. Now there is a queen called Elizabeth the Second. She is not so powerful but she is very expensive because everyone has to pay for her palaces and castles. She wears different clothes every day so that is expensive too. This year she will have a Joolybee but we won't take any notice. Some people think she should ab-dick-ate to save everybody money. But other people think she should stay because she is nice and has corgis. The End.'*

Layla beamed in triumph and everyone clapped, even Malcolm.

'Well, Gordon, I must admit you seem to be doing a pretty good job after all.'

I'm sure Gogo would have liked to tell Malcolm what he really thought of him, but he would have known well enough how important it was to keep him sweet.

'I think that calls for a glass of wine, don't you? I hope you'll join us, Malcolm – blackberry and elderflower, vintage '76.'

'Don't mind if I do,' said Malcolm expansively. 'Just a small one.'

Two large glasses later he was looking around him with a faintly bewildered air. 'I must say…this is all surprisingly…'

'Surprisingly what?' said Pete, who had joined us. 'Was "civilised" the word you were searching for?'

'I suppose I was expecting…'

'Filth and disorder? We've given that up for Lent.'

'He's only joking,' said Shine. 'We're always clean and tidy, mostly. Especially him. That's why he's called *Neat* Pete.'

Malcolm tittered. 'Well, hippies, you know… you do have a certain reputation. Drugs, free love, that kind of thing.'

'So now you can go back and spread the word that we are *evolved* hippies and our reputation is unfounded,' said Pete. Fortunately this year's marijuana plants hadn't yet sprouted in the Garden.

'And I thought there'd be – well, more of you.'

'There are more of us,' said Marjoram. 'But we don't all stay here every minute of the day, you know. We have to go out sometimes into the big wide world.'

'Oh yes. You have to go and pick up your dole, I suppose.'

'Certainly not,' said Bill, so sharply that Malcolm gave a little jump. 'We would consider it deeply immoral to live off a State and a System of which we disapprove.'

'What – you mean you have *jobs*?' Malcolm seemed shocked, almost disappointed.

'Not quite, perhaps, what you would consider normal employment,' said Bill. 'But perfectly legitimate methods of earning a living. For instance, one of us is a musician, certain others sell home-made goods in the markets. And so on.'

'So you pay taxes and all that?'

'In my own case, yes. The others do not find it necessary to earn enough to be above the tax-paying threshold,' said Bill. 'Our requirements are small. We are virtually self-sufficient as far as food is concerned.'

'Well, I would never have realised – '

'But now you do, Malcolm,' said Pete. 'From today you can just think of us as law-abiding, hard-working *non*-citizens.'

At this point we spotted Sean meandering towards us, stopping now and then to marvel at a tree root or a spring flower. He'd probably been having a rest and a few spliffs after his morning work-out. Malcolm was sitting with his back to him, but those who could see him looked worried.

'Ah, Brother Sean,' said Pete, getting up smoothly. 'The very person I hoped to see. We were having such a fascinating discussion last night about classical music and there are still a few points I want to take up with him.' He strolled over to Sean, turned him round, and steered him away. Everyone relaxed.

Malcolm was obviously struggling to order his thoughts. 'Now then – what I'm still concerned about – it's this non-citizen bit,' he said finally. 'It really isn't fair on your kids to deprive them…'

'Of what?' asked Ginnie sweetly.

'The whole – experience – of being in society and knowing how to deal with it.'

'We believe it wouldn't be fair to bring them up *within* that society, when we so strongly oppose its values. As you've seen, our children are all healthy, stable and well-educated. They'll be amply equipped to deal with any environment they choose to live in as adults.' She smiled her special loving I-know-best smile. 'You can trust us, Malcolm.'

Bill stood up. Looking down on Malcolm he gave him a full blast of charisma, and then gently took his arm to help him to rise as well. 'I'm sure you'll agree that this has been an extremely useful meeting, Malcolm, but I think that now it's time for all of us to get on with our lives. You in particular must be a very busy man. Thank you so much for taking the time to visit us.' He held out his hand.

Hypnotised, Malcolm shook it limply. 'Yes – well – thank *you*, Mr Bennett.' He was too impressed to call him by his first name.

We skipped after him to his parked car – a modest black Ford Cortina, I think it was.

'His real name isn't Mr Bennett you know,' said Jelly Bean. 'It's Electricity Bill.'

'Gracious, you kids – you've certainly got a lot of imagination, haven't you?'

As we passed Pete's caravan we saw him sitting once again on the steps, having already disposed of Sean somewhere. He'd put on an opera tape, but not the kind I liked. It was something discordant and jarring: Schoenberg, or perhaps just Berg.

Malcolm smiled uncertainly at Pete. 'Unusual music.'

'Schnitke's *Cantata for Dead Feet*. So moving.'

'Can't say I've ever heard of it.'

'No? You might care to come over one evening and we'll have a singalong. I've got the libretto. It's wonderfully deep. Life-changing, really.'

We turned away and tried to stifle our sniggers. Malcolm gave a nervous laugh. 'And to think I imagined that you'd all be singing folk-songs all day long.'

'You see? Another false prejudice ground in the dust.'

Malcolm seemed much relieved to see Loose running up. She sparkled at him. 'Monsieur Malcolm, I jus' wanted to say au revoir.'

He blinked. 'Um – I don't know whether – if you ever come to Chandleford –'

'Alas, I belong to anuzzer. But eet 'as been *so* lovely to meet you.' She blew him a kiss and he got rather sadly into his car.

'Why did you say that about the dead feet and the singalong?' I asked Pete, as the Cortina laboured up the track.

'Because, my dears, I wanted to make absolutely sure that he'd never come back.'

10. MOVING ON

'OH WOW,' SAID Sean. 'Shit!! That is just *totally unreal...*'

'Mm,' murmured Stella. 'It makes you feel so small.'

'No man, I'm *huge – stretched* – I'm up there with them... Jesus Christ! I'm on a giant roller coaster in the sky and it's a cosmic neon WOW – I'm sliding down the W – now I'm going up again – down again – up again... FUCK! Now I'm on the O and it's *so unbelievably round* – I'm SWOOOOSHING round the O – I *am* the O...'

Stella giggled. 'He's hopeless. But I love him.'

'Great picture, though,' said Tiger Lily. 'I'm gonna paint that. I'll call it *Sean's Vision*.

Erryk got up and disappeared into the night. I guessed immediately that Sean's cosmic WOW had reminded him too much of Wing's initials, still engraved on his heart even though I had painted over them on the caravan door months ago.

'I can't see any WOWs,' said Layla, 'Just billions of magic fairy tadpole tails.'

'Not billions,' corrected Shine. 'Hundreds. Ooh – look at that one! It's really long!'

'Must be a specially big one,' said Rain.

Stella sat up suddenly. 'What if one lands on top of us?'

'Impossible,' said Shine. 'They burn up in the atmosphere.'

'The bats are watching too,' said Jelly Bean, pointing at the small black shapes flitting erratically in the dim starlight.

It must have been about one in the morning, and we were lying in the Sheepfield beneath the Perseid Shower, which was doing its sensational stuff in a cloudless, moonless sky. All the adults were passing round joints, but Sean had also dropped a few of the magic mushrooms which were just coming into season.

By this time – 1977 – Sean was still the only truly unreconstructed hippie amongst us; everyone else had, to a greater or lesser extent, evolved somewhat. It wasn't that the basic principles of Lothlorien no longer held true: it was rather a question of image. Not long after cutting her own hair, Zoë had turned her scissors first on Stella – who now had a fetching style which was short on one side and longer on the other – and then Rick. She shortened his ponytail and removed all facial hair, including his long luxuriant sideburns. He had cherished these as they had been so much thicker than the hair on his head, but she was adamant.

'I don't look like a musician any more,' he said bitterly. 'I look like an accountant.'

'Nonsense. Musicians can look like anything these days. You look younger and sexier.'

'It makes you look more intellectual,' added Marjoram, which helped.

Zoë even managed to make a start on Ashley, having persuaded him that he would have more success with women if he was tidied up a bit. So now he had a much less matted look – and it seemed to have done the trick. He drove more often into Chandleford, and he had a new song:

'I bought her a beer and said come over here

'She was raring to go so I couldn't say no

'And she panted for more as she lay on the floor...'

'What floor?' I asked. 'Behind the pub,' said Ash shortly. 'And it's none of your bloody business.' But he sounded quite the opposite of annoyed.

'Wouldn't it be more comfortable to bring her back here and do it in the tree house?'

'Hell's bells, we don't want the woods invaded by hoards of females fighting over my body.'

'What he means is, she doesn't fancy sleeping in a tree with a slobbering dog,' said Stella.

'But man, she gets the dog anyway, because Chip always goes with him,' said Sean.

'They're not so squashed up together, though. And she doesn't have to go all the way to the shower block if she needs to go the toilet.'

'Ash just pees out of the window.'

'Well, he would, wouldn't he. I can't imagine a woman doing that.'

Stella herself, having completed her jewellery-making course, ordered supplies through her old teacher and set to work in her caravan. Her jewellery wasn't bright and shiny; it had a satin lustre which I grew to appreciate. And it was always highly asymmetrical. I found that peculiar at first, but later realised that therein lay her originality – it was a useful lesson in design which I must have subconsciously retained.

'I've got enough to show people now,' she said after a few months, and took off in her sky-blue Mini to London, where she had a few ex-model friends who'd set up boutiques where they sold fashion accessories.

'They love it!' she exclaimed with some amazement, and from then on began to sell quite regularly both to her mates and to a few other shops elsewhere.

'You know,' she said, 'I used to think I was as thick as shit, but now I'm not so sure.'

It was fun watching her work; she had slim delicate fingers and always kept her nails manicured and varnished with interesting colours. As she finished each piece she stamped it with her trademark, a small star.

'That's you, babe,' said Sean.

*

One evening in the middle of a communal Fireplace dinner Ginnie stood up, clapped her hands and called for silence.

'A miracle has taken place in Middington,' she announced.

Rick looked up from his plate. 'Is that possible?'

'I expect it's because of the prayers we send out beyond our boundaries,' said Ginnie, causing Ashley to snort quietly into his beer. She looked at him disapprovingly. 'You may not realise it, but Lothlorien does have an effect on Outside – at the *subliminal* level.'

'I've always loved that word,' mused Pete.

'Then you can tell me what it means later on,' said Tiger Lily.

'Please be quiet everybody, and listen: *the butcher's shop is closing down*.'

'Thank God for that,' said Marjoram. 'I hate walking past that place.'

'Oh, me too,' said Stella. 'I always cross the road. And I can't help thinking, what if all those bits of carcasses hanging up were human beings.'

'Probably are,' said Rick. 'People who can't afford funerals. They sell their bodies in advance to meat suppliers. It's a well-known fact.'

Zoë gave him a sharp dig in the ribs. 'Don't talk such crap.'

'Worse things happen.'

'Of course we'll all be glad to see the back of it,' said Gogo, 'but that doesn't mean the good burghers of Middington are going to stop eating meat, does it? They'll just get it from the supermarket, nicely wrapped up in sellophane. Then they won't have to think at all about where it came from.'

'Right,' said Rick. 'And it's easier to disguise what it really is. Loin of baby going as choice stewing veal.'

'It's the same thing, really,' said Ginnie quietly.

Bill frowned. 'Rick, I think that kind of comment is unhelpful. And kids, there is absolutely no need to laugh.'

We stopped. Everyone fell silent as we contemplated the awfulness of eating flesh.

'Are you – how do you know it's closing?' asked Erryk eventually.

'I was in the library. The librarian was talking about it with another lady. I just wanted to jump up and down and sing, while they were saying what a shame it was.'

'Don't know why you call it a miracle, though,' said Ashley. 'The place'll just get taken over by another butcher.'

'Not if –' Ginnie raised herself on tiptoe – 'not if *we* take over the lease.'

'What's a lease?' I asked. Everyone else seemed for a moment too surprised to say anything.

'It means that we give some money to the people who own the shop and then we can do whatever we like with it.'

'Within reason,' said Bill.

'Who owns it?' asked Marjoram.

'The couple who live upstairs. Bill and I have already had a word with them. They seem pretty cool about the whole thing.'

'Don't hang about, do you?' said Ash. 'Who's supposed to pay for this bloody lease, anyway? Because you can forget about me, for a start.'

'Ashley, you're the very last person I'd ask for money, and in fact I don't have to ask anyone, because last year I was left a small legacy. From my great-aunt Rose, bless her. I know she'd want me to use it wisely – she was quite a spiritual woman, in her way.'

'Never came to visit here though, did she?'

'Don't be silly, Ash. She was very old and I hadn't seen her for years. But I remember her as being somehow on the right *track*.'

'So what exactly is your plan for this place?' asked Gogo.

'First of all it'll need a huge amount of ritual cleansing. To get rid of the – the memories of blood and slaughter. All that terrible, terrible, undiluted Yang. But just think – there's so much talent in Lothlorien. *Yin* talent. Stella's jewellery – Marj's herb mixtures – Tiger Lily's paintings – Zoë's hairdressing – my aromatherapy oils of course... And Loose – you're something of a photographer, aren't you?'

'Oh I see – it's going to be a girlie thing,' said Rick.

'Well, why not? Unless Erryk...'

'No... no. I'd rather stick to the markets. Thanks.'

'And not me,' said Loose. 'I need to work alone. People might ask me to do wedding photos – ha! And I would do it, just for fun – but in my style!

So they would *hate* them!'

Ginnie looked slightly relieved. 'No, we don't want to disturb anyone. It must be an oasis of calm. Outsiders are so stressed. They need to be *healed*.'

'Wow, it'll be enough to heal the world...' Sean was smiling the smile of the truly stoned. 'All you chicks grooving together, doing your little thing... Fa-a-ar out.'

Ashley made a hurrumphing noise. 'Sounds more like an excuse for a bit of bourgeois capitalism.'

'No,' said Bill patiently, 'it would simply be a case of conducting honest transactions with Outside, not for reasons of greed or exploitation, but simply as a means of providing, we hope, a little extra income for the community from the sale of entirely ethical goods.' He turned to Jack, who had been listening quietly throughout this conversation. 'What do you think about the whole idea?'

Jack drew on her Gauloise. 'Frankly, I can't see much wrong with it. Providing you're prepared to bear the cost, Ginnie, if it doesn't work out.'

'It will work out,' said Ginnie, her eyes glowing with conviction.

*

First all the fittings were stripped out and transported to the tip by Ashley, who grumbled as usual but helped anyway; then it was time to banish the evil meaty vibes which lingered inside. All of us children participated in this cleansing – I recall a great deal of splashing of blackberry wine and essential oils on to walls, floor and ceiling, while Ginnie waved incense sticks and invoked the souls of the animals whose carcasses had been dismembered at the back. 'Now their new lives will be free of bad karma,' she said. 'They can gambol in fresh mountain pastures.' It was a nice picture – skipping pigs, leaping sheep, frolicking cattle.

Much discussion went into the choice of décor.

'It's got to be true to the spirit of Lothlorien,' said Marjoram.

'Of course,' said Zoë. 'Nothing punk.'

'But it can't be too... well, trippy hippie,' said Ginnie. 'We don't want to alienate our clientèle.'

In the end Tiger Lily painted the outside a dark and rather dusty violet, very different from the vibrant purple of her Tarot booth, and on the wall between the door and the window she added a simple logo, a light green leaf shape with the words *Nature's Way* inside it, the name which had been settled on as being accurate but un-scary. The interior, extremely pale lavender, was enhanced by some Ginnie-chosen pot plants and plain wooden furniture with faintly flowery linen cushions.

'So tasteful,' remarked Pete. 'But then of course she was conceived in the John Lewis soft furnishings department.'

'*Really*?' asked Rain. 'You mean in *public*?' There was a branch of John Lewis in Chandleford.

'Rain, you must try to curb your literal-mindedness. She's from Cheam, that's all you need to know.'

'Where's Cheam?'

'Don't even ask. With any luck you'll never have to go there.'

'Neat Pete speaks in riddles, ' Rain grumbled to me.

Finally the stock was brought into the shop: Marjoram's herbal infusions and lotions scattered artistically in big wicker baskets; Ginnie's oils arranged on rustic shelves; Stella's jewellery on the wall and in a glass display case. Zoë put up a notice to advertise her home hairdressing; she didn't want to cause any ill-feeling in the High Street by competing too directly with *Hair Today,* just down the road. Tiger Lily hung up a selection of her new paintings. These were rather blurry and abstract, very different from her earlier psychedelic style. They were quite pretty, but I didn't like them so much.

'They're to contemplate if you need to change your aura,' she explained. 'People will buy them, you'll see.'

But they didn't – to begin with, they scarcely bought anything. People stared into the window rather suspiciously and only occasionally ventured in for a quick look round. Enthusiasm faded into discouragement: even Ginnie started to wilt around the edges.

Until Tiger Lily's revelatory experience. 'It came to me in a dream, girls,' she said. 'The whole thing's too low-key. We need more action. Look, Zoë – why don't you give some sort of make-up counselling? Tell your private clients about it, they'll bring their mates. You can use Marj's stuff.'

'I don't do make-up, though,' said Marjoram.

'Get hold of some natural pigments – ocres and that. You can get them at Chandleford artshop. Mix them up in a bit of Vaseline or something, and stick them into dinky little boxes. Those tiny wooden ones – I know a bloke on the market who sells them. Stell – you can do jewellery-making demos. And Ginnie – you should give people some aromatherapy treatment sessions. That'd be a whole lot more of a draw than just having the oils sitting on the shelf. It's still a new thing – you gotta *coax* the folks. Pamper them. Make them feel special.'

'Yes... maybe you're right...'

'Course I am. You'll see. And you'll love doing it.'

'Well, it would be much more *healing*. But what about you? Will you do something?'

'Too right I will. I'll give aura readings. With crystals. I can get those on the market too.'

'Yes – but we can't all be doing things at the same time,' objected Ginnie.

'No, of course not. We can each have a special day of the week.'

'And let's get some leaflets printed,' said Stella. 'You can do us a good design, can't you Tiger? Then we'll take them round everywhere.'

Marjoram laughed. 'I can hand them out at the Women's Institute Fête. I'll get a skirt and a cardigan from the Oxfam shop so I can blend in.'

'And we can invite a journalist from the local paper. Give her a couple of free treatments.'

Thus *Nature's Way* got its second wind, and business started to pick up.

*

If I was in Middington on a library expedition I often looked in to the shop to see what was going on. It wasn't possible to actually watch Ginnie or Tiger Lily with their clients; both practised their arts in an alcove they had curtained off at the back of the shop, formerly occupied by the dead flesh in the butcher's big deep-freeze, now by the living flesh of Middington's ladies of leisure, who were encouraged to relax comfortably on a small couch while ambient music swished and burbled from a tape recorder concealed beneath it. Sometimes I positioned myself discreetly outside the curtain, so I could enjoy a gust of Ginnie's perfumes or listen to Tiger Lily's soft murmurings.

Almost all the auras she examined turned out to be in some way unhealthy, but curable by the right kind of energy source, usually one of her pictures plus a crystal or two. I liked the crystals a lot. I memorised their names and recited them like an incantation: rose quartz, smoky quartz, black agate, amethyst, moonstone, lapis lazuli, malachite, aventurine… My favourite was labradorite, its oddly doggy name so different from the magical blue-green glimmers which only appeared if you held it at the right angle to the light.

Zoë didn't use the alcove but sat her clients in front of a softly-lit mirror in the main part of the shop. A major part of her counselling seemed to be flattery. 'Basically, you've got this really fabulous skin texture,' she might say. 'It just needs to be enhanced a little.' Then she would smooth on one of Marjoram's herbal creams. 'There! Do you see that *glow*? And look how this eye-shadow brings out the lovely subtle colour of your eyes… Now – maybe a firming neck massage with this really *sumptious* penetrating elixir…'

'You've got such a great line in bullshit,' said Marjoram.

'Oh I know, I know,' sighed Zoë.

Once they found out that she could do hair as well, clients sometimes asked her to their homes for a touch of coiffure, thus adding to the number of customers she'd already acquired through the builder's wife. They liked to talk to her about their preoccupations – mostly domestic strife or illicit romance.

'Spoilt bitches, most of them,' she said. 'Sometimes I feel I shouldn't be pandering to their crappy little fantasies. It's contaminating.'

'No, no,' said Ginnie. 'It's just the opposite. They're unconsciously absorbing your purer energies. Think of it as spiritual osmosis.'

'I think of it as cash,' said Zoë. With her new earnings she bought a second-hand Mini – not pale blue like Stella's but a bright tangerine colour, which I loved. Now she could be fully independent.

'*Aromatherapeutics*' was the name Ginnie gave to her own brand of spiritual osmosis, and as Tiger Lily had predicted its appeal spread quite quickly. In fact within months the whole shop became an accepted fixture of the High Street, no longer an object of suspicion.

'I just love it in here,' said Stella. 'It's so holistic.' This was a word which could be heard more and more often in Lothlorien.

Personally, although I quite liked going to the shop, it wasn't half as much fun as when Tiger Lily set up her little tent as the Aboriginal Seer – but she did this less and less often now. 'Auras are easier,' she said. 'The Tarot really takes it out of you, it's so bloody powerful.'

For her, indeed for all the women involved, this concerted foray into commerce meant that their time had to be more structured than before; routines had to be established to fit in with the rhythms of Outside in a way which I'm sure would have been anathema to them in the pioneering days of Lothlorien. But as I said, everyone had moved on a bit.

They all enjoyed their time in the shop – 'womanning' the premises, as they liked to say. Some years later I realised that this was a feminist term coined as an alternative to 'manning', but at the time I just took it to be a normal verb. 'Womanning my arse,' said Ashley. 'They're shop-girls, working in a shop. Not that there's anything wrong with that. I could tell you a thing or two about shop-girls…'

'What?'

'Not now. Too complicated.' He chuckled into his beard.

Nevertheless, the shop-girls of *Nature's Way* preferred to think of themselves as Spiritual Therapists. When on duty they wore one of the special uniforms which Stella had found for them in London – jumpsuits, I suppose you would have called them, though they seemed to make their wearers glide rather than jump. They were one-piece garments in some kind of jersey material, the same pale green as the logo. 'Elf-green,' said Layla approvingly.

Elf-green: Wing would have liked that, I thought – though without any deep feeling of nostalgia. I honestly didn't miss her.

Layla adored the shop. To begin with she spent as much time there as she could, and was undoubtedly an asset.

'What a pretty name!' people would say. 'Like the song.'

'No, the song's like me. I came first.'

This was true; '*Layla*' hadn't been released until several months after her birth, and it was just a coincidence that Rick and Zoë had settled on a name which was later to take on such fashionably musical associations. 'I always said that track would be a hit,' said Rick.

'Just like our daughter,' said Zoë. 'It's a sign.' Perhaps it was.

At any rate, Layla was a big hit with the customers. Looking disgustingly cute she would open a bottle of, for instance, herbal body lotion, and gently rub it into the skin first of her own arm and then that of her Sindy doll. 'Look!' she would exclaim to enchanted onlookers. 'See how soft and smooth it makes us!' And they of course would walk out with a bottle or two, and tell their friends about the adorable little girl in the new shop in the high street.

This went on until the morning when a woman gave her a searching look and said: 'Shouldn't you be at school?'

'We don't go to *school*,' said Layla. 'We have a *proper* teacher.'

The woman looked questioningly at Zoë, who forced a smile. 'Home education,' she said brightly. 'We believe it allows more room for real development.'

'It looks like child exploitation to me,' said the woman. 'Maybe I should report you to the Social Services.'

'Feel free. We know them well.'

'Social Services is called Malcolm,' said Layla. 'He liked my essay.'

The woman sniffed and walked out.

Zoë and Marjoram told us about this little exchange when they got back to Lothlorien that evening.

Ginnie looked serious. 'I think it would be better in future if Layla only goes into Middington on Saturdays and during school holidays. We really don't need any interference from Outside which could disrupt our healing practices.'

'But we *need* to be there!' exclaimed Layla in dismay. By 'we' she was of course referring to herself and her Sindy doll.

'I'd like to strangle that doll,' said Rain later, and indeed we all shared this sentiment sometimes.

'Drowning would be better,' said Shine. 'We could sacrifice it to Galadriel.'

'Chop it up and bury it,' said Jelly Bean.

Despite these occasional murderous impulses we were generally pretty tolerant of the Sindy doll, probably because it gave us so many opportunities to tease Layla.

'Sindy sleep-walked into my bed last night,' I once told her. 'She told me she's tired of being a lesbian and she wants to be my girlfriend.'

'You're just being silly,' said Layla loftily. 'Sindy doesn't sleep-walk. And she'd *never* be unfaithful. Not even with Loose and Jack.'

These two were by now so well embedded in the community that it was hard to imagine a time when they hadn't been among us. Jack, although she could occasionally become irritable if her writing wasn't going well, was in general a benignly stable presence, slightly apart and yet accessible. And I noticed that both Bill and Ginnie often asked for her advice. Looking back at that period now, I see her not so much as a grandmother as a kind of Buddha figure. 'She just gives off such a good calm vibe,' said Marjoram. She did – she was happy in those days.

And while Jack wrote and typed and smoked her Gauloise cigarettes, Loose bounded around singing – but she did plenty of other things while she sang. She fashioned her own eccentric musical instruments out of bits and pieces salvaged from Ash's and Erryk's work-benches, and she did her best to dragged Rick out of his winter depression by banging or twanging on these until he reluctantly agreed to jam with her a bit.

Most of all, she took photographs. She had a Nikon camera filled with black and white film and she took pictures of everything: us, the woods, the shop, the sheep. In the streets of Middington and Chandleford she took candid photos of startled passersby. Then she had them developed at the Middington photo shop – God knows what they made of them. Loose's pictures were wild – the subjects slanting, grainy, often out of focus; they were art photos, and alternative ones at that.

I can't say I liked them – though now I probably would. Most of the adults seemed pretty impressed. There were a few which took my fancy: a sheep, apparently standing on a forty-five degree slope and looking terribly pleased with itself; Jelly Bean leaping in the treetops like a flying squirrel. Following Jack's advice, she sent the pictures she thought were the best to underground art magazines in England and in France, and some were published and paid for. Through Jack's contacts she even had a couple accepted by a magazine in New York.

Jack was immensely proud of her. 'You're a phenomenon. You'll bring out a whole book one of these days.'

'Wowee! I'm going to be FAY-MOUSE!' She pulled her bunches above her head like horns and pirouetted.

One day she showed us some close-up pictures of Sean's naked flesh. While I don't think they were in any way erotic, they did imply that a certain amount of physical closeness had taken place – although all she'd asked him to do was lie down and flex his muscles, which came out looking more like duny desert landscapes than anything else.

Sean loved them. 'Man, that's sooo cool. Look at those shadows... Wow, those pecs aren't bad… and are those my *biceps*? Awesome.'

When Loose caught sight of Stella's face she rushed over to give her a hug. 'Don't worry, Stella! For me Sean's body is just an object – I mean *neutral*. Like a table or a tree.'

'Don't you like men at all?' I asked her later on.

'Of course I like them. But not for sex, not now. Here they are all my good friends.'

'Which ones do you like best?'

'There's no best. They are all different, so I like them in different ways. Gogo is so sweet and so clever. Erryk is sweet too, although he is so sad… I think I must do something about Erryk. Rick is brilliant even if he has bad moods. But I *love* to sing when he plays.'

'Ashley?'

'He pretends to be bad, but he is good. Just a bit smelly.'

'Sean?'

She exploded with laughter. 'Sean is a WANKER. But he is funny, and he is not nasty.'

'Pete?'

'He is *very* funny. But I think he is unhappy underneath.'

'Bill?'

She shrugged. 'Bof. Bill is Bill. Like a big rock, or the rain. A force of nature.' She threw her arms around Jack. 'And this is the person I love best.'

Jack turned pink and grunted.

I was interested in what she'd said about Pete, because in fact he seemed unusually bouncy of late – far from unhappy. He'd been away a lot on what he called his 'business trips', eternally mysterious because he would never say the slightest thing about what this business was. 'Nothing of interest,' he told me when I asked. 'All rather boring, really.'

'What do you think Pete *does* when he's not here?' Stella mused once at a communal dinner. He himself had once again disappeared for a few days. 'Do you reckon he's got a boyfriend tucked away somewhere?'

'He's a very private person,' said Bill. 'That's his choice, and we must respect it.' Ginnie nodded emphatically. I wonder if she and Bill knew more about Pete than they were letting on.

At any rate, each time he returned after one of these absences he had a zippy new waistcoat – with less embroidery than on his older, hippier ones, but very chic. He always wore these over a spotless white shirt. From one such trip – longer than most, at least ten days – he came back deeply tanned. This was during the summer, but that year we certainly hadn't had the kind of weather which could have turned anybody that colour, certainly not in ten days.

'Where have you been?' I asked, amazed.

'I've been where southern zephyrs blow. To the isles of the blessed.' He wouldn't be drawn any further.

'You've got a lot of secrets, haven't you Pete?' I felt I was old enough now – eight – to talk to him man to man.

'Oh my dear, I'm *stuffed* with secrets. I am brimming with a million hidden mysteries. But I never let them overflow. I'm relentlessly discreet. Now then – shall we gaze at that fabulously kitsch sunset over there behind the trees? Doesn't that make you want to weep?'

'Not really. It is pretty though.'

'Pretty! Curly, sometimes I fear for you.'

*

I hadn't taken Loose seriously when she said that she ought to do something about Erryk, because what could be done? We'd all tried, and failed, to bring him out of what Pete called his 'shroud of pain'. His eyes still filled with tears as he strummed '*Forever Young*'; he still couldn't get through '*Don't Think Twice*' without breaking down in the middle. I'd become so accustomed to his despair that I'm rather ashamed to say I hardly noticed it any more.

But one afternoon that autumn Loose marched up the steps to our caravan, barged in, and yanked the guitar out of his hands. 'That's enough!' she shouted.

I was in my bedroom, reading, and looked up in surprise. I knew that Loose had her moods – she wasn't always a little ray of sunshine. When crossed she could become as spiky as a porcupine and then sulk and pout for hours, (in a way that I've since rediscovered in certain other Frenchwomen). This didn't happen very often, but when it did her ill humour spread through Lothlorien like black squid ink, as she didn't keep it to herself but stamped around the settlement thumping her fists on trees and caravans, and cursing in French. At such times we all became very jumpy and did our best to stay out of her way.

Luckily these caprices never lasted for more than a few hours. On one occasion I'd taken shelter with Jack in the campervan; she was suffering from a migraine, no doubt brought on by Loose, but was bravely trying to distract herself by teaching me how to play chess. I couldn't concentrate, and we were in danger of snapping at each other. The door burst violently open and there was Loose, eyes narrowed, as if she were about to spit at us.

Instead her face broke into a dazzling smile. 'Ha! I was angry. Now I'm not angry any more.' She gave a screech of laughter and everything was back to normal.

This assault on Erryk didn't seem to be part of one of those episodes, however. Her manner was sharp but not really bad-tempered.

'I have been here for thirteen months – thir*teen* – and I am *sick* of hearing that music. Now you are going to stop playing and come to help me.'

'Help –?' Erryk looked as if he were the one in need of help.

'Yes. You will help me to build my darkroom.'

'Dark –?'

'Room. I have it in a packet, a little cabin. I went with Ashley to buy it this morning, to the garden centre.'

'Ash? Then he's the one to help…'

'He's gone again. He went to Chandleford for a screw. And you also, you are very – *manual,* so you must do it.'

'But can't it wait…'

'*No*. Ashley will screw for hours, and I need my dark-room *now*. Come.'

She took his hand and pulled him to his feet. In a daze he allowed himself to be led outside, like a man going to his execution. I jumped up and followed.

Against the wall at the back of the shower block was propped a tall flat box with a picture on it of a small wooden garden shed without windows. I hadn't been aware of its arrival that morning as we'd been out with Gogo on a field trip.

Loose patted it happily. 'We will put it here, because the ground is flat and it's near the electricity.'

Erryk stared at the box. 'Shit, it's a kit,' he said.

'Why shit?' asked Loose. 'It's so easy.'

'Oh God… they want us to be – all the same. Doing it their way. Like robots.'

'They? Who are *they*?'

'Business. The System.'

'You are talking *rubbish*, Erryk. Take off your sunglasses.'

What did she mean? Erryk never wore sunglasses.

'The ones *inside* your head, stoopid,' said Loose. 'If you take them off you will see that the world is not so black. Only in my darkroom!' She tapped the box. 'Now you will build it. Curly, get some tools.'

By late afternoon the shed was up, the roof was on, and I'd gone inside to cover up any small knot-holes in the planks with black masking tape. Loose was ecstatic. Erryk seemed, if not exactly jovial, at least relieved. But then came a slight structural hiccup.

'Now I will get the shelves!' cried Loose. 'Ashley has cut them for me. And he has given me the –' She drew in the air.

'Brackets,' said Erryk gloomily. He began to droop again. 'We should have put them up before the roof went on. It's getting too dark… And the screws – they'll stick through to the outside…'

But Loose had already run off to fetch the shelves and the brackets.

'I'll get a torch,' I said. 'And a drill and an extension lead – and some more wood from Ash's place.' I could see that the screws wouldn't stick out if we put some battens on the outer wall.

So while Erryk softly groaned and mumbled I crouched behind him directing the torch beam, and Loose held the battens in place against the outside of the shed and sang cheery French folk-songs.

The widest shelf had four large rectangles cut out of it. 'For the chemicals,' she explained. 'In special trays. And also the water for washing afterwards.'

'What about your red lamp? And the enlarging thing?' I asked. Loose had been explaining to me the basics of what she would be doing in her darkroom.

'I have those already. Bill will fix the wires tomorrow. That is what he is *for*.' She cackled with delight.

Erryk emerged for the last time from the shed, exhausted. 'There's no room… You'll never be able to work in there.'

'Of course I will! I am small and I am skinny and bendy.' She hugged him energetically. 'You did it, Erryk! You are *marvellous.* My darkroom is alive. Like a butterfly that has come out of its cocoon.' She clapped her hands. 'And now it's your turn. You must open your wings!'

I winced. Surely she shouldn't have used that word, even in the plural?

'I haven't got….' Erryk sounded a bit desperate.

'Of course you have!' yelled Loose. 'You don't need anybody else for having wings. We all have wings!'

Those words made a lasting impression on me. These days, they could be the title of some psychobabbling self-help manual: *We All Have Wings.* But at that moment they didn't sound soppy or pretentious in the least – just Loose-like. And somehow, combined with her forced shed-building therapy, they flipped a switch in Erryk – or as she would have said, they took off the dark glasses in his head.

That evening he cooked the best meal he'd made for ages. When I expressed my approval he nodded slowly and took a deep breath.

'I think… she's right.' There followed a longish pause while he screwed up his features in an effort to squeeze out the next sentence. 'We can't – go on hoping – she'll come back to us.' I understood that there were two different 'shes' being referred to here.

'No.' There didn't seem to be any point in saying that I'd never shared his deep grief at Wing's disappearance, or that I'd long considered her gone for good. In the note she'd left me she'd said she wanted to 'find herself' – well, that couldn't have taken *this* long. Besides, I reasoned, she'd left with Arjuna, and he definitely wasn't going to come back, so why should she? She must have found herself with him, and that was that.

'We'll be OK,' I said, and reached across the table to slap his shoulder in what I hoped was a comforting manly way.

'Yes… yes. Yes.'

Not much of a discussion, really, but I could tell that Erryk had at last, in today's jargon, drawn a line under the past and was ready to move on.

*

And move on he did, though in a gentle, quiet and completely Erryk-ish way. He started cooking again regularly, performing a new range of culinary experiments for which we were on the whole willing guinea pigs, though I drew the line at curried beetroot – (yes, curry had crept back into the Lothlorien diet) – with clove-flavoured yoghourt sauce. Layla liked it because the yoghourt turned pink.

With some pushing from Stella he changed the style of his leather goods so that they became less fringed and shaggy. 'Beads are *out*,' she said, and gave him some of her small bits of silver as alternative trims for his belts, bags and purses. His output and sales improved.

'Now for the rest,' said Zoë. 'That means your hair, first of all. It's got to go.'

Erryk looked alarmed. 'All of it?'

'Of course not,' said Zoë. ' You've got lovely thick wavy hair, I'm just going to bring out the best in it.' And before he realised quite what was happening she had done exactly that, watched with fascination by myself and the twins.

It was a remarkable transformation. Gone was the furry bloodhound with long fluffy ears – the re-styled Erryk had a comparatively short, layered cut. She removed most of his beard, leaving a much smaller, neater affair which joined up at the sides with a slim-line moustache. When she'd finished she brought a mirror out to the caravan steps, where the operation had taken place.

Erryk gazed with dismay at the new shorn him. 'I feel – sort of naked…'

'You'll soon get used to it,' said Zoë. 'It only feels strange because it's been so long since your face was exposed to light and air. And you must have lost over a pound.'

'I've lost my… self.'

'No you haven't, it's fantastic!' exclaimed Shine. 'You've just got a new outside. You look like a Spanish conquistador.'

'Mind-blowing,' said Sean wonderingly. 'Totally metamorphic.'

'Wow, you look so *glam*!' said Stella. 'And your eyes seem so much bigger.'

In order to continue the process of glamorisation, Zoë went with Erryk to Chandleford to help him choose some new clothes, including cord trousers and a smart leather jacket to replace his ancient frayed jeans, holey old jumpers and shapeless duffel coat.

'But I *liked* those…' said Erryk hopelessly.

'Then keep them! Frame them! Just don't wear them.'

'It's really not my…'

'Yes it is,' she said firmly. 'You look really good.' Everyone else agreed.

Not long afterwards he began playing non-Dylan songs on his guitar: his own adaptations of Pink Floyd numbers. They made a welcome change. Then one evening he came back from Middington wearing a completely new sweater, quite different from those he'd got with Zoë in Chandleford. This one was dark chocolate brown with a few rather dashing orange stripes round the upper half.

'That's nice,' I said. 'Where did you get it ?'

Erryk coughed. 'It was a – um, present.'

'Who from?'

'No-one... I mean – er – no-one you know.' He looked distinctly bashful.

But we all knew soon enough, because she came to visit one afternoon. Her name was Miriam, and she was everything that Wing wasn't: a few years older than Erryk, dark, plump, good-humoured and very *un*stoned. She was also divorced, had her own small house, and worked part-time for an estate agent. If she was surprised by Lothlorien she didn't show it. We liked her – but not her horrible five-year-old son who came with her on that first occasion, burst into tears when encouraged to play with us, and threw sticks at Jelly Bean. Miriam hardly ever brought him again, but came alone from time to time while he was at school.

'He's not so bad when he's at home,' said Erryk, who soon took to spending the night with Miriam in Middington once or twice a week. This arrangement seemed to suit them both very well. Naturally we were all delighted for him, not least myself.

Harmonious, constructive... that's how I remember that period in Lothlorien. For us children life was full of interesting stuff to do, as Gogo devised all kinds of projects for us on subjects ranging from archaeology to the evils of advertising. Marjoram gave us wonderful botany lessons with the aid of a real microscope she had bought with proceeds from the shop. Any friction between the adults passed largely over our heads, and even Elvira wasn't a problem any more. We now called her El, a compromise which she found acceptable, and when she was around she was at least not actively unpleasant. As for some time now she had no longer shared a bedroom with Layla, her former bed had been converted into what Layla called Sindy's Super-World.

Idyllic days? Perhaps... No-one was remotely prepared for the major disturbance which was soon to erupt into our lives.

11. OPERATION HAMSTER

'YOU DON'T KNOW what you're missing,' said Ashley. Ketchup and mayonnaise dripped into his beard.

Admittedly, the smell was delicious. But both Rain and I knew what lay beneath the red and yellow gloop: the cooked flesh of dead animals. We'd been so thoroughly conditioned about the horrors attached to the production and consumption of meat that it wasn't difficult to resist the temptation of a double hamburger, the treat that Ash liked to give himself when in town. Instead we had each settled for a portion of chips and a chocolate milkshake – although we knew they weren't 'real' food. The chips were thin, paltry things, nothing like the garlic-and-herb flavoured wedges that Marjoram made. And Stella had told us that the milkshakes were thickened with edible plastic.

Everything I'm eating at the moment might as well be made of plastic, because I seem to have largely lost my sense of taste.

'Ah, it's psychosomatic,' said Marco knowingly. 'You have lost your taste for life.'

'Or it could just be the food,' I said. 'Half the time I can't tell what it is.' I swirled my fork in the soft pinkish-brown mass on my plate, presumably some kind of reconstituted vegetable. I'm able to eat simple meals now, but they still seem to be mainly slop, accompanied if I'm lucky by a rubbery omelette or a triangle of processed cheese: on the label is a picture of a cow having a good laugh – at human folly, perhaps. I doubt whether the cows forced to over-produce milk in factory conditions find their own life particularly amusing.

In this part of the world, vegetarians are regarded by many people with deep pity. 'But at least you eat chicken,' they say. 'And fish.' 'No, nothing with eyes,' I explain. 'And no shellfish either.' Pity turns to alarm, even suspicion. 'But that's unhealthy!' is a frequent observation. One of the hospital orderlies here has more or less blamed my accident on the lack of meat in my diet. That's one thing I've retained from my childhood – I've never eaten it. Even the smell repulses me now, for a reason which I shall have to write down eventually. That's not going to be easy.

Apart from Marco, I have a fairly steady trickle of other visitors to my sick-bed. To be honest, most of them I could do without. I resent being dragged back into the present by people who, I now realise, are not so much real friends as people I just happen to know. Nice enough – but there's no real intimacy between us. They come to see me out of some sense of social duty, I imagine, and perhaps a touch of morbid curiosity too. Over the years I've lost touch with the good friends I had when I was younger – not just in Lothlorien, but later on in London and abroad – and it seems I no longer have the capacity (or the time) for making new ones. If that sounds self-pitying it's not supposed to – I haven't noticed the lack. I've been too busy. I enjoy my work.

A couple of ex-girlfriends have been among my visitors. It's true I've had a fair share of women, even if they haven't left much of a lasting impression – at least not during the past ten years or so. This isn't cold-hearted machismo speaking; I don't think I meant much to any of them either, except as a temporary distraction. We generally parted on fairly amicable terms, usually because one of us was about to go away somewhere.

And then there's Mrs Evans, who I simply don't seem able to address as Jeanette. For reasons I can't fathom she's established a routine of popping in once a week on her way to fetch her daughter from her piano lesson. She never stays long. 'Just checking,' she said last time.

'Checking what? That I'm still alive?'

'Could be.'

Quite often she brings me some fruit or a decent piece of cheese, which I can eat now and am genuinely grateful for. When I thank her she just raises one narrow black eyebrow and gives me an odd look. 'No-one ever been nice to you before?' she says, or something similar.

Recently she saw me for the first time without the bandages on my head. She stared at me critically. 'It's growing. Your hair.'

'I have been aware of a certain fuzziness, yes.'

'There's a few grey ones in there now – you didn't have those before.'

'Is that so.'

'Not surprising, considering what you've been through.' She reached over and gave me a light tap on the top of my skull, a gesture I found unpleasantly over-familiar. 'Must be a lot going on in there.'

'Well yes, I am still capable of lucid thought.' She doesn't bring out the best in me.

'What do you do all day? You must be bored out of your mind.'

I tend to slide my exercise books under the bedcover when visitors arrive. 'I read,' I said. 'I watch television. I listen to music.'

Only Marco, in fact, knows that I'm writing. I haven't told him what, and he hasn't asked. He brings me gossip and jokes and news of the two big design projects we'd been working on before I ended up in here: one in Milan, the other on a super-yacht belonging to some mates of Mrs Kalashnikov. Two things are clear – first, he can manage perfectly well without me, as he has talent and flair, good technical understanding, and wonderful social skills. Second, he is the one person I can now count as a true friend.

But I'm straying too far from the subject in hand.

*

Back in the burger bar Ashley removed a biggish piece of meat from his bun, licked off the sauces, and wrapped it in a paper napkin. 'Chip's share.' He swallowed his final mouthful and wiped his beard vigorously. 'Come on gang. Off to consumer heaven.'

He meant Waitrose, where he was going to buy biscuits for Chipolata and various necessities for Lothlorien only obtainable Outside – things such as coffee, citrus fruit, large packs of loo-paper. (Erryk made coffee from dandelion roots but the others, apart from Marjoram and Gogo, had never managed to acquire the taste). Rain and I liked to come along for the Waitrose run; the store was still a relative novelty in Middington, and we enjoyed its bright lights and the displays of peculiar food which filled its shelves, fridges and freezers. We loved reading the packaging. Arctic rolls! Angel Delight! And the strangest of all: packets of Vesta Ready Meals. 'You just add water!' said Rain, amazed.

And then there was the dazzling array of cleaning products, which we found inexplicable because of what was universally used in Lothlorien – Marjoram's Magic, we called it. It works better than anything else I know – for dishes, laundry, and the filthiest of bathrooms: 40 grams of grated pure soap dissolved in a litre of warm water, plus one tablespoon of white vinegar and another of bicarbonate of soda, which when added will produce a satisfying fizz. Bottle up the resulting creamy liquid and use as required, leaving it in place for ten minutes on really dirty surfaces before rubbing it off. Magic indeed – who needed Omo and Ajax? 'It's the fucking capitalist System,' said Rick. 'Forcing people to buy chemical crap they don't need.' Our community was definitely in the forefront of Western green consciousness.

Waitrose was a short drive from the burger bar. Rain and I and squeezed into the long front seat of the pick-up next to Chip in his basket. 'Here, give him this,' said Ash, handing me the napkin in which he had wrapped the piece of burger. 'Break it up a bit. I don't want him to choke.' Chip ate the pieces with relish, but delicately – he was a good-mannered dog. 'Won't be long,' Ash said to him when we stopped in the supermarket car park. He patted Chip lovingly before shutting the door.

'You haven't opened the window,' I observed. Ash had closed it for the drive and put on the heater – it was a cold day – but I knew he always liked to let a bit of air in when he had to leave Chip in the pick-up alone.

'Shit, yes,' said Ash. He unlocked the door and wound down the window a little. 'Can't have you suffocating, can we old mate? Hey, slow down you two!' he shouted, as we raced towards the doors of the shop. 'And no messing around with the trolleys, right? We don't want a repeat of last time.'

He was referring to the incident a few weeks before when Rain and I, intoxicated by the number of shiny new trolleys – (we only had the one in Lothlorien and it was a bit worse for wear) – had got hold of a couple of them to use for a battle of Roman chariots. Although the battle was conducted outside on the forecourt the manager had been very upset, and we had to apologise abjectly in order not to be banished for life. 'Good thing you sound posh,' Ash said. 'Because you don't look it.' It was years before I really understood what he had meant.

We slowed down and walked sedately inside. Then Rain gave me an immense dig in the ribs and I jumped sideways. 'Look over there – in that queue!' he said.

Waiting at one of the tills was Janet the Great.

'Don't let Ash –' But Ash, not far behind us, had already seen her.

In recent weeks he'd being doing a lot of work up at the House: 'There's enough dry rot in that staircase to last me a lifetime,' he said. If he happened to see Janet he would, as usual, greet her with an oily politeness which she completely ignored. Her only comment had been directed at Chip, out of his basket one day and lapping at the water in a silver fruit bowl that Ash had purloined from the kitchen. When Chip drank, there was always a certain amount of water and general dribble which ended up on the ground, which in this case was covered by a Persian rug.

'*Disgusting*,' hissed Janet.

Ash fumed but kept quiet. 'Stupid cow,' he said to me later. 'I'll give her disgusting.'

'Did you clean up the carpet?' I asked.

'Of course I did. With Fairy sodding Liquid. *And* I scrubbed her precious bowl out – with bleach. I used wire wool, for fuck's sake. It's never been so clean in its life. And do I get any thanks? No I bloody do not.'

Now he was walking purposefully towards the till. With a flourish he swept off an imaginary hat and bowed deeply. 'Janet!' he called. 'What a wonderful surprise!'

The other people in the queue looked at him. So did the cashier. Janet stared expressionlessly into the middle distance.

'Excuse me,' said Ashley to the woman being served at the till, 'would you mind just catching the attention of the lovely lady behind you, the one in the blue coat? I don't think she can hear me – must be those gorgeous ear muffs she's wearing.'

'Those look like rabbit tails,' Rain whispered to me.

'They probably are. Her husband kills rabbits.'

'How do you know?'

'Sean told me. He was up at the House giving Our Lord an exercise class, and Janet's husband came in with two dead rabbits.'

Rain was horrified. 'Why didn't you tell me before?'

'I forgot. And anyway, I didn't think you'd want to know.' Rain had become very sensitive to animal welfare in the past year or two.

Janet's husband Greg didn't look much like a killer – he didn't look much like anything, in fact; although quite a tall man, he had small and curiously forgettable features. We sometimes spotted him in Middington – or did we? We were never sure if it was really him or not. When passing by the Lodge we would occasionally see him stooped over something in the garden, but he never looked up.

'He's got no aura,' said Tiger Lily. 'He must be depressed.'

'Wouldn't you be?' said Pete. 'Imagine having to... No, it's too ghastly to think about.'

By now Janet was the centre of everyone's attention. She had turned very pink. Her eyes swung round in search of an escape route, but she was hemmed in by trolley-pushing shoppers and was too large to squeeze past them.

'May I say how particularly elegant you're looking today?' said Ash loudly, leaning towards her. 'I'm just mad about your muffs.'

Rain and I started to giggle, and so did the girl at the till, though she put a hand over her mouth to try and hide the fact. Other customers in the queue turned to each other with puzzled smiles. Janet had become alarmingly red by now, molten with rage and embarrassment. She seemed incapable of speech. As she reached the till Ashley seized her purchases one by one.

'No, let *me* bag these up for you. Gingernuts? What a sensible choice. Ah, spaghetti hoops. I always knew you were adventurous. And there's nothing like a nice fish finger, is there?' He was having a field day.

Fumbling furiously with her purse, Janet let some coins drop to the floor. Ash swooped to pick them up. 'Every pee counts these days, doesn't it? Let's pop these back in there –'

'This man is a lunatic. I've never seen him before in my life,' she finally declaimed. Everybody murmured sympathetically. Then with a massive shove she forced her way past Ash and hurried towards the exit.

He ran after her. 'Janet! Wait! Don't you want to say hallo to my little Chipolata?'

We watched her sweep through the doors like a river in full flood. Then with tears of laughter in our eyes the three of us made our way into the body of the store. Ash was almost prancing with glee.

'I hope she doesn't cause any trouble,' said Rain.

'She can't do a thing. Our Lord won't listen to her. Anyway, he isn't even here at the moment.'

We whizzed round the aisles and were finished within ten minutes, though there was a hold-up at the till when the roll of paper stuck and the supervisor had to come and un-stick it. Ashley was still in excellent humour, singing snatches of song as we made our way back to the pick-up.

'There once was a woman called Janet,

'The stupidest cow on the planet...'

He threw the shopping into the back of the truck and pulled the keys out of his pocket. But before his hand reached the door he suddenly stopped short as if paralysed. 'What the fuck...?'

We stood on tiptoe to see what he was looking at inside the cabin. He was looking at nothing: the front seat was empty. No Chip, and no basket.

'Shit, he's fallen off the seat...' He hadn't. It was obvious that the floor was totally Chip-free. 'He must be in there somewhere.' Ash inserted the key into the door lock, but it didn't turn. The reason for this was instantly obvious.

'Great bollocking balls of fire – I didn't fucking lock it again, did I! When I opened the window – I forgot... Oh Christ, he's been stolen.'

'Maybe somebody just let him out for a run,' I said hopefully.

Ash swung round in fury. 'The BITCH! She opened the door and frightened him off!' He began to look desperately around the car park, and then took off at a run. 'CHIP!' he roared. We ran after him, up and down the rows of cars and then back into the supermarket.

'*CHIPOLATA!*' Ashley's voice was becoming hoarse with distress as he tore through the aisles, scattering outraged shoppers.

'Sorry, sorry,' said Rain and I repeatedly, trying to limit the damage by righting trolleys and smiling wildly. 'He's lost his dog, you see...'

Finally the supervisor and the manager, alerted by the general commotion, succeeded in catching up with us. With the help of two other staff members they pinned a struggling Ash against a shelf of canned baked beans, most of which clattered to the floor.

'Unless you leave these premises immediately I shall have to call the police.'

'My dog! I've got to find my dog!' Ash trampled in the rolling tins and staggered.

'You've got no business bringing a dog in here. It's against the rules.'

'I didn't,' moaned Ash. 'He was outside in the car...'

'Then I suggest you go back outside and look for it there. This type of in-store behaviour is quite unacceptable.' By now an indignant crowd had gathered round us.

'I do apologise, ladies and gentlemen. We are in the process of ejecting this person.'

I pulled at Ash's arm. 'Come on, Ash. Chip's not in here.'

The manager turned to me and Rain. 'Don't I know you? Weren't you the boys who –'

'Yes, but we're trying to help you now,' said Rain. 'Come along, Ashley.'

The fight abruptly went out of him; he seemed about to burst into tears. Limp with despair, he allowed us to lead him outside.

'And don't let me see you in here again!' the manager shouted after us.

'It's all my fault – how could I be so fucking stupid...' Ash muttered wretchedly.

'He can't be very far away,' I said. 'Perhaps he's gone to the shop.'

'He wouldn't find it – he's never been there on foot -'

We went, anyway – craning to look out of the windows on either side in the hope of spotting him.

Ginnie and Tiger Lily were on shop-duty that day; I could see Tiger Lily through the window, smiling her beautiful wide smile at a woman who looked like most of those who patronised *Nature's Way*, that's to say well-off and smartly dressed. The alcove curtain was closed; Ginnie was presumably behind it, casting one of her perfumed spells. I could tell that it wasn't the sort of scene into which Ash, in his current state of physical and psychological disarray, would be a welcome intruder.

'You stay outside with Rain,' I said. 'I'll go in and find out if he's there.'

I darted into the shop, surprising Tiger Lily and the lady customer. 'Ashley,' I panted. 'He's lost Chip… Did he come in here?'

'Lost Chip?' Tiger Lily was horrified. 'When?'

'Just now. In Waitrose car park.'

The smart woman looked out at Ashley, who now had both hands flat on the window and was staring in like a madman. She backed further into the shop.

'He's not dangerous,' I assured her. 'He's just worried.'

'Chip's definitely not here,' said Tiger Lily. 'What happened – did he jump out of his basket?'

'No – he was in the pick-up – it wasn't locked – we think Janet took him out and scared him away…'

'Janet!' Tiger Lily stiffened. 'Hey – have you been to the vet?'

'No – why?'

'Something Zoë told me…' She gave me a push. 'Just *go*. Quick.'

I relayed this message to Ash, who gazed at me with growing horror. He leapt back into the pick-up and then collapsed over the steering wheel. 'Oh Jesus Christ. I don't know where it is. The vet's place.'

'I do,' said Rain. 'I went with Gogo. When we found that badger by the road with the broken leg.'

Ash had never taken Chip to the vet; he'd never had anything wrong with him. 'And I don't want him filled up with all those chemical vaccines,' he'd said once. 'No bloody point. He's in a much healthier environment than other dogs.' I'm not sure if this was true, but it was typical of Ashley to distrust anything he didn't know all that much about.

Rain gave directions while Ash skidded round corners, almost running down a couple of pedestrians. 'But why are we going there?' I whispered to Rain. 'I can't even say it,' he whispered back. 'It's too horrible.'

At last we got there. There wasn't a free parking space, so Ashley double-parked on the road. 'Urgent, urgent…my dog –' he gabbled when rebuked by a passing motorist.

The receptionist gave a start as we burst through the door, as well she might. It didn't help that Ash was yelling 'Chipolata!' over and over, like a war cry.

'Be quiet, be *quiet*,' begged Rain, holding him back from the reception desk as best he could.

The other people in the waiting room were equally alarmed, and so were their pets; a big dog began to bark, and a cat in a closed basket started miaowing. A small child hid behind his father.

I ran up to the desk. 'Did a lady bring a dog in here?'

The receptionist examined me with distaste. 'Ladies bring dogs in here all day long, young man.'

'No – this would have been just now – about –' I turned to Rain for help. We weren't very good at measuring time in Outsiders' terms.

'Not very long ago,' said Rain. 'A sort of sausage dog.'

'With curls,' I added. 'Brown and white, all mixed up.'

The receptionist frowned. 'Are you the owners of the dog?'

'Of course, of course – my dog, my dog,' gibbered Ashley. 'Chip. Chipolata.'

'As a matter of fact a lady did come in with a dog like that.' The receptionist spoke reluctantly. 'In a sort of gardening basket.'

'What did she look like?' I asked quickly.

'Well – she was quite a big woman. In a blue coat.'

Ash let out out a terrible wail. 'She kidnapped him…'

'The dog didn't have a collar. She told me it was a stray that had been worrying the sheep on her farm. It bit her husband and he's got an infected arm. She thought it ought to be put down.'

'She's a fucking liar! He wouldn't bite a fly! Let alone a sheep – or her sodding husband… she just hates dogs…' He was on the point of breaking down completely.

'Shut UP, Ashley,' I said. My heart was beating rapidly, and felt like a hammer in my chest. I turned back to the receptionist, unable to utter the dreadful words. 'Did you – have you –?'

'I don't think so, no,' she said. 'The vet's busy operating at the moment. We've put the dog in the basement for the time being.'

'He's operating on my hamster,' said the child, who had emerged from behind his father's chair. 'He's got a growth. And you shouldn't say fucking, it's naughty.'

An immense surge of relief swept over all of us. 'Let me see him!' pleaded Ash. 'How do I get to the basement?'

'You can't go down there, I'm afraid. But I could bring him up… I should check with the vet first though.'

'Check with him afterwards – just bring him up – *please*.'

She softened, perhaps at the sight of me and Rain – we must have looked so anxiously hopeful. At any rate, she went and got Chip.

It was a heart-warming reunion. I could see that even the other pet-owners in the waiting room were touched. Chip yapped quietly but ecstatically and began to lick Ashley's face. Ash groaned with happiness and hugged him tightly.

'Yes, I suppose he must be yours,' said the receptionist. 'He's quite a nice little dog, really. I didn't think he looked as bad as she said, to be honest. But she must have had a reason...'

'Like he said, she hates dogs,' I said. 'And she hates Ashley too -' I touched his arm – 'because – because of Chip. She doesn't even have a farm, she's just... she lives near us.'

'Do you have a licence for this dog?'

'No, I'll get him one. I *promise*.' Ash planted an enthusiastic kiss on the receptionist's cheek. 'You're a pearl among women,' he said. She flushed, though probably not from pleasure. He was very sweaty.

He turned and patted the head of the little boy. 'And your hamster's a hero. I'm sure he'll get well soon.'

'His name's Chewy,' said the boy.

'Well, you tell Chewy he saved my dog's life.'

*

We went first to the shop, laughing and singing like maniacs. 'Got him!' Ash mouthed through the window at Tiger Lily, holding up Chip in his basket. Her customer had gone, so she came out on to the pavement.

'You were right,' said Ash grimly. 'But how did you guess? Even I didn't think... '

'Zoë says she's really weird at the moment – more than usual. She's probably going through the menopause.'

'I don't care if she's going through the straits of Gibraltar. That's no sodding excuse.'

'And she loathes the pair of you. You know how you tease her – and Chip's always with you when you're up at the House, isn't he? As far as she's concerned he's just making the place dirty. She said to Momma Lord that she'd like to have him put down. Momma Lord was quite shocked – she told Zoë. When Zo was doing her hair one day. And Zo told me.'

'And why the fuck did no-one tell *me*?'

'Didn't seem to be any point in upsetting you. Besides, we didn't think she'd ever have the chance to get her hands on him. I'm just glad you've got him back.'

'Snatched from the jaws of Death,' said Ashley. 'Thanks to you. And a hamster called Chewy.' He began to giggle hysterically. 'Operation Hamster.'

'It's the after-effects of the shock,' said Rain.

'I'll tell you about the hamster later,' I said to Tiger Lily.

Back in the pick-up Ash stopped his giggling and became totally silent. I could sense that he was working himself up into a rage. Rain and I didn't feel like talking either. We knew that human wickedness existed – from books, from Gogo's history lessons. But now we'd seen it right on our doorstep, as it were, and it was horrible.

As we neared Lothlorien Ash began to drive faster and faster, one hand on the steering wheel, the other fondling Chip's ears. He turned sharply through the gates and brought the pick-up to an abrupt halt next to the Lodge. Janet's car was tucked into the car port but there was no sign of either her or her husband.

Ash jumped out and paced to and fro, looking at the ground. Rain and I didn't move. Very soon he stopped and picked up a large stone from the side of the drive.

'MURDERER!' he bellowed. Then he hurled the stone with great force at one of the front windows of the Lodge. The leaded panes caved in and shattered. He leapt back into the driving seat and we lurched at top speed down to the woods.

12. *THE WORLD FALLS APART*

'YOU *WHAT?* SHIT, I don't believe it – you can't have – ' Marjoram gazed at Ash with horror.

'She's lucky I only broke her window. Should've broken her bleeding neck.' Ashley spoke with placid satisfaction, his anger sated by the violence of his stone-throwing.

'Are you *drunk*?' asked Gogo despairingly.

But Ash was drunk only on the triumph of his revenge. He was sprawled like a conquering hero in the torn leather armchair next to his workbench, drinking nothing stronger than the mug of tea that Rain had made for him. Between sips he munched his way through a packet of Chocolate Digestives. Chip lay in his lap with a bowl of his own biscuits balanced by his nose.

Ash fondled his ears. 'We showed her, didn't we Chippo? Sodding killer bitch.'

Everyone had gathered in Ash's caravan to find out the reason for the great war cry that had rung through Lothlorien as Ash got out of the pick-up, holding Chip in his basket high above his head like a battle trophy. Everyone, that is, apart from Bill (away on a job), Ginnie and Tiger Lily (still at the shop), and Sean (asleep). We were squashed around Ash's blow-heater, Rain and I perched on the back of his armchair, Shine, Layla and Jelly Bean crouched at his feet.

'She's sure to have called the police,' said Gogo. 'We'd better get up there – quick. Before they come down here. And that means you too.' He tugged on Ash's arm. 'Come on. We haven't got much time.'

'Are you being funny? You think I'm going to *apologise* or something? She fucking well tried to kill my dog!'

'I know, Ash, I know. Just *listen*. You broke her window. She may even have been injured. She's rung the cops – or her husband has. If you're up there to meet them you won't seem so guilty. And besides – do we want them swarming all over Lothlorien? *Think* about it.'

'Gogo's right. It's better to confront them head on,' said Jack. 'Tell them your side of the story before she can tell hers.'

'We'll all come with you,' said Erryk. 'Moral support – solidarity –'

'Maybe not *all*,' said Gogo. 'Not Sean. Where is Sean, anyway?'

'Napping,' said Stella.

'Just as well. Jack – do you mind coming along? You'd add a bit of –'

'Weight,' said Jack. 'And age. They do help sometimes.'

'Oh bugger – Janet will have rung the House as well,' said Marjoram. 'Our Lord must be at the Lodge by now.'

'Unlikely. He left for London last night,' said Pete.

'How do you know?'

'Nothing escapes my eagle eye, my dear. And by the way, I think I shall remain quietly here in the woods. I'm not wild about policemen. Such unflattering uniforms.'

'I'll stay too,' said Loose. 'They'll think I look weird.'

'Let us away to my caravan, darling. We can put on some soothing Chopin and play at being a quaint little couple in case they do decide to drop by.'

'Come along, Ashley. You owe it to us all.' Gogo heaved him to his feet as Rain and I pushed from behind.

'I'm not leaving Chip.'

'No, you're bringing him. He's Exhibit A. They'll see how cute and harmless he is.'

Rick stopped suddenly as we hurried outside. 'Christ – the shit.'

There was a contingency plan in Lothlorien to cover just this kind of possible emergency. We all knew where everybody's dope was kept, and if someone was absent anyone else could go and grab it, since the caravans were never locked during the day. One person would go round and gather it all together, another would collect all visible roaches, someone else would pull up the plants in the Garden. Then the whole lot was to be hidden inside a hollow tree in the woods. All this of course depended on our getting a certain amount of notice; we did, however, always hear if an unexpected vehicle was coming down the track. This routine had already been put into practice at the time of Malcolm's visit, but I doubt it would have been really effective had the police really wanted to have a good poke around; there would have been too many stray roaches lurking under mats and furniture, too strong a smell in some of the caravans – and in Sean's hair.

'I'd better stick around and do the necessary,' said Rick. 'Thank Christ it's winter – no plants.'

Shine ran after him. 'I'll help you.'

'And I'll hide it,' said Jelly Bean. 'But I won't put it in that tree. I know a much better place higher up. I bet they can't climb trees.'

'Me and Sindy want to go and meet the policemen,' said Layla.

We drove up to the Lodge in a convoy of three vehicles. Gogo went with Chip and Ashley in the pick-up, to make sure Ash didn't change his mind on the way. The rest of us piled into the two Minis. 'They look clean and innocent,' said Zoë. She was right – both Erryk's estate car and Gogo and Marjoram's old Cortina had a worn and seedy appearance, whereas Stella and Zoë managed to keep their Minis respectably sparkling and scratch-free.

'Now just keep quiet and look cute,' Zoë warned Layla.

'OK,' said Layla. 'But if Sindy wants to say something I can't stop her.'

Our hearts sank as we rounded the last bend in the drive before the gates; Gogo's fears had been well-founded. Parked by the Lodge was a big shiny black car with a flashing blue light on the roof. I confess I found this rather beautiful and exciting. Less so was the sight of Janet and her husband talking to a couple of policemen in the porch. One of them seemed to be taking notes.

They broke off their conversation and turned to stare at us as we drew up and got out of the cars. We approached them slowly, in a solid block, and stopped by the Lodge's front gate.

'There he is!' cried Janet, pointing. 'That's him – Ashley Tippins. The man who nearly killed me.' Rain and I instinctively stepped forward to stand in front of Ash.

'Don't let them see Chip yet,' whispered Gogo. 'Remember she doesn't know that you know. Or that you got him back.'

The older of the two policemen began to walk heavily towards us. 'And who might all these other people be?'

'They're his... neighbours. They all live in an – an – alternative compound, down there. In caravans.' Janet waved dismissively towards the woods.

'What – hippies or gypsies or something?'

'Hardly,' said Gogo, 'Do we look like it? We are a community of people who prefer to live simply, in natural surroundings – at the invitation, I should point out, of -' (he named Our Lord). His voice was calm, polite, and – as I realise now – must have sounded very well-educated.

The cop looked nonplussed. He eyed us up and down with suspicion.

'Hello, policemen,' said a tiny high voice. It was Layla, trying to be a ventriloquist.

She tilted her head winsomely and waved her Sindy doll. The younger policeman smiled. He looked quite friendly, almost comical, in his helmet with the silver star. But the older one ignored Layla and frowned. He wore a peaked cap and had V-shaped stripes on the sleeves of his jacket. As he walked up very close to Ashley his breath steamed in the air. Rain and I stood our ground; now our heads were more or less on a level with his waist, which stuck out instead of going in. I looked up at his very bright buttons which glittered in the falling dusk. They had crowns on them; I wondered why.

'Now then, Mr Tippins – I understand that you deliberately propelled a rock through the window of this lady's residence.'

'Too right I did. *Very* deliberately.'

'And may I ask the reason for this assault?'

'She kidnapped my dog. She wanted –'

'Absolute nonsense!' interrupted Janet briskly. 'The man is insane. A psychopath. He ought to be put away.'

'Don't you mean put DOWN?' shouted Ash.

'You see, inspector? He's probably schizophrenic. I've always thought so.' (I made a mental note to ask Pete what that meant. 'Psychopath', too. Both words sounded alarmingly sinister).

'If he's lost his dog I'm very sorry,' continued Janet, 'but I can't imagine why he thinks I'm responsible.'

'But you were!' cried Rain, unable to contain himself in the face of such a blatant untruth.

'And what's the matter with you, sonny?'

'The pick-up was unlocked – in Waitrose car park. She got Chip out and took him to the vet and told him to put him down!'

'The child's hysterical, don't listen to him.' Janet's voice had risen shrilly. 'He's just repeating the lies he's been told.'

'It's true!' I said. 'Go and ask the vet.'

'They're all liars!' Now Janet was beginning to lose control. Her husband, who hadn't uttered a word up till now, put a hand on her arm and murmured in her ear.

The inspector sighed. He looked at Janet and then back at us. 'I think I'd like to have a word with your employer, madam.'

'He's away! In his absence *I* am the person in charge here.'

'No you fucking aren't –' Ash tried to push past the the inspector. Erryk and Gogo yanked him back. At that moment Zoë broke away from the group and headed towards her car, pulling Layla after her.

'And where might you be going, young lady?' called the inspector sharply.

'My daughter – she needs –'

'Sindy wants to wee,' said Layla. At a look from his superior the constable turned his laugh into a cough.

Janet was still shouting. 'Keep him away from me! He's dangerous – a public menace.'

At that moment we heard a voice from beyond the police car, near the gates. 'Fuck me, what's going down?' It was Elvira, I mean El, on her way back from school.

'Another neighbour, I presume?' said the inspector, his voice freighted with sarcasm.

'I live here, yeah, if that's what you mean.' El wheeled her bike towards us, totally unfazed by the policemen. 'Wassa matter? Janet gone berserk?'

The inspector looked at her more closely as she passed him. 'Haven't I seen you somewhere before? Loitering around in Middington with those teenagers?'

'Probably. That's what teenagers do, innit? Loiter. It's our hormones.'

'She must be on something,' Gogo whispered to Marjoram. He beckoned. 'For heaven's sake, El, come over here and keep quiet. The police don't want to know about your hormones. We'll fill you in later.'

Jack put her hand up, fortunately diverting the inspector's attention. 'May I say something, officer?'

'If you must.'

'As it happens, I believe Mr Tippins is telling the truth about the dog, as are the two boys who were with him today.'

'And why would that be, sir?' asked the inspector wearily.

'Arrest her – she's a lesbian!' screamed Janet.

'That is not a criminal offence, madam, and under the circumstances is neither here nor there.'

'Quite so,' said Jack. 'Now then, perhaps you should take a look at this.' She marched to the pick-up and removed Chip in his basket. 'Here is the dog which was taken from the front seat of this vehicle when left unlocked by Mr Tippins…' (she was interrupted by a screech from Janet) '… and which was fortunately recovered from the veterinary surgery before the vet had time to put him to sleep.'

'Because he was operating on a hamster!' said Rain. The constable looked up again from his notebook and blinked.

'According to the receptionist's description, the woman who brought in the dog and requested its euthanasia was clearly Mrs Janet Fitch,' finished Jack.

'Because it's a filthy, vicious little creature!' snarled Janet. 'And you're a filthy dyke!'

'Bitch Fitch!' shouted El. 'She's a –' Stella slapped a hand over her mouth to shut her up.

With admirable calm, Jack ignored Janet and walked up to the inspector. She held the basket under his nose. 'Vicious and filthy, would you say?'

Chip, remarkably placid after his eventful day, wagged his tail but otherwise didn't stir. He looked as clean and groomed as the Minis, and luckily wasn't dribbling.

The inspector closed his eyes and took a deep breath. 'We're not here to investigate the character of a dog, *madam*. Serious damage to property has occurred and I shall have to ask Mr Tippins to accompany us to –'

A car door slammed behind us. Zoë was back. As Layla emerged from the rear, her mother ran round to the passenger door to assist the unfamiliar figure who was struggling out of the front seat. To our astonishment, it was Momma Lord. Both Janet and the inspector fell silent.

Zoë took her arm but she shook it off. Unsteadily, but with great determination, she wobbled towards the policeman – small, frail, yet with a surprising air of authority. I'd never seen her close up before, and I was awed.

'Good afternoon, officers. To what or to whom do I owe this pleasure?' Her voice carried clearly in the cold still air, like a little crystal bell.

'Go home! Go home!' yelled Janet. 'You know perfectly well you shouldn't be out on your own.'

'I am scarcely on my *own*,' replied Momma Lord with hauteur. 'I am with all these good people.' She gestured vaguely but grandly around her.

'Might it be possible to ascertain the identity of this lady?' The inspector was beginning to sound very, very tired.

'I am the owner of this estate.'

'Well fancy that. Then why was I under the impression that the owner was –'

'You are probably thinking of my son. He manages the place for me, after a fashion, but I am answerable for everything that goes on here. Now tell me – has this woman been bothering you?'

Janet made a strange sound, half sob and half cry of rage.

Momma Lord glanced at her with dislike. 'She is a bully and a brute and is not to be trusted.'

'Go for it, Momma!' called El from the background.

The inspector sighed deeply again before once more addressing

Momma Lord. 'And are you by any chance also acquainted with Mr Tippins here?'

'Of course I am. He is our carpenter. He is an excellent worker and I can vouch for his good character.'

'Are you aware that he has severely damaged Mrs Fitch's property?'

'It is *my* property, inspector. Kindly bear that in mind. And if he has done so it is because he was sorely provoked.'

'She tried to kill my dog!'

'Yes, so I have been told, Mr Tippins. I really can't say I'm surprised. That is the sort of woman she is. A troublemaker and a sadist. Whereas the dog is most delightful.'

'Nevertheless, and with all due respect to you madam, Mrs Fitch could have been seriously injured by flying glass. She is perfectly entitled to press charges, as she intends to do.'

'She will be doing nothing of the kind. She knows quite well what will happen if she does. And I shall be reporting her to the R.S.P.C.A. for abject cruelty.'

El punched the air. 'Go Momma, go go go!'

By now Janet had collapsed onto her husband's shoulder and was sobbing loudly. Momma Lord regarded her with some satisfaction. 'The unfortunate Mrs Fitch is a hysteric who appears to be having a nervous breakdown. Take her inside, Mr Fitch. She needs a stiff gin. I shall of course have your window repaired at the earliest possible convenience. I am sure Mr Tippins could do it himself, but under the circumstances I think it would be preferable if I telephoned that rather nice tradesman in the village.' She turned back to the inspector. 'Well – I think your work here is done, officers. As you will no doubt have understood by now, this is a purely internal matter. Thank you so much for your visit.' She fumbled in her coat pocket. 'Would either of you care for a Rolo?'

*

I hadn't long finished putting the events of that day on to paper when a nurse came in to perform the routine early evening checks and administer my cocktail of tablets. She remarked on my accelerated heartbeat. 'Don't worry, it's only because I've been thinking about something exciting,' I said. She gave me a rather coy look. 'You're not well enough yet for that sort of thing. You should concentrate on subjects which calm you. Why not turn on the television and watch a nice nature documentary?'

Maybe I should. But growing up in Lothlorien was a nature

documentary in itself, albeit one which we children took completely for granted – we'd always been familiar with the trees, plants, birds, plus the habits of rabbits and all the other fauna. And what went on there, with all the emotions and tensions, are the only things that matter to me at the moment. It's strange, inhabiting a virtual world – though it was real enough at the time. Is it the same for those people who devote so much of their lives to video games? Do their imaginary universes mean as much as my remembered one? The big difference, apart from the fact that mine doesn't come out of a machine, is that the games-players assume a persona of their choice, whereas I'm simply reliving how I felt as a child.

I still think it has something to do with all the drugs I'm required to swallow. 'Médicaments' they call them, which sounds quite dainty but doesn't alter the fact that they're drugs – and I've never been a heavy drug-taker before now. I got that kind of thing largely out of my system when I was still pretty young, around the time of the 1979 Glastonbury Fayre. But for the present, dosed up to the eyeballs with chemicals, I'm only too happy to dive back into Lothlorien, even to that deeply anxious period brought on by the Chip'n'Janet affair – which didn't, of course, all end happily with Momma Lord and her Rolos.

However, there was no doubt that she'd saved the day – or rather Zoë had, as it had been her inspired idea, when Layla wanted to pee, to go up to the House and enlist Momma Lord's support. This would have been impossible had Our Lord been around, as he insisted she should always stay quietly at home. 'They keep me shut up in here because of my condition,' she had told Zoë during a hairdressing afternoon, though she refused to divulge any details. If someone was with her she could walk in the gardens, as she sometimes did with her son, or with Zoë, who was fond of her. In general she seemed to be content enough in front of her TV – (probably she too was drugged) – but occasionally she was overcome by an urge to get out on her own and wander further afield. Then she would be hauled back by Janet, part of whose job was to keep an eye on her.

'That woman is worse than a rampaging hippopotamus,' she said to Zoë on their way back to the House after the police had been seen off. 'And believe you me, I've seen more than my fair share of hippopotamuses.'

This was a fascinating piece of information.

'But she should have said "hippopotami," ' said Shine.

'Who cares,' said Jelly Bean. 'Do you think she used to live in Africa?'

'Zoë asked her but she changed the subject.'

'Maybe she used to go to the zoo a lot,' said Layla.

'Yes!' said Rain. 'And one day she fell into the hippo enclosure and got savaged by an angry one, and that's why she's got a condition.'

Everyone really liked this idea.

What we liked a lot less was the Meeting called by Bill the next day. Summoned by an urgent phone-call from Ginnie, he had arrived late the previous evening and was not at all pleased. He'd had to abandon the job he was working on – only temporarily, but at a Bad Moment, according to Ginnie – in order to try and sort out a situation which was both ridiculous and nasty, and, as it turned out, potentially catastrophic. He didn't come to see any of us that night, but his displeasure seeped into all the caravans, an invisible miasma, and we dreaded the next morning. Even then it was only after he had already spent some time up at the House that we eventually saw him; we guessed, correctly, that Our Lord was back too, contacted in London by either Janet or her husband.

A little before lunchtime we heard the Spitfire coming back down to Lothlorien. A few minutes later Bill knocked on everyone's door and coldly announced that we should all assemble around the Fireplace as soon as possible.

The atmosphere was awful. The weather didn't help – still, dank and chilly, with a sky completely veiled by thin cloud behind which the low winter sun cast a weak whitish gleam. It looked like a baleful poached egg. As I gazed at it through the black lace of the damp leafless branches around us I desperately wished I was somewhere else – preferably inside Tiger Lily's cosy combi, sitting on her beanbag with a bowl of hot soup, watching her paint. But of course she wasn't in there, she was here with the rest of us, looking as pale, shivery and glum as everyone did. Marjoram tried to light a fire but it just smoked sullenly and refused to get going.

'I believe we all know why we are here,' Bill began, and then proceeded to tell us. There were, however, one or two things we didn't know. When Janet rang the police she had also rung Our Lord, who had arrived back a few hours later, before Bill. He went first to the Lodge, where Janet's husband gave him a heavily abridged version of events, leaving out the kidnap of Chip. Then up at the House he found his mother tottering around the kitchen looking for something to eat, because naturally Janet hadn't brought any dinner up to her room. But she was in exceptionally good spirits, singing snatches from *Salad Days* as she searched for lettuce and tomato. She told him her own garbled story, very different from that of the Fitches, and then broke into *How much is that Doggie in the Window.* In this skittish mood she refused to go to bed and asked to be taken out dancing; it had been difficult to persuade her that this was not the moment.

Much worse was to come. First thing in the morning Our Lord went up to see if she had calmed down enough to have had a good night's sleep, and discovered her half out of bed and only semi-conscious, one side of her face ominously distorted. Our Lord called an ambulance; she was now in Chandleford hospital.

'She has had a stroke,' said Bill. 'We don't yet know how serious it is.'

'Who stroked her?' queried Layla. For once no-one laughed.

Instead Bill glared icily at Zoë. 'It is unfortunate, to say the least, that she had to be involved in a situation that was sure to over-excite her. And from what I can gather, it was also entirely unnecessary for so many of you to gather up at the Lodge, which obviously caused an even more inflammatory state of affairs.'

'Obviously my arse,' said Ash. He was in fully defiant mode. 'Come off it, Bill. They weren't inflaming anything, just trying to help. If you've got to blame somebody, blame me. Though personally I blame Janet, because she started it all. If she hadn't –'

'Allow me to make my own judgment,' interrupted Bill. 'I understand that in fact you yourself were the source of this incident. Apparently earlier in the day you had humiliated her in a public place.'

'Humiliated her! Fucking hell mate – I was *complimenting* her. And I helped her with her sodding shopping.'

'Knowing your relationship with Janet, I'm not surprised if she took that as an insult.'

'That's hardly a reason for taking Chip to be put down,' said Jack mildly.

'I am aware of that. Nevertheless, Ashley got him back –'

'Thanks to you, gorgeous.' Ash put an arm round Tiger Lily's waist. 'And the hamster, of course.'

'– so it would have been far more in keeping with the principles of our community to have taken no further action, certainly not one so intrinsically dangerous. She would have been sufficiently chastened once she knew she had been found out and her intentions thwarted.'

'And I think it's important for us all to know,' said Ginnie, 'that Janet is going through the menopause at the moment. Her moods and reactions are bound to be... erratic.' That was the second time in two days I'd heard that word 'menopause'. Tiger Lily enlightened me later.

'Erratic!' growled Ash. 'Bloody-minded, more like. She's always been like that, anyway.'

'Ashley, we really shouldn't allow ourselves to take a backward step on our spiritual path. Rather than criticise, we should try to understand. We must all *meditate* for Janet, and wish her peace and happiness. I'll hold a special session this evening.'

Ash gave a mirthless guffaw. 'Well you can count me out of *that*, for starters.'

Bill cleared his throat. 'Thank you, Ginnie. Now let us return to the essentials. You have performed an excessively violent action, Ashley. That is undeniable. Janet is currently incapable of carrying out any of her duties. Our Lord's mother is in hospital with a stroke. Our Lord himself is in despair. The only possible thing for you to do is first to go and give a full apology to Our Lord – and I think you should go too, Zoë. It's lucky that he has a soft spot for both of you. And all of us must meditate for his mother, at least. Janet and her husband certainly won't want to see you yet, Ash. But you must write to them – I'll help you draft the letter – in an attempt to make amends.'

'Oh must I? And if I don't?'

'Then I do not see how our community can continue to exist in its present form.'

'You mean I'll have to fuck off.'

'Basically, yes. In the interests of us all.'

*

'You can't go, Ash, you can't!' I was distraught, as everyone else was.

When the meeting broke up we had all, apart from Bill and Ginnie, followed Ash as he stomped back to his caravan. Straightaway and without a word he started to take his tools down from the long panel above his work-bench and throw them into a big metal box. Jelly Bean jumped onto the bench; Rain, Shine and I retrieved the tools and handed them to her to put back. Ash took them down again. 'Thanks for the kind thoughts, kids, but you're wasting your energy,' he muttered.

Layla started to cry. 'Don't leave us, Ash! Sindy loves you too much.'

At this, Ashley himself seemed to break down. He didn't actually burst into tears, but he looked as if he might do. He dropped into the armchair and sank his head onto his knees. 'I'm sorry folks, I'm sorry,' he groaned.

Tiger Lily knelt by his chair and put a hand on his knee. 'Look, Ash, we aren't going to let you go like this. No way. Just tell Bill to write that bloody letter and you can sign it. And I'm sure you can sort things out with Our Lord. He really likes you.'

'We'll go up and see him together,' said Zoë. 'Then we'll go and see his mum in hospital. Visitors will do her good.'

'She probably hates me now.'

'Nonsense,' said Marjoram. She rubbed his shoulder. 'She knows you're a good guy. And so do we, and that's all that matters.'

'How can you leave your house in the tree?' said Loose. 'It's too beautiful. And Chip would miss it so much. He would miss us a little bit also.' She knew that the way to Ash's heart was through his dog.

'If you leave, the bitch wins,' said Pete succinctly.

'Absolutely,' said Jack. 'Don't let her think she's beaten you. Bill's got a point about that letter. The way I see it, if you send that you'll show them you're bigger than she is.'

Ash gave a weak chuckle. 'Not possible.'

'Man, we *need* you here,' said Sean. 'The caravans would fall to pieces without you to do the repairs.' Rick, Gogo and Erryk murmured comradely words of agreement.

'I think we'd *all* fall to pieces,' said Stella sadly. 'Please stay, Ashley.'

This onslaught of concern seemed finally to be bringing Ash round. He lifted his head – and then let it drop back sharply. 'No, it's no good. If I stay I'll be sure to bump into her sooner or later. I just couldn't bloody well cope with that. There's no knowing what I might do.'

But as it turned out, he never did have to see her again.

Lothlorien had an unlikely guardian angel: Momma Lord, who was pretty soon diagnosed as out of danger and likely to make a good recovery. When she was brought back to the House Our Lord engaged a rather dour but not unpleasant local couple to look after her – and take over not only Janet's other functions but those of her husband as well. This miracle came about because, wonder of wonders, Janet and Greg were moved to Our Lord's house in London to be the custodians of that instead. 'They requested a transfer,' Bill said.

Momma Lord confided the truth of the matter to Zoë as soon as she was fit enough to ask for a hairdo. 'I said to him, 'If you don't get rid of that woman I shall jump out of the window. I may have had a stroke but I'm sure I can manage to heave myself over the sill'. Anyway, you'd help me, wouldn't you my dear? Or that nice Mr Tippins.'

*

So life went on.

'Our Lord has been merciful,' said Pete.

It strikes me now that perhaps there was another force at work behind the scenes apart from Momma Lord. At the time it certainly didn't occur to me – like everyone, I was just relieved that the drama was over.

Relations between Bill and Ashley were strained for quite a time, however. And we had all been badly shaken. At the same time the incident had proved beyond doubt how glued together we all were. Amazing, really, when so many other similar communities had foundered years before, as I discovered later. What was this glue?

One essential component must have been the efficient organisation which underlay Lothlorien, largely thanks to Bill at the beginning, but maintained by the fact that everyone went along with it without complaint. Then there was the relative comfort we lived in. The caravans were spacious, well-lit, well-heated and had decent cooking equipment. The cost of our electricity was still met by Our Lord, and his support, though distant, must have been a huge help.

Tiger Lily's combi was of course much smaller, but she was perfectly content with it. She had her own little electric stove and hot plate, and didn't care that she didn't have the kitchen sink and small washroom that were part of each caravan. Instead she used the shower block for all her washing. 'I'm an Aussie, I can rough it,' she'd said when she was settling in. 'I'm not a softie Pom like you lot.'

Jack and Loose didn't have all that much room either, but as they usually slept in the upper tent-like section of their campervan, (except when it was raining really heavily), the main part gave them sufficient space to live in – and anyway, Loose was outside most of the day, taking photos or in her darkroom. Bad weather didn't bother her. 'My camera has a *mackintosh*. And the light is often more interesting when there are big clouds.'

In any case, I don't remember anyone in Lothlorien ever moaning about a lack of space, other than El. Life was perhaps more cramped in those communities whose members lived in smaller caravans, the kind that could be towed by a car. One advantage they had was that they could move if they were hassled. But we were never hassled, and I think the stability of our surroundings gave us a strong sense of belonging to one place – which was, let's face it, pretty idyllic. We were also lucky to have such good food, thanks to the Garden – and of course the chickens.

When these periodically fell victim to a fox there was always much lamentation and ceremonial before we got new ones and strengthened the defences of the coop. Once it was my fault – I hadn't shut the door of the coop properly after going to collect the eggs. I would have been four or five, but the appalling shame I felt is still fresh in my mind. The adults were more sorrowful than angry. Ginnie told me that the dead chickens would have lovely peaceful future lives to make up for their violent death, which made me feel a little better. I was encouraged to give each of the replacement chickens a name, and get to know them well – (those unfamiliar with chooks generally don't realise that each has a distinct personality) – so that I would be more careful in future.

So during my admittedly limited lifetime there had been occasional changes in the chicken coop, and of course the arrival of Chip, but the human hard core of Lothlorien had stayed pretty much the same. Arjuna's presence was by now just a blip on the horizon, and Wing's disappearance had never been a major tragedy as far as I was concerned. She had flown away and the air had closed behind her, leaving only the faintest of scars. Although Jack and Loose had arrived less than two years ago it felt as if they had been with us for ever. Our community had the permanent feel of a small clan.

I don't mean to idealise it. We had our dodgy patches. But – and I think this was perhaps the stickiest part of the glue, even more than our shared system of values – there was a real affection between us all. And being on the whole an easy-going bunch we were generally tolerant of each other's eccentricities and weaknesses. You could compare Lothlorien to a cake whose ingredients all go together well – like our Solstice cakes. I've since been in plenty of groups in which one person, though not essentially toxic, ruined the whole ambience – as soy sauce would ruin a crème brulée.

*

A glorious spirit-lifting May day: trees were bursting into leaf and wild flowers danced in the sunshine. Us kids were completely intoxicated by the warmth, the light, the scents, and all the new life to be seen in the woods; we stayed outside till early evening. We'd prepared egg and cheese sandwiches to take with us, and for salad we nibbled hawthorn buds and the leaves of saxifrage and wood sorrel. After this healthy snack we decided to go mushroom-picking, as following a couple of rainy weeks the spring fungi were abundant.

'Those eat meat,' said Jelly Bean, when we discovered some magnificent clusters of oyster mushrooms on the beech trees.

'How can they?' protested Layla. 'They haven't got teeth.'

'They suck the juices out of worms in the tree. With their feet.'

'Yuk!'

But we knew how delicious they were, so we picked them anyway. We found morels too, and fairy ring mushrooms in the Sheepfield, and had filled two baskets by the end of the afternoon.

'Let's cook them ourselves and take them round to everybody as a surprise,' said Shine, so we did this in the twins' caravan, as Marjoram and Gogo were still out working in the Garden.

'I'll take some to Tiger Lily,' I said.

I found her sitting peacefully behind the combi, gazing at the sunset. Her painting gear was still outside, and the picture on her easel showed what looked to me like a pink exploding star surrounded by flowers.

'What is it?' I asked.

She smiled. 'Dunno. I'll have to wait and see.'

'These are for you. We picked them today.' I held out the dish of mushrooms.

'Wow! That's far out, Curly – thanks.' She gave me a big kiss on the cheek and I purred inwardly. But then she peered at the mushrooms and poked them with a finger. 'Can I really eat all of these?' she said softly, as if she was talking more to herself than to me.

'Of course you can!' I was indignant. 'We'd never touch anything poisonous.'

'I know you wouldn't. I wasn't thinking that.' She put an arm round me and pulled me close to her. 'Look at that sunset. Isn't that just totally knock-out?'

It was. Streaks of cloud in the west were turning crimson in a glowing sky. As we silently watched it fade, from pale orange to lemon yellow to liquid green-blue, I experienced an intense moment of pure happiness. To watch the sun set and the evening star come out, all the while pressed to the warmth of Tiger Lily's body – I couldn't ask for anything more. Of course, ever since I could remember I'd been in love with her – as far as a child can be in love, which is in fact very far. In the depths of my heart I'd always carried the knowledge that one day, one day… But for now, all I needed was to be near her.

Her long paint-scented curls touched my face as she leaned to whisper in my ear. 'If I tell you something special, will you promise to keep it to yourself? I don't want the others to know yet.'

'Yes, of course.' I was proud to be such a trusted friend.

She paused for a moment before speaking again. 'I'm going back to Australia.'

I pulled away in surprise. 'For a holiday?'

'No, Curly. For ever.'

It was then that the world collapsed around me.

13. *FAIRGROUND BLUES*

'SO DOES SHE go?'

For a second I was completely thrown. In the groggy daze between sleep and waking, the voice sounded so much like Tiger Lily that it took me a moment or two to register the wholly unwelcome sight of Mrs Evans perched on the end of my bed. She was flipping through the exercise book I'd been writing in before I'd dozed off. I hadn't heard her come in.

I couldn't speak – I was too angry. It must have been obvious from my face.

She put the exercise book down. 'Sorry. Something private?'

'Yes.'

'Writing a book?'

'No.'

'What is it then?'

'Just a story. For a child I know.' Anything to shut her up.

She gave me a strange look. Nothing unusual there – strange looks are her speciality. Her jacket was bright pink and hurt my eyes, so I closed them again.

'I'd still like to know if she goes back to Australia.'

'Why? Are you thinking of going back yourself?'

'Oh, very funny.'

'How's Terry, by the way?'

'Who?'

'Your husband.'

'Haven't a clue. Good mate of yours, is he? Comes to see you a lot?'

'Look... I'm not in the mood to chat.'

'So what else is new.' She stood up and dropped something on the bed. 'Enjoy. Catch you later.'

When I was certain she'd gone I opened my eyes. I was still tense with annoyance – and with something else too, which I unwillingly have to admit was fear. I'd had the same feeling one frightening time in Lothlorien – (when I was ten, so not yet written down) – a visceral alarm at the invasion of my territory by hostile Outsiders. Ridiculous, but there it is.

To distract myself a bit I opened the plastic bag the invader had deposited on the bed. Inside were a wedge of Salers cheese – (how could she have known that's one of my favourites) – and a couple of pears. Also a short note: '*Great combination. Try it.*' I experienced the usual blend of mild gratitude and profound irritation that she is so good at provoking in me. Why does she keep on coming to see me? I'm told I'll soon be ready to be moved to a convalescent home some distance from this hospital, so that should put a stop to her visits.

But thinking like this takes me precisely nowhere. I need to return to Elfland and the past. Even that time of personal anguish is preferable to a present in which I lie brooding about my dislike of the peculiar Mrs Evans. I shall, however supply the answer to her question, even if she herself will never get to know it.

*

On that terrible evening when Tiger Lily told me she was leaving I was at first stunned into a kind of numbness. Like someone who returns to their house to find it devastated by a bomb, or disappeared down a sinkhole, I was unable to take in the ghastly truth in front of me. When it finally began to penetrate, all I remember is repeating: 'Why, why, *why*?' over and over again.

She pushed me into the combi and onto the beanbag. 'I'll explain, Curly, I'll explain.'

I gazed at her speechlessly while she made me my favourite drink, cinnamon-flavoured cocoa. I didn't touch it; I just carried on staring in horror at what I was going to lose. She came and sat next to me on the edge of the beanbag.

'Now then, just listen and try to understand. I've been here almost ten years, you know. It's time I went back to see the oldies. Make it up with them before they cark it – my mum's pretty crook at the moment.'

I knew Tiger Lily sometimes got mail from her family, but she'd never talked about them in any detail. 'We don't see eye to eye,' she'd told me.

'Can't you just go and see them quickly and then come back?' I asked desperately.

'No. That wouldn't work. Besides – I'm thirty years old. It's time I did something with my life. Get my own little gallery, maybe.'

'But you're doing lots already! And you've got the shop!'

She sighed. 'Sometimes you just gotta make a change. It's a… gut feeling.'

'But what about *us?*' What I really meant, of course, was: 'What about *me*?'

'Oh Curly, of course I'm going to miss you. You can't imagine how much.'

'I *can* imagine. Because I'm going to miss you even more.'

She put her arms around me. 'You know I love you.' It was then that I dissolved into a slush of tears and snot, shot through with bursts of wild fury and utter frustration. In Lothlorien no-one had ever told us that boys don't cry – it was expression, not repression, that was encouraged. So I expressed, immoderately. Tiger Lily hugged me, she tried in vain to comfort me, and she ended up crying too.

'I knew you'd take it worse than the rest of them… That's why I told you first. So's you'd have a bit longer to get used to it.'

'How long… When…?'

'Coupla weeks.'

'*Two weeks?*'

'Yeah. I've booked my flight.'

Another paralysing crack around the head. How could she *do* this, without telling anyone?

I gulped. 'Are you *sure* the others don't know?'

'Positive. I don't want them making a big drama out of it. No Ginnie-style ceremonies. I just wanna shoot through without any hassle. I'll tell them at the last minute – when I start packing.' She shook me gently. 'It's not going to be easy for me – you must realise that.'

I moaned softly.

'And Curly – you can come and visit! You'd like that, wouldn't you? When you're a bit older.'

A tiny gleam of hope. 'How old?'

'Well – when you're big enough to travel on your own. And when you can earn the money for the fare.'

'I can go with you now! The others will give me the money.'

'No Curly, you belong here. No-one would let you go. Not yet.'

It was then that a new resolve took root in my heart. Somehow, and sooner rather than later, I would get to Australia. Concentrating hard on that, I sank deeper into the beanbag, wrung out by all the emotion and with no more tears to cry. Emptied, exhausted, I fell asleep.

That night I had a terrifying dream. Huge cannonballs the size of armchairs were thundering down around me from the sky, breaking open a hole in the earth into which I fell; roots and soil filled my eyes and mouth and I woke in a cold sweat, sure I was about to suffocate. After that I lay awake for what seemed liked hours in a state of total desolation. When the fabulous woodland dawn chorus struck up it seemed to be laughing at my unhappiness.

*

For the next ten days or so I slept in the combi, hoping that my presence might somehow anchor Tiger Lily to Lothlorien. No-one remarked on my being there – us kids often moved around at night; Layla, for instance, had recently taken to dropping off in Sean and Stella's caravan after an evening of experiments with Stella's make-up. But what everyone did notice was my distinct lack of bounce: I was silent, lethargic, uninterested in everything – even food. Bad moods were respected, even lengthy ones in Rick's case, but no-one had seen me like this before. After a few days they began to worry.

'For God's sake Curly, what's got into you?' asked Marjoram. I recognised the love and concern in her voice and for a moment I was on the point of telling her. But I didn't – I just shook my head and walked away. And all during this time Tiger Lily was exactly the same as usual – cheerier than ever, if anything. Such duplicity! I felt even further betrayed, but I was helpless. In the combi at night we never spoke about her departure any more. I would just crawl in as dusk fell and go to sleep, or at least pretend to. I knew how hard it must be for her to see me like this, but it was my way of punishing her, to show that I wasn't going to 'get used to it' as she hoped.

I realised that I had to think up some excuse in order to stop the others pestering me about my sorry condition. The twins and Layla were the most persistent and the most difficult to fend off. 'Sindy thinks you're in love,' said Layla. 'She wants to know if it's with me or with her.' I wanted to hit her. In the end I invented a long and involved story of a favourite rabbit I'd found half-eaten in the Sheepfield, which I felt guilty about because I'd seen a fox earlier on and if only I'd chased the rabbit down its hole at the right moment… etc.

Ginnie gave me one of her Loving Holy Hugs when she heard this tale of woe. 'That rabbit won't want you to grieve any more,' she whispered in her sweetest voice. 'You must let him go, and wish him well. He's sure to have a wonderful reincarnation – perhaps his spirit's hopped into the frogspawn in the Pool! He'll be reborn as a new kind of friend for you, a lovely little frog. Shall we meditate about it together?' I wanted to hit her as well.

One afternoon Pete called to me as I trailed dejectedly past his caravan. 'A spot of jasmine tea, Curly?'

Because it was Pete and I knew he wouldn't badger me with questions, I followed him wordlessly inside. He put on the kettle and made the tea in his little Japanese iron teapot, then pulled a packet of biscuits out of a cupboard.

'Jaffa Cakes,' he said, handing me one. 'Don't tell Marjoram. They're appalling commercial junk, but *so* energising.'

Just to please him I took a small bite. It was delicious. After finishing it I accepted the packet which Pete held out to me and ate a few more.

'You must *never* go without food if you can possibly help it,' he said. 'One needs strength to fight off the demons of despair.'

I didn't say anything. I remembered how devastated he had been the previous autumn when Maria Callas had died – and how he had, indeed, indulged in a flurry of new cookery books. We'd been treated to banquets of vegetarian moussaka, spanokopita, bean and feta casseroles… 'It has to be Greek. We have to pay homage,' he'd told us.

'I'm well aware,' he said as he watched the Jaffa Cakes go down, 'that all this has absolutely nothing to do with rabbits.'

Dismayed, I paused in mid-mouthful and looked up at him.

'Remember – I am the All-Seeing Eye, Curly. But my lips are sealed, and I'm certainly not going to probe.' He turned briskly to his record player. 'Now – shall I put on a touch of Maria? It never hurts to jerk out a few tears.'

At the opening bars of *Un Bel Di'* I began to shiver. I'd heard it so often, and I knew what it was about. Time and time again I had made an attempt to sing along, whereupon Pete would say, 'It doesn't help to know the words, Curly,' and we would both laugh at my atrocious lack of singing ability. Now those words of longing seemed horribly apt – except that I knew that no white ship was ever going to appear on the horizon bearing my loved one back to me. I burst into sobs.

'Weep, Curly, weep. It always helps,' said Pete softly. In fact I hadn't cried at all since the evening of Tiger Lily's revelation – I'd been too stupefied by my sense of impending loss. And Pete was right, I did feel a little better afterwards.

'Ah life, life…' murmured Pete. 'Just another word for strife. We simply have to seek out the beauty and go on.'

*

Not long after that, Tiger Lily invited everyone to a communal casserole dinner that she was planning to cook in the Fireplace. There was nothing unusual in this – it was something everyone did from time to time. But I knew only too well what this particular dinner signified.

Once the meal was over – (I was too tense to register what she'd prepared, though it was no doubt delicious) – and spliffs were being passed round, Tiger Lily stood up. I felt sick.

'Hey everybody! I've got an announcement to make.' Conversation ceased. She took a deep breath. 'Basically it's – well, a great big thank you. You've been the best bunch of mates that anyone could hope for and I'm gonna miss you all like buggery because –' her voice was shaking a little now –'because I'll be leaving you the day after tomorrow. I've gotta go back to Oz. Personal family reasons. And I won't be able to come back here.' She sat down again abruptly.

Silence. Then a cacophony of voices. I couldn't bear it any more, so I slipped away. Shine ran after me and grabbed my arm. 'Curly – did you know already? Is that why…?' I nodded miserably and dashed off into the trees.

When it was almost dark I went back to the combi. I didn't go in, as I could hear Tiger Lily talking to someone.

'I couldn't tell you before,' she was saying wearily. 'I woulda spent the last few weeks crying, with all of you guys trying to make me come back.'

'We can still try!' said a voice that I recognised as Ginnie's. 'We *need* you, Tiger Lily. What about the shop?'

'You can take over the crystals and the auras yourself. You'll be good at it.'

'If it's a question of money, I'm sure we could lend you the return fare -'

'No way.'

'But –'

'But nothing, Ginnie. I've gotta go. I'm going, and I'm staying there.'

I crept away to my own caravan.

Next morning everyone was occupied in one way or another with Tiger Lily's departure. I hovered on the edge of the proceedings, watching in horror as the combi's interior was dismantled. Erryk took all Tiger Lily's canvases off their stretchers so that she could lay them flat in her big portfolio along with her works on paper. Ash helped her to arrange her paints and brushes into their carved wooden box.

'I made that,' he said flatly.

'How could I forget? I'll always treasure it.'

Although it was a day when Ginnie and Zoë would normally have gone to the shop, they stayed behind to help too. With Marjoram and Stella they took down the hangings and folded them with Tiger Lily's clothes into a large sturdy suitcase – I'd never even known she had it, because it had always been covered in sarongs and cushions to serve as a seat.

'No point taking the cushions or the bean bag,' said Tiger Lily. 'Share 'em out. Same with everything else – cooking stuff – incense – lamps – candlesticks… And you can just chuck the bedding tomorrow, unless you can use it for anything.'

'Chip'll use it,' growled Ashley. He stared at the stripped-down interior of the combi, with all his handiwork laid bare: cupboards, shelves, the fold-up bed. He looked almost as shattered as I was.

Rick zoomed off to the shop on his bike to fetch a couple of jars of Marjoram's herbal face-cream to give to Tiger Lily. Marjoram herself gave her a folder of own veggie recipes; Gogo presented her with a small trowel from the Garden: 'So you can think of us when you plant your own garden.' Sean wandered about in a trance. 'Freaky, man, freaky. Life without the Lily – heavy number.'

'You'll survive,' said Stella, a touch sharply.

I watched Tiger Lily carefully wrap her bamboo flute in a sarong and place it on a pile of things to pack. It broke my heart to think I'd never hear it again.

Pete came over with a cassette tape. 'Just a few tunes, darling. To remind you of some happy times.'

Tiger Lily threw her arms round him. 'Thanks Pete. Thanks *everybody.*' There were tears in her eyes.

Loose whispered in my ear. 'We're making a picture for Tiger Lily. Come and help us.' So I followed her the campervan, where I found the other children making a collage with some of Loose's Lothlorien photos stuck onto a sheet of cardboard. Jack was helping, too. The photos included portraits of everyone – not conventional portraits, but shots taken when the subjects were unaware, and they were all skewed in some way or out of focus. There was one of me eating a sandwich, shot from a strange angle which made me look like a mini troll. It was quite funny and almost made me smile. I would have liked to give Tiger Lily a better-looking picture of myself as well, but I didn't have one. Until Loose's arrival, Lothlorien-dwellers had never really been into cameras, although Bill and Ginnie had a couple of albums filled with photos of their early trips to India. But no one took happy snappies, probably because we saw each other all the time – we didn't need reminders. Gogo often said that it was better to live in the present than stare at the past. Now it seemed to me a dreadful pity. What

I longed for was a picture of Tiger Lily looking her usual gorgeous self.

'Can you take one for me?' I begged Loose. 'Not a weird one – just normal.'

But Tiger Lily wouldn't let her. Maybe she was right – she didn't want me worshipping a photograph, which is no doubt what I would have done.

That night I went back to the combi. Tiger Lily was curled up on the floor in her sleeping bag, reading the Tarot cards. Her I Ching book and the three Chinese coins with the holes lay beside her also. So did her tapestry bag, with her passport on top of it. I picked it up.

'It's like Ginnie's passport.'

'Yeah.'

'Aren't they different in Australia?'

'That's a British passport. I've got what's called dual nationality – I'm an Aussie but my mum was from London so I can have one of those as well. Without that they wouldn't let me stay in the country so long.'

'Who's they?'

'Those buggers at immigration. The guys who decide if foreigners can come in. Even Outside has its own Outside.'

I opened the passport and then looked up at Tiger Lily in surprise. 'Teresa ...?'

'Teresa Lia. Maltese name. That's where my dad's family came from.' She sighed. 'Don't ask questions, Curly. It's a long story and I don't feel like talking about it right now. I had enough hassle renewing this bloody thing last year. Remember when I went up to London with Stella?'

I did, but only vaguely. 'So you're not really Tiger Lily?'

'Course I am. Passports only show what you are officially. They're just another invention of the System, that's to say a loada shit.'

The System. I didn't want to think about it.

'Why aren't you on the bed?' I asked.

'Don't feel like it. It's easier to lay the cards out down here.'

The beanbag was still there, and I realised she'd been waiting for me. Without a word I pulled it close to her and lay down.

'You must keep the beanbag, Curly.'

'I don't want it. Chip can have it.' It was too soaked in happiness turned sour.

She turned back to the cards. 'Look – they're good. So's the I Ching.'

'Not for me they wouldn't be.'

'Oh Curly – they would be. You're going to have a fantastic future. And you're going to come and see me one of these days, remember?'

'I might be dead before that.' My self-pity seemed to know no bounds.

She leaned over and took my hand. 'If I tell you a *really* big secret, will you promise not to tell anybody?'

'I don't know.' I was sick of keeping things to myself.

'It'll make you understand why I absolutely, totally can't stay here.'

Curiosity got the better of me. 'OK,' I said reluctantly.

'I'm pregnant.'

That took me completely by surprise, of course. But I didn't see what on Earth it had to do with her leaving. 'You can have a baby here! We'd all be really pleased.'

'I don't think so. It's Sean's baby.'

It took me quite a few seconds to register that little revelation and all that it implied.

'But it can't be – Sean can't –'

'That's only what Stella says. She's desperate to have a kid, and she can't bear to think that she's the one with the problem. That's why she was rooting Arjuna, to try and get pregnant. At least that's her story. Personally I reckon she'd've been doing it anyway. She was nuts about him.'

'And is that why you were doing it with Sean? Because you're nuts about *him*?' I could feel a new and frightful spiky serpent beginning to crawl its way into my heart: jealousy. I'd never been the least bit jealous of her casual lovers. I knew they were simply there for what Loose called 'hygienic reasons'. But Sean…!

'Well, I've always fancied him rotten, but it's only physical – I know he's an airhead. I never had any intention… Because of Stella, of course.'

'So WHY?'

'It was kinda accidental, really. I was up in those fields behind the House, you know? Doing some sketching. And Sean comes jogging by... It was quite a warm day, after all that snow had gone. And there's that old barn up there… We were both pretty stoned.' She paused. 'After that – well, Stella's out and about a lot these days, and I think Sean's been feeling the lack.'

'So you kept on doing it.' The monster flicked its tongue and writhed within me.

Tiger Lily sighed. 'I reckon I must've wanted to get pregnant too, unconsciously. But you must see why I've gotta go, Curly.'

'No! You could still stay – you can say ...'

'What? That I had a quick naughty with some bloke in Middington? And what if the kid turns out looking like Sean? Even if it doesn't, I couldn't live with a lie like that. Sean would guess, anyway, and he'd be so bloody proud of himself he'd be sure to spill the beans sooner or later. I just couldn't do that to Stella.'

I looked away stonily. But I did, finally, understand.

Tiger Lily stroked my hair. 'You mean far more to me than Sean does, Curly.'

Then I forgave her – I think I would have forgiven her anything. But I still howled and clung to her, and fell asleep in her arms.

She left very early next morning, in the Spitfire with Bill. He had to go up to London and had volunteered to drop her off at the airport. Everyone was gathered by the car, even El, who normally stayed in bed until the last possible moment before getting ready for school. 'Go for it, Tiger!' she said, and slapped Tiger Lily energetically on the shoulder.

Everyone else was pretty subdued. Despite all expectations, Ginnie couldn't bring herself to perform any rituals. 'Don't forget to write,' was all she could manage to say. Layla presented her with the photo collage. Tiger Lily gazed at it. 'It's bloody fantastic – shit – I can't...' She bent and gave Layla a big kiss. Then she went round and hugged each of us in turn. No-one spoke. I'd placed myself so she would come to me last. She opened my hand and put into it one of her most precious possessions: the dragon charm that used to hang in her Tarot booth. Smaug. 'It'll look after you,' she whispered.

I stared at it in amazement. 'You always said you were going to keep it for ever.'

'It's yours now. I'm sure I can get another one back home.' *Back home* – those words sliced through me like a butcher's knife.

She got swiftly into the passenger seat of the Spitfire. Gogo and Erryk tried to squeeze her case into the boot, which wouldn't close, so there was an agonising delay while they got some rope to hold it down. Bill revved the engine. Then, with a last wave, Tiger Lily was gone.

Gone.

So there you have it, Mrs Evans: the answer to your question.

*

'You and me both, eh old son?'

I nodded morosely as Ashley laid down his chisel. He'd begun to teach me wood-carving, something I'd long wanted to learn, but the lessons weren't progressing very fast because we both kept stopping to stare into space.

Ash, too, had been badly hit by Tiger Lily's departure; in spite of his adventures with women Outside, she had always remained the principal object of his devotion. We didn't talk about her much – that would have been rubbing salt into our wounds. But just being with him, in the knowledge that we shared a similar pain, afforded a kind of comfort.

Everyone missed her, of course. 'It's as if a hole's been torn in Lothlorien,' said Marjoram sadly. She and the other adults did their best to fill it with distractions for all of us; frantic busy-ness was the order of the day. Erryk completely repainted the combi, in the same pale green as the *Nature's Way* logo, and it was moved to a different place. From then on Ginnie and Marjoram used it as a store for their products. I couldn't bring myself to go inside it, and I tried to avoid looking at the bald patch of ground where it had stood before.

Gogo and Marjoram were constantly organising events and outings, most of which passed me by in a kind of blur: treasure hunts, charades, visits to museums, a ruined castle, botanical gardens... And there were a lot of trips to the seaside; I must admit that ice-cream and swimming did offer at least temporary consolation. That was the summer when all of us children learned to swim properly – even Layla discarded her water-wings.

Jack taught us to play chess, at which the twins excelled – and, curiously, Layla, though her strategy was illogical, based on surprise rather than careful reflection. Loose invented a singing version of Chinese Whispers, in which she liked to involve as many people as possible: instead of being close enough to whisper to each other we had to be spaced far apart in a line through the woods, and pass on the words and tune of a snatch of nonsense song which she herself, at the head of the line, would make up on the spur of the moment. This game occasioned a lot of laughs, even from me. I was good at the words but hopeless at the tune, while Rain was just the opposite, so the end result always turned out to be completely different from the original.

After all this frenetic daytime activity I found it a relief to get back to the caravan and spend some time in quiet mourning. Some evenings Erryk was away at Miriam's house, but when he was around he was, as ever, a restful presence, strumming and humming peacefully or else occupied at his work table with bits of leather. Now I understood how he must have felt when Wing disappeared, and to make up for my previous lack of empathy I tried to help him as much as possible with cooking and housework. There was, however, a difference between his grief and mine: he'd got over it eventually, whereas I was sure I never would. I didn't spend every minute of the day moping, but I felt older, darker – as if a flame which had always burned somewhere inside me had been snuffed out.

One day El said to Rick and Zoë: 'You ought to take them to see Star Wars.' She had seen it the previous year with her mates, and now, due to popular demand, it was showing again at the Regency cinema in Chandleford. The posters looked interesting, but due to our hitherto screen-free existence – impossible to imagine these days – it hadn't occurred to us to ask if we could go and expose ourselves to what Bill called 'the pernicious value-system of Hollywood.'

'Oh for Christ's sake, it won't do them any harm,' said El when her parents expressed their disapproval. 'It's just a bit of fun. It'll do them good – you too. You need to lighten up.'

Layla, always more tempted than the rest of us by the vicious lure of glamour, turned up her charm to maximum. 'Please, Daddy,' she said, 'Sindy wants to go.'

Cringe-making though it was, this kind of thing always made Rick crack, especially when he was addressed as 'Daddy.' And so, only a day or two later, we found ourselves crammed into the back of Zoë's Mini, on our way to our very first movie experience. 'I hope this isn't going to damage our brains,' whispered Shine.

In the event we were completely overwhelmed by the whole thing – the hugeness of the spectacle, the story, the sound, the special effects – especially the hologram of Princess Leia. 'And her name's almost like mine,' said Layla wonderingly. 'But I'm prettier. I think he'd like me better.' She was referring to Luke Skywalker.

'Dream on, babe,' said Rick, but he couldn't resist his daughter's pleas for him to fork out for a Luke Skywalker doll, on sale in the foyer. Sindy must have regretted her desire to go to the pictures, because once back at Lothlorien Layla stuck her into a drawer and switched her affections seamlessly to Luke. We teased her without mercy, of course. 'Those boots look like bandages,' said Shine. 'I think he's turning into an Egyptian mummy.'

Nonetheless, the twins and I had also been much affected by the movie. For weeks afterwards we raced around the woods battling each other with imaginary lightsabers and shouting 'May the Force be with you!' From the treetops would come an answering yell: 'You all arseholes are!' – for Jelly Bean's favourite Star Wars character was Yoda.

Soon after this life-changing expedition came what was perhaps the most successful distraction of all, in that it brought us a new friend – although it was one we were only to see for a brief period in the year.

It was Stella, coming back from the shop one evening, who brought us the exciting news. 'Guess what! There's a big fair setting up on Middington

Common.'

We'd been on rides at the seaside, little roundabouts and mini dodgems, but this, according to Stella, was the real thing. There was a Big Wheel and a Big Dipper, wonders never before seen in Middington.

'Oh wow,' said Sean. 'We have to go, baby.'

Sometimes when I looked at Sean I still felt a burst of loathing. But then I would remember that Tiger Lily cared for me much more than she did for him – and that I knew something that he would never know. Then the hatred would fade away.

There was one other person who, I came to realise, was also aware of her secret: Pete. Not long after she'd left I was moodily slurping a cup of jasmine tea in his caravan when he suddenly said, apropos of nothing at all: 'I go for walks, you know. I don't spend my whole life in here reading Czech poetry and grieving over Maria.'

I glanced up at him. 'What are you talking about?'

'Sometimes I find myself straying as far as the House. Even beyond. I tend to notice things up there that other people don't see.' He looked at me with great compassion. It was then that I knew that he knew, and that like me he would never breathe a word to anyone else. Of course Tiger Lily's secret is out now, at least on paper. But in view of all that's happened since, I can be sure she wouldn't mind. Nor would Stella. As for Sean.... well, there's no point getting into that now.

He was wild with enthusiasm about going to the fair. 'I've still got some dried mushies somewhere,' he said. 'It'll be the ultimate psychedelic experience. The kids'll love it too – we'll take them with us.' We were all delighted by this idea.

'Well I'm not having any of those mushrooms,' said Stella. 'I'm past the age for tripping in public. And don't expect me to hold your hand if you start freaking out.'

Loose wanted to come too, so somehow we all squeezed into Stella's car – Layla and Jelly Bean on Sean's lap in the front passenger seat, the twins, Loose and I in a contorted pile in the back. You'd never get away with that now.

I think we found the fair even more thrilling than Star Wars, because it was real and we were part of it. We sniffed the air, revelling in the warm unfamiliar blend of smells: hot dogs, candy floss, diesel. We loved the coloured lights flashing all around us, and the fabulously lurid scenes which decorated the rides. And the sounds! Hurdy-gurdy from the horses which pranced sedately up and down on their silver columns; blaring rock songs; hideous groans and cackles issuing from the Ghost Train; shrieks from the giant slopes of the Big Dipper. Its name was attached along the side in huge twinkling letters: 'STEEL STELLA'. We all exclaimed in delight.

'Baby, I can ride you in the sky!' said Sean.

He had eaten a substantial mushroom sandwich in the car, kindly fed to him in bite-size pieces by Layla and the Bean, and it was now beginning to take effect. Of course we couldn't let him go on Steel Stella alone, so we queued up and then shrieked along with all the other passengers as we hurtled down. I adored it, even though I was sitting right behind Sean, whose hair flew out behind him and kept getting in my eyes.

'I'm a great golden bird,' he exulted at the end of the ride. 'I am the phoenix.'

'OK, sweetie, just don't go laying any eggs,' said Stella. 'And don't go up in smoke.'

I wanted to try everything – everything apart from the Rotor, that is, because Stella told us that we'd stick to the side and might turn upside-down and be sick. But it appealed immensely to Loose and Jelly Bean, who went on it and not only slid themselves upside-down on purpose but turned flat cartwheels against the swiftly spinning wall. We were lost in admiration.

Then we squealed and giggled our way through the Ghost Train and whooshed screaming round the Octopus. After that came an exhilarating go on the Dodgems – huge, grown-up Dodgems where we had to be aggressive to hold our own. Even Layla, in a car driven ferociously by Jelly Bean, forgot about being cute – she stuck out her tongue and hurled colourful insults at surprised adolescent boys. Exhausted by all this, we then wandered down a quieter alley of food-stalls and shooting ranges. It was captivating to watch the pink fluff of candyfloss form from a tiny spoonful of spinning sugar; Sean was particularly enchanted. 'Man, we're seeing the birth of the Universe,' he marvelled, so Stella bought him a stick. Layla wanted some too, but the rest of us opted for toffee apples – candyfloss was pretty but not very substantial.

At one of the shooting ranges a small group of unpleasant-looking skinheads were taking shots at a line of cut-out squirrels with big eyes and goofy teeth, which stood on their hind legs on a hill which rotated them up and over and out of sight. The skinheads weren't hitting very many, and were taunting each other with raucous laughs. They all had HATE tattooed on the knuckles of one hand, and FUCK on the other. I saw that one of them, bent double with his version of mirth, also had a red tattoo of the flag of St George on his shaved head. He straightened up and spotted Sean.

'Fucking hell – look what's here. Fucking hippie. Peace and love. Bet he's never touched a gun in his life.'

Sean smiled magnificently and threw back his golden mane. 'The Orc-hordes must be vanquished.' He turned to Stella. 'Pass me the gold, Princess.' Sean never liked to carry money on him if he could help it. Stella gave some coins to the man looking after the range, who looked rather squirrelly himself. He pointed to a shot-gun which Sean picked up and stroked thoughtfully for a long moment.

'Look at him! Playing with it like it's his fucking donger. Get on with it, Goldilocks.'

Slowly Sean lifted the gun to his shoulder and began to fire. We held our breath.

Ping! The first squirrel went down. Ping! Ping! One after another they all keeled over. He didn't miss a single one. We all cheered, though not the skinheads, who had fallen silent.

'He was a sniper in the SAS,' Stella said to them, deadpan. They melted away.

'Is that *true*?' asked Loose.

Stella giggled. 'Of course not. But he did do an archery course once. And when he's tripping he can get incredibly *focussed*. Not like when he's stoned.' She nudged him. 'Go on – you can get a prize now. Maybe two.'

'He can have *one* of anything,' said the squirrel man rather grumpily. 'But he can't have another go.'

'I must consult the Princess,' said Sean. 'What do you require, fair lady?'

Stella gazed at the array of soft toys stacked at the back of the stall. 'I require that big pink teddy.'

'Look – ducks!' said Jelly Bean. She'd spotted one of those stalls where you're given a rod with a hook on it to pull out plastic ducks floating round in a circular trough. We all tried this, apart from Sean who was now lost in wonder at the softness and lustre of the pink teddy bear's fur. 'This is something *essential*,' he murmured. 'A new element in the Cosmos.'

'It's called nylon,' said Shine.

Hooking the ducks turned out to be trickier than it appeared – except, amazingly, for me. Now it was my turn to be a champion – I picked them out as if I'd been doing it all my life.

'He's been practising,' said the duck woman. Like Sean I was denied a second turn, but she gave me an extraordinary prize: a pair of real live ducklings in a small box lined with straw. 'Keep them warm for a day or two,' she said, 'and then give them a go in the bath.'

'What should we give them to eat?' I asked.

'Oh, bits of bread. They don't need much.' She didn't sound as if she cared a great deal.

'We'll put them in the Pool,' said Jelly Bean. 'The water's warm now and they can eat pondweed. That'll be much better. I'll look after them.'

She was obviously dying to play Mother Duck, so I gallantly handed her the box. Anyway, I didn't really feel up to the responsibility at the moment.

Our attention was now caught by the loud thumping noise coming from one of those test-your-strength machines. We strolled towards it and saw a large man pounding a huge rubber mallet on to a round disc at the bottom.

'Nearly there. Good try,' bellowed the man in charge. He was short and beefy, and had the brightest hair I'd ever seen – a deep flaming orange. He was puffing on a cigar.

'Behold, the Dragon Smaug,' said Sean, and strolled closer.

The redhead looked Sean up and down with a slightly condescending air. 'Want to flex your muscles, gorgeous?' Sean gave him a friendly smile. He was wearing a loose long-sleeved shirt with large mauve flowers on it, which gave no hint of the muscles about to be flexed.

'Three goes for the price of two. Special bargain – don't miss this chance.'

'One will do nicely,' said Stella.

'Can Rain and I have a go too?' I asked. 'Then we can have the three goes for two.'

'Smart lad. But it don't work like that, sonny boy.'

Smaug softened a little when he saw my disappointment. He glanced at Stella. 'Maybe just this time.' She smiled nicely and gave him the money, and was rewarded with a wink and a lift of the orange eyebrows. I'd noticed that Stella often got this kind of reaction from men Outside.

A man from a neighbouring stall sauntered up. 'Got any change, Bluey? The punters've only got fivers tonight.' He too gave Stella an admiring once-over as he exchanged his notes.

'Bluey?' said Rain.

'Cause I've got red hair,' said Bluey, who had heard him.

Loose giggled. 'English logic.'

'You got it, love.' Bluey handed the mallet to Sean. 'There you go.'

Sean lifted the mallet easily, nonchalantly, and this time we all knew exactly what was going to happen. He smashed it down; the ball zoomed up the groove in the tower and struck the gong at the top loudly. Bluey and his mate gawped in a very satisfying way, and once again we felt immensely proud of Sean. He turned to me. 'And now 'tis your turn, Elf-child.'

I did my best and struck with all my force. Then Rain did the same. We didn't hit the gong, of course, but we could see that Bluey was impressed.

'Bloody hell. You're a bit strong for kids, aren't you?'

'They have a healthy lifestyle,' said Stella.

He looked at her again and then at me. 'She your mum?'

I nodded, because I knew Stella would be pleased.

'Lucky boy.' He examined Sean again. 'Then Mr Flower Power here ain't your dad.'

Sean had turned away and was staring at the Big Wheel. 'I need to fly in the sky again.'

It had been decided that we should leave this treat for last, when dusk would give us an even more spectacular view of the sparkling fairground below. I shared a seat with Shine, who didn't want me to swing it too much when we were at the top. Suddenly I thought what it would have been like had I been there with Tiger Lily. She would have swung the seat wildly and laughed, and put her arm round me as we marvelled at the lights below, and I would have been happy. A frightful sadness swept over me. 'What's the matter?' asked Shine. I couldn't speak.

Back on the ground I slipped away from the group, and headed towards a dark gap between two rides. Here I was in an entirely different world; generators thrummed and lines of enormous caravans gleamed palely in the dusk. Sunk in gloom, I wandered aimlessly among them. They weren't like ours at all – they were very shiny, often with lace curtains in the windows, and they were clearly made to roll.

I was standing on tiptoe trying to look into one of them when I jumped back in embarrassment, because sitting on the steps in an open doorway was a boy who was staring at me. I tripped over a cable and fell over. In spite of the pain in my ankle I picked myself from the ground and stared back. He seemed to be around my own age, and was eating a doughnut. The light from the interior of the caravan shone brightly on his brilliant orange hair.

14. UNEXPECTED RELATIONS

FRIENDSHIP AT FIRST sight? Not exactly.

'Wot you doing here?' said the boy, his mouth full of doughnut.

'Just looking...' I wanted to turn and run, but something held me to the spot – my ankle, which hurt considerably when I tried to move it.

'Nothing to look at. It's private.'

'Sorry. Your caravans are really nice...' I was aware how feeble this sounded.

'Trailers.'

'I live in one too,' I said, hoping to soften his hostility.

'In a trailer?' He stared at me suspiciously.

'Yes – well – we call them caravans. They're different from yours.'

'Oh, so you're on your holidays then.'

'No...' I still hadn't quite grasped this concept of holidays. 'I live in one all the time.'

His expression of distrust deepened. 'You a gypsy?'

'Not at all. We sometimes get called that, though. Are you?'

'Fuck no.' The boy spat on the ground.

'Don't you like gypsies?'

'It's cause of them we're here. We had a barney with gypsies at Otfield last summer. Council wouldn't let us back. So we come here instead.'

'We're really glad you did.'

'S'alright. Bit small for a gaff this size.' He inspected me carefully. 'If you live in a trailer, how come you talk like that?'

'Like what?'

'Like you live in a big house or something.'

I didn't understand. 'I don't know. There's a big house near where we live, but I don't go there. Some of the others do.'

'What others? Your family?'

'The people in the other caravans. There's seven caravans and a campervan and -' I stopped short. The combi was only a ghost.

'So it's a caravan *site*, then. Where you can live all year round.'

'It's a wood. We're hippies.'

'Oh... *hippies.*' His face cleared. 'Long-haired dope-heads. You stoned?'

'No. I don't smoke.'

'I do. Only fags though, when my mum's not looking, else she'd wallop me. Not a lot of hippies left now, is there? Used to be all over the place, didn't they. That's what my dad says.'

A thought struck me. 'I just saw a man with hair like yours. He's called Bluey. He's looking after that thing where you -' I gestured.

'The High Striker. Yeah, that's my old man.'

'Is your name Bluey as well?'

'Just Blue. I'm shorter than him, so my name's shorter. What's your name?'

'Curly.'

'Ha! Should be Straighty.'

We both laughed. It was around this point that a tentative mutual respect began to take root. It wasn't only because of our hair-based first names; I think we both realised that we each inhabited worlds which, although totally different from each other, were neither of them part of Outside.

'Got any brothers and sisters?'

I thought about this. 'Sort of.'

'What, you mean your mum and dad got some kids with other people?'

This was getting too difficult. I wasn't up to explaining the Lothlorien kinship system, or lack of it, so I just shrugged vaguely. 'Do you have any?' I asked.

'Brother. Micky. He's eighteen.'

'How old are you?'

'Ten next October. My mum says I was an afterthought. What about you?'

'Nine – quite soon I think. Has your brother got red hair too?'

'Nah, he's more blond, like our mum. He's a diamond, is Micky. That's his trailer, next to ours. He's out there working at the moment.'

'Why is he a diamond?'

'Well, f'rinstance, if he hears our dad having a go at me or our mum, he comes over and sorts him out. Flattens him. Cause our dad, he can get a bit out of order sometimes. If he's had a few too many, like. So Micky lands him a couple of punches – boom, boom – and he's out like a light.'

I was keen to know more – but at that moment I heard my name being called from some distance away. It was Stella, and she sounded rather desperate. The others were calling too. I'd temporarily forgotten all about them.

'Sounds like you're wanted,' said Blue.

'Yes –' I turned, reluctantly, and nearly collapsed.

'Got something wrong with your foot?'

'When I fell down – I must've done something to my ankle.'

'Here, I'll give you a hand.' Blue got up from the steps. He was shorter than me, and broader – (I was the skinny, sinewy type) – and proved to be an excellent prop as I limped towards the voices, feeling rather ashamed of myself and distinctly unmanly.

'Cur-LEE!' yelled Loose, the first one of the group to see me as I re-emerged into the bright lights.

'Shit, Curly, where did you get to? ' cried Stella. 'We've been looking for you everywhere.' I could see that I must have strayed quite a way from the Big Wheel.

'And what have you done to your leg?'

'My ankle. I fell over.'

'It's all right, he's been with me,' said Blue. Everyone looked at him. 'Curly's my new mate,' he explained. I was touched.

'This is Blue. He's been helping me.'

Blue frowned at Stella. 'You a hippie? You look quite normal.'

Sean, swaying gently between the twins, suddenly opened his eyes very wide. 'Oh man, you've shrunk! Bluey's SHRUNK!!'

'No, that was his father –' I began, but as Sean sank to his knees in wonder I realised there wasn't any point going on.

'He's off his head,' observed Blue correctly. '*He* looks like a hippie. Is he your dad?'

'No.'

'He's our *friend*,' said Layla. 'He ate a mushroom sandwich.'

Blue took in Layla. 'This your sister?'

Layla flashed him her baby-doll smile. 'We're all one big happy family.' She was quoting Ginnie, and to me she sounded pretty much off her head herself. Perhaps she'd been eating too much candyfloss. 'Thank you very much indeed for bringing Curly back,' she said.

'Pleasure.'

Sean put his hands on Blue's head. 'Keep shrinking, Bluey, and I'll put you in my pocket.'

Loose and the twins hauled him to his feet. 'Hey – now it's *me* that's *growing*!' he exclaimed. 'I am the Jelly Beanstalk. Look – jelly beans are sprouting from my fingernails.'

'We'd better get him back,' said Shine. 'He's starting to hallucinate. And he's been trying to climb things.'

'Ha-LOOSE-inate!' said Sean. 'Is Loose growing too?'

Blue was eyeing Layla very thoughtfully. 'Any chance of coming over to your place one of these days?' he asked. 'I wouldn't mind having a dekko at that wood of yours.'

*

Blue was a hit in Lothlorien. As it happened, almost everyone was around on the day of his first visit, so he got to meet a good cross-section of the community. A day or two after our fairground excursion, my ankle well bandaged up by Marjoram, I drove with Erryk to a pre-arranged pick-up point on one side of the Common. I'd told Blue to look out for me there every afternoon after lunch, and I'd come to collect him when I had the chance – I knew I'd have to check first with Bill and Ginnie about the suitability of his coming to Elfland. 'Of *course* we must welcome your friend,' said Ginnie.

Once in the car, Blue examined Erryk closely. 'You Curly's dad then?'

'Er... I suppose... in a way.'

'Lots of ways,' I said loyally.

'Sort of step-father?'

'Um... yes.'

We were both sitting on the long front seat of Erryk's old estate car. Blue craned to look in the back. 'Little blond girl didn't come with you?'

'She's making you some biscuits.'

'That's all right then.'

'This private property?' he asked, as we turned in through the gates. 'Not Council or anything?'

'It belongs to -' I guessed that 'Our Lord' would sound a bit strange – 'to a guy who has the big house I told you about. You can't see it from here.'

Blue nodded. 'Nice. So he doesn't mind hippies then.'

'No – he likes us.'

Ginnie glided up to meet us as we emerged from the car, wearing a dark blue kaftan and a string of Tibetan prayer beads. 'Hello Blue,' she said, and gave him a kiss on both cheeks, as Loose had taught us to do.

Blue seemed a little surprised. 'Cor, you smell nice,' he commented. He looked her up and down. 'I thought hippies didn't wear bras.'

Ginnie gave a tinkly laugh – a faint echo of Arjuna. 'Perhaps we're not ordinary hippies.'

'You Curly's mum?'

He was treated to her let-me-enlighten-you smile. 'Well now – here in our community everyone is *everybody's* mother. And father.'

'Bit confusing, ain't it?'

'Oh no, it's really simple. It just means that *spiritually* speaking, we're all related, and we all look after each other.' She took his arm. 'Wouldn't you like to come and sit down by the fire? I've made some scones.'

Preparations for tea were in full swing around the Fireplace. Bill stopped splitting logs as we approached, and leaned down to shake Blue's hand. 'Good to meet you. Welcome to Lothlorien.'

'You must be the gaffer,' said Blue cheerily. 'The big chief, eh?'

'Why do you say that?' Bill looked amused.

'Oh, I can tell.'

'Such perspicacity!' said Pete, who was buttering the scones.

'Percy who?'

'He means you are clever,' said Loose. She and Jack were setting out mugs and plates on the flat stones around the Fireplace.

'Hey, I've seen you before, haven't I? Bona riah.'

'What?'

'He means he likes your hairstyle,' said Pete. Recently Loose had taken to pulling all her hair onto the top of her head to create a kind of fountain effect. She had bleached a wide streak and then dyed it bright green, which I too found very attractive.

'Oh, *thank you*! Yes, I came to the fair with the others.'

'That's a point – where are the others?'

'The children are cooking, they will be here very soon.'

'How about the blond lady? My dad fancies her.'

'Stella? She's at the shop.'

'What shop?'

Blue seemed puzzled as I explained about the shop. 'I didn't think hippies went out to work.'

Bill smiled. 'We don't believe in living off government hand-outs. So we do what we can to earn money, but in ways which won't turn us into slaves of the materialist capitalist system.'

'Ah... So is that stoned hippie at the shop as well?'

Loose snorted. 'No. He is very, very asleep.'

Blue scrutinised her. 'Sounds like you're foreign.'

'Not just foreign! I am from *France*.'

'I been there. *Parly voo onglay*, that's what I had to say to everybody. My mum taught me – she knows a bit of Froggie.' He looked at Jack and frowned. 'You a Froggie too?'

Both Jack and Loose burst into laughter. 'She is my Rosbif piggie sweetheart!' said Loose, and gave Jack a noisy kiss on the nose.

'Oh, you mean you're palone-omis,' said Blue. 'I know all about those. My auntie's one of them. And I got an omi-palone cousin,' he added, addressing Pete. 'Ugly bugger, my cousin. You're much better-looking.'

'My God! The child is a miracle of tolerance. What a marvellously varied family you seem to have.'

'Yeah, it's not bad.'

'BLOO-OO-OO!' Layla was approaching with a large plate in her hands. 'Look what I've made for you!' She broke into a run. The twins and Jelly Bean followed her, retrieving biscuits from the ground as they fell from the plate.

'Come along, everybody – teatime!' Ginnie picked up the little Nepalese gong which she often used to summon us, and struck it several times so that it resonated through the trees. 'Now then Blue, what would you like to drink? We've got delicious mint tea, otherwise there's elder-flower syrup or wild strawberry crush.'

'Got a Coke?'

'We never buy products made by large American companies,' said Shine.

Ginnie registered Blue's look of bafflement. 'Especially not the ones which make fortunes poisoning the whole world with toxic mixtures of sugar and chemicals,' she explained kindly.

'Does that mean you haven't got any Coke?'

'It makes your teeth fall out,' said Layla.

I saw Blue's face change as he looked at her, Coca Cola no longer foremost in his mind. 'All right then, I'll give that strawberry stuff a go,' he said, sounding rather absent-minded.

Teatime was a very cheerful occasion. Ashley, Rick, Marjoram and Gogo all came to join in the fun, and Blue enjoyed himself memorising everyone's name in between mouthfuls of scone. As far as I was concerned, Ginnie's best attribute was her scone-making ability. Marjoram's bramble jelly was, as it were, the icing on the cake. The biscuits went down well too, especially with Blue.

'You made these all by yourself?' he asked Layla.

She fluttered her eyelashes.

'We helped her,' said Jelly Bean. 'Otherwise she burns things.'

'She can burn me up anytime,' said Blue gallantly.

Rick had brought over his acoustic guitar and jammed for a while with Erryk, their different styles linked by Loose's improvised singing – her usual wild swooping sounds, rather than tunes with words. 'This is *surrealist* music,' she said.

'You ought to make a record,' said Blue. 'Might catch on.'

After this musical interlude we took Blue on a full guided tour of Lothlorien, starting with the Garden, where Gogo and Marjoram showed him all the different fruit'n'veggies. 'Blimey, it's a living supermarket,' he said. He flicked the row of handsome marijuana plants growing in the middle of the tomato patch. 'Ha! I bet *those* ain't tomatoes. Don't worry, I won't tell the cops.' We hadn't bothered to hide them because it hadn't occurred to us that he would know what they were.

A few of the sheep and a couple of big lambs had strolled down to suss out what was going on and inspect the new visitor. 'And there's the meat counter,' said Blue. 'Bit of mutton hot-pot, eh? Very tasty.'

'Oh no!' said Rain. 'They're not for eating. They belong to the House up there – they're sort of pets. And lawn-mowers.'

'Pity. So the owner don't slip you the odd lamb chop, then.'

'We wouldn't eat them,' said Marjoram. 'We're vegetarian.'

Blue was shocked. '*Honest*? I've heard about that. It's not healthy.'

'Well, *we* are. You can see.'

'I s'pose you eat those chickens though.'

'Only the eggs. Being vegetarian means you eat no animals at all. Nothing alive except plants.'

Blue scratched his ear and looked at her sideways. 'Do you make bread?'

'Yes, of course.'

'My mum makes bread. She says yeast is little animals. So when you stick your loaf in the oven you're burning them alive.'

We hadn't thought about that before. We looked anxiously at Marjoram and Gogo to see how they would respond.

'You're quite right,' said Gogo. 'But yeast is made up of micro-organisms. They don't possess any form of consciousness.'

'They don't have *faces,*' said Jelly Bean.

'So you could eat, like, oysters and that. They ain't got faces.'

'No, but they're much bigger than yeast. They still might be able to think,' said Rain.

'They haven't got brains,' said Shine.

'Maybe they use something else to think with.'

'I'd like to know what oysters think *about*,' said Blue. 'Must be a pretty boring kind of life, just stuck to a rock.'

'They think about pearls,' said Layla.

Jelly Bean started to run on ahead. 'Now come and look at the Pool,' she called. 'And the DUCKS!'

As she approached the water's edge the two fairground ducklings paddled towards her cheeping loudly. Blue was surprised. 'They're not really meant to *last*,' he said. 'She only gets 'em to use as prizes. People don't know how to look after 'em, so they croak. Then the punters come back and complain.'

'That's because they're taken away from their mother too early. They get cold at night. These ones sleep next to me in my tent, over there. So that keeps them warm, and the foxes can't get them.'

Bill and Ginnie had long ago given in to Jelly Bean's attachment to solitary outdoor accommodation, and had given her a small tent for her sixth birthday. It seemed preferable to the space beneath a caravan or inside a hollow tree – or indeed a nest of branches and grass, which she sometimes made for herself during dry weather. 'In your last life you really *were* a gorilla,' said Layla – (a reference to the famous gorilla suit, resurrected after Arjuna's departure, but now sadly a little too small). 'I wish I still was,' replied Jelly Bean.

If snow or tempest raged she would spend the night on the settee in one of the caravans, generally ours, but most of the time she slept in her tent. She moved it around the woods according to which particular item of fauna or fauna she wanted to be close to at any given moment, so she made an ideal foster mother for the ducks. I think Ginnie must have felt something of a failure in the motherhood department, which is perhaps why she felt compelled to dispense so much sweetness, light and aromatherapy elsewhere. Of course I could be wrong.

From the Pool we showed Blue round all the caravans. He particularly liked Pete's. 'Reminds me of my Gran's,' he said. 'Same cups. And she likes that sort of music, too. Shopping, mostly. Piano.'

He was even more enthusiastic about Ashley's tree-bedroom. I didn't go up there so much these days, as I hated to see Tiger lily's old duvet and bean bag, now transformed into Chip's bed. Ash had also taken one of her lamps, which glowed warmly through its crimson shade.

'*Very* nice,' said Blue. He glanced at Layla. 'We could have some fun up here, eh gorgeous?'

Layla simpered. 'I can be your girlfriend for now, but not *like that*, because I'm engaged to Luke.'

'Luke?'

'Skywalker.' She pulled the horrible doll out of her candy-striped shoulder bag. 'He's with me all the time.'

Blue guffawed. 'That's all right darling, I'm not jealous.' He turned to me. 'Cutest thing on two legs, eh Curly?'

*

Following this memorable visit Blue invited all five of us children to tea in his own caravan. 'Remember to call it a trailer,' I said to the others.

'I hope Blue wasn't a nuisance at your place,' said his mother. 'He can get a bit over the top sometimes.'

'Not at all, Mrs...'

'Call me Cynthia, love.'

Her hair was so blond it was almost white. Who did that remind me of? It came to me with a slight shock of guilt – Wing. But Cynthia's hair was thick and bouncy, caught up at the back in a tortoiseshell clip. And she was taller and plumper than Wing – and definitely jollier. Had Wing been like that I might miss her more, I reflected. Still, missing another person would have been too much for me.

We found the interior of the trailer very beautiful, and we admired everything: the tapestry-covered cushions, the lacy mats and curtains, the cabinet full of ornaments stuck in place with Blu-tack. There was a glass-fronted bookcase in which we spotted a good number of children's books and an encyclopaedia.

'Do you go to school?' I asked Blue. He made a face.

'Not as much as he should do,' said Cynthia. 'In the winter, mostly. Social Services give us a bit of trouble sometimes.' I thought of Malcolm.

'My mum taught me to read and write,' said Blue, 'and my dad showed me how to count up money. What else do you need? Anyway, at school they treat me like I'm a fucking gypsy.'

'Mind your language or you'll get a crack round the head,' said his mother.

'But it's true. School's rubbish. You lot don't go to school, do you?'

'Don't you really?' asked Cynthia. 'You sound like you do.'

'We have a teacher called Gogo,' I said. 'His lessons are really interesting. Not like school at all.'

'He used to work in a school, but he didn't like the System, so he left,' explained Rain. 'He says school stifles the natural urge to explore and ask questions.'

'Does he now. Well, so long as you're learning enough to cope all right in the world.' She offered round a plate of assorted chocolate biscuits. Most of them would never have found their way into Lothlorien, but we didn't care. But we did draw the line at Coca Cola, and settled for Rose's Lime Juice instead – a new and fascinating taste.

During the next two weeks visits to and fro continued, a particularly high point being my birthday party. Blue brought me a present: a set of darts with bright blue flights. 'You got a dartboard here, I s'pose,' he said. I had to confess that he supposed wrongly. 'I'll have to get you one then,' he said. I also received, to my great delight, the communal present of a new bike – a mountain bike, slightly too big in order to allow for growth, but hugely superior to the old one which I'd had for three years and was now used more by Jelly Bean and Layla. What with these gifts, the cake, the music and funny poems, and the huge card made by the other children, I felt truly happy for the first time in what seemed like ages.

A few days later we made our last visit to Blue's trailer, minus Jelly Bean who had a prior engagement with the ducks. Blue presented me with the promised dartboard: 'Micky's. He's got himself a new one.'

'That's really nice...'

'You can tell him yourself. He'll be over in a minute – he's been wanting to meet you.'

Micky the Flattener: that's how I'd privately thought of him. And he certainly did look as if he could flatten anyone he wanted. Beneath his T-shirt, emblazoned with the legend 'S.U.C.K.', his muscles looked even bigger than Sean's. Like Cynthia his hair was pale blond, but cut very short, and his face was pinker and covered in freckles. He flexed his biceps and cracked his knuckles loudly.

'Don't worry, he's not dangerous,' said Blue, seeing our expressions.

'Only when I want to be.' The Flattener laughed genially. 'You the hippie kids then? Where's all your beads?'

'We don't wear beads any more,' said Shine. 'We're modern hippies.'

'Modern, eh?' He looked at Layla. 'You must be the one that's been leading my little brother up the garden path.'

'He's just my *tempry* boyfriend,' said Layla primly.

'That's the way, my darling. Treat 'em mean, keep 'em keen.'

'Thank you very much for the dartboard,' I said.

'Never played?'

'No, but Blue's going to teach me.'

'Future champion, that's what Blue is.' Micky gave Blue an affectionate cuff round the ear. Blue responded by pummelling his brother's abdomen.

The blows bounced off as if from a bullet-proof vest.

The Flattener grinned at me. 'We'll have a few games next year. So as I can see if you've been practising.'

An alarming prospect: but mixed with pleasure, as it meant that the fair would be coming back.

Blue gave Layla a nudge. 'Then you 'n me can have a few games too, eh sweetheart? Up in the tree.'

Layla wriggled coyly. 'I'll have to ask Luke.'

'Well you can tell him from me, if he gives me any grief I'll shove his light-whatsit up where it won't shine at all.'

Blue came back with us that afternoon, as he was going to spend the night in Lothlorien. 'You're our first guest!' said Shine, which was true, because although the adults had friends and occasionally family to stay from time to time, we'd never asked anyone our own age for a sleep-over before – simply because we didn't know anyone we wanted to ask. Looking back now, I can see that we had incredibly limited contact with other children. At the time it was something we didn't miss at all, perhaps because we were so used to the adults treating us more or less as equals. And as I've already mentioned, children Outside seemed rather silly. Blue, on the other hand, was a different matter altogether.

We met up with Marjoram and Ginnie in the car park behind the High Street, after they'd closed the shop. While we were waiting for them Blue put his arm round Layla. 'You got an extra bed in your bedroom, haven't you?'

'No, that's for Luke,' she said. 'You're going to sleep in Curly's caravan. He's got a proper spare bed.'

Blue sighed. 'Ah well. Have to wait till next year then.'

Once we were back in Lothlorien I asked Ashley to find a good place for the dartboard, so he fixed it securely in the fork of a tree where it would be easy enough to remove in bad weather. Then, while the twins helped to prepare the meal and Layla went to ask Zoë for a special hair-do, Blue gave me my first darts lesson. I wasn't doing too badly until Jelly Bean ran past.

She stopped and took two of the darts from my hand. 'Do these have to go in the middle?'

'It depends...' I began, but Jelly Bean had already aimed one dart after the other. Both landed in the dead centre of the board. 'Blimey, two double-bulls!' said Blue.

She ran on, laughing. 'I'm good at those things,' she called.

'She's got a bow and a whole lot of arrows,' I explained. 'She made them herself.'

'What, for shooting birds and that?

'Oh no, she'd never *kill* anything. It's just for fun. Sometimes she'll climb a tree and put some paint on a leaf or an acorn or something, and then come back down and shoot it off the branch.'

'Right little savage, that one.' I could tell he was impressed. He went to pluck the darts out of the board, and handed them back to me with a serious look on his face. 'Know what Curly, I been thinking.'

'What about?'

'The other kids here – they've all got, like, real *parents*. A mum and a dad.'

'Yes – I suppose so...' It was always hard to remember that Jelly Bean had parents, especially ones like Bill and Ginnie.

'But you ain't got neither.'

'No – but with us that sort of thing doesn't matter.' I'd realised by now how much more important family relationships were in Blue's world than in ours.

'Yeah, I know how Ginnie goes on, you're all related blah blah – but you're not, are you. So what I thought is, if I make you my blood brother, then you'll have a kosher family. Cause that'll make you related to all of us. Through the blood.'

Bluey Senior my father? Cynthia my mother and the Flattener my big brother? And what about all those aunts and uncles and cousins he'd told us about – would they be mine as well? I just couldn't believe in the reality of it all – but on the other hand I did like the idea of having Blue as my blood brother. I knew that his offer came from the heart, and I deeply appreciated it. 'Ok, that'd be good,' I said.

He sat down on a big tree stump. 'This is how you do it...' Without hesitation he plunged the point of one of the darts into the tip of his forefinger, which began to bleed copiously. 'It's easier if you do it quick,' he said.

'Have you done it before?'

'Nah, but I've watched Micky. Now it's your turn. Here – sit down next to me.'

I tried to be as brave as he was, but only succeeded in making a dent. Determined not to be a total wimp, I pushed and rotated the dart until a small red hole appeared and a thin trickle of blood began to ooze out. The operation was quite painful, but I certainly wasn't going to admit it.

'Now we mix the blood.' Blue held up his finger, I did the same, and we pressed them together for a few seconds.

'Right. We're blood brothers for life,' said Blue. We shook hands solemnly. It had been a short but powerful ceremony.

He stood up. 'I can smell cooking. Must be time for that veggie dinner. Hope it don't poison me.'

15. LOWS TO HIGHS

SOON AFTER THAT the fair left town. My sadness crept back, like a nagging stomach ache that had been quelled for a while by a good dose of pain-killer. I say stomach ache because it really did feel like a physical entity lodged somewhere behind my diaphragm, which at times threaded its tentacles into the rest of my body. Paradoxically, I got so used to this sensation that I reached a point where I hardly noticed it any more.

But sometimes I dreamt about Tiger Lily, and in my dreams she was always back in Lothlorien and I was delirious with joy. Then, while still asleep, I would realise I was dreaming, and wake up flooded with a black, oily tide of grief which took hours to drain away.

It didn't help that she was still talked about a good deal – unlike Wing who, once twinned with Arjuna, had become more or less taboo.

'Oh, I do miss Tiger Lily,' Marjoram would sigh.

Ginnie agreed. 'She was such a breath of fresh air. I do wish she'd write to us.'

'I expect she will once she's really settled down,' said Zoë. 'It can't be easy, adapting to life Outside. Particularly in Australia.'

Why so difficult? According to the stories Tiger Lily used to tell me, there were plenty of marvels to be experienced in Australia if only you went to the right places. She was probably having such a wonderful time at some sacred waterhole or other that she'd forgotten all about us. I imagined her floating in circles on her back, her baby a smooth round bulge rising ever higher above the water.

Ashley never mentioned Tiger Lily, but I knew that like me he thought about her more than the others did. With him I felt a sense of shared manly sorrow, profound but unspoken. I took to spending more time in his company, and began to concentrate properly on carving, and wood-work in general. There seemed to be so much to learn: how the grain in each type of wood behaved differently; which species resisted insects; what tool to use for each particular task. I owe a huge amount to Ash.

He quite often took me along when he had some work Outside –

which might be anything from fitting a kitchen to repairing a window frame or a piece of furniture. Several of these jobs came through Zoë, whose hairdressing clients often seemed to need things done around the house. 'You can be my minder,' Ash said to me. 'These bored housewives are rampant nymphos. I need to conserve my energy.'

He had a stock answer if any of these predatory houris ever asked why I wasn't at school: 'My nephew attends a progressive boarding school which encourages the acquisition of certain extra-curricular skills.' I had to try hard not to giggle at this statement, which he always delivered in a very solemn, un-Ashlike tone. It was generally met with approving murmurs. 'How fabulously *advanced,*' I remember one woman saying. 'Where is this school? Anywhere near here?' 'No,' said Ash, and named the neighbouring county. 'They give them a week off at a time. I go over and pick him up.'

Those houses were an eye-opener. Most of them were spotlessly clean, tidy, and enormous – at least they seemed so to me. If Ash and I were alone, I had fun running up and down the soft carpeted staircases, bouncing on vast sofas and opening doors to peer at other immaculate interiors – but why did these Outsiders need so many rooms? And those great expanses of lawn – what were they *for*? I knew not all Outsiders lived like this – I'd seen plenty of more modest houses, at least from the exterior. 'Typical bourgeois excess,' said Ashley. Excessive or not, the atmosphere inside rarely struck me as cosy or welcoming. But I did find the bathrooms fascinating: acres of shiny patterned tiles, an abundance of fluffy pastel towels warmed on heated rails – and bathtubs big enough to swim in. I was terribly tempted; we only had showers at Lothlorien, so I'd never had a bath, unless you counted the deep laundry sink in the shower block where we'd all been bathed as babies.

On one job, when Ash knew the house owners would be out all day, temptation got the better of me. I ran the water as hot as I could bear and watched my skin turn red as I slowly lowered myself in. Once I was used to it I rolled like a seal, floated and splashed, blew hot bubbles under water, and emerged brick-red and steaming. Then I ran around in the kitchen to dry off, as I didn't dare use the towels.

'Yes, nothing like a bath for warming yourself up,' said Marjoram when I told her, 'but not awfully healthy, at least not the way we do it in England. You soak in your own dirt. The Japanese have a good shower before they get in a bath.'

Nature's Way had recently been transformed: Rick now called it 'Little Japan'. After Tiger Lily's departure Ginnie had decided that the shop needed a new 'emphasis', and after a good deal of discussion all those concerned had decided that this emphasis should be Japanese. Marjoram liked the idea of Japanese herbal medicine; Stella was attracted to Japanese contemporary design; Zoë had started taking weekly Shiatsu lessons in Chandleford. She practised on anyone who was willing to serve as guinea-pig, which most of us were only too happy to do.

'Japanese culture is all so *refined*,' said Ginnie. 'So spiritual.' Hello Kitty hadn't yet impinged on her consciousness. She had pale green kimonos made as new shop-wear, and began to buy books on Zen Buddhism.

'She'll have us all committing hara-kiri soon,' said Pete.

'Sooner the better,' said El.

During her school-free weeks that summer El had moved more or less permanently into Pete's spare bedroom, where she'd been sleeping off and on for several years when she wasn't bedding down on the settee in the main part of Rick and Zoë's caravan. This new arrangement, completely separate from her parents and sister, suited her better. Pete didn't mind. 'She's no trouble at all,' he said. 'I hardly know she's there, except when she's kind enough to share her dinner with me. The perfect lodger.'

The scope of El's cooking was limited to pasta, enhanced with some of Marjoram's tomato sauce; when she got bored with this she would deign to drop into her parents' caravan in order to check out what was on the menu. I frequently did the same, as Zoë was a good cook and it was always a treat to find that there was enough for me as well.

'The occasional *word* would be appreciated,' said Zoë one evening, as El silently helped herself to a large bowl of food and then headed for the door. '"Please" or "thank you" for example. Remember those? Or don't they feature in the punk vocabulary?'

'No point speaking to her,' said Rick. 'She only talks to Pete these days. Or Jack and Loose. Don't ask me why.'

El spun round to face him. 'Well I'll tell you why. It's because they're *real*. Not like the rest of you. You all think you're so bloody alternative but you're just play-acting. Jack and Loose are authentic. So's Pete. They know what it means to suffer.'

'Oh, so you *suffer*, do you? Do you think that's what authenticity is all about? And are you gay as well?'

'Get stuffed,' said El coolly, and walked out.

'She isn't gay,' I said.

'How do you know?' asked Zoë. 'Not that I'd mind if she was, of course – I just wish she could get over all this teenage angst business and *talk* to us.'

'I saw her snogging a boy in Middington.' I liked the word 'snog', fairly new in my vocabulary and introduced to me by Blue. It had a nicely gross ring to it which corresponded well with what I'd seen El doing behind the hot-dog stand in the market a week or two earlier. She seemed to be a pretty ferocious snogger. The boy in question had been a few inches shorter than her, and was standing on tiptoe as he tried to respond adequately to her assault.

Rick looked glum. 'So any day now we'll be grandparents.'

'And I'll be an auntie!' said Layla.

'For God's sake shut up, the pair of you! Just because she's kissed a boy or two doesn't mean...' Zoë stopped. 'I suppose I ought to give her a few packets of the Pill though, just in case.'

'She won't take them, not from you. Give them to Loose – she can pass them on.'

El's behaviour didn't stop her from being a star pupil; her school reports were always full of praise. Rick and Zoë found this hard to believe, but I knew from Pete that she applied herself to her studies with great diligence, and spent a lot of time reading and writing when in his caravan. And I quite often bumped into her in the campervan, talking to Jack about feminism or history; the latter was her favourite subject. Jack lent both of us books, though my tastes were rather different from El's. I'd developed a passion for murder mysteries – Jack had a box full of old green-and-white Penguin paperbacks, and after reading my first Margery Allingham I was hooked. I wrote murder plays and persuaded the other children to act in them; Layla usually had to be the corpse because she couldn't be bothered to learn many lines but didn't mind lying down for a while in an attempt to look both dead and glamorous. 'The new Marilyn,' remarked Pete.

He himself was studying Italian. 'Why?' I asked him. 'You know it already, from the operas.'

'That wouldn't help me order an espresso, or even ask for directions to the post office. They just don't do that kind of thing in *La Traviata*. And I want to be able to wander through Venice and converse freely with the gondoliers. I have to prepare myself for my future existence.'

'What, you mean when you die?'

'Not at all. Much as I relish the idea of an afterlife of Roman debauchery, I'm actually thinking of when I move to Italy.'

At that, I must have looked totally aghast. Pete smiled. 'Don't fret, I'm not about to leave these sacred woods. Not until my ancient aching bones begin to yearn for that bijou sun-drenched villa on Capri. By that time you'll be long gone from here. You can come and drink grappa with me on my vine-shaded terrace.'

'Grappa?'

'One of the world's finest intoxicants. We shall get drunk and solve the secret of the universe.'

It was hard to visualise this scene; Pete hadn't really furnished me with enough detail. I'd seen pictures of gondolas, but my knowledge of Italy didn't extend much beyond the Venetian canals. I couldn't imagine myself 'long gone' from Lothlorien, either. 'Have you been to Italy already?' I asked. 'Is it nice?'

'You *have* to stop using that word! "Nice" can be used to describe, let's say, a little folk-ditty penned by Erryk, or perhaps one of Ginnie's scones... but *not* the splendour that is Italy.' He closed his eyes. 'Yes, of course I've been there. The first time was a school trip when I was fifteen. To Florence. I was overwhelmed by art while my philistine classmates spent all their time ogling girls and moaning about the food. The only ravioli they knew was a slimy brown mass in a tin from Sainsbury's. When they were confronted with the real thing they panicked.'

*

Subsequently, of course, I got to know Italy quite well, and I understand why Pete wanted to live there. It would have suited him perfectly. I've visited Capri – and been marked for ever by the five minutes you get in the Blue Grotto, an experience which was just as Pete described. In spite of all the other little boats packed with tourists and rowed by singing boatmen, the colour is so sublime you want to drink it in and die. Peace be with you, Pete.

And now here I am 'convalescing', which means I've been moved to this pleasant establishment where I get heaved around by charming physiotherapists and the food is definitely better than it was in the hospital. My strength is coming back – but without any desire to start picking up my life at the point where it left off. That life always seemed surreal: now it seems simply *un*real, insubstantial, of no significance. Faithful Marco still comes regularly to see me, though rather less often than before, as this place is further away from what he calls 'civilisation'. An advantage of this is that I no longer get dutiful visits from people I can't really be bothered to talk to. And Mrs Jeanette Evans seems to have lost the scent, so I don't have to put up with her enigmatic remarks or her inexplicable gestures of generosity.

Thinking of Pete reminds me of the apartment I've been renting for the past couple of years in San Remo, which used to be handy for some of my work. And then of course there's the other one in Villefranche. Not remotely jet-setty – they're just small studio flats, nothing I've ever thought of as home. (Have I ever thought of anywhere as home since I left Lothlorien? I suppose not – but it's never bothered me). The leases on those studios must be due to run out in a couple of months. I don't want to renew them. Marco will no doubt ask me why and I won't be able to give him a satisfactory answer. 'Because once I've finished reliving my youth I might want a change of direction' – he wouldn't think much of that.

*

Gogo took a stick and drew a large spiral in the gravel of the Lothlorien parking place. 'Now imagine that, hundreds and hundreds of miles wide. Inside it the air's warmer than it is outside, so it's rising and making the pressure lower. The centre's dead calm, like the middle of an LP going round. That's called the eye of the storm. But the colder air outside it is getting sucked in faster and faster, and the winds are already spinning at over eighty miles an hour. They might even reach hurricane speed.'

A rapidly deepening Atlantic low: that was the phrase which had prompted this lesson on meteorology. Rain had heard it on the radio. Lately he had developed a great interest in the weather and listened to the forecast regularly; the one that autumn morning had worried him.

'It's coming towards us! Will we get blown away?'

'No. The worst of it will come in a lot further north. Scotland will probably get hit quite badly. Down here we'll just feel the side effects, because it'll still be pretty blowy round the edges of the depression.'

It was. They say that schoolchildren become unsettled when the wind is high; it certainly had an effect on us lot, and we roared around the woods screaming and leaping as we avoided falling twigs and branches. It wasn't as dangerous as you might think; Outside children would probably have been kept indoors, but being so well acquainted with the woods we knew where the largest branches were likely to fall. Then we ran to the top of the Sheepfield with the wind pushing us, and whooshed back down again with our arms out, pretending to fly. As the air rushed past I had the sensation that it was forcing its way through my whole body, and once back at the bottom of the hill I felt an exhilarating feeling of cleaned-out emptiness.

'I'm a bird! I'm a bird!' cried Jelly Bean ecstatically. But later that day she was sunk in misery, having discovered that both the ducks were missing from Galadriel's Pool. They were adult now, with handsome white plumage – real farmyard ducks.

Ginnie tried to sooth her. 'They've flown away with the wind to find a bigger pond,' she said. 'Or perhaps they've gone to get married with some other ducks.'

'Ducks don't get married,' hissed Jelly Bean. 'They *breed*. And not in the autumn.' She mourned their loss for weeks.

Several trees were also casualties of the gale. Ash and Erryk sawed most of them into logs, so we had plenty of wood for the Fireplace. This gave rise to a lot of baked potato evenings.

It was during one of these convivial occasions, on a dryish winter evening, that Zoë made an announcement.

'I think I shall have to sleep with that guy from the hardware store,' she said loudly.

'What, you mean the young good-looking one who's always popping into the shop for a chat?' asked Stella, equally loudly. It all sounded somehow rehearsed.

'That's him.'

'He's got lovely brown eyes. And a really cute little bum. I'm sure he fancies you.'

'Go ahead,' said Rick listlessly. 'Might as well work your way down the High Street, while you're at it.'

'Why not?' said Ash. 'The greengrocer looks like he's a bit of a goer. And I could put in a good word for you with Alan at the garage, if you like.'

'Let's not forget the estate agent,' said Pete. 'He's probably longing for you to rip off his tie and unleash his hidden tiger.'

Sean roared and pounded his chest, and we all laughed – apart from Zoë.

'How dare you! You know perfectly well I would *never* sleep with the estate agent. Or *any* guy in a tie.'

Erryk picked up his guitar and launched into a tuneful murmur. 'Butcher, baker, candlestick maker...'

'... a guy in a tie and the undertaker...' continued Ashley.

'Hey! Cool lyric!' said Sean. 'Did you guys just make that up?'

'No – well I – not the first bit -' began Erryk.

He was interrupted by a shout from Stella. 'Stop laughing, everyone. This is serious. Rick – can't you see she's trying to get a *reaction* out of you? To make you *jealous*?'

'Jealous? Why should I be jealous? You live your life babe, and I'll live mine.'

'*Exactly*!' retorted Zoë. 'So you can feel good about shagging all those groupies.'

Rick frowned. 'Can't say I recall...'

'Come off it – what about all that recording you did in London last summer? With that band? There must have been loads of them hanging around. Hordes of panting girlies waiting to get their sweaty little hands on you.'

'I'm a session musician, not a rock star.'

'You get the rock stars' leftovers though, don't you?'

Rick gave a sardonic snort. 'Their excess baggages. Sadly, no.'

Zoë glared at him. 'Do you realise that this is the longest conversation we've had for at least two months?'

Rick ran a hand across his eyes. 'Oh Christ. She wants me to talk.'

'He never talks in the winter,' said Layla.

Gogo nodded. 'You should be used to that by now, Zoë. You've been together long enough.'

'A sight too long, if you ask me.'

'I could move into the shower block, if you like.'

'No!' squealed Layla. 'I need you in the caravan. Both of you together.'

Rick put out an arm and patted his daughter's shoulder. 'Thank you, baby.'

'And anyway, you're perfectly *capable* of speech,' Zoë went on. 'You've just been talking now. These so-called depressions of yours are just an excuse to lie around and do bugger all except feel sorry for yourself.'

'It's fairly common to feel down in winter, you know,' said Jack. 'Especially in Scandinavia, for instance.'

'This is England, not Lapland.'

'Even here it's not that unusual. It's a kind of hibernation state some people seem to fall into. You should probably just let Rick hibernate in peace.'

'It seems to me,' said Bill, 'that this discussion isn't so much about your respective sexual adventures, or lack of them, but rather Zoë's growing, and if I may say so understandable, frustration at your inability to find, or indeed seek out, a solution for this problem of yours, Rick.'

Rick looked surprised at this onslaught of Bill-speak. 'So what the fuck am I supposed to do about it?'

'Light therapy might be the answer. Exposure to simulated sunlight for a certain length of time every day can apparently be a extremely effective way to combat winter depression.'

'So you know how to simulate sunshine, do you? I hadn't realised your electrical prowess stretched so far.'

Bill sighed. 'I'm sure it won't be difficult to obtain the necessary piece of equipment. I'll look into it for you.'

Rick grunted.

'And Rick – I'm sure you're aware that in the interests of domestic harmony, and ultimately the harmony of the community, it really is advisable to be open to communication with your partner.'

Ginnie nodded vehemently. 'It's absolutely essential. It's what keeps us bonded.'

Bill ignored Rick's groan and turned to Zoë. 'What you choose to do with the hardware store's unmarried personnel is of course none of my business, but I do think it would be preferable, for the sake of the good reputation of *Nature's Way*, not to encourage the attention of any of your own clients' husbands.'

Zoë reddened and shot a furious look at Ginnie, who looked away.

'What have you been saying to him? Is this what "communication with your partner" boils down to? Telling tales?'

'I have eyes of my own, Zoë,' said Bill mildly, 'and I pass through Middington fairly frequently.'

'Come on, eat up everybody', said Marjoram. 'Let's get on with living in the moment. This is a delicious baked potato moment.'

Thinking back to that time, (because, with apologies to Marjoram, I'm not that interested in this convalescent present) – it seems to me that she and Gogo were the most organically joined of the Lothlorien couples, in a state of near-perfect symbiosis, like the tree-roots and fungus Gogo taught us about. I never heard them raise their voices to each other in anger or even disagree very much. On the other hand, despite Ginnie's claims, her relationship with Bill was held together by high tension wires rather than true bonds of communication. I think they were both very conscious of being Leaders, however much Ginnie might witter on about us all being equal, and there was competition between them, a kind of power struggle between their often differing opinions on how matters within the community should be handled. I only became really aware of this when I was a bit older.

Sean and Stella were a different case altogether. His looks and behaviour belied the fact that he was the oldest member of Lothlorien – he must have been at least forty by this time. Stella was in her early thirties; she was only nineteen when they first met, during the filming of the fabled deodorant ad, and his magnificent stoned hedonism must have seemed the epitome of hippie chic. In time she realised that there wasn't an awful lot going on beneath it, but her adoration never wavered. 'He'll grow up once he's a dad,' she used to say, until it became pretty clear that parenthood was likely to elude them. Perhaps I'm being over-simplistic, but I think that Sean, unchanging, became in a sense her child, so it was in her interest to collude with his unchangingness. Occasionally she would come back from a trip to London or elsewhere in extra-sparkly mode, which makes me think that she probably had the odd hopeful fling, if only in the interests of potential conception.

Where did Sean spring from? I knew that Stella was originally Scottish – her mother usually came to visit every year. And everyone else occasionally mentioned parents or relatives, and the places where they grew up, in spite of the fact that they didn't have much contact with them any more. Even Pete had a mother and a father – I'd heard him speak of them as 'those benighted and ill-favoured moles of Basildon', which I found rather poetic. But Sean's origins were a mystery.

I asked him once; he threw back his head and roared with laughter. 'His father was a lion and his mother was a sunbeam,' said Stella, from which I gathered that the subject was closed.

All this reminds me: one day towards the end of that winter Ash came down from our mailbox by the Lodge with a card from Australia. It was postmarked Byron Bay. On the front was a picture of a kangaroo on a surfboard. '*Hi Guys,*' read the message, '*all good here – loads of cool new stuff going down. Missing you like crazy – come and visit.*'

'But she hasn't put her address!' wailed Ginnie.

'Bet she's got herself a new fella,' said Zoë. 'That kind of thing can make you absent-minded.'

'Oh can it,' said Rick. 'Is that why you forgot to bring back your bag from the shop today? With those chocolate éclairs I asked you to get?'

'Must be,' said Zoë. 'You're getting too fat, anyway.'

There was no malice in this exchange, for Rick had undergone a magical transformation. Bill had procured a light box for him; although at first he'd been utterly scornful of it Zoë had insisted on switching it on every day at dinnertime, when he was least likely to disappear, and after only a week or so his mood had improved to a point where he was capable of playing his guitar and even cracking jokes. It had increased his appetite too, especially for cakes. I empathised, and encouraged him to share some of them with me.

So normally I would have been disappointed that Zoë had left the éclairs in Middington. Now, I hardly gave them a thought – because I knew, of course, what Tiger Lily's 'cool new stuff' must be. Thinking about it gave me a headache. But I took the postcard from Pete, who was the last to read it, and shoved it under my sweater. He put a hand on my shoulder.

'Cup of tea?'

I shook my head. In a fit of gloom I wandered over to the campervan and sat down on the steps. It was cold, but I didn't care. I stared at the darkening grey sky through the bare trees and imagined the hot sunny Australian summer and the giant blue-green waves in which Tiger Lily would no doubt be frolicking with Sean's baby. Perhaps it'll drown and she'll come back, I thought. But I knew this was a wicked idea and tried to push it away.

Jack opened the door. 'Come inside, Curly.' She pulled me up and sat me on the settee. I watched dully as she sat down too, took up some typed sheets from the table and began to make notes in the margins. I appreciated her silence. She must have known how much I still missed Tiger Lily, even though she wasn't aware of the whole horrific truth.

'You know,' she said eventually, 'even if it's not quite the same as before, Lothlorien's still a good place to be. All the people here basically wish each other well, which is pretty damn rare, believe you me. So enjoy it while you can, because nothing lasts for ever. It'll be an excellent base for your life to rest on – a boat for when you sail away.' I liked that image, though sailing away was still far beyond my imagination.

We heard Loose leaping up the steps. 'Hey!' she shouted happily as she burst through the door. 'Look what I have to show you! From the darkroom. My Waitrose photos of yesterday – people doing their shopping. They are so funny!'

They were – even I had to laugh. I think it was with one of those pictures that Loose later won a prestigious competition, and she sold quite a few to a French photographic magazine.

'This calls for a celebration,' said Jack. She pulled up part of the settee to reach for one of the bottles underneath. 'Fetch the corkscrew and three glasses, Curly.'

For some reason the Lothlorien rule about no alcohol apart from that brewed on site had never seemed to apply to Jack and Loose. I suppose Bill turned a blind eye because of Jack's age and natural authority. So I did as I was requested and Jack opened the bottle and poured us each a full glass of red wine – considerably more than she usually gave me, but I gulped it all down.

Its heat began to creep all through my body and into my brain. I lay back and thought about what Jack had said, and a vision came to me of everyone in Lothlorien as a length of bright cord of a different shade, woven together to form a rainbow-coloured coracle. Bill was dark metallic blue, Layla was pink, Marjoram was leaf-green... I was rocked in a warm and comforting current which swirled me gently into a deep sleep.

*

'I don't see any reason why not,' said Stella.

'Astrologically, it does look very auspicious,' said Ginnie. 'And they're going to lay on special facilities for children.'

We looked expectantly at Bill, who was deep in thought.

He cleared his throat. 'It seems to me, in view of the fact that several of us will be going anyway, we could indeed turn this into a communal event. And take the kids along.'

We cheered.

And so began the planning for what would be an unprecedented expedition: The Great Lothlorien Outing to Glastonbury Fayre, or GLOG, as it came to be known.

The twins and I wrote down all the arrangements. Erryk and Stella were taking leather items and jewelry to sell on a stall they'd reserved, and Marjoram and Ginnie thought it would be a good idea to display some of their smells and herbs as well. Ginnie was to set off with Bill a few days before everyone else, as Bill was involved in some electrical way; he knew friends of the organisers who had offered to put them up in their house a couple of miles from the festival site. Rick had a musician mate in one of the bands booked to play, and had been invited to stay with him in the latter's large caravan, along with Zoë and Layla. The rest of us would establish a settlement in the camping area nearby, supervised by Gogo; he and Marjoram had bought a tent specially for the occasion. They were going to take Ashley's pick-up and set up his 'nookie parlour' arrangement in the tray as an excellent bedroom for the twins and me. Loose would sleep on the front seat, while Erryk was perfectly happy to bed down in the back of his own car. Sean was going to use what he called his 'survival skills' to construct a shelter for himself and Stella out of an old tarpaulin and some branches brought from our woods. Jelly Bean would take along her tiny tent.

Jack didn't like crowds, so she elected to stay behind and look after the chickens in our absence.

'We shall tend them together,' said Pete, 'because not for anyone or anything would I spend three days sharing a Portaloo in a field with several thousand people. But of course I shall be thinking of you all very warmly.'

'And the ducks!' cried Jelly Bean. 'Please, please check on the ducks. Make sure they're on their island at night.'

It had been a time of great rejoicing for Jelly Bean when on a fine spring morning one of the ducks had come back to Lothlorien and splashed down into the Pool – not with its old companion, but a new, slightly smaller, brown duck. Together they had produced six ducklings, by now well into adolescence and interestingly mottled. Jelly Bean had spent several mud-covered days heaving earth and stones into the centre of the Pool to create an artificial island, on which she got Ashley to construct a small wooden duck house so the family would be safe from foxes.

'Fear not, I shall protect them with my life,' said Pete.

Like Pete, Ashley decided not to go to Glastonbury. 'Too stressful for Chip. He doesn't like crowds either. But I can look after the shop if you like. Chat up your customers a bit.'

'*No*,' said Ginnie. 'We'll just put a notice in the window saying we're closed for Solstice celebrations.'

El, naturally enough, scorned the whole idea of the festival. 'A billion old hippies on a farm? Don't make me laugh.'

A month or two earlier, along with her friends, El had morphed from punk into Goth. When we were first treated to a glimpse of this new look we had made the mistake of laughing, at which El turned and opened her mouth to display a pair of long and pointed canine teeth tipped with red. 'Wanna lose some blood?'

Layla screamed.

'They're false,' said Shine scornfully.

'Yeah. They're to hide the real ones I got growing underneath,' said El with a leer.

'I wouldn't be surprised if she really was a vampire,' muttered Rain afterwards. 'She probably doesn't go to school at all, she just sleeps in a coffin somewhere.'

He was quite worried about the prospect of spending two whole nights away at Glastonbury. 'It's a long time to be Outside,' he said. 'What if we get lost or abducted or something?'

'Rubbish,' said Shine. 'We're *ten*, for goodness sake.'

'Cheer up mate, it'll be a home-from-home,' said Ash, who'd been to Glastonbury in pre-Chipolata days. 'Just like here, but a thousand times bigger.'

He was right. Our little convoy arrived around halfway through the first day, and I was instantly enchanted by the array of coloured tents dotted thickly over the camping areas. And so many hippies! – full-on, hairy, heavy-duty hippies, who looked just like my early memories of the Lothlorien adults before they opted for a rather more clean-cut style.

They all seemed stoned and happy and we soon felt completely at ease – particularly as some of them appeared to be conducting Summer Solstice rituals not unlike those that Ginnie had insisted we perform with her at dawn, before setting off. She had asked the relevant Powers for continuing fine weather, and they obliged – no doubt thanks to our hearty rendering of '*Let the sun shine in*', one of our favourite anthems.

'Oh man, feel the vibe….' said Sean – but once we'd selected our campsite he soon began to flex his shoulders tensely, a habit of his when the flow wasn't going his way. His branches refused to stay upright, because the ground was too hard to dig them in.

'Try it like this, sweetie.' Stella picked up a branch and leaned it diagonally against the side of the pick-up.

'Yeah, cool, I was thinking of that,' said Sean. He arranged the rest of the branches in the same way and tucked the tarpaulin around them. 'See, babe? That's what survival's all about. Adaptation. Innovation.' He pushed their foam mattress and sleeping bags inside and lay down.

Ginnie came tripping up the slope towards us. She was wearing a tiara of daisies and looked radiant. 'I knew I'd find you! I could sense that Lothlorien vibration.'

Vibrations were definitely the order of the day, not only psychic but aural. Music thrummed over the fields from an inviting structure which was topped with a roof like a kind of huge balloon. 'That's the main stage,' said Gogo.

Although we were longing to get closer to the action we had to wait while the adults went through tribal bonding rites with our immediate neighbours. Marjoram brewed up herbal tea on our camping gas stove and offered it to everyone with homemade bread: in return the neighbours gave us chocolate cake and whole-wheat ginger biscuits, which seemed to me a very good omen. Spliffs were circulated.

'Now kids,' said Gogo, when at last we set off to explore, 'here are some plans of the site, one for each of you. Stick together and stay with me and Marj. If anybody gets lost, just head back to our camp. We'll stop every so often to make sure you can all spot where it is.'

'That'll be easy – our nookie parlour's taller than the tents all round it.' Shine had a carrying voice; one of our female neighbours looked at her a bit doubtfully.

First we helped Erryk and Stella set up their stall, with Marjoram and Ginnie's produce on a folding table beside it. Then, as arranged, we met up with Zoë and Layla in the children's area. Layla had blue flowers drawn round her eyes and was carrying a stick with a silver star on the end. 'It's a magic wand,' she explained. 'The face-painting lady gave it to me because I look like a fairy.'

'There's just no hope for you, is there,' said Shine.

*

'Sean's right, it *is* cosmic,' sighed Rain happily as we settled into our makeshift beds, exhausted by all the excitement, loud music, and an extensive tour of the vegetarian food stalls. The next day promised even more treats, especially as Rick had arranged to introduce us to his friend's band. We fell asleep to the sound of Sean's snores. They shook the side of the pick-up, but they scarcely disturbed us.

Once again the morning dawned bright and summery. We were joined by Zoë and Layla for a leisurely breakfast of porridge with honey, after which we prepared to head off towards the heart of the Fayre. I'd been puzzled by the spelling of 'Fayre'. 'It's an old way of writing it,' said Marjoram. 'It's supposed to make it seem quaint and traditional.'

'Names are always better with a "y",' said Layla smugly.

'Well I've got one too,' said Jelly Bean.

'So've I,' I said.

'Yes, but not in the *middle*,' retorted Layla. 'I'm the only quaint and traditional one.'

'Thank God for that,' said Shine.

'Shut up and listen, gang,' called Gogo. 'There's probably going to be a lot more people here today, so it's even more important to stick to what I told you yesterday. Do you remember what that was?'

'Keep together, stay with you, head back to the camp if we get separated,' I said.

'Cool. Let's go.'

He was right about there being more people – crowds were streaming through the entrance and spreading everywhere – which is perhaps why no-one noticed when Jelly Bean peeled off from the group. We were heading over to inspect the alternative medicine stands, which Marjoram wanted to see before the music really got going, when all of a sudden I spotted Jelly Bean sprinting away to the left towards the other camping area on the far side of the site.

'The Bean! I'll go and get her!' I shouted, and ran off in the direction I expected to find her. But she'd vanished. I looked around and realised that the others were nowhere to be seen either.

It didn't worry me particularly, because I knew where they were going

– but I felt a certain responsibility towards Jelly Bean, whose wildness might get her into trouble, so I made my way further into the campground to look for her. She couldn't be that far away, I reasoned. Sure enough, she suddenly popped out of a tent in front of me.

'Bean! You know what Gogo said.'

'Oh, I wasn't lost. I'm never lost. I saw a monkey! A *real* monkey – but it's gone into a tent and I can't find which one.'

'You can't go poking your nose into every single tent. Come on, let's get back to the others.'

She followed me reluctantly, stopping now and then to peer behind an open tent flap.

But we both paused when we came across an especially long-haired and bead-laden hippie who was sitting cross-legged outside a tent and swaying rhythmically from side to side like Rick's metronome. His face was a grey-white colour and had an unhealthy sheen. Round rimless glasses magnified his pale blue eyes, which were staring straight at us.

'Children, children!' he called softly. 'Come, sit by me.'

He had stopped swaying, but was obviously off his head. 'I am a holy man,' he explained. 'How did you seek me out? Where have you come from?'

'Mars,' said Jelly Bean. We were used to stoned adults and quite enjoyed entering their fantasy lands from time to time.

The hippie looked suddenly alarmed. 'The Spiders! The Spiders from Mars! You've come back!'

'That's right.' Jelly Bean waggled her hands above her head.

'So many antennae...' The hippie looked as if he might faint. 'So many, so many antennae...'

I felt a giggle bubbling up but turned it into what I hoped was a friendly smile. 'It's OK, we're not poisonous or anything. We're just here to be sociable.'

'But how did you get here?'

'On our threads, of course,' said Jelly Bean. 'You just keep letting one out till you've slid all the way to Earth. It's quite quick.'

The hippie shook his head in wonderment. 'Then you are welcome. Let us drink to your coming!'

We nodded, as we were thirsty, and had seen the jug of juice on the grass next to him. He poured it carefully into three plastic beakers. It looked like Ribena, a rather opaque version because of the darker speckles in it, which I took to be pieces of some kind of fruit. Grapes, perhaps. We gulped it down.

It was indeed Ribena, but it had a peculiar aftertaste and Jelly Bean pulled a face. 'What's in it?'

'The Elixir of Life...'

At that moment a girl stuck her head through the tent flap. She was dishevelled and seemed half asleep.

'Hey Jonno, who you talking to? Oh... hi, kids.'

'Hi,' we chorused.

'Where's Pie-Face and Julie?'

Jonno waved vaguely. 'Elsewhere in the Galaxy. And these are not kids. They are Spiders from Mars.'

'God, you're hopeless.' Her eyes lit on the empty jug. 'Shit, have you finished all that off? You selfish prick! You were supposed to leave some for me.'

'He didn't drink it all – he gave most of it to us,' said Jelly Bean.

'WHAT?? I don't *believe* you...'

'It's true,' I said.

'Jonno, you stupid, *stupid* fuckwit...' The girl seemed about to burst into tears. She squatted down next to us. 'Kids, where are your parents?'

'Over there somewhere,' I said, and pointed. 'We're going to join them.' I could sense it was time to get away from these two.

'Listen.' The girl gripped our arms. 'Go *now*. Run. You better tell them – oh *fuck* – tell them you drank some whizzed-up mushrooms by mistake.'

We stared. 'What – dried magic ones?' asked Jelly Bean.

'Yes, yes... now GO.'

16. *INVADERS*

ONCE WE WERE out of sight of Jonno's tent we stopped running and stared at each other with dismay.

'How soon before we feel something?' asked Jelly Bean.

'I'm not sure...'

The psyllocybin mushroom was of course revered within Lothlorien. 'It's the gateway to other realms,' I'd heard Stella say. Most of the adults took the occasional trip, but I'd never paid much attention to the timetable. Sean always had a bag of mushrooms culled during the previous season and carefully dried; he liked to chop them up small and stuff them into a marmalade sandwich for breakfast, and although I was aware that he was usually far away by mid-morning I couldn't have pinpointed the moment when he actually took off. I thought of his trip at the fair the year before; the effect must have taken at least an hour to kick in – or was it less?

Even Sean wasn't that frequent a tripper; unlike marijuana, an everyday staple, mushrooms were for special occasions only.

'Your head's got to be in a really good place,' he said.

It had also been impressed upon us, by Sean and everyone else, that magic mushrooms were most definitely Not For Children; that an adult should have given us some came as a terrible shock. Perhaps he wouldn't have done so if he hadn't been under the influence – but all the same, no-one in Elfland would ever have been so irresponsible.

'Your brains aren't big enough yet,' Marjoram told us. 'You could do yourselves lasting psychological damage.'

'You might have a bad trip,' said Sean. 'Get blown into outer space and lose the way home.'

These words came back to me now.

'We must find the others and tell them,' I said. 'They'll know what to do. Perhaps there's something you can drink to make the effect less powerful.'

'I know what – let's try and throw up.' Jelly Bean stuck a finger down her throat.

'I can't stand puking.'

'Neither can I, but it's better than leaving all that stuff inside us, isn't it?'

So we headed for a patch of grass where there weren't too many tents or people, and did our best – without success.

'Maybe we should just go to the camp and lie down,' said Jelly Bean. 'Someone's sure to come looking for us there soon.'

It was hard to decide – in fact, it was hard to think clearly at all, and I began to panic. 'Camp,' I said finally.

We hadn't gone very far when my stomach began to churn alarmingly. 'Now I really *am* going to throw up,' I muttered, and turned away. I retched a bit, but the mushrooms remained resolutely inside me. Meanwhile the cramps were becoming more and more violent. I sat down, doubled over in agony, for what seemed like ages. Was I going to die?

Suddenly I remembered having seen a first aid place marked on the site plan that Gogo had given to each of us. I pulled it out of my jeans pocket and unfolded it. Oh shit, I thought helplessly, it's the wrong one. The piece of paper was covered with signs which didn't make any sense.

'Bean, can you look at this...' But Jelly Bean had disappeared again.

The pain in my gut had gone too, as quickly as it had come. Relief washed over me. Everything would be all right – Jelly Bean had gone to fetch the others – I could just lie down here and wait for them. And it was a beautiful day...

As I lowered my head to the ground I began to realise just *how* beautiful. I hadn't the faintest idea of where I was, but it didn't matter, because I was *part of the grass*. The sunlight shone fluorescent green through the long blades by my nose. I breathed it in – it smelt delicious. It began to stream into my blood. So this is what it feels like to photosynthesize, I mused, remembering Marjoram's botany lessons.

Enthralled, I watched a ladybird climb a stalk. So red and shiny! Such perfect black spots! Yet not a lady, nor a bird, so why...? People were confused, they'd muddled up the name with something else. Then it dawned on me: it didn't have a name at all, as far as *it* was concerned. It didn't need one.

I laughed and rolled over to stare at the sky, which had splintered into endless shifting patterns. This was fascinating – why hadn't I noticed clouds do that before?

'Are you OK?'

A woman's face swam above me, dissolving and reforming as if under water.

I gave her a big smile and sat up. 'Oh yes, I'm fine, thank you. Just enjoying the sun.' How fantastic to be able to utter these words – and obviously the right ones, because she smiled back and walked off.

The whole world was now shimmering with fine nets of coloured light – blue, pink, gold... Amazing. I glanced with interest at my sandalled foot with its grubby toes. Was all that strange meaty thing really attached to me? And what did 'me' mean, anyway?

From accounts of mushroom-eating that I've heard or read since, this loss of self is a common experience, and generally a restful one. I certainly found it so. And like me, many people seem to have an almost total recall of their trip. Even today, though I haven't thought about it for God knows how long, it emerges from some recess of my mind still glittering diamond-sharp.

It wasn't all ecstatic oneness with the universe. When I eventually stood up I had a moment of intense anxiety, unable to make any decision about what I should do next or where I should go. I was hot – should I change my clothes? Where was our camp? My sense of direction had completely deserted me. Then I realised that these things didn't matter, and I began to drift. But quite soon wave after wave of vile emotion began to crash over me – anger, hate, jealousy, guilt, fear; each was a different horrible colour – (bile-green, violent mauve...) – and full of spikes. They seemed to come out of nowhere, with no specific cause or object. I thought I was going to drown, so I buried myself in a hedge.

Just when I was sure I was going to pass out, some words of Rick's flashed before my eyes like a neon autocue. '*Emotions are just chemicals in the blood, and the mushrooms make those chemicals, so then you feel the emotions...*' I'm not at all sure about the accuracy of this information, but at the time it was immensely comforting. The lurid chimeras began to dissolve and I was overtaken by a soft, translucent euphoria. Now I felt hopeful and generous, so I extricated myself from the hedge, and saw that I had passed into a very different world. I began to notice countless extraordinary details around me: a blue skirt swirling like water in a rock pool on the beach; a blackbird *dancing* on a branch; needles of light sparking from a passing beard.

So I wandered on, in a state of what I can only describe as rapture. For how long? I can't say, because I'd lost all sense of time, but it must have been for a good hour or two – and all the while the others, who I'd completely forgotten about, were frantically searching for Jelly Bean and myself. I imagine both of us were moving around a good deal, but nowhere near the camp. And I wasn't always out in the open, as I was frequently invited into a tent or a caravan and offered food and drink. I was neither thirsty nor hungry, so I always declined. This turned out to be a mistake.

Quite often I was asked where my parents were. What a ludicrous question! I just beamed and pointed: 'Over there.' I was tall for my age and can't have appeared to be in any way lost or worried; I was still incredibly calm, a floating bubble, utterly content within my emptiness. I think it must have been this serene and ego-free aura which made so many people want to talk to me. And they all wanted to tell me about their lives. It was very, very odd – so much strangeness, so many problems. I listened and smiled benevolently as their stories wove intricate glistening tapestries.

There were other times when I was on my own once more and the music vibrated and sparkled through me like audible light. But each time I tried to approach it the sound started to make my bones ache, so I moved away again. At some point I realised that I was sweating a lot and thought it would be a good thing to have another lie-down, so I found a patch of long soft grass beneath a tree which grew by what must have been one of the boundaries of the site. The universe throbbed and unveiled its mysteries one after another. I looked on and marvelled, and didn't feel the need to move any more.

It was here that Marjoram eventually found me.

'How nice to see you!' I said sincerely, not yet understanding either what she was doing there or why she seemed so distraught. Of course she grasped straight away that I was in a very much altered state.

'Curly! Have you been smoking or something?'

I smiled. I *was* a smile. 'We drank Ribena with mushrooms in it. Jonno the Holy Man gave it to us. We didn't know – his girlfriend told us afterwards. He thought we were spiders.'

'Christ Almighty...'

'It's OK, I'm fine,' I assured her.

'You don't look it.'

It was true that I was feeling a little weak.

'You need water,' said Marjoram, ever practical, and passed me an opaque blue flask. I sat up slowly.

'Drink it, don't stare at it!' she urged, as I gazed entranced at the light playing on the plastic surface. 'Have you drunk anything since that bloody Ribena?'

I shook my head.

'And I bet you haven't eaten either.'

'I'm not hungry.'

'Come on, let's get you back to the camp.' She helped me to my feet.

Immediately my head filled up with a thick mist and I sagged towards the ground. Marjoram sat me down again and gently pushed my head down on to my knees.

After a while the mists cleared. 'I'm all right,' I said, 'just a bit wobbly.'

'Hang on to me.'

We made it to within sight of our camp – which I recognised with some relief – and then I collapsed a second time. Nothingness overtook me, though in quite a pleasant way.

When I regained consciousness I was stretched out on my back. I observed that the clouds were behaving normally again. Turning on to my side I saw I was wrapped in a blanket on the grass next to Gogo and Marjoram's tent. Beside me, similarly swaddled but lying on her front, was Jelly Bean. She was making clicking noises.

'She's talking to insects,' said Stella, who was watching over her.

I understood entirely.

'Mother Ginnie's going to freak when she finds out,' said Sean. 'So will Father Bill.' Bill and Ginnie had been spending the day with some of their mysterious Contacts to whom no-one else seemed to have access.

'Don't tell them,' said Loose.

'They'll know,' said Rick. 'The kids'll still be weird tomorrow. Maybe longer.'

I didn't care.

It was Loose who'd found Jelly Bean, having had the bright idea that she would probably be up a tree. After several fruitless arboreal searches she had spotted a pair of small bare feet hanging below a leafy cluster of branches. Hooting noises came from behind the leaves where Jelly Bean was calling to the owls.

Our neighbours wandered up. They'd been watching a band performing on the main stage. 'Wow, guys! You should've been there!'

Gogo explained.

'Luckily I don't think they had a full adult dose,' he finished. There followed a suitably horrified conversation about the fucking imbecile who'd... etc. I felt quite removed from their horror.

'Eat this.' Marjoram had made me an egg-and-tomato sandwich.

At first it felt strange and unnecessary to have food in my mouth, but gradually it became more interesting, especially when I was given an orange and some fruitcake.

'Is it dinnertime?' I asked.

'It soon will be. You were lost for ages.'

'I was just somewhere else.'

And now I'm *here*, here in this unreal present, wishing that what I can see sashaying across the lawn could be just another hallucination. No such luck.

*

'I knew you were here. I've just been too busy to come over. Sorry.'

'Don't be.'

In my head I'm still at Glastonbury, floating back down into my usual self, but not quite there yet. So how can I cope with this woman in any lucid and rational way?

'Divorce takes up so much bloody time... Ever done it?'

'No.'

'Well don't. Especially not with a total bastard like Terry Evans.'

'I'm not really likely to.'

'Witty as ever, aren't you?' She looked around. 'Nice garden. Sit out here a lot?'

'Yes.'

'How much longer? Before they let you out, I mean.'

'I don't know.'

She stepped closer and narrowed her eyes. She seemed to be wearing less make-up than usual. A long swathe of black hair flopped over one shoulder. It's grown.

'You're looking pretty good. Relatively speaking. Can't you walk without those things yet?' She pointed to the crutches leaning against the back of the long chair where I'm sitting with my feet up. I shook my head.

'So what's still to fix?' she asked.

'A knee. A foot. The odd internal organ. A few nerves.'

'Nerves?'

'I'm told they haven't all knitted together as they should.'

'Knit one, purl one. Yeah, you don't want any dropped stitches.' She gave a hard little laugh. 'That's what I've got – too many frigging dropped stitches. Mental ones though. I feel like I'm unravelling.'

'You don't look as if you are.'

'Thanks for the compliment. But looks can lie.'

Her feelings of falling apart were not a subject I wanted to explore. I changed tack.

'And they're still checking me for brain damage,' I lied. 'I may have a touch of psychological... impairment.'

'Such as?'

'Oh... I sometimes get very violent for no reason. I tried to strangle a nurse the other day.'

She looked at me sceptically. 'So you've got a bright future as a serial killer.'

'Probably.'

'Seriously though – what really happens when you leave here? Business as usual?'

'I expect so.'

'Looking forward to that?'

'What about you – I mean after your divorce?'

'Hey, a question about me for a change! Progress at last.' She cocked her head on one side. 'Well now. I might just go back to Australia. Not Sydney though. That's where I'm from, but it's got too expensive. Byron Bay, maybe. Been there?'

I said nothing.

'Used to be a just a really long beach with a few hippies and surfers. Now it's full of New Age rich people. You can make money out of those guys. I could open a little shop – selling magic crystals and all that shit.'

I shut my eyes and willed her to go away.

'You hate me, don't you?' she said brightly. I opened my eyes again and blinked.

She laughed. 'Don't look so surprised. I'm not a mind-reader – you're just crap at hiding what's going on in there.' She pointed at my forehead. 'And you're stuck with me today. I didn't drive all the way here just to turn round and go back again. Besides, you make me forget my own problems.'

'So glad to be of help.'

'Well you are, even if you don't mean to be.' She sat down on the grass and kicked off her sandals – she was wearing high heels as usual, this time topped with a lattice of thin black and gold straps. 'Nice, eh? They're new. I needed a touch of retail therapy.' From a big straw hold-all she pulled out a series of brown paper bags. 'Your fruit supply. Melon, strawbs, flat peaches... cute, aren't they? Like pincushions. But they taste better.'

Pincushions... Do people still use pincushions? I saw one in my mind's eye – whose? It was covered in dark red velvet, faded and balding in places. Someone was taking it out of my hand: 'That's not to play with, Curly. You might hurt yourself.' Erryk, guiding me away from Wing's sewing box. A very ancient memory.

I accepted a flat peach. It was delicious. She took one as well and we chewed in silence, until she tossed her stone away and began to twist little clumps of grass between her fingers. 'You haven't met my daughter, have you?'

'No.'

'I hate doing this to her... But there's no alternative.'

'You could stay married – live separate lives or something.'

She shook her head. 'I don't want her growing up around a bloke like that. He's toxic.'

'I don't seem to be having much success at taking your mind off things.'

'Oh, sod you.' She stared off into the distance and then abruptly turned back to me. 'You might find this hard to believe, but I used to be quite a nice person. Before I landed myself with that shit of a husband.'

'So why did you?'

'I fancied him like crazy at the time. Lust can make you stupid.' A new expression flickered across her face and for a moment she seemed fractionally softer, or at least less brittle. 'The one good thing that came out of it is Melanie. That's my daughter.'

'His daughter too, surely.'

'She's nothing like him at all. Thank God.' The softness disappeared as she forced her features into a wide artificial smile. 'OK then, change of subject. Shall we have a nice chat about the weather? That's what English people like doing, isn't it? Or how about that -' she pointed to the exercise book on the low table beside me, open but turned over. 'Tell me about your kids' story. Is that what you're writing still?'

'Yes.'

'Must be pretty long by now.'

'It passes the time.'

'There's something you're not telling me, isn't there?'

'I don't see why I should tell you anything at all, actually.'

'Because, *actually*, I'm interested.'

'Why?'

'Christ. You're bloody hopeless. I don't know why I bother.'

'Neither do I.'

She glared. 'Righto. I might as well have a siesta then. I'm totally wiped out.' She lay down with her back to me. 'Just ignore me, why don't you.'

This proved impossible. I picked up my exercise book but soon realised I couldn't concentrate with Jeanette lying there only a couple of metres away. So I closed my eyes again. I tried at least to organise my thoughts, which were darting chaotically, like bats. But I must have dozed, because when I next looked she was no longer there. On the cover of my exercise book was a message scribbled in red felt pen: '*C u soon. I promise to be in a better mood next time, maybe u 2 with a bit of luck, you sarky bastard. And by the way u have a very musical snore.'*

A quick glance around me reveals no trace of her. So she's definitely gone – but she's left an unsavoury aftertaste. Am I really a sarcastic bastard? It's not how I've ever thought of myself. She just brings it out in me. And no-one's ever told me that I snored, either. Well stuff her, as Ash would have said; I've got better things to think about than Jeannette Evans. So I pick up my biro and scribble over her message and then stare out across the garden. Leaves are shifting in the breeze and the sky is the rich bright post-card blue of spring. In a few months it will be dulled by that enervating summer heat-haze, a blend of humidity and dust and pollution. And where will I be then? Does it matter?

Down by the rose bushes a nurse is chatting to the gardener – chatting him up, to be more exact. I can tell from her body language. She's not exactly a beauty, but she's lively and smiles easily, so I'd say she has a good chance of success. I watch them as I'd watch something on television which is vaguely interesting but of no relevance. I've already said that the present doesn't seem real: in fact the whole world I'm inhabiting now, both post- and pre-accident, no longer seems to have anything to do with me at all. Only the past does.

That sounds maudlin and melodramatic, but I don't feel that way – I feel remarkably light and weightless, in spite of my less than perfect physical state. It's just that the past is all I can currently be sure of, the only thing that prevents me from floating off into a state of semi-insanity.

So I turn the exercise book over and am back in that summer of '79.

As yet, there was absolutely no sign of the dark clouds which were beginning to gather below the horizon of Lothlorien. The first one was about to come into view.

*

'Bugger me. That must've done your head in.' Blue stared at me closely.

The fair was back, to our great delight, and we'd been itching to recount the tale of GLOG and the mushrooms. Blue's shock reaction was very satisfying.

'Sure you're not going schizo or anything?'

'We're OK,' said Jelly Bean. 'We're tough.'

'Micky had a mate who used to do mushrooms and he started hearing voices and smashing up his mum.'

'Well, we only had a smallish glass each. Maybe if we'd had more...'

'You're fucking lucky.'

I did feel lucky – or privileged, rather – set apart in some way. I'd had magic mushrooms, my brain had survived unharmed as far as I could tell, and I felt I'd discovered many, many things, though I couldn't begin to describe them properly. But I knew that the adults understood – all but Bill and Ginnie, that is, as it had been decided that this was one event they really didn't need to know about, and luckily they hadn't guessed.

Jelly Bean and I had been grateful to the others for being sympathetic and for not making jokes about our experience – also for not going on too much about all that we'd missed at Glastonbury. On the day following our trip we'd both been pretty feeble, jittery and irritable, so had stayed in our camp and dozed a lot, always with someone else present in case either of us had a flash-back and freaked out. Jelly Bean had plenty of them. During each one she was back in the tree, deep in conversation with some kind of fauna.

'Don't go!' she shrieked as the visions faded.

'Shut it,' I snapped.

Even now, several weeks later, she still got an odd look in her eyes and I knew she was remembering. But otherwise she seemed quite sane, or at least no different from usual. Layla, however, remained wary of her for some time. 'She could turn into a big vole or something,' she said. 'Or a rat that bites.'

'No she couldn't,' said Shine.

'Don't worry darling, I'll protect you,' said Blue.

His relationship with Layla had taken a leap forward this year. 'He's much better at kissing now,' she told us. 'His auntie's been teaching him.'

'Triple yuk,' said Jelly Bean. The twins and I shared this feeling up to a point, but it was nonetheless mixed with admiration for Blue's new advanced talents. It was presumably these which had caused Layla to relegate Luke Skywalker to the same drawer as the Sindy doll.

'I suppose I ought to start learning those things,' said Rain. 'But I can't think who with.'

'Blue's aunt might still be available,' said Shine rather caustically.

'Nah, she's in Yarmouth with her new fella,' said Blue.

It was a fine day. The six of us were sprawled on the yellowing grass of Middington Common under a tree, just beyond the edge of the fair but not far from Blue's trailer. His mother Cynthia had given us some plastic beakers and a big thermos of chilled orange juice, which we were consuming along with the last fragments of my birthday cake. I'd reached double figures just a day or two earlier, much to my delight; the cake had been particularly large and delicious, cooked in the earth oven to a new recipe of Marjoram's.

'You're too sweaty,' said Layla, and lifted her head from where it had been resting on Blue's chest.

'Not my fault, darling. Fancy a nice cold shower in Micky's trailer? You and me together?'

While Layla was considering this proposition I caught sight of a small group of Goths emerging from the fairground. Blue had seen them too.

'Hey – in't that your big sister and her mates?'

Layla grimaced with disgust. 'Just ignore them. They won't want to see us, anyway.'

But now El detached herself from the others and began to stride purposefully in our direction.

'Looks like a bloody daddy-long-legs, don't she,' observed Blue. Layla turned on to her stomach and buried her head in his chest again, sweat obviously preferable to the sight of her sister.

'What's the matter?' I asked, as she approached and stood over us, lowering. She was wearing opaque white lenses in her eyes which covered the irises; only the pupils showed, small black dots.

'I just saw Sean and Stella on the dodgems. They said you'd probably be somewhere round here.' She sat down and picked a dry stalk which she began to chew. Her presence was so unexpected that we all felt a little uneasy. The eyes didn't help. At least she wasn't wearing her vampire teeth.

'Something you ought to know,' she said finally.

'Well?' said Shine.

'The Middington Skins. Know who I mean?'

We did. They were a group of five or six, boys not much older than El and her friends but far, far tougher-looking. We recognised them as the same pair of skinheads who had taunted Sean at the shooting range the previous year. If we caught sight of them in town we always avoided getting too close.

'They're going to attack Lothlorien,' said El casually.

Everyone sat up, even Layla, and stared at her with disbelief.

'They can't possibly know about Lothlorien,' said Shine.

'Well they do. It's not exactly on another planet, even if it feels that way. Loads of people have heard a bit about it, even if they don't know the name. And the skins know where it is.'

'How?' squealed Layla.

'They've got scooters. They could've followed Stella back from the shop one day, at least as far as the Lodge. They were talking about her and Sean. 'That's fucking Goldilocks and his blond tart from the hippie shop'.'

'*Where* did you hear them talking?' asked Rain.

'In the queue for the dodgems, just now. They're pissed as farts so they weren't exactly keeping their voices down. The youngest one, he's only fifteen but he's huge, and he's a fucking nutcase with it. I know because he goes to my school.'

'Did he recognise you?' asked Shine.

'Course not. I don't look like this at school, do I? Anyway, he's not even in my class, they kept him down a year.'

'He doesn't know – that you sort of live in Lothlorien?'

'They think it's just hippies in there. They reckon Goths live in the cemetery.' She gave a vampirish laugh. 'And by the way, next Friday night, that's when they're going to turn up. After the pubs shut.'

I felt a surge of relief. 'The Lodge gates are closed in the evenings. You can't get in without a key. If you try and climb over an alarm goes off.'

'They won't go that way, dickhead. They'll go over the wall.'

'It's too high,' objected Shine. 'You can't carry ladders on scooters. Anyway, what about the broken glass? That's all the way along the top.'

'Not where that tree fell on it a couple of years back. When there was that big storm, remember? It's never been repaired. Down by that little ruin. There's a gap big enough to get through – you wouldn't have to climb much. And it's close to the road. They've done their homework, they know about that place.'

'But they won't know how to get from there to Lothlorien itself,' I pointed out.

'Oh yes they will. They were talking about the path and how they'd need torches to get to it. Maybe they've been in already and done a bit of a recce.'

It had been ages since El had really talked to any of us, but in the shock of her revelation I didn't register how odd it was to hear her speak at length. What I felt at that moment was an electric current of pure fear. Up till then I'd felt completely protected within Lothlorien. Arjuna, Malcolm, Janet: none of them had managed to destroy this illusion of inviolability. Rather the reverse, as after each episode our community seemed if anything to become stronger. And now, a handful of skinheads was out to destroy it – and *might have already been inside*... That was the most frightening thing of all.

'Do they want to kill us?' whispered Rain.

'Course not, stupid. They just want to trash the place. They reckon at that time of night everyone will be too stoned to do anything.'

'But *why*?'

'They must be sexually repressed,' said Shine. 'Or from very unhappy homes.'

'Just thick as shit, more like,' said El. 'Thick and bored. They need a bit of action to occupy their tiny minds.'

'Will they have weapons?' I asked anxiously.

'Knives and chains maybe. Knuckledusters. And their boots, of course. They wouldn't have much trouble kicking down a caravan wall.'

'What are we going to *do*?' wailed Layla.

'Tell Bill, of course,' said Shine. 'He'll ring the police and they'll send a patrol car.'

Blue shook his head. 'The skins'd just come back another time. Besides, the sharpies wouldn't believe you.'

'They'd believe Bill.'

'Might do – but they wouldn't just sit there on the road in their car. You'd have 'em crawling all over the place. No-one wants that, do they? Pity to have to pull up half your Garden just when it's coming along so nicely.'

'But what else can we do?' I was numb with alarm.

'You gotta put the frighteners on 'em. So as to show 'em you're more dangerous than they are.'

'But we're not, are we?' said Rain helplessly.

Blue rolled his eyes and pulled on his lower lip, as he always did when he was thinking hard. 'Got any shooters?'

'Shooters?'

'Shotguns. Rifles. That sort of thing.'

'Of course not!' Shine was horrified.

'What, not even Ashley?'

'No! We're all totally anti-violence.'

'Pity...'

'But Shine, sometimes you've *got* to be violent,' said Jelly Bean. 'If it's self-defence. I'll use my bow and arrows. There'll be a moon on Saturday night – I'll easily be able to hit them. In the throat.'

Layla gasped. 'That might *kill* them.'

'Yes, they'll probably bleed to death.'

'That would make you a *murderer*.'

'You can't risk that,' said Blue. 'Then you'd really be in trouble. I'm just talking about giving 'em a proper scare. Not shooting *at* them.'

'What about a catapult? I'm good with that too.'

'Nah, you'd still be doing too much damage. Mind you... I spose if you used something a bit softer than stones...'

'Ping pong balls? We've got some of those.'

'*Too* soft.'

'Potatoes!' said Jelly Bean suddenly. We all stared at her, but Blue nodded in approval. 'That's more like it... not too big though, and not too small neither.'

'We've got all sizes.'

'Reckon you could hit 'em in the basket?' He pointed.

'The goolies? Course I can.'

'What a terrible waste of food,' said Shine.

'No it isn't,' said Jelly Bean. 'We can pick them up afterwards.'

'I'm not eating anything that's touched a skinhead,' said Layla. 'Especially not *there*.'

For once Blue ignored her. 'OK then, we'll go with the spud attack – but it's still not enough.' He pulled at his lip again. 'And you haven't even got dogs, have you. Not real ones.'

I thought about Chip. 'No, we haven't.'

'Hang on a sec!' Blue brightened. 'Micky's got dogs. Fierce buggers. Least, they are when he wants 'em to be.'

Layla shivered.

'They wouldn't hurt *you*, gorgeous. They'll be eating out of your hand if Mick tells 'em to. He's got 'em well trained.' He looked slowly round at each of us to make sure we were all paying full attention. We were, even El. 'Now I *think*, if we all *cooperate*, we can make a plan. But we don't tell no-one else, right? *Nobody*. Only Micky.'

17. *ILL MET BY MOONLIGHT*

FRIDAY EVENING: THE moon was a couple of days past full; from the top of the Sheepfield we watched it rise over the rolling hills to the east.

'It looks like an apricot,' said Rain.

'I'd like to taste a little bit,' said Layla. 'It might be sweet, mightn't it?'

'No,' said Shine. 'It's just rock.'

'Seaside rock's sweet.'

'Not as sweet as you are, darling.' Blue patted Layla's head. 'I'll ask my dad to get you a chunk, if you like.'

'Could he really? A piece of the moon?'

'Course. He can get hold of anything you want, my old man.'

'But how would he go there?'

'No need to *go*. Those astronauts brought bits back, didn't they.'

'That's true,' said Rain, 'but they must all be in places like science labs, for research. Does your father know any scientists?'

'Oh, my dad knows anyone he needs to know,' said Blue airily.

'Can he really get *anything*?' asked Jelly Bean.

'Put it this way – I've never known him *not* get something. People ask him for all kinds of stuff. Mind you, they have to pay for it. Nice little earner for him in the winter.'

'Could he get me an elephant?'

'Easy. Whole herd, if you want. Ask me something difficult.'

Jelly Bean thought for a moment. 'A driving licence?'

'I said *difficult*. That's even easier. He's always getting asked for driving licences.'

Like the twins and myself, Jelly Bean was learning to drive on Ashley's pick-up. We spent happy hours swerving around the gravelled parking place, which was permitted when the majority of the vehicles were Outside. Being the tallest I could reach the controls more easily than the others could.

Blue looked sceptically at Jelly Bean. 'You're too small though. You'd get stopped if you went out on the road.'

'No I wouldn't! I always put loads of cushions on the seat.'

'So how do you push on the pedals then?'

'Ash lends me a big mallet.'

'Blimey. You could be in the circus, you could.'

'Yes! I'd let all the lions and tigers out of their cages and bring them here, to be free.'

'They'd eat the sheep,' I said. 'And Chip.'

Blue guffawed. 'And then they'd have a good old chomp on you lot.'

'Oh, do stop being silly, all of you!' shouted Layla. 'We're supposed to be *serious* tonight.'

'You started it,' said Jelly Bean.

'*You* started it. Talking about elephants.'

'BE QUIET!' snapped Shine.

We were all, in fact, in a state of high suspense, although we'd been trying to hide it while we ate our picnic dinner and watched the night fall. Only Blue seemed his usual calm and jovial self. He must have been used to this type of situation.

He pressed the button on his watch to light up the dial. He always wore this watch, which we found impressive but strange, as within Lothlorien watches were not a normal accessory at all. Bill and several of the others had one, but only used them Outside, because, in Ginnie's words: 'In here we are beyond time.' But not, apparently, beyond invading hordes.

Blue stood up. 'Let's get moving.'

*

El had been right: the skins had already been inside. We'd seen that clearly enough while we were going over the plan in detail on the previous day. Vegetation had been roughly chopped away and flattened all the way from the gap in the wall, over the fallen tree and up to the path – the path which ran from the ruined chapel through the stand of beeches and then on towards the caravans. It was a truly terrifying thing to see.

This evening, as we approached the ruin, dread descended on me like a dark fog. We'd gone quietly down the Sheepfield and climbed through the bottom fence into the woods well beyond the caravans, so no-one would see us pass; as far as the others were concerned we were still up the hill admiring the night sky, hoping to spot a few shooting stars, stragglers from the shower of two nights before. Bedtime was a fluid, indeed virtually non-existent concept in Lothlorien, so we knew no-one would be worried if we were still outside late at night. So perhaps they'll find our corpses in the morning, I thought grimly.

We heard a rustle in the undergrowth near the wall, and a low growl. The light of a torch flickered among the leaves. My heart gave a bound.

'Good, Mick's here,' said Blue.

The two dogs emerged on to the path, each on a long chain lead, followed a moment later by their master. He was wearing a policeman's uniform with a flat peaked cap. We knew he was going to be thus attired, but it still seemed surreally incongruous.

'Evening all. Ready for the fun?'

'I am,' said Jelly Bean. 'I don't know about the others. Hello Killer, hello Hulk.' She tickled the dogs under the chin and they licked her hand.

Blue had taken us to meet these two already, a couple of days earlier. 'So's they know you're family,' he'd explained.

To me they appeared utterly fearsome, twin Hounds of the Baskervilles. Their pointed ears had shot up like arrow-heads when they saw us entering Micky's trailer. They looked hideously alert and ready to pounce.

'Dobies,' said Micky affectionately. 'Best guardians in the world. Let 'em give you all a sniff.'

'Do they bite?' whispered Layla.

'Only if I tell 'em to. Done your fair share of biting, haven't you my beauties? Come on then, give us a smile.' The Dobermans opened their mouths and displayed their ghastly fangs. 'This here's Killer, that one's Hulk.' He slid his hand between Killer's canines. 'See? Wouldn't hurt a fly, normally. They only go for the baddies. So you're safe as houses.'

'How do they know we're goodies?' asked Rain.

'Cause I'm being friendly with you.'

I remained doubtful; tonight I stood well back. The brightening moonlight glistened wetly in their eyes.

'Where's the car?' asked Blue.

'Up a track, other side of the road.'

'Goths here yet?'

'Yeah, down by the wall.'

'What about their bikes?'

'Hidden. Skins won't see a thing.'

We hadn't expected El to offer much in the way of support. But I suppose that in spite of all her defamatory remarks about Lothlorien she was secretly quite attached to us – although of course she would never have said as much. 'Skins are total scumbags,' she told us flatly. 'They hate Goths so we hate them back.' She'd insisted that her two best mates, the builder's sons, should be involved as well; Blue and Micky had reluctantly agreed on condition that they swore an oath of secrecy.

'Swear on the blood of your vampire ancestors,' Micky had commanded, which we thought was rather clever of him. 'And don't forget I know where you live. So do these two.' He was referring to Hulk and Killer.

Now, as I was looking with some apprehension at the two Dobermans, they suddenly swivelled their heads towards the wall, ears pricked.

'A car!' Rain exclaimed – and sure enough, we could hear it approaching along the road from the direction of Middington. There was very little traffic on that road at night.

Layla squeaked in alarm. 'It's them.'

'Nah, they'll be coming on their scooters,' said Blue.

The car passed by without stopping.

'Shouldn't be long now though,' said Micky. 'It's past closing time. Better get into position.'

Blue gave Layla a squeeze. 'Off you go, love.' She ran some way back up the path, her job being to alert the adults in the event of something going drastically wrong; this would be signalled by a long rising whistle from Blue. I confess that I envied her being so relatively far out of harm's way.

'Get your stockings on,' said Micky. He took them from his pocket and handed them round. They were black and shiny – his girlfriend's? Solemnly we pulled them over our heads until we were able to see out of the two small slits cut in each leg, and then knotted the foot section so that it wouldn't dangle down and hide our view. With our faces contorted into squashed masks we looked rather comfortingly horrible. The ladders that had begun to form beneath each eye-hole gave the impression that our eyes were oozing grotesque tears. Rain giggled nervously. I began to feel a little better. The dogs bounced eagerly on their toes and wagged their stumpy tails.

At a nod from Micky, Jelly Bean shinned up the tree which she had calculated would give her the best view of the path. A large leather bag was slung on her shoulder.

'Now into the bushes, you lot,' said Micky. 'I'll make sure the wires are covered up.'

He had with him two rolls of electrical wire coated in black plastic. He passed one to Rain and one to Blue. Rain gave the end to his sister, then each twin backed away from opposite sides of the path until they had melted into the darkness. Blue silently handed me the end of his roll and we did the same, a few yards further up. My place was beneath one of the yews. I crouched down, heart beating wildly, willing my fear to go away.

We heard Micky sweeping woodland debris over the sections of wire which lay across the path. The dogs made horrid snuffling noises. Then all of a sudden they became dead quiet; they'd detected the sound of the scooters advancing up the road.

'OK gang,' called Micky cheerfully. 'Let the magic begin.'

The scooters drew to a halt – three of them. That meant up to six skinheads. Huge, violent skinheads, armed.

Laughter, muffled but nasty, floated up into the woods. I forced myself to think of what Blue had said earlier: 'They'll be well tanked up and we'll be stone cold sober. So that means we'll have one over 'em already. And don't forget David and Goliath.'

'Who?'

'Oh yeah, you wouldn't know, would you. You're all Hari bloody Krishna, or whatever it is Ginnie goes on about.' He laughed. 'So here's a bit of proper religion for you. David was this midget in the Bible who killed a giant because he was cleverer. Which just goes to show that it's brains what count.'

As I waited under the yew-tree, my brains felt about as efficient as cold scrambled eggs. But then, as the drunken little group began to push their way through the gap in the wall, their torches flashing haphazardly, my fear gave way to a surge of pure territorial fury. I held tight to my end of the wire and stopped thinking altogether as the adrenalin took over.

Swearing and sniggering, the skinheads stumbled up the makeshift passage they had hacked out during their reconnoitring foray. The one in the lead reached the path and turned on to it. ''Ere we go, 'ere we go, 'ere we go,' he chanted under his breath, and the others chortled vilely and spat on the ground. They were very close now. Although I couldn't see them clearly through the drooping branches of the yew I crouched as low as I could in case one of their torches lit up my hiding place.

A low hoot sounded from the trees. One of the skinheads grunted in alarm. 'What the fuck?'

'Owl, you plonker,' hissed the leader.

But in fact it was Jelly Bean's first signal. I yanked with all my force on the wire and felt Blue's simultaneous tug on the other end. The leading skinhead tripped, cursed and fell with a thud. I saw the glint of a knife-blade flying through the air. A second hoot: the next skin went down as the twins pulled up their own trip-wire. The other four froze – and then Jelly Bean's potatoes began to zip down from the trees in rapid succession. I can still remember that sound of the slap of spud on jeans. Judging from the squeals and curses quite a few landed right on target. And then total mayhem broke out as Micky let Hulk and Killer off their chains.

They didn't bark – they just snarled and leapt. They seemed to be everywhere at once, monsters from hell. There were sounds of fabric ripping, mixed with shrieks and shouts and the foulest language I'd ever heard. Some of the skinheads must have been trying to lash out at the dogs with knives or chains, because Micky called out menacingly: 'Drop those or they'll bite. I mean *really* bite. Fancy losing a hand or two?'

'Bugger me, a fucking cop...'

Micky gave a soft whistle and the dogs drew back a little, panting and growling. The skinheads were all on the ground by now, their torches scattered and their weapons surrendered. One of them was moaning and vomiting. There was a foul smell in the air.

'Shit your pants, did you? Better run off home quick and get your mum to clean you up. Oh, and you can take those boots off and leave them here. Not just him – all of you.'

With a muttered chorus of obscenities they untied their laces, slowly at first and then a lot more rapidly as Micky clicked his tongue and the dogs began to advance again. He tossed the boots into a patch of brambles. 'Now get the fuck out of here. If I catch you again you're dead. Dog food.' The skinheads struggled to their feet and fled, trampling through the undergrowth and hollering as they trod on stones and caught their already shredded jeans on thorns and branches.

Once they managed to reach the gap in the wall a final surprise was waiting for them. A loud and hideous wailing struck up as the three Goths, stocking-headed like us but holding red torch-lights in their open mouths, charged after them on to the road. They let the six of them make it to their scooters, but once the engines were starting to rev they darted over and grabbed each passenger round his neck with one slime-coated hand. The scooters jerked forward and the Goths backed off, screeching with unearthly laughter. In the meantime Micky had set off the police siren he'd brought along.

Once the scooters were out of earshot he turned it off and we all converged on the path, pulling off the stockings and giggling with hysterical relief. So many hours – days! – of planning, suspense, foreboding: all over in a matter of a few minutes.

Hulk and Killer were sitting on their haunches looking disgustingly pleased with themselves, tongues lolling out like giant slugs, while Micky collected up the abandoned weapons and torches.

'Well, that turned out all right, didn't it? You done a good job, all of you.' It was as if he were talking about an event innocuous as a garden fête. He took off his policeman's cap. 'OK folks, time to drop the awnings.

You ought to get back and explain to your elders and betters what that little bit of noise was all about. Tell 'em it was a cop car chasing a few drunks on scooters.' He put the leads back on the dogs and patted them affectionately. 'Bloody stars, you are. Better be getting along so you can have a few extra bikkies, eh? Coming with me, bruv?'

'No way. Haven't said goodnight to my girlfriend yet. I'll get a lift into town tomorrow.'

'All right then. Bona nochy.'

*

While I was setting that down on paper I realised that my heart was pounding all over again; I don't think I've ever felt so afraid again since that night. I didn't see the whole operation, obviously – my account is made up of everyone's slightly different version, replayed a hundred times afterwards. Blue and Micky brushed the whole thing off as if it had just been a bit of a laugh. No doubt for them it was, but we knew that without them our world would have become a disaster zone, and we were intensely grateful.

'Gotta help my blood brother,' said Blue cheerfully.

Those of the adults who'd heard the commotion down by the ruin that night – (only Ginnie, Marjoram, Gogo, and Pete, the others being already too deeply asleep or simply absent) – appeared to accept the explanation we gave them when we got back to the caravans. They were already outside with torches.

'Was that racket anything to do with you?' asked Gogo.

'No – there were some drunk guys on the road,' I said, trying hard to keep my voice steady. It wasn't easy to act normally, and we didn't like having to lie, but even Shine understood that for once it was necessary.

Gogo frowned. 'It sounded closer than that. As if it was coming from the woods.'

'There were lots of them. Really loud. I think they were having a fight.'

'I thought you were all up in the Sheepfield,' Marjoram said.

'We were,' said Blue, looking very innocent. 'But when we heard a bit of bother we run straight down to see what was happening.'

'In case there was someone who was hurt,' added Layla, opening her eyes extremely wide.

'We couldn't really see much,' said Rain. 'There was an awful lot of yelling, though. Really rude – worse than Ash.'

'Yeah, they were totally off their tits,' said Blue.

'*I* saw them!' Jelly Bean said blithely. 'I climbed up a tree near the wall. There were six boys on scooters, wobbling all over the place and shouting stuff. Then a police car came and chased them down the road. I expect they got arrested.'

Ginnie sighed. 'How very sad. It makes me realise how *lucky* we are here. We're so *protected* from that kind of thing.'

Only Pete looked a touch sceptical, but he didn't say anything.

Very shortly afterwards a strange thing happened. We were in the woods with Gogo, learning about lichens I think, when we heard the sound of chain-saws which seemed to be coming from somewhere near the ruin. No-one in Lothlorien owned a chain-saw, not even Ashley: 'I'm a carpenter and joiner, not a sodding lumberjack.' Besides, Ginnie thought they were barbaric. So we walked down to investigate.

A couple of men were sawing up the big fallen tree which had been the cause of the breach in the boundary wall. They were wearing T-shirts which bore the words 'TOM'S TREE SURGEONS' in large green letters, and we could see the roof of their lorry which was parked on the roadside.

'Owner of the place needs to have this cleared away,' they replied to Gogo's inquiry. 'Can't get the wall patched up otherwise.'

On the following evening Jelly Bean brought us the news that the repairs were already complete. Our Lord had evidently engaged a reputable builder to do the job, as weathered bricks had been used which blended in well with the old ones. New shards of glass had been cemented on to the top.

'Yes, that did need doing,' said Bill when we told him. 'It was certainly something of an eyesore, from the road. And possibly an invitation to trespassers.'

'Oh, I don't think so,' said Ginnie. 'It's terribly jungly down there. I can't imagine anyone wanting to battle through all that.'

We managed to borrow her I Ching book on some pretext or other – she never really liked lending it to us – and settled down to a session of divination by candlelight in Layla's bedroom. Layla always presided, putting on a suitably priestessy voice to read out the often baffling pronouncements of the oracle. She was good at interpreting them, too. Ginnie had shown us how she herself consulted the I Ching by means of her sacred set of dried yarrow stalks, but she wouldn't lend them to us 'until you're older.' In any case, we preferred the far quicker method of throwing Zoë's three ancient Chinese coins.

Sitting cross-legged on the floor, we concentrated hard on our question as Layla took the coins from their jewelled pill-box and threw them reverently in the air one by one. We peered at them closely as they fell. 'One moving line,' muttered Shine. Layla searched in the book for the corresponding hexagram. "*The Taming Force... small restraint*", she intoned. "*Progress and success... dense clouds, but no rain coming from our borders in the west*".

'Middington's to the west!' I exclaimed. 'And so is that part of the wall.'

'Exactly,' said Layla placidly. 'It means that we're small, but we tamed the skinheads. And they're really angry – that's the dense clouds – but they can't do anything about it.'

'What about the moving line?'

"*The danger of bloodshed is thereby averted and his ground for apprehension dismissed*".

That seemed to us all a wholly satisfactory prognostication.

The skins never did come back, of course. For a while we didn't even see them in Middington – perhaps because they couldn't immediately get the cash together to buy themselves new boots. The twins and I put on old pairs of gloves and extracted the discarded ones from the brambles; they were pleasingly scarred with teeth-marks. We put them in a bin bag, covered them with twigs and sheep droppings, and tipped the lot into the garbage skip up at the Lodge. When Rain and I did finally spot a couple of the skinheads near the chip shop one day we swiftly changed tack. The sight of them made us feel sick.

But they did make an attempt to get their revenge – eventually. It came in a rather indirect form that we could never have foreseen.

*

A repeated cough woke me from a deep sleep. Almost immediately after reliving our epic battle I was towed away for a rather gruelling hour of physiotherapy, and I was wiped out. I fuzzily imagined that the coughing was coming from one of my fellow inmates, but as my eyes focussed on the chair next to my bed I got an unpleasant jolt.

'Terry.'

'Yes – yes. That's me. Hi there, mate. How's it going?'

'This is rather off your usual beat, isn't it? Don't tell me you're a patient here too.'

'No, no, nothing like that. I was passing nearby so I thought I'd drop in... I bumped into Marco the other day, he told me you were here.'

'Oh, I see.'

'I must say you're looking pretty good, considering. Back to work soon, eh? I expect you're straining at the bit to get out of here. Mind you –' he raised his eyebrows as one of the prettier nurses looked in to check that I was OK – 'there must be quite a few perks... bed-baths and stuff... can't be all that bad.'

He's a reasonably attractive man I suppose, in a square-jawed, hunky kind of way, but like a lot of the British ex-pats down here he's beginning to show the signs of heavy drinking. When he leaned forward I smelled a whiff of pastis and tobacco.

'Well now,' he said confidentially, 'I've got a nice bit of business I reckon I could put your way, when you're ready that is. I sold a mega-yacht last week. Can't tell you the buyer's name, but believe you me, he's not short of a bob or two. Uber-loaded. And his girlfriend wants a total refit of the interior. Egyptian style. Sphinxes and obelisks, the whole malarkey. Right up your street.'

Pyramids on the aft deck? Mummies in the cabins? 'That's kind of you – but in fact I'm not sure if I'm going to stick around in this part of the world.'

'Hey, that won't do! We need you here.'

Do we? I hardly know this person. In the past few years he's recommended my services to two or three yacht owners and I've given him a commission for his pains, and that's about it.

'Not thinking of going down under, by any chance?'

I stared.

'You know – Oz and all that. Land of the cuddly koala and the jumping kangaroo.' He chuckled.

'Er – no.'

Terry ran his tongue around his teeth for a moment. 'Look here mate – have you been seeing my wife?'

So that was what all this was about.

I gave a weak laugh. 'Terry, I haven't been the least bit capable of "seeing" anyone for months. Certainly not in the sense that you mean.'

'Not before your accident?'

'Of course not. What gave you that idea?'

'I found your name on her phone – in the diary. Several entries, actually. One of them was just three days ago.'

'That would be because she's been to visit me a few times. She's got the insane idea that she was somehow responsible for me driving into that wall. Because she was rude to me at that party of Mrs Kalashnikov's.'

'You mean you'd had a row?'

'Not at all. She was just – drunk, as far as I could tell. And a bit aggressive. I'd never seen her in my life before that night.'

'That's a pity. If it's true, that is.'

'It is true, I swear it. But why...?'

'Um... don't know if she's mentioned it to you... we're going through a pretty messy divorce at the moment and – well, to be honest with you, I haven't always been an entirely good boy in the past, so I was hoping that if I could find something on her as well... She's trying to hang on to the house, see, and I don't bloody well see why she should. I paid for the fucking thing.'

During this little speech Terry's face had turned quite a dark shade of crimson. He took a few deep breaths. 'Anyway – I was hoping you might be able to help me out. Maybe you still could, eh? I'll scratch your back if you scratch mine, and all that jazz. Know what I mean?'

'Not really.'

'Well, I slip a couple of top-end clients your way, you admit to a touch of hanky-panky with the bitch... I'd make sure it all stayed discreet. Wouldn't land you in the shit or anything.'

'That's very good of you, but no, I'm not prepared to tell a lie so that you can keep your house.'

He leaned towards me again and leered rather nastily. 'Reckon she's after you, though.'

'I can't imagine why she would be.'

'No accounting for tastes, is there mate? She's a fucking weirdo.' He got up. 'I need a fag.'

Fortunately, like the skinheads, he didn't come back. But I found it impossible to fall asleep again.

*

After the invasion the woodland air seemed to me to be tainted with a slight but persistent odour of pollution. I knew this was entirely in my imagination, but it took weeks to fade away, and from time to time a feeling of profound disquiet would sweep over me, in spite of the upbeat prophecy of the I Ching. When I confided this to Rain he admitted that this happened to him and Shine as well. I don't think Jelly Bean was affected – she was too fearless. And Layla was preoccupied with other matters by now. After the fair left Middington, taking Blue with it, she began to sit around languidly and sigh a lot.

'She's moping,' said Shine scornfully. 'Can't live without her *boyfriend*.'

'You're jealous,' said Layla, a remark which may well have had some truth in it. 'I like having a boyfriend. I think I'll have to find another one, at least for when Blue's not here.'

'You're *nine*, Layla. Real boyfriends are for later.'

'Maybe they are for you.'

'You know perfectly well that the female human being should never let her life be defined by her relationships with males,' said Shine pompously, quoting Marjoram.

Layla took no notice and carried on applying her make-up.

That autumn she, the twins and myself went to Middington with Zoë one afternoon to buy new winter shoes. Jelly Bean still stuck to the leather bootees that Erryk made for her: 'They're like paws,' she said. But the rest of us by now preferred rather more conventional footwear.

We were in a fairly sensible kind of shoe shop when Layla became restless. 'Everything's too clumpy in here,' she complained. 'I'm going over there. The shoes are much prettier.'

'And much more expensive,' said Zoë, but Layla was already out of the door and crossing the road.

A few minutes later we heard a high-pitched yell, clearly Layla's. We all turned and ran outside. On the opposite pavement Layla, looking oddly taller than usual, was surrounded by a small crowd. She waved as we approached.

'Is this your daughter?' a woman asked Zoë. 'What on earth do you think you're doing, letting her walk around alone looking like that?'

Zoë grabbed hold of Layla. 'What's going on? Where did you get those shoes?' Layla was tottering about in a pair of red high-heels, a small adult size but still far too big for her.

'I was only trying them on. One of the ladies inside let me.'

'That's not the half of it,' said the woman. 'Tell your mother what happened next.'

'Oh, I came outside to look at the colour in the daylight, like you do. To see if it would go with my handbag. While I was looking a man came up and asked if I wanted to go to the pictures with him, and –'

'WHAT?' shrieked Zoë.

'Of course I said no, and then he said he'd take me to the sweetshop instead, so I said "Fuck off, you filthy pervert" like you taught me, and then I screamed and whacked him with my bag and he ran off – that way.' She pointed down the street. 'Then these people stopped to see what was the matter.'

Zoë looked round wildly. 'Did any of you see him?'

Everyone shook their heads and muttered.

'He wasn't very old, but he was quite ugly,' said Layla.

'Right,' said Zoë, pulling her away from the onlookers and into the shop. 'That's the last time you go off anywhere on your own, understand?' She was shaking. 'Now take off those ridiculous shoes and we're going home straight away. And you will *never* wear make-up Outside again until I let you.'

'I don't know why she made such a fuss,' said Layla afterwards.

'I do,' said Shine. 'He could have dragged you off and raped you and then cut you up in little pieces and scattered them in all the Middington litter bins.'

'Don't be silly,' said Layla. 'I would've just hit him again – but *there*. Like Jelly Bean did with the potatoes. Men don't like that.'

Indeed no. The two youngest members of Lothlorien made Rain and me uneasy at times, since both of us were becoming more and more conscious of our expanding testicles.

This incident with Layla was another reminder, if we needed one, that Outsiders could be the embodiment of evil. But we didn't dwell on it for long – some new winter excitements were soon under way which occupied a good deal of our time and concentration.

Best of these was the play; we often put on plays, but this one was particularly special because Loose had written it and it was in French. She'd decided that our grasp of the language was now sufficient for us to handle such an undertaking, and what we didn't understand at first we soon learned. I say she'd written it, but in fact she improvised it as rehearsals progressed, incorporating all our suggestions. The plot was crazy: a mixture of pirates, punks, poets, Parisian cafés and tropical islands, interspersed with lots of songs. We all played several different parts and spent hours making our costumes, helped by Stella and Zoë. Loose of course directed the whole thing and encouraged us to over-act.

'Like this it will be easier for the others to understand,' she said, and it was true that most of the audience didn't know half as much French as we did. Only Erryk's girlfriend Miriam spoke it well; she was still a fixture in his life and so she was of course invited. Unfortunately this was one occasion when her son had to be invited too; he was still as horrible as ever. He yawned all the way through until Loose, in her cameo role as a sea monster, jumped into the audience and kidnapped him.

'You will be our dinner!' she yelled, in English, and yanked him behind a tree while we cheered and gnashed our teeth. 'Ugh!' she shouted a moment later. 'This meat is rotten!' She threw him back. After this shock he kept quiet.

The show was such a success that we put on a repeat performance when Stella's mum came to visit for a couple of nights in the New Year. Today someone would have filmed it on their phone and posted it on YouTube. I prefer it to remain a glorious chaotic memory. But Loose took lots of photos, and some of those may have survived – where? Out of reach: who knows where Loose is now.

Another momentous event at the end of that winter was when Rain, not long before the twins' twelfth birthday, had his first wet dream. He discussed this endlessly with me, because Shine didn't want to know; the twins, previously so close, were becoming a little distant from each other. Although we knew in theory what the stages of puberty were, and what it all signified, the whole thing remained mysterious and deeply fascinating. We compared our soft sprouts of new hair; we were desperately impatient for it to grow longer and stronger, along with everything else.

Funnily enough, we found it easier to confide in Pete rather than the heterosexual males of the community, perhaps because he didn't represent any threat of competition to our budding masculinity. He was brilliant: matter-of-fact, funny and packed with useful information. 'My darlings,' he said, 'when you start to get really *gorgeous* erections you must look for *older* women who'll know what to do with them. Forget girls – they'll be a dead loss and you won't learn a thing.'

'But where on earth will we find older women?' asked Rain.

'Well now... I just might know of one or two not so far away who'd be only too happy to oblige. You'd be surprised.'

This was a great relief to hear. We trusted Neat Pete, and in those days we didn't think that anything about him could surprise us.

18. THE HORROR

WE'D BEEN LOOKING forward to our veggie Lebanese dinner – Pete's latest culinary special that he'd promised to prepare for us that day. 'Lebanese is so divine,' said Stella. 'It's detox food.' Detox was a recent buzz-word in Lothlorien.

'My taste buds are tingling already,' said Rick. 'Might as well intensify the pleasure, eh Sean?' They went off to roll a spliff or two.

But at six in the evening our chef de cuisine still hadn't got back from Middington.

'He normally pops into the shop when he's in town,' said Stella, 'but we didn't see him today, did we Zo?'

'I can't think what's keeping him,' said Ginnie. 'He only went to get some aftershave from Boots.'

'Maybe the kind he uses was out of stock so he went to Chandleford.'

'All that way, just for aftershave? He could have had some of my Tarragon Skin Tonic for Men,' said Marjoram.

'Oh, you know what he's like,' said Zoë. 'Once he's found something that suits him he sticks with it.'

By seven o'clock it became pretty clear that something more than simple brand loyalty was detaining him.

'He might have had an accident,' Ginnie said. 'Or a puncture. Do you think we should go up to the House and see if there's a message?' (Lothlorien still depended on the telephone that Bill had had installed in one of the old stables; it's difficult, now, to imagine that far-off time before the instant accessibility provided by the mobile phone. That said, these last few months without one have been a treat – I've kept it switched off).

By 'we', Ginnie meant Bill, of course. He shook his head. 'He's unlikely to have had a puncture next to a phone box.' Nonetheless, shortly before eight he jumped into the Spitfire and zoomed up the track.

We hung around the Fireplace while we waited for him, staring at the unlit fire; Rain and Jelly Bean had built it up earlier in a specially neat wigwam of branches that they thought Pete would appreciate. Everyone was becoming hungrier, and more worried too, as Bill seemed to be gone for ages. Ashley passed round some of his home-brewed beer; Sean banged on his bongos, though without much conviction. Night began to fall. Ginnie lit candles in the coloured glass jars scattered on the ground.

At last we heard Bill coming back. He got out of the car very slowly, and walked towards us looking even more serious than usual.

'I think we should light the fire and get some dinner together,' he said. He paused for dramatic effect and took in our speechless expressions of alarm. Bill enjoyed creating a bit of tension. 'Pete won't be back this evening. He's at the police station in Middington. He's been arrested.'

Gasps and expletives flew.

'The charge,' he continued, 'is 'importuning'. In plain language, he's accused of trying to pick up an underage boy in a public lavatory.'

General cries of 'He couldn't have! He'd never –'

'No. I find it hard to believe myself. Unfortunately there are still plenty of people around who are strongly prejudiced against homosexuals and will go to great lengths to attack a person they perceive to be gay.'

'Tell me about it,' muttered Jack grimly.

'But who – who –' whispered Ginnie.

'We don't yet know who reported him.'

'Why did you take so long to listen to his message?' asked Shine.

'The message wasn't from Pete. I don't think he'd be allowed to phone us. The police rang to check on the address and number he gave them. Of course they only got our answerphone, so then they rang the House's number direct.'

'So Our Lord –'

'He knows, yes. It's most regrettable. We talked at some length.'

'What will happen? Will Pete go to prison?' Layla was in tears.

'It's impossible at this stage to know what the outcome will be.'

'But what can we *do*?'

'For Pete, nothing, at the moment. But for ourselves it would be advisable, as I said, to prepare some food.'

'I don't think we're very hungry any more, are we?' said Ginnie.

'Cheese sandwich'll do me,' said Ashley. He stood up and turned in the direction of his caravan.

'NO!' shouted Loose. 'We must send to Pete a big positive vibe. We must make a good meal and eat it all together and *sing* – really loud, so he can hear us. At least in his heart. It will be like a magic spell. A spell of the elves.'

These fiery words were magic in themselves, because they ignited the Lothlorien spirit of solidarity. Although for the past few years most of the adults had been looking and behaving a lot less like traditional hippies, they were still citizens of Elfland, and capable of reacting as such.

'She's right,' said Gogo firmly. 'Let's get this fire going.'

'Bring out the bong, Rick,' said Sean. 'We'll blow Pete some smoke rings.'

Shine jumped to her feet. 'I'll cook some spaghetti. Someone else can make a sauce.'

Erryk turned to me. 'There's – we've got those, um, nettle-tops, haven't we, Curly? In the fridge. They should still be fresh. Well... fresh*ish*.'

'Fine,' said Marjoram. 'We'll also need a couple of onions, plenty of garlic, and a large tin of tomatoes. And Parmesan, of course.'

'And parsley?' queried Stella. 'Maybe a few walnuts?'

'I'll fetch the blackberry wine,' said Gogo.

Thus galvanised into communal elf-action, all our spirits lifted. The resulting nettle and tomato sauce was the best ever – I remember it well. Once everyone was sated, and the adults suitably stoned, Rick and Erryk brought over their guitars and began to jam. Loose improvised one her wild sound-songs while Stella made pretty 'La la' noises in the background. The rest of us clapped and stamped, even Bill.

Sean pounded his bongos vigorously. 'Feel the beat, Pete,' he roared. 'Feel the beat.'

*

The following afternoon Pete was back. He'd been up before the magistrate that morning, pleaded not guilty, and was currently out on bail pending trial. Our Lord had put up the bail. At the time none of this made any sense to us, even when explained by Gogo. But the essence of the matter was clear enough: Pete had been the victim of an evil Outside force, and was now in the grip of the System.

He himself made light of the affair. 'That magistrate really should change her look,' he said. 'She's got a hairstyle that could bring out criminal urges in the mildest of men. Zoë darling, you should get in touch.'

'But Pete, *what happened*?'

Although the adult males of Lothlorien steered discreetly clear of questioning Pete too closely at this stage, the women and children showed no such restraint. We'd all gathered round the steps of his caravan, where he sat calmly smoking through his elegant cigarette holder. In fact he didn't need much coaxing to tell his story: he probably needed to get it off his chest.

'Well, I was unfortunately caught short in Boots. No sooner had I made my way into those so-called conveniences by the market than I was overcome by a powerful odour of beer and old sweat, which was obviously emanating from a couple of brutish louts who seemed to be comparing notes, as it were, by the urinals... Of course I instantly averted my gaze and nipped into one of the cubicles. If there's one thing I can do without, it's proximity to a skinhead.'

'Skinheads?' I said, horrified. Of course the twins, Layla, and Jelly Bean were all thinking the same thing as I was.

'Yes, pasty creatures with unpleasant tattoos. I suppose they believe that a shorn head and those beastly boots will somehow distract from their acne. They are tragically mistaken.'

'What did they do?'

'I was naturally hoping they hadn't spotted me and would simply zip up their flies and leave me in peace. Instead they started chanting 'Death to queers' and other poetic phrases. They also kicked the door quite a few times, and I'm not ashamed to tell you I was trembling like an aspen leaf.'

So were we, as he recounted this. 'Do you think they knew where you were from?' Rain asked. His voice was shaking.

'I presume so. Amongst their vile mumblings I caught a phrase about "perverts in the woods". Lothlorien isn't a secret, you know – after all, we've been knocking around Middington for years. They also made a fragrant reference to the shop, with which they were evidently aware I had a link.'

'Oh my God!' exclaimed Ginnie. 'We'll have to protect it... put in an alarm or something.'

'I shouldn't think that's necessary, my dear. It's me they object to. Anyway – they did finally leave, laughing like trolls, if one can dignify those grunting noises with the name of laughter. Then they must have hatched their nasty little plan and hurried to the police station to denounce me, because the next thing I experienced, as I was strolling gently towards the car park, was the heavy hand of the law upon my shoulder.'

'What will happen now?' breathed Stella.

'I shall eventually be called to stand trial, probably in Chandleford Crown Court, whereupon I shall either be handed a hefty fine, if the judge is lenient, or sentenced to a maximum of five years in prison if he isn't, which is far more likely. He'll take one look at me and think, "Fucking faggot, needs putting away". '

'That's impossible!' cried Zoë. 'You're *innocent*, Pete.'

'Rather difficult to prove when there's two of them and only one of me, and no other witnesses. And let's face it, I don't appear strikingly heterosexual, do I? Public opinion in this part of the world being what it is, most people probably think cottaging is my favourite pastime. In vain will I insist that I am far too refined ever to indulge in that rather sordid activity. Even vainer will be my attempts to stress that a skinhead could *never*, even if he were the last male in the entire cosmos, appear to me as a potential source of carnal delight.'

'We'll all be character witnesses for you,' said Marjoram staunchly.

'Yes!' said Zoë. 'Even Our Lord would be, I'm sure. They'd have to believe *him*.'

'I rather doubt it.' Pete's voice, so flippant up till now, had begun to falter. We all rushed to hug him. His cigarette holder fell to the ground.

'Darlings, *please*,' he said faintly, 'much as I value your affection and support, I'm not ready to die from suffocation just at the moment.'

And yet... A couple of weeks later the charge was withdrawn, and Pete never had to appear in court after all.

*

'You see,' said Ginnie, 'that's proof of Intervention by Higher Powers.' She was convinced that it was her offerings to the relevant Cosmic Forces which had secured Pete's deliverance, so as part of the evening of feasting and music laid on to celebrate the good news she performed another ceremony – (of course) – to thank them for their help. It smelt nice, because as she chanted she poured quite a lot of her essential oils on to the embers of the fire.

'She means well,' sighed Pete.

Ashley snorted.

'Higher Powers my arse,' he said next day. 'Unless you count Our Lord as a Higher Power.'

Zoë was trimming his hair in front of her caravan while Rick sat on the steps looking glum; it was his turn next. Rain and I were collecting up the red-brown wisps as they fell to the ground. We intended to use them to make ourselves a false beard, to give us an idea of what we were going to look like when our own facial hair grew. Jelly Bean too was snatching up as much as she could, as lining for a nest she was making in the hole of a tree as a potential wild-life refuge.

Rick agreed with Ash. 'Yeah, I reckon the great man had a hand in it.'

'Our Lord? Yes, I suppose he might have,' said Zoë. 'After all, he's known Pete the longest of all of us.'

We all knew that way back in the mists of history it had been Our Lord rather than Bill who had invited Pete to join the community.

'Only through a friend of a friend,' said Rick. 'It's not like they're bosom buddies.'

'More like his royal highness didn't want any scandal attached to himself and the House,' said Ashley. 'So he put a bit of pressure on. Bill told me that one of those skinhead tossers lives with his mum in a tied cottage over on the Baxford road.'

'What's a tied cottage?' I asked.

'It belongs to this estate. Our Lord can boot the tenants out if he feels like it.'

'I don't think he'd do that,' said Zoë. 'I think he just had a quiet word with the fuzz, and persuaded them to get that little idiot to tell the truth. Our Lord's fond of Lothlorien, you know, even if he doesn't come down here much any more. He sort of looks on it as his creation.'

'Perhaps the police *tortured* the skinhead,' said Jelly Bean. 'I hope so, anyway.'

'Well he'd better watch out, because if I get my hands on him I'll bash his sodding head in,' said Ash.

I very much hoped he wouldn't get the chance.

Fortunately his mind was soon otherwise occupied; it was not long after this shock to the community that Our Lord asked Ashley to do some work for him up at the House.

'Coming to give me a hand?' he asked me. 'He wants these new built-in wardrobes for his dressing-room. Got too many clothes for his own good.'

'Um –'

'No-one's going to eat you, you know.'

Although Ash, Bill, Zoë and even Sean were fairly frequent visitors to the House, to me it had always felt somehow out of bounds. Perhaps this was a hangover from the days of Janet the Great – even though we knew that Our Lord was well disposed towards us, and that the local couple who had taken over from Janet and her husband bore us no ill will. We just referred to them as Mr and Mrs Lodge, as no-one could remember their name. Sometimes I'd go and fetch our mail from the Lodge and if the woman was around she would give me a wan look of recognition – not quite a smile, but often accompanied by a biscuit.

So I went to the House to work with Ash. I knew it would be nothing like the houses where I'd worked with him up till now – it was older and of course far bigger, with dark corners, unexpected staircases and a totally different smell. Though clean, it was also shabbier, and all of the rather sparse furniture appeared to have seen better times in some fairly distant past. Light flooded through the tall windows, but it was nonetheless easy to imagine vampires concealed in upright coffins behind the panelling, waiting to break out at nightfall. 'It's where El goes in the daytime,' I told Rain, and he almost believed me.

Our Lord's dressing-room was the size of our caravan. I peeked inside one of the two huge free-standing wardrobes and was met by a musty scent of mothballs and ancient clothes – which, when I looked at them more closely, reminded me of those I'd seen illustrated in Jack's Sherlock Holmes stories.

'Does he *wear* these?'

'Haven't a clue. Probably belonged to his great-grandfather or something. People like him never throw anything out.'

The other wardrobe contained newer-looking outfits, but of a kind never seen in Lothlorien: suits which even I could see had been beautifully hand-stitched, plus a plethora of shirts and ties.

'Why does he need all this?'

'He doesn't. He's got the cash and he likes shopping. You could build a new hospital with the money he's spent on that lot.'

I opened a drawer which turned out to be stuffed full of thick woollen socks, and pulled out a pair of strange elastic objects I'd never seen before. 'What on earth are these?'

'Sock suspenders. Stops him getting wrinkly ankles in public.'

That struck me as ludicrously funny; but I quickly choked back my laughter when I heard a soft tapping in the bedroom beyond. The next moment Momma Lord appeared in the doorway to the dressing-room.

She looked even frailer than I remembered – (I hadn't seen her since the Janet fiasco) – but she beamed radiantly as she leaned on her stick.

'Mr Tippins!'

'That's me. How's life?'

'It couldn't be better. And what a pleasure it is to see you on this happy, happy day!'

'Glad it's OK for some.'

'Oh, I have had the most *marvellous* news! But I'm not allowed to divulge it, as I'm under strict instructions to *keep mum*!' Her eyes fell on me. 'And who is this young man?'

'My apprentice. Curly.' I always felt proud when Ashley called me his apprentice.

'Curly! What a charming name.'

I felt this called for a little bow.

'And such charming manners! So rare nowadays... particularly on the television... Do you live down in the woods with Mr Tippins in that delightful *settlement*?'

I nodded. 'Well, not *with* him exactly. But quite close by.'

'Oh, how I have always longed to visit you all. It must be quite enchanting. Mrs Maxwell has told me all about it.' It took me a second or two to realise that she meant Zoë. 'Ah, the lure of the forbidden... Never mind, never mind... one cannot always...'

Her voice had momentarily taken on a fading, wistful note, but she swiftly brightened up again. 'And yet today – such joyfulness!' She tottered away.

'What was all that about?' I asked.

'Search me. Old dear's a touch gaga, if you ask me. No harm in that so long as she's happy.'

'Why doesn't she call you and Zoë by your first names?'

'She's the old-fashioned type. Likes a bit of formality.' Ash chortled. 'I tried calling her Alice once. That's her name. She acted like she hadn't heard me.'

'So what *do* you call her? "Madam" or something?'

'Don't make me laugh. I don't call her anything. Doesn't stop her speaking to me when she wants to.'

'What about Our Lord? What do you call him?'

'Cecil.'

'And he doesn't mind?'

'He loves it. Makes him think he's one of the boys, being on first-name terms with the tradesmen.'

As we were on our way out of the House that afternoon we came upon Our Lord himself, strolling meditatively around the entrance hall. I hadn't seen him for some years, and still found him difficult to focus on clearly; there was a slightly viscous quality about him which had always made me think of a melting jelly. He was tall, with smallish eyes set in a large pale face which seemed somehow soft around the edges. He no longer had the pony tail that I remembered from those earlier years when he used to stray down to Lothlorien from time to time; his hair was now short, and thinning at the crown. I suppose he would have been in his mid forties by then.

'Hi there, Ash. Getting on all right?'

'Yup. Like a house on fire. You'll soon have enough space to stock the whole of Harrods' menswear department.'

'Harrods? I really prefer...'

'Don't tell me. That little man in Jermyn Street.'

'Well, sometimes...' Our Lord laughed uncertainly and turned to me with a vague smile. 'Gracious me, you've grown.'

What did he expect? I didn't know what to say, so I just smiled back equally vaguely.

'Your mother seems cheerful today,' said Ash. 'Got a new boyfriend, has she?'

Our Lord chuckled weakly. 'Yes, yes.' He stroked his chin. 'I mean no. But yes, she certainly is in good spirits, I'm glad to say. And in relatively good condition, don't you think? For her age. All things considered.'

'You keep on treating her right and she'll live to be a hundred.'

'Goodness – do you really think so?' A look of alarm passed across the face of Our Lord. He coughed. 'Well now – I'd better be getting ready for – for –'

'A night on the tiles?'

'Ah, if only... Cheerio then, Ash.'

'Ta-ta, Cecil. Remember – if you can't be good, be careful.'

*

The remainder of the summer was peaceful – too peaceful in fact, because to our immense disappointment the fair didn't come back to Middington that year. Where was my blood brother? There seemed to be no way of finding out. Today we'd both have been on Facebook and no doubt in touch all the time.

Layla seemed the hardest hit of all by Blue's absence. She'd been getting more and more excited for weeks, trying out new hairstyles and make-up, and was now slumped in despair. She cast a pall over my birthday party that August.

'It's heartbreaking to see her like this,' said Zoë, 'but to be honest, I can't help being a bit relieved as well. God knows what they might have got up to.'

'I hate you!' wailed Layla.

'Daughters, who'd have 'em,' sighed Rick.

'We didn't ask to be born,' said El, who was helping herself to some of my cake. She took her plate and moved off to eat it on her own.

'Did I really give birth to *that*?' said Rick, staring after her.

'I was the one who gave birth, in case you've forgotten,' said Zoë.

'She probably came from an alien sperm.'

'No chance. She might have my hair and my freckles, but otherwise she's just like you. Tall and short-sighted and bloody-minded.'

'Oooh,' moaned Layla, her hands clutched to her heart. 'Be *quiet*. Can't you see I'm in *pain*?'

She perked up remarkably quickly one day in Middington library when she caught sight of a boy who none of us had seen before. He was about the same age as the twins, and had smooth dark hair and olive skin. He was peering at the shelves as if he didn't know what was where.

Layla sidled up to him. 'Excuse me – are you new here? Would you like me to show you around? I know where all the best books are – even for boys.'

He turned and immediately flushed; it was sickeningly clear that he wouldn't be able to resist Layla's charm offensive. No-one seemed able to – except, of course, those who had grown up with her.

'His name's Gee-o-varni,' she told us afterwards. 'His parents are Italian and they've moved here from London to open a restaurant. We're going to meet for coffee next time I'm in Middington.'

'Oh no you're not,' said Zoë. 'Or only if I come with you, at any rate.'

'You don't even like coffee,' said Shine.

'Yes I do. Now I'm ten I'm different.'

'Not different enough,' said Jelly Bean.

Zoë heaved a very deep sigh.

*

On an afternoon in late October Bill summoned us to an Important Gathering. It was a dank day with drizzle in the air and a good deal of mud and wet leaves on the ground; Gogo had to struggle to get the fire going. It fizzed and smoked and gave out little warmth. We sat grumpily around the Fireplace with mugs of hot drinks, and whinged gently while we waited for Bill to join us.

'Couldn't he – can't we do this on another day?' murmured Erryk.

'Yes, tomorrow would be better,' agreed Stella. 'It's going to be fine. I heard it on the radio.'

'It has to be today because we're all here,' said Ginnie. 'You and Marj will be at the shop tomorrow – and you've got a gig somewhere, haven't you Rick?'

'So the news is so earth-shattering that Zo can't be trusted to tell me about it afterwards?'

'Well, it is rather big news, yes. And it does concern us all.'

'Perhaps Our Lord's going to bring some wild animals into the grounds,' said Jelly Bean hopefully. 'Like at that other place. But he'll have to keep them out of the Sheepfield.'

We scoffed at this. And yet, in a way, she was closer to the truth than we could have guessed.

'Here he comes,' said Sean. 'Prepare yourselves to be blown away.'

Bill came striding towards us with an even more purposive air than usual. He rubbed his hands together over the fire and looked around at everybody. After the requisite dramatic pause he cleared his throat and began to speak.

'There are going to be some changes here. Productive ones, I hope. Cecil – Our Lord – is going to be married.'

Was this really so amazing? The adults seemed to be pretty surprised, however.

'Didn't think he was the marrying kind,' said Rick.

'No – he's sort of neuter,' said Zoë. 'There *are* people like that – asexual.'

'Can't imagine him humping anyone,' said Ash.

Bill looked at him with disapproval. 'Whatever you can or cannot imagine, Ashley, the fact remains that he has found himself a fiancée.'

'What's her name?' asked Shine.

'Rosemary.'

'Well, that sounds all right,' said Marjoram. 'Have you met her?'

Bill nodded.

'What's she like?'

'Extremely pleasant. She's been some kind of champion athlete – a pole vaulter, I believe – though I presume she'll be giving that up.'

This caused an eruption of raucous laughter from almost everyone. 'Sure she's not a pole dancer?' spluttered Ashley.

Bill ignored him.

'Ash, there's really no need to be vulgar,' said Ginnie. 'She's seems a very nice person. I've met her too.'

'Is she pretty?' asked Layla.

Ginnie hesitated. 'She has a very... *kind* face.'

'You mean plain.'

'Looks aren't everything, Miss Superficial,' said Shine.

Sean's eyes lit up. 'Hey! Maybe we can do some training together. She must have mind-blowing leg muscles.'

'That explains why Our Lord's been getting you to do all those fitness sessions with him lately,' said Stella. 'So he'll be able to cope.'

Bill coughed. 'Can we stick to the point please? She is, apparently, a little worried about the continuing existence of Lothlorien.'

That brought us all to attention.

'Woah!' said Rick. 'She thinks we're a sinkhole of vice and sloth! She's afraid of our contaminating influence on her hubby-to-be!'

'Not quite. Her concerns are primarily financial. Our Lord's support of our community is in fact a sizeable part of his expenditure...'

'Crap,' said Ashley. 'Mrs Lords don't come cheap, that's his problem. She wants all his piddling extra cash to spend on lampshades and handbags. I know what women are like.'

'Thanks, Ash,' said Marjoram. 'Remind me to show you my handbag collection some time.'

'And my lampshades,' said Jack.

'Sod it, you know what I mean.'

'To get back to what I was trying to say –' Bill was becoming annoyed; everyone fell silent. 'He feels it would be more appropriate for us to become fully autonomous. In other words, he is no longer prepared to pay for our electricity, water and general repairs.'

'So. Our Lord giveth, then he taketh away,' said Pete acidly.

Bill frowned. 'He has been, and remains, exceptionally generous towards us all. Without that generosity we certainly wouldn't have been able to build the kind of life that we have here. And let's not forget that he's quite happy for us to stay – rent-free, I should remind you – providing we show ourselves ready to adapt to his changing circumstances.'

Gogo pulled on the point of his goatee, which meant he was about to reach a decision. 'In actual fact it'll better for us to be independent. We can all afford it now, can't we? I've often felt that being partially maintained at Our Lord's expense for so long was somehow – I don't know – degrading. As if we were his children.'

'Well, he can have some real kids of his own now,' said Marjoram. 'Unless... How old is she? Is she still young enough?'

'Oh yes,' said Ginnie. 'She's quite a bit younger than he is. Not much more than thirty.'

'Momma Lord must be over the moon,' said Zoë. 'She's been worrying for ages that he wasn't going to produce a son and heir. I reckon she was giving him a really hard time, and that's why he's finally getting hitched. To keep the old girl quiet.'

'Oh!' I said. 'That must have been her wonderful news – remember, Ash? But it was still a secret then.'

'Must be why he needed ten more acres of wardrobe. For wifey's ball-gowns. And her designer maternity outfits.'

'So we'll be seeing Baby Lords and Lordesses gambolling in the Sheepfield,' said Rick. 'I can't wait.'

Bill lifted a hand to cut short any further flippancy. 'And by the way. They've been kind enough to ask everyone here to attend the wedding reception. In the interests of future public relations I think it's essential that we all honour the invitation. *All*,' he repeated, looking at Sean, who had begun to sway and groan.

'But man, that's such a heavy number,' said Sean, fairly predictably. 'Small talk with straights – I can't hack it.'

'It'll be a doddle, love. Just keep your mouth shut and smile.' Stella stroked his hair. 'You get on fine with Our Lord, anyway. And you can talk fitness with Rosemary. I think it's sweet of them to ask us.'

Erryk was looking worried. 'We won't – we haven't got the right kind of gear. They'll be expecting ties – suits...'

'No, it's going to be a relatively low-key affair,' said Bill. 'Smart casual will be quite all right. But we must all be straight as well – no red eyes. And no hair and clothing smelling of grass. Try to think of it as a unique and far-out experience, Sean. A new kind of trip.'

*

The date of the wedding was fixed for the following March, giving everyone plenty of time to get used to the idea.

Erryk, for one, had doubts about the whole thing. 'I don't think – I mean I can't help thinking...'

'What?' I asked.

'It's going to be more than just... I'm not sure.' But he never clarified these cloudy ruminations.

Ash, up at the House one day to discuss further home improvements, had the privilege of coming into contact with the future Mrs Lord.

'Did she do any vaulting?' asked Rain.

'No, but she looks as if she still could. Wouldn't want to find myself alone with her in a dark alley.'

'Ash, you've been exaggerating,' said Zoë when a little later she too met the lady in question. 'She's certainly a touch... beefy, I suppose, but she seems really nice. Not at all snobby.'

Layla, although heavily preoccupied with her new boyfriend Giovanni that winter, was the most excited of us all about the forthcoming wedding – and became even more so when shortly before the event she heard the news of the Prince Charles's engagement to Lady Diana Spencer.

'Isn't it thrilling? *Everybody's* getting married! Now we'll have a real new Princess, and she'll live in a real palace, and get a chance to try on all the Crown Jewels!'

'How on earth do you know about *that*?' said Zoë, disgusted.

'Giovanni's parents showed me the pictures in the paper. She's so beautiful! They're going to take us to London so we can see her in the golden coach!'

'Let her go,' said Gogo. 'It'll be a lesson in the abuse of privilege and the conditioned subservience of the masses.'

'I doubt it,' said Zoë.

*

To my surprise, even Shine and El showed a certain enthusiasm for Our Lord's marriage. Rain, Jelly Bean and I were more interested in what the food would be like.

'Will there be stuff we can eat?' we asked.

'Oh yes, they'll be sure to cater for vegetarians,' said Zoë.

'Because they *care*,' said Pete. 'They want to fatten us up for the sacrifice.'

I thought this was a slightly odd remark, even for Pete, but he'd been listening to a lot of Wagner recently. I was interested in the story of the Ring Cycle, although I couldn't warm to any of the characters. 'Is it the same ring as in the Lord of the Rings?' I asked him. 'Just a bit earlier on?'

'Of course! It's always, always the same tired old story, over and over again. Good and evil, love and hate, chance and destiny, life and death – going round and round eternally. But Wagner's version is entirely Hobbit-free, for which let us be thankful.'

I stood up for the Hobbits.

'It's natural you should love them, Curly – you are a child of the Elves, you were born here. Whereas I have never *truly* belonged.'

'Of course you have!'

'No. Much as I value all the tolerance and affection I've enjoyed in here, I do not possess an inherently Elf-like soul. Now be quiet and listen to the music.'

Some of it was exciting; Rain and I loved the Ride of the Valkyries. Mostly I found it too sombre and oppressive, however. 'But look how it matches the sky!' said Pete, when one grey and windy day in February I asked him to play something more cheerful. 'Can't you see Wotan sweeping towards us on that cloud?' I could, sort of, but it made me feel gloomy. Even Pete seemed plunged in melancholy.

In early March the weather must still have been quite miserable, as Stella, Zoë and Layla all started to fret about the possibility of rain on the wedding day. So Ginnie did a little anti-rain ritual, and lo, dryness prevailed, even a little sunshine. 'How exceptionally fortunate we are to have a weather goddess among us,' said Pete.

I was feeling hungry when we assembled by the Fireplace, so it must have been around midday. It had been decided that we should all walk up to the House together, as there were likely to be a lot of cars there already and we didn't want to clog the place up with any more. 'But it's too windy!' complained Layla. 'My hair will be spoilt.'

Everyone, finally, had made the effort to be tidily groomed, and in some cases quite smart. Loose, in purple leggings and a huge pink mohair sweater, was perhaps the most eccentrically dressed of our party. 'I am French, so it doesn't matter,' she said. For once, even El was wearing a reasonably neutral outfit, dark trousers and a jacket that Stella had lent her. 'Only because no-one I know will be there,' she said. She'd told her friends she had to go to a funeral.

Pete came out of his caravan in a black waistcoat embroidered with a golden dragon, his hair tied back with a scarlet silk scarf. He had an expensive-looking carrier bag with him, striped red and white, which he swung jauntily. 'Just a little prezzie for the happy couple,' he said when I asked him what was in it.

'Bill told us they didn't want us to bring any presents,' I said.

'I know, but I simply couldn't resist. In any case, it's not so much a present, more a *gesture*. In fact, if you'll excuse me, I think I'd better go on ahead so I can find a suitable spot for it.' He laughed lightly. 'And now, my dears, let me extend to you all my most sincere and heartfelt thanks. To you I owe -' He broke off and turned away with a small skip. Then he set off rapidly up the track out of Lothlorien before anyone had a chance to ask him what he meant.

Rick shrugged. 'Too much opera.'

'I think he's been drinking,' said Gogo.

Bill was looking around irritably. 'Where the hell is Sean?'

'Oh...' Stella ran to their caravan and soon re-emerged pulling Sean after her. His eyes weren't bloodshot and he didn't smell of dope, but he had an unmistakeable aura which we recognised only too well.

He smiled lazily. 'Had to change my sweater. Wrong colour – bad vibe.'

Bill closed his eyes. He looked furious.

'It's OK,' said Stella. 'I'll make sure no-one notices anything, I promise. I don't think he ate all that many.'

We set off up the hill. As we drew closer to the House the new marquee came into view within the gardens; its bright white sides rippled in the wind. Party noises drifted down – music, chatter and sometimes an explosion of laughter. From another part of the gardens, further off, a plume of dark smoke began to curl into the air. A few minutes later I detected a smell which was foreign to Lothlorien but nonetheless familiar to myself and Rain: charred meat. It was reminiscent of the pork chops that Ashley sometimes treated himself to at the Grill'n'Sizzle in Middington, an occasional alternative to his usual burger.

'They're having a barbecue,' said Rain.

'They must be roasting a whole pig,' said Ashley. He sounded hopeful.

As we approached the odour intensified, now laced with a whiff of petrol. When we reached the gardens of the House nothing untoward had so far been detected: everyone was in the marquee eating and drinking, sheltered from the chilly wind outside. But as we were about to go into the marquee a high, terrifying scream cut through the sounds of merriment – and then Mrs Lodge, who had presumably gone to check on the source of the smoke, came careering towards us. She was shrieking Our Lord's name, between hoarse sobs and gasps.

Our Lord rushed out of the marquee, followed by a group of guests. Mrs Lodge grabbed his arm and pointed behind her. 'A man! A man!'

We found ourselves pushed towards what we still thought of as the barbecue site, ahead of the crowd swelling behind us. The smell of burning meat and petrol was overpowering now. The smoke was thick but blowing sideways, so the blackened figure within it was clearly visible, flickering with tongues of fire, cross-legged on the ground against the orchard wall. It began to topple forward. The fire whooshed up, a mass of orange flame. A few yards away on the grass a petrol can lay on its side, next to an empty red and white striped carrier bag.

And after that: hysteria, chaos, the abyss.

19. THE EYE BEGINS TO SEE

'YOU LOOK A bit crook,' said Jeanette Evans.

Not surprising. I've just spent several hours dwelling in detail on an event so traumatic that for many years I'd chosen not to think about it except in the most fleeting and superficial fashion – as in: yes, it was ghastly, but life goes on, and anyway he wouldn't have wanted... etc.

Now, the remembered smell is making me feel nauseous, and my head aches. At the time it had ached for days, as if the matter of my brain had been contaminated by the smoke and the stench.

'Catch yourself a virus?'

'Possibly.' I realised that my defence mechanisms against this woman weren't functioning properly, because I had a frightening urge to tell her everything. I also wanted to cry.

'Sorry, this is a bad time,' I said.

'So when isn't it?' She dropped a plastic bag of food offerings on to the table beside me and scrutinised my face. For too long. Then she looked down at the open exercise book open on my lap.

'I see the sad story's still coming out.'

'It wasn't all sad.' *Christ!!* I had to get rid of her.

But she turned away of her own accord. 'Hallelujah, you're starting to get real. Keep going.'

*

My memories of that darkest of dark times are jerky and confused. I have an image of a wedding guest throwing up against the side of the marquee. Or was it me? I've absolutely no recollection of how or when we got back to Lothlorien, but I know the door to Pete's caravan was open, and we all stared at it as if we hoped he'd appear on the steps, cigarette holder poised elegantly in his hand, one eyebrow raised: 'Whatever's got into you all? You didn't really think that was *me* up there, did you?'

'Perhaps he left a note,' said Marjoram dully, but no-one moved, as if we were afraid to go inside.

It was El who eventually went up the steps. She came out with a sheet of Pete's ivory-coloured writing paper with the crinkly edges. Her face was streaming with tears.

'It was on the table... it says – "*From this wood forth I wander, never to return*".'

'Oh Pete, you were poetic to the last,' sobbed Ginnie.

'It's from an opera,' I said. Pete would sometimes hand me the English librettos to read so that I could follow the story, as all his opera recordings were in the language of the original. That particular line from The Ring had stuck in my mind; I wondered whether one day it might apply to me. And I'd enjoyed Pete's comment on it: 'Ah, Siegfried! He thinks he's so heroic but he's really just a pompous little shit. Utterly insensitive. And yet, alas, I can't help loving him.'

*

'Do you want to take any of these?' Pete's brother pointed at the shelf full of cassette tapes and LPs.

His wife glanced at them. 'I don't think so. Too highbrow for me.' She opened the cupboard next to the kitchen area. 'I quite like these cups and saucers. They'd look pretty on the kitchen dresser.'

'No!' I couldn't help myself. I was deeply attached to those cups with the violets on; they were redolent of so many tranquil and Pete-enhanced cups of tea.

'Why? You don't want them, do you?'

I nodded.

'*Really*? I'm surprised a boy like you would appreciate that kind of thing.'

'We're full of surprises,' said Shine, very grim.

'Yes, well...'

The twins and I were standing just inside the door of the caravan, watching in despair as the frightful brother and his wife picked over Pete's worldly belongings. They had driven to Middington to attend Pete's funeral, held earlier that day, and to deal with various administrative business. At first they didn't want to accept the legality of his will, written on one of those forms you can buy at a stationer's, and witnessed by the couple at the Lodge. Pete had made it two weeks before his death; he'd left it on his bed. He had bequeathed everything he owned to the community of Lothlorien. Bill assured the couple that it was in fact perfectly in order, but out of courtesy suggested that they should choose a few things for themselves to take from the caravan.

'You don't all have to stick around gawping,' said the brother. He was a short-haired and tubbier version of Pete, which somehow made him seem all the more horrific. 'We can do this perfectly well on our own.'

'Of course you can,' said Rain. 'But we're here out of respect.'

'Someone's got to be respectful,' said Shine, 'even if you aren't.'

The wife raised her eyebrows in amazement. 'There's no need to be rude.'

'Bloody cheek,' said the brother. 'We didn't come all this way to be insulted by a bunch of hippie kids.'

'You didn't respect him though, did you?' I said. I hated these people. The brother went very red but said nothing. Instead he began yanking cushions off the settee and chucking them on to the floor. We picked them up.

'Don't tell me you want those as well!' said the wife.

'Yes, we should very much like to keep them,' said Shine, speaking with great formality. 'They will remind us of all the happy times we shared with our dear friend Neat Pete.'

The brother made an exploding sound, like Bill's Spitfire when it backfired.

'Talk about precocious,' said the wife. 'And you smell as if you've been drinking.'

'We have,' said Rain coldly. 'To Pete. And we're not precocious. Young people Outside are rather backward, that's all. It's not their fault, it's just their conditioning.'

The brother made strange clawing gestures with his hands, as if he wanted to strangle us – which no doubt he did.

'Look – just get out and leave us alone, will you?' said the wife. 'This is hard enough as it is.'

We shuffled out, clutching cushions and bone china. Walking backwards down the caravan steps I tripped and dropped one of the cups, which hit a stone and shattered. I let out a howl. Layla, waiting for us outside, leapt to pick up the fragments of gold-rimmed porcelain. Each of the broken violets in her hand glared at me with reproach.

'Don't worry, Curly,' said Layla. 'You can make it into a beautiful mosaic. On a rock or something. It can be Pete's Memorial Rock, and it will be there for ever.'

I loved her at that moment.

*

Pete's remains were cremated, though there can't have been much of him left to put in the coffin. He must have died long before the fire was put out, probably while we were watching. It would have amused him to be cremated. 'Double roasted!' I could hear him saying.

We were all there, of course – in our best and brightest clothes, to the clear disapproval of the black-clad brother and spouse. Neither of them wanted to say anything during the service. It wasn't the conventional religious kind; each member of Lothlorien got up, spoke a few words and laid a flower on the coffin. I can't remember what any of us actually said, except for Sean: 'Hope you're having a great trip, man.' Ginnie tried to chant but broke down. Bill was strikingly impressive. Our Lord was present, as was the new Mrs Lord. They held hands and seemed as stricken with grief as we were. Pete's recording of Maria Callas singing *Un Bel Di* was played – at which the Chapel of Rest, or whatever it was called, was awash with tears, (though not the brother's). And at the end, The Ride of the Valkyries boomed out to accompany the coffin as it slid behind the terrible blue velvet curtains.

*

Back in Lothlorien afterwards, Gogo gave each of us a glass of blackberry wine so that we could drink a solemn toast to Pete around the Fireplace. Once again I heard his voice: '*Toasted*! But how perfect!' These words in my head didn't strike me as in any way bizarre or inappropriate. They were simply reassuring proof that Pete was still somehow with us and that his sense of irony was intact. I tried to hold on to that.

Ginnie, still weeping, called on something or someone – all the Forces of the Cosmos I suppose – to watch over him during his passage to his Next Life. We drained our glasses. The brother and the sister-in-law, although invited, hadn't joined us for this ceremony, but had instead gone straight to Pete's caravan to see what, if anything, they wanted to take away: they'd brought a number of cardboard boxes. Once the toast was over the twins and I went to watch them and make sure they handled Pete's things carefully, but after the cups-and-cushions incident we stayed outside. Layla, however, went in.

She came out with a swirly candle-holder in her hand. 'I said I loved this, it was so Pete, and that man said I had a nerve, just walking in and taking stuff, so I said that's what they were doing too, and then *she* said it was shocking how all the kids here were given alcohol to drink. So I told them it was an exceptional occasion and that *we* thought it was shocking that they hadn't come to toast Pete as well.'

'You should have told them we were usually drunk all day,' said Jelly Bean.

Eventually the brother emerged, carrying two small chairs and a couple of table lamps. 'Not a lot we wanted, really. Just these and a few kitchen bits. And the cassette player – for our daughter.' He waved the lamps. 'Not altogether our taste but at least the light bulbs will come in handy.' He gave a half-hearted chuckle which was not returned. We watched forlornly as he went to pack the things into the boot of his car.

His wife followed a few moments later, carrying a couple of cardboard boxes with a pile of pictures on top of them. 'I've taken the some of the artwork as well, because we can use the frames. For photos.'

'We'd like to keep the pictures,' said Stella. 'So can you take them out of their frames please?'

The wife tipped the pictures on to the ground. 'Blooming heck! You people!'

Ashley exploded. 'No – YOU people! You're nothing but scum-bags and thieves!'

The couple stopped and looked at him and turned cochineal pink. At any other time it would have been funny.

'*Pardon*?' said the brother. 'We have been instructed by Mr Bennett here to examine my late brother's effects and take anything we choose. As his next of kin...'

'His *kin*? His sodding murderers, more like.'

'Repeat that,' said the brother, menacingly.

'Ash, for God's sake –' Bill tried to pull him away, but he might as well have tried to stop a lava flow.

'*You* killed him! You and everyone like you, with your fucking petit bourgeois prejudices and your fucking frilly dressin tables and your fucking fucked-up heads! If he'd been able to lead a normal life –' He broke off, choking.

During this outburst the woman had pulled her husband towards the car door and pushed him in. She ran round to the passenger side: both doors slammed.

'Good riddance,' said Marjoram, as the car rocketed up the track. 'Well done, Ash.'

*

They weren't the only visitors. The police had been the first. We knew they'd come, of course; grass and mushrooms were well stashed away and not consumed by anyone for days, even Sean. His last trip had turned so bad at the sight of Pete in the flames that he was still trembling, partly from fright and partly from a real fever, as he had flu. It was rare that anyone fell ill in Lothlorien, but what had just happened was enough to lower anyone's resistance. Rick and El had bad colds; several of us, including me, had an unpleasant stomach bug. We assumed we'd picked up these complaints from guests at the wedding.

Even Ginnie, although she was meditating more than ever, broke out in cold sores. But we knew it was essential to keep ourselves well washed and brushed in readiness for the cops' arrival, and we were in any case in such an obvious state of devastation that the inspector and his woman constable were quite kind to us, in a plodding sort of way.

Everyone vouched for the goodness of Pete's character. No, he wasn't being treated for depression as far as we knew. Yes, he might have been ill but he hadn't told us. Bill dazzled them with charisma in the politest way imaginable, leaving no doubt in their minds that we were anything other than a group of vegetarian eccentrics – weirdos perhaps, but law-abiding ones. Naturally they knew about Pete's arrest the previous summer, and very likely assumed that being a gay man was enough to make anyone want to top himself. 'The fuzz couldn't give a monkey's about the Petes of this world,' said Rick bitterly. 'One less to corrupt their kids, that's their attitude.'

A journalist from the local paper made it as far as the Lodge one day, but was seen off by Our Lord. According to Gogo, the article which appeared was a very vague and watered-down version of events. Our Lord's powers must have been fairly extensive.

He himself, with Mrs Lord, came to see us again; they both looked washed out. I have to hand it to them: Pete had, after all, totally fucked up not only their wedding day but their honeymoon besides, and yet they were as solicitous towards us as if it had been all their fault and the suffering entirely on our side. We'd been afraid that they now might really want to put the kybosh on Lothlorien, but not a bit of it. That was some slight relief in the midst of all the anguish.

For the first week or so I don't remember anyone speaking very much. We were all feeling hideously guilty – because why hadn't we seen it coming? At that time we tended to eat our meals huddled together, for comfort – either round the Fireplace if it was fine, or else squashed into someone's caravan; one evening at dinner we at last began to talk.

'He must have been so, so depressed... we should have realised and *done* something,' said Zoë.

Stella nodded hopelessly. 'Funny people are often like that, aren't they? Depressives. Look at Tony Hancock.'

'But how could we have realised?' said Marjoram. 'He may have been depressed, but he didn't let on. He seemed pretty normal.'

'All the same,' said Gogo, 'he had been a bit more – I don't know – vitriolic lately. Perhaps that whole skinhead business got to him more than he wanted to admit.'

The vengeful skinheads: had they really been the cause? I was racked with a ghastly unease. Supposing we'd handled the whole skins thing differently, if we'd just alerted the police instead of going along with Blue's plan, would they still have been so intent on getting their own back on Lothlorien in some sneaky and indirect way – through Pete, in fact, who they would have considered an easy target? And could he have had another bad encounter with them that he hadn't told us about, but which had been enough to push him over the edge?

'No,' said Jack, as if reading my thoughts. 'Those guys could never have made Pete want to kill himself, not even if they'd landed him in jail. He was quite strong enough to cope with prejudice – he'd been fighting it all his life. Just think of his brother. His parents were probably worse.'

'Then why...?'

'I think his heart was broken,' she said after a pause.

'But he didn't have...' I said.

'We don't know that. He spent quite a lot of time in London, didn't he? Or so he said.'

'You mean he was in love with someone there?'

'It's a possibility. One true love gone wrong can do far more damage than forty years of insults.'

'I thought of that too,' said Zoë. 'There was so much we never really knew about Pete. If only we'd asked him more about his life Outside. It would have helped him so much to be able to talk.'

'No,' said Bill, quite forcefully. 'If he didn't tell us it was because he couldn't. He absolutely didn't want to.'

'But why – like *that*?' said Erryk softly. 'And why *there*?'

'You don't suppose -' began Stella.

'I don't think we should suppose anything at all,' said Bill very firmly.

'Pete was *dramatic*,' said Loose. 'He wanted to be a *spectacle* – like one of his operas. So no-one would forget.'

Those present at his death could never have forgotten. And for all of us in Lothlorien the recurring flashbacks and nightmares were so frequent that after a time we stopped telling each other about them, and just accepted that they would be an integral part of our life from now on.

But of course there were things which remained unsaid; like Bill, I think this was almost certainly for the best.

*

We made the Memorial Rock, from a suitable boulder I found by the river. Ash and Erryk rolled it to a spot near Pete's caravan. There were enough pieces of broken cup to form his name; I cemented them on to one side. Ashley engraved the dates of his birth and death underneath, and Stella partially buried an earthenware vase at the rock's base, into which everyone placed wildflowers from the edge of the Sheepfield.

Some days after the funeral Bill collected Pete's ashes and brought them back to Lothlorien. We all gathered at the rock and took turns to scatter them around it. I'd imagined that the urn would be made of pottery, with handles, something along the lines of a classical Greek urn. I was dismayed by the gold-coloured plastic jar with its smooth bland sheen. And the ashes, which I'd thought would be powdery, like the cooled embers from our fires, turned out to be hard little pieces of grit. 'Bone,' whispered Shine. Bill silently dug them into the ground. Gogo sprinkled wine on top, and Marjoram various herbs. Ginnie recited some Sanskrit sentences and poured sweet-smelling oils on the rock.

That evening the woods were particularly calm and beautiful. A blackbird sang piercingly in the tree-tops, and feathery pink clouds fanned out in the west against a turquoise sky.

'Pete's wings,' said Layla.

*

From that day on, there was never a time when the vase at the foot of the rock was empty. Even in winter, when there were no flowers to be found in the fields or woods, someone would bring a bunch from the florist in Middington – or we simply cut strands of ivy or fluffy old man's beard, and decorated them with coloured ribbons. Ginnie regularly offered her prayers and perfumed libations. 'How divine, my personal priestess,' said Pete. I found I was hearing him more and more, and sometimes even had conversations with him: my way, I suppose, of coping.

And life did indeed go on – but at half mast. Lothlorien had received such a colossal shock to its system that everything seemed muted and lacking in colour, even though we did our best to continue with business as usual – shop, Garden, chickens, jobs, lessons… 'It's as if a light's gone out,' said Rain.

Everyone agreed that the money in Pete's bank account – more than expected, apparently – should be put into a fund for repairs and improvements to Lothlorien. First we painted and re-tiled the shower block, and put in two new washing machines.

'Thank you, Pete,' said Layla. 'Now we shall always have shining clean clothes.'

'I'd rather be dirty and have Pete,' said El.

Since his death El had undergone another metamorphosis: she had shed her chrysalis of Goth-dom and emerged, if not as a gorgeous butterfly, at least as someone surprisingly presentable, even mildly elegant. Now she wore long dark floppy jackets over normal jeans, and even asked Zoë to restyle her hair. It wasn't possible to get rid of all the frizziness, but Zoë managed to tame it into a shortish halo and removed some of the black dye. The resulting colour was strange, a kind of pale uneven charcoal, so El accepted Zoë's suggestion of a golden-brown tint with lighter streaks. All of a sudden she seemed much older than seventeen. She moved differently: her slouch disappeared, and she began attending Alexander Technique classes given by the mother of one of her friends in Middington. She still didn't have a great deal to do with the rest of us, but communication, when it took place, was on the whole polite. Most of her time in Lothlorien was spent in studying for the A-levels she was going to take the following year.

By common consent she had completely taken over Pete's caravan; she had, after all, been living in his spare bedroom for some time while he was still alive. 'Maybe he'll haunt it,' said Layla. 'I hope he does,' said El. She changed the coverings and other decorations, but constructed a small shrine to Pete on a low table with which she covered with one of his silk scarves. She added two photos, one taken by Loose, recognisable although oddly angled, and another of him as a very young man which she found in an old pre-Lothlorien album, one he'd never shown us. Next to these she placed his cigarette holder, and a small statuette of Michelangelo's David. Pete had been very fond of this. 'Kitsch as all get out,' he used to say, 'but loaded with memories.' El usually kept a stick of incense burning next to it.

'Isn't that a bit too hippie for you?' I asked.

'I have to face up to that aspect of my upbringing,' she said seriously. 'There's no point trying to repress it – I've gone beyond that. Some things you just have to accept, whether you like it or not.'

*

At the end of July we received an unexpected boost of energy: the fair came back.

'Our gaffer got a chance to try this other place last year,' said Blue. 'Shithole. So here we are again. Good eh?'

It was just the kind of distraction we needed. Erryk had spotted the rides being built up on Middington Common and offered to take us in to town the next day. The twins, Jelly Bean and I all jumped at the chance, but Layla was distraught. 'What can I tell him? I can't two-time Giovanni. I don't even want to.'

'Tell him the truth,' said Shine. 'He's a big boy, he can take it. '

She was perfectly correct.

'Bugger me, so you've gone and fallen for a spaghetti twister!' Blue roared with laughter. 'Hope he treats you right, darling. Bit of a stallion, is he?'

'He's a real gentleman,' said Layla demurely.

'That's all right then. Come to think of it, I got an auntie who's married to a wop, and he's quite a gent...' He coughed. His voice was breaking, and he continued in his new voice, which was disconcertingly deeper than mine. 'Matter of fact, I'm what you might call otherwise occupied myself.' He gave me a nudge. 'Tell you all about it later.'

Layla's face fell. 'You mean you've got a new girlfriend?'

'What, you were hoping you'd break my heart? No such luck, doll.' He gave her a big noisy kiss on the lips before she could stop him. 'There, that's for old time's sake. Now I want to hear what you guys been up to.'

We told him about Pete.

'Fuck me...' For a long moment Blue was lost for words. He shook his head. 'He was a diamond, that one. Went out with a bang though, didn't he? You gotta admire that. Not a lot of people with that sort of courage. Know why he did it?'

'No.'

Blue pulled on his lower lip as he reflected. 'Ain't easy, being omi-palone. My cousin, he don't have what you'd call a happy life.'

'But he should have!' exclaimed Shine. 'When I'm older, I'm going to try and change all that.'

'How?'

'I'll be a lawyer. Or a barrister. So I can fight prejudice and injustice.'

Blue looked at her sceptically. 'Don't see how you can do that through the law.'

'You've got to work inside the System if you want to fight it. That's what I think, anyway. Gogo and Marjoram don't agree, but that's too bad.'

'You going to be a lawyer too?' Blue gave Rain a punch on the shoulder. 'I'll hire the pair of you when I land up in court. Twin defence – can't lose.'

'No, sorry,' said Rain. 'I want to be an engineer. So I can invent things. Not stupid things – useful stuff. Spaceships.'

'Blimey.' Blue gave Layla a little squeeze. 'Bet gorgeous here ain't going to be a brain-box, are you darling? Brightest star in Hollywood, that's what you'll be. Remind me to get your autograph before the rush starts.'

'That won't be necessary,' said Layla rather huffily. 'I don't want to be a film star – you can't have a proper private life. Anyway, I want to do something useful too. I'm going to create my own fashion and make-up range. Stella says she'll help me.'

'Another great leap for mankind,' I said, and I had the weird sensation that it was Pete speaking through me.

'Well it will be. I'll be giving everyone the chance to look nicer, so they'll be much happier. That's far more useful than floating around in outer space.'

'I'll have the best job,' said Jelly Bean, 'because I'm going to be a game ranger in Africa. Animals are far more interesting than stupid humans.'

'Right up your street – shooting lions and tigers with your catapult.'

'Are you mad? I'll shoot the poachers. With a gun.'

'Bet you would, too.' Blue chuckled. 'And how about you then, Curly? Got an exciting future lined up?'

'Not really. I think I'll just stay here and work with Ash.' I'd never told anyone that I was saving most of the cash he gave me in a box under my bed, for my ticket to Australia. It was in a brown envelope wrapped in an old sweater, together with the little silver dragon that Tiger Lily had given me when she left.

Ashley had a lot of work on that summer; this was just as well because it meant that between Gogo's lessons, Ashley's jobs and the usual round of Lothlorien chores, I had little time for reflection. Thinking wasn't something I wanted to do very much after Pete's death. There was also another, very different, cause of my brainlessness: my body. By now it was a seething mass of hormones, ready to boil over at any minute – especially when Blue regaled me with lurid stories of his new girlfriend, a cousin two years his senior. 'Cor, is she a goer,' he said, licking his lips. 'Can't get enough of it.'

'You mean you go... all the way?'

'All the way and round the houses and then back again!' He elaborated in some detail, while my erection throbbed with envy. I secretly wondered if he wasn't simply regurgitating material from Micky's porn magazines.

'You just gotta go for it,' he assured me when I confessed I had no idea how to set about satisfying my own desires. 'You'll be amazed how many women are absolutely aching for a good shag with a nice young lad – best way to learn all about it. And you got an advantage, you look a bit exotic. They love that.'

Exotic? Me?

'Any rate,' Blue went on, 'no good standing around with your hand in your pocket shaking hands with the unemployed.'

But that's all I seemed destined to do for the foreseeable future.

There may have been some truth in what Blue said, however. More than once, while out at work with Ash, I noticed a woman client looking at me in a strange way. To begin with I presumed this was because they thought I appeared too wild, or too young, to be Ash's apprentice, in spite of the little spiel he used to give them about me being seconded from a progressive school in order to get some work experience. On the other hand, I was now already at least as tall as the average fifteen-year-old, and although I never knew what to say to these women I always smiled politely. So perhaps it was something else – a suspicion which was borne out when one day when we were fitting a kitchen. Ash had gone to fetch a tool from the pick-up and I found myself alone with the lady of the house, who would probably have been in her late thirties. I pretended to ignore her and carried on with my work, but she came over to me and casually ruffled my hair.

'You're rather an attractive young man, do you know that? Sort of different.' She swished out of the kitchen with a light laugh while I blushed to the roots of my curls without saying a word. After this I began to fantasize about her in a big way. Sadly that job ended before I had the chance to find out if these fantasies might blossom into reality, but from then on I was perpetually on tenterhooks when I was working in those houses, longing for Ash to leave me alone with some sex-starved housewife who would take my hand and sweep me into her bedroom.

Within Lothlorien, however, I began to sink more and more into an uncharacteristic lassitude. All the adults must have known what I was going through, but it was Elfland policy not to be pushily inquisitive. I'm sure any of the men – or women, for that matter – would have been only too happy to offer sympathy and advice, but at the time I was far too self-obsessed and self-conscious to want to share anything with them.

Pete had been a wonderful confidant, but Pete... I often remembered his advice about older women. Rain was the only person I could to talk to now, as he was more or less in the same condition as I was, although he was lucky in that he seemed able to sublimate his sexual desires to some extent by throwing himself into his studies; at that time he was deeply into physics and cosmology. These were subjects largely beyond Gogo's range and also that of the Middington library – though not, luckily, the library in Chandleford. He tried to get me interested too; I dimly understood his fascination for the outer reaches of the Cosmos, but what seemed to me far, far more worthy of exploration were the inner reaches of a woman.

Jack came to my rescue. 'If you want to stay lying down all the time, then at least read,' she said, and introduced me to a throng of authors hitherto unknown to me – Salinger, Hemingway, Henry Miller, Lawrence Durrell, Gore Vidal, Philip Roth. *Portnoy's Complaint* I found particularly comforting, though I couldn't relate to his mother fixation. I read, and read, and attended to my dick, and read, and that was how I spent the greater part of my spare time during that earliest year or so of my manhood. I also had frequent moments of intense grief, as we all did. Much of that period, however, passed by me in a fuzzy haze of frustrated longings.

But there was a moment during the Solstice which comes back to me vividly. The celebrations were subdued that winter, for gaiety was still noticeably absent from Lothlorien even though we did sometimes have a shot at being jolly. We made an effort for the Solstice, and began to make a cake as usual – but Marjoram, while pouring the mixture into the cake tin, slipped on the wet surface around the earth oven and spilt most of it on the ground. It looked like vomit.

'Oh, for Pete's sake!' she cried, furious, and then realised what she'd said. She threw the tin down and burst into noisy tears. It was awful to see Marjoram collapse – like watching a tree fall without warning. Of course she'd cried at Pete's death, but quietly, and no-one had ever seen her give way to such a storm of emotion.

Everyone was silent – until Loose, as ever the wild card of the community, began to jump up and down and shout. 'Yes! For *Pete's* sake! We must *laugh*, because he would laugh too – and we must make more cake *now*. Lots and lots of cake!'

Somehow she released a spring in us – her great talent – and all of a sudden we started to cheer and yell and, finally, to laugh. We laughed until we ached, and when eventually the laughter died down we rushed around frenetically getting the ingredients together for a fresh batch of cake-mix. The cake, baked overnight, came out of the oven next morning risen and triumphant. For the first time since Pete's suicide we felt a real lightening of our spirits.

We went back to holding impromptu music sessions, and began to put on theatrical events again, either our own plays or else highlights from the classics. Although I couldn't summon up much energy for this kind of thing any more, I did quite enjoy our rendering of the death scene from *The Duchess of Malfi*. Layla played the garrotted duchess, and choked and gurgled most convincingly while Rain and I, as the garrotters, pulled on the cord with enthusiasm. This caused a certain unease among some members of the audience.

'Isn't that reinforcing stereotypical gender violence?' Ginnie asked Gogo, who'd directed our efforts.

'They're quite mature enough not to confuse their present lives with the out-dated morality of a Jacobean tragedy,' said Gogo. 'It isn't going to influence the code of ethics they've learned here.' I thought of all the times Rain and I would have quite happily garrotted Layla, or at least one of her dolls.

Thanks mainly to Gogo, us younger members of Lothlorien were well versed not only in Jacobean tragedy but also in a richly varied range of other subjects – from plate tectonics and the fauna and flora of Madagascar to the social life of both Neolithic farmers and the Pre-Raphaelites. We could have told you, among other things, about the Romans, the Renaissance, the Enlightenment and the evils of the Industrial Revolution. But we hardly knew the first thing about current affairs.

This was a deliberate strategy on the part of our elders, who wanted us to grow up untouched, as far as possible, by the preoccupations of Outside – we were seldom aware of what year it was, let alone what date. They themselves didn't pay much attention to politics and global events either, though lately we had begun to hear fairly frequent grumblings about 'That Woman'.

There was one subject, however, which we noticed cropping up more and more often in conversation: Greenham Common.

Jack and Marjoram seemed to be the most interested in this place, with Ginnie a close second. 'Heard about that,' said Blue when I mentioned it to him in the summer. 'Loada women demonstrating against the nukeler. You oughta get up there – not a bloke in sight, they say. Good chance to get your leg over.'

Not long before the Solstice of the following winter Jack announced she was going to make a trip to this paradise.

'It looks as if there's going to be a huge protest. I want to be part of it and I want to write about it.'

'Can Rain and I come too?' I was mentally dribbling at the idea of so much female flesh concentrated in one location.

'Sorry, Curly. Women only.'

Marjoram, Ginnie and Loose went with her. They took Pete's car, loaded up with two tents, plenty of warm clothes, and provisions for a couple of days. It had been decided the previous year that his car should be kept in Lothlorien rather than sold, so that Jack and Loose would no longer have to depend on anyone else's vehicle when they needed to go Outside: the campervan was too much hassle to move, as the wheels were by now sunk several inches into the earth and the grass grew past the hubcaps.

They returned three days later, muddy and elated. 'Absolutely amazing,' said Marjoram. 'Thirty thousand women. Thirty thousand! We held hands all around the base. I can't tell you what it felt like to be part of that solidarity. Such a force for good.'

'I wish I'd come with you,' said Ginnie, Zoë, Stella and Shine.

'Next time. There's bound to be plenty more action.'

Jack explained to me some of the reasons behind the existence of the protest camp, including nuclear weapons, Hiroshima... It was hard to take in. For a while I forgot my sexual obsessions as I pondered the terrifying nastiness of Outside.

'Yes, it isn't very nice,' said Jack. 'But that's the way of the world, unfortunately. Here, have a glass of sherry.'

We sipped in silence for a few minutes.

'Oh – I've been meaning to show you this.' Jack took a book from the table and handed it to me: an anthology of modern American poetry. 'It was Pete's,' she said. 'He left a bookmark in it – I've only just noticed. Read that page – the left hand side.'

I opened the book. The poem began: '*In a dark time, the eye begins to see...*' A shiver went through me as I continued to read; although at the time I didn't fully understand all of the poem I knew that it was giving me a glimpse into Pete's state of mind before his death. When I reached the end I realised I was crying.

'Can I borrow this?' I asked.

'Of course,' said Jack.

I copied out the poem and learnt it by heart. Perhaps one day it might come in useful.

*

Such as now. Nothing brings back so intensely the atmosphere of that period: it also reminds me of the necessity to get a new angle on my own existence.

Unlike Pete, I have absolutely no suicidal urges. I'm only too pleased I didn't manage to do myself in by accident. But I do know my vision has changed: I'm no longer the person I was when I began to write this account. Then, it was as if I was peering into Lothlorien from Outside, whereas now I'm inside looking out – and yet I feel a whole lot freer.

Marco came to see me today – a visiting Outsider, though always a welcome one. Such optimistic good humour is a tonic. I must have been looking reasonably bright and cheerful myself – the couple of days spent writing about Pete have finally provided me with a kind of catharsis.

'So you will soon be back!' he exclaimed with delight. 'They will be so happy when I tell them.'

'Who will?'

'Your clients! There is especially a friend of Mrs K who is hassling me to know when you will be available. She says she met you at that party and saw that you were the only person who really understood her need for a feng shui solution to her villa problem.'

I thought backwards, outwards, to another world. 'Oh God, her. Why didn't you tell her you understood it too?'

'Because –' Marco put his hand over his heart – 'I am certain that it is only you who can offer her full satisfaction. And anyway, when you get out of here you will need – how do you say – something to get your teeth into.' He winked.

'Marco – I think you'd better tell her – everyone – that my availability from now on is non-existent. Zero. You can say I've gone to Tibet or something.'

Marco stared. 'You are going crazy...'

'No – but I want a change. New job, new place. You can take over all my stuff – you know the business backwards, you're really good at it. It's all in your name anyway. *And* you know how to flirt – better than I do. '

'I don't want to work alone! It's too much for me! And we have so many good times together.'

'I'll miss those too. You'll have to take on a bright young assistant. A female one.'

He looked very doubtful. 'You will change your mind. I will try to change it for you.'

'No chance.' I gave him a big smile. 'My decision is final.'

20. ARRIVALS

'SHE'S PREGNANT! MRS Lord!' Zoë had just come down from the House; Ashley and I were putting a couple of new window frames into her and Rick's caravan.

Rick looked at her quizzically. 'And is that steaming nugget of news supposed to bring joy into my life?'

'It's official – four months already. She didn't want to tell anyone before, just in case anything went wrong. I did have my suspicions though. Momma Lord's going wild – she's drunk on champagne. I could hardly get her curlers in – Mrs Lord had to hold her down.'

'What a charming family scene.'

'So he managed it,' said Ash. 'Got it up and got it in.'

'Must you always be so vulgar, Ashley?'

'Blimey, you're beginning to sound like Ginnie. I'm not vulgar, I'm factual.'

Ash was in surprisingly good spirits these days. Whenever he wanted me to come and help him with a job he sang outside my window to wake me, instead of banging on it as he normally did.

'*Hi ho, hi ho, it's off to work we go...*' I soon began to get sick of that song.

He still sang even when he contracted a heavy cold, which streamed from his eyes and nose for days.

'Where the hell did you pick up those germs?' asked Marjoram, passing by on a morning foray into the chicken coop.

'It's all the low company I keep Outside.' Ash trumpeted snottily into an old rag. He began to pull lengths of timber from under his caravan. 'Ha! These should do the trick. Give us a hand then, mate.'

I heaved out some planks. A fine frost shimmered in the sunlight and our breath steamed in the air. 'New job?' I asked hopefully. Some days earlier we'd finished working in a house which had been disappointingly empty of females, at least during the hours when we were in it. Ever optimistic, I was looking forward to a new and more fulfilling location.

'Spiral staircase,' said Ash. 'Round the tree.'

'What tree?' I asked stupidly.

'My house, thicko. Needs a more efficient means of access. Ladders aren't so great for ageing joints.'

I looked at him with some scepticism as he energetically hauled out more wood. 'Nothing much wrong with your joints. And you're not all that old either.'

'Might as well prepare a few creature comforts while I still can. Besides, Chip's getting a bit arthrickety these days. He'll like a nice staircase.'

'But you always carry him up the ladder in his basket.'

'Exactly. He needs some exercise.' He picked up a saw and a pile of planks. 'Run and get my sander, there's a good lad. I lent it to Gogo. You can give it a quick run over the floor while I'm sorting this lot out.'

'The floor of the tree house?'

'No, Buckingham Palace. Then it'll need varnishing.'

'How about a fitted carpet?' I was feeling tetchy now; I didn't feel in the least like spending time in Lothlorien on Ashley's home improvements.

My sarcasm was completely lost on him. 'Not a bad idea... couple of new rugs might be better though. Sort of fluffy.'

Fluffy? I began to be suspicious. 'Is that woman coming to visit?'

Ash looked at me innocently. 'What woman?'

'The one you go to screw behind the pub.' She seemed to have been a fairly reliable sexual partner for several years now, though Ash had never brought her to Lothlorien.

'That old slag? She's history.' He moved off towards the tree house. '*Hi ho, hi ho, it's up the stairs we go...*'

Rather sulkily, I walked over to Gogo and Marjoram's caravan and knocked on the door. As it opened I was greeted by the warm scent of scrambling eggs and grilling tomatoes.

'Come for breakfast? ' asked Marjoram.

I'd already had breakfast, but only a bowl of Erryk's home-made muesli, so I wasn't going to refuse.

'Ashley's got a new girlfriend,' I announced, once I was full of hot food and therefore feeling more cheerful.

'Really?' said Marjoram. 'He hasn't said anything. What makes you think so?'

I explained.

'Knowing Ash, I doubt if it's anything serious,' said Gogo. 'He's never had what you'd call a real relationship.'

'He just hasn't found the right woman,' I said.

'Maybe... but perhaps he doesn't want to. He has a commitment problem.'

'He's committed to Chip, isn't he?' said Shine.

'That's not quite the same thing,' said Marjoram. 'And anyway, I don't think he attracts the right type. He's a bit too rough around the edges.'

'But he's a really good guy underneath,' said Rain. 'There must be *some* women who could see that.'

'Possibly... though not many of them would want to sleep in a tree with a dribbly middle-aged dog. Or cook in a carpenter's workshop.'

It was indeed pretty obvious that Ash's caravan, furnished mainly with his work benches, lathe, tool boxes, and various piles of wood, didn't leave much room for the practice of *fine cuisine*. He had a tiny oven perched next to the sink and two electric plates on the draining board, all of which were well coated with blackened grease.

'We're not all into cooking,' protested Shine. 'And lots of people like dogs. And there's sure to be a few hippie women out there who'd love to sleep in a tree.'

'There could be – at Findhorn or somewhere like that,' said Marjoram. 'Not in Middington or Chandleford.'

'Let's just wait and see,' said Shine.

While we waited, Ash and I went full steam ahead with his renovations. It didn't take us long to complete a handsome staircase and smarten up the floor of the tree house; that done, however, the rest of the interior looked shabby in comparison.

'Needs a touch more TLC, eh Curly?' said Ash. 'Definitely those rugs... lick of paint on the walls... tell you what, you're artistic, you can be in charge of all that.'

'Why not ask her what *she* likes?'

'Her? I never said anything about a *her*. You're jumping ahead of things. Just pick some nice stuff for me and Chip, OK?'

And so began what could be called my very first interior design job, and it turned out more enjoyable than I'd imagined. I decided that the plank walls, until now unadorned, should be white – apart from the one behind the bed which I painted dark blue and decorated with a sparkly Indian wallhanging from Ethnic Imports in Chandleford. While we were there I chose a few cushions, a bright striped bedcover, and two Afghan sheepskins for the floor. The small cupboard and set of drawers, torn long ago from his caravan and installed in the tree to store clothes, were also in urgent need of a makeover; I stripped off the formica and painted them white as well.

Then I insisted that we had to replace the ancient and rather smelly bedding. Ashley and Chip had been sharing a sleeping bag and a pile of hairy blankets on top of Tiger Lily's old mattress, pillows and bean bag; although it caused me pain, I could see that even these last items had to go, as by now they were too heavily Chip-impregnated. So we got a new mattress, pillows, and a duvet with a couple of covers – one blue like the wall and the other sunshine yellow, with sheets and pillowcases to match.

'Bugger me,' said Ashley, 'you're turning it into a suburban love-nest.'

'No I'm not,' I said. 'I'm just brightening it up. It'll be a hippie country retreat.'

Finally I persuaded him that he needed a mirror and a few pictures, and curtains for the windows. He accepted my choice of two framed prints of Rousseau reproductions – exotic felines in jungle settings. Stella provided the mirror and a chunky wooden candlestick, and cut up a paisley kaftan that she didn't wear any more to make curtains – she'd become very enthusiastic about the project. Ginnie gave him a new bedside lamp, as the old one with the red shade, once Tiger Lily's, had become extremely grubby.

'Now you can be *proud* of your home,' she said.

'I was proud of it before.'

'Yes of course – but now it's so much more cosy and *welcoming*, isn't it?' She tilted her head to one side and raised her eyebrows archly: this was the Ginnie equivalent of a wink. 'Are you expecting a guest quite soon?'

'Swarms of 'em,' said Ashley. 'It's going to be one long arboreal orgy.' He clapped me on the shoulder. 'Curly'll have to help me out.'

If only. Ginnie tinkled with laughter and tripped away.

But for the time being not a single orgiastic invitee materialised.

'Told you it was just for me and Chip,' said Ashley, but he didn't seem in any way downhearted. Instead, he started clearing up the kitchen area of his caravan, so I presumed that hope was not lost.

Inspired by my design work, I took a look at my own bedroom and found it wanting. I was so used to it that I hardly noticed it any more, but now I saw that it belonged to my younger self, and needed to be shed, like an old skin. The children's books, the home-made mobiles, the odd soft toy, model cars and planes and so on – I packed them all away under the bed, together with my Star Wars posters and pictures of rabbits. Then I realised that my faded orange candlewick bedspread simply wouldn't cut it with today's woman, so I found, in the Oxfam shop in Middington, a slightly peculiar light grey quilted cover with a geometrically textured surface, which struck me as masculine but not off-puttingly so; I had been well conditioned by the women of Lothlorien to avoid the overtly macho. I added a couple of bright crimson cushions, because I remembered Tiger

Lily telling me that crimson was the colour of passion.

It seemed like a good idea to take advantage of the dark blue paint left over from the tree house, and as I wanted an atmosphere a bit more eccentric and modern than Ashley's bedroom I used it on all the walls and the ceiling too, producing what I hoped was a cool, mysterious and slightly wacky effect. As wall decoration I made a collage of pictures from old National Geographic magazines which Gogo gave me: Machu Picchu, the Pyramids, coral reefs and other far-flung parts of the world. This, I thought, would show how well-travelled I was, at least in the imagination. I made another collage with some of Loose's photos, and Rick supplied me with pictures of Talking Heads, Bowie, the Clash and of course Laurie Anderson, who I fancied something rotten. I pinned her photograph on the ceiling next to a large poster of the moon, and gazed at it lustfully while I imagined her seducing me to the hypnotic beat of *O Superman*. Oh, those electronic arms...

So now my own love-nest was ready – if not for Laurie Anderson, then for some glamorous American tourist who would be visiting the House one day. She would cruise slowly up the drive from the Lodge in her open-topped sportscar just as I reached the top of the track on my bike – and of course she would stop and ask for directions, which I would give her in my new, husky, and I hoped sexy voice. Full of gratitude, she would whisper: 'You're so kind – how can I thank you? Maybe with a little surprise...'

A real-life surprise soon came from another direction – one which was much less thrilling for me personally, although interesting in its way.

Erryk and I were having a quiet dinner in the caravan. He'd wanted to try out a new recipe on me before inflicting it on anyone else: a heap of swede mashed with cream and parsley, filled with an onion and red bean mixture topped with cheese. 'Inflict' is actually the wrong word, as it was delicious.

Although I expressed my appreciation he didn't seem convinced; he was nervously tapping the fingers of one hand on the table top.

'Curly,' he said at last, 'do you think you'd mind if...'

I waited for a while.

'...if, er, someone else, that's to say another person, was living here? I mean with us, in this caravan?'

'Who, Miriam? I wouldn't mind if it's just her. Not her son, though. We all hate him. Jelly Bean would probably drown him in the Pool.'

'No need to – I mean Miriam – it's not her. You see, she gave me a kind of – ultimatum. She wanted me to move in with her, into her house, but...'

'I can't imagine you living in a house.' I really couldn't – in my mind

Erryk and the caravan formed a single unit.

'No – I don't think – no.'

'So you've broken up with her and you've found a new girlfriend.' New girlfriends were all the rage this winter, it seemed – though not for me, I thought bitterly.

Erryk's face relaxed in relief. 'Yes – that's just it.'

'Who is she? Did you meet her at a market?'

'Um... no. In the shop. She was getting some of Ginnie's oils. I was passing by in the car but I stopped – and I went in... I'm not sure why.'

'You felt a psychic pull.'

'I suppose I did. Ginnie told me afterwards – she comes in often and they talk... she's been through a bad time and she needs a different... you know, environment. So Ginnie thought that maybe... well, it was sort of her idea.'

'You mean Ginnie arranged the whole thing, just like that?'

'No, no – we went for tea quite a lot, and things –'

'*Things*?'

'Well, she's been renting this bed-sit'...

'OK, you can spare me the sordid details. What's her name?'

Erryk smiled shyly. 'Gail.'

*

'What, as in violent wind?' Rain asked me, smirking.

'No, arsehole, it's with an "i."'

'The eye of the storm!' declaimed Shine. 'Perhaps she's tempestuous, like Cathy.' Shine was very much into the Brontës at that time, and had rather unexpectedly begun to reinvent herself as a romantic heroine. She wore long skirts and had grown her hair. It was darkish brown, slightly wavy, and she had started to take care of it with her mother's herbal conditioners. In fact, as I realised now, she wasn't bad-looking; her face was on the broad and heavy side and her features were strong rather than dainty, but she had wonderful clear grey-green eyes – the only thing she shared with her brother.

'I can't think where those came from,' Marjoram used to say.

'They're just a mixture of yours and mine,' said Gogo. 'Genes don't mix bright blue and brown as if they were paint.'

Everyone had always remarked on the fact that the twins didn't resemble either of their parents very much – or each other, for that matter, apart from the eyes. Shine was quite tall and rangy, whereas Rain was more solidly built and, to his great annoyance, a little shorter than his sister. His hair was fair and completely straight and floppy, always a matter of wonder to Gogo whose blackish locks were almost as curly as mine. 'He takes after my dad,' said Marjoram.

'Rain, you're going to be a stunner,' said Stella, 'and you too, Curly. You've both got something special.' Of course we didn't believe her.

It was only recently that I'd taken much notice of how we all looked. My own appearance was not a source of any pleasure to me; I was far too tall and gangly, my ears stuck out and despite my brownish skin I had freckles on my nose, especially in summer. Layla was of course the only obvious beauty among us, and she had the kind of confidence which comes from being told constantly from early childhood, and often by strangers, that you're gorgeous. But neither she nor Shine – to all intents and purposes my siblings – were in any way sexually desirable as far as I was concerned. And Jelly Bean, now twelve, still seemed more like a wild animal than anything else, though her pointed features and fierce eyes had already attracted the attention of a rather odd, silent boy who lived on a farm some miles away. They went on long cross-country rambles and sometimes stayed out all night watching for bats and hedgehogs.

Ginnie had given up worrying about her daughter. She busied about more than ever; apart from the shop she took part in aromatherapy workshops in London from time to time, and had started a correspondence course in homeopathy. Yoga and meditation were still part of her daily routine, but now she launched herself into these activities with an energy bordering on desperation, and her stillness had an aura of tension rather than transcendental calm.

One day I spotted her in front of Pete's caravan, crying silently. Stella was comforting her: 'But you know he's had a brilliant reincarnation. You said so yourself – he's going to be an opera singer.' Ginnie shivered and said nothing. Perhaps she was losing her faith.

That caravan had become a sad place; while El was living there it still seemed to have some kind of soul and purpose, but these days it was nearly always empty, as El had gone to Brighton University the previous autumn: she was reading history. Apart from a few days over the Solstice she had spent her winter vacation with friends elsewhere, and although she occasionally popped in for a quick visit she was now more or less a complete Outsider.

'As long as she's happy, that's the main thing,' said Zoë. 'Kids – you have them on loan for a while and then they go off and do their own thing. It's natural.'

'Ah yes, Nature, doncha just love it,' said Rick. 'Years of care and expenses and then it's fuck you, Mum and Dad.'

'Well, that's what we did with our parents, isn't it? At least she's not a Goth any more and she's stopped being so rude to us.'

'Yeah, and now it's Layla's turn,' said Rick. 'Farting about all over the place with Mister Smoothie I-tie and his royalist parents.'

'That is a racist and totally uncool thing to say,' said Zoë. 'Go and sit next to your light box.' Rick still used this in winter and on the whole it did seem to keep his depressions at bay. Since Pete's death several of the others used it from time to time.

Giovanni was certainly smooth but by no means unlikeable. He was always impeccably polite to everyone when Layla brought him to Lothlorien; although he often seemed surprised or amused by us, he wasn't in any way supercilious. Rain and I rather envied him his easy charm, which to us seemed very sophisticated. But we felt he was on an entirely different wavelength from us – it would never be possible to be real friends with him.

'He's a Londoner,' said Layla. 'He's streetwise. You're just woodwise.'

'Blue's ten times more streetwise than Giovanni,' I said. 'But he's ten times easier to be friends with.'

'That's because Giovanni likes being with me more than with anybody else.'

'I suppose you fornicate,' said Shine.

'Don't be so disgusting. We're going to wait until I'm fifteen, then I'll go on the Pill, and then we'll *make love*.'

*

Gail's arrival was supposedly just around the corner: Erryk was getting jittery, especially in the kitchen. He burned soups and confused salt with sugar. Most annoyingly, he put food in strange places and then forgot about it. I was relieved when Ashley proposed a baked potato dinner, complete with his own home-made fillings.

It was a relatively mild and windless evening, one when the spring begins to feel like a possibility. Ash had lit the fire well before nightfall; from my bedroom I could smell the smoke and hear him singing:

'She'll be hot as baked potatoes when she comes,' (repeat)
'She'll be baking hot potatoes,
Raking hot potatoes,
Shaking hot potatoes when she comes.

Singing yi yi yippee yippee yi...'

At least someone's happy, I thought with a touch of resentment, but soon sank back into my muddy wallow of self-absorption. I was trying my hand at erotic poetry; Gogo had rather sensibly suggested that for our next literature assignment each of us should write as many poems as we could. The twins, Layla and myself had all plunged into this project with great seriousness. Jelly Bean couldn't see much point in it, so she just wrote *'I'm a cat, I'm a rat, I'm a bat, and that's that'*. Gogo found in these words a certain naïve freshness, but we knew she was just being lazy. On the other hand, it's the only one of our poems that I can remember – which is fortunate, as they were no more than long outpourings of adolescent angst or, in Layla's case, lollipop sentimentality.

My poetic trance was broken by a frenetic rapping on my bedroom window.

'Curly! *Viens vite!*' Loose often lapsed into French when she was excited. Thanks to her, all five of us by now spoke the language much better than any of the adults. She had also taught us plenty of lurid slang, which we used among ourselves when we were Outside to make rude remarks about Outsiders.

I looked up and saw her leaping up and down. *'Vite! Bouge-toi le cul!'* she yelled.

So with an effort I rather unwillingly shifted my arse and went out to see what was up.

'Elle est là – la nana!'

'Gail?'

Loose cackled. She took hold of my hand and pulled me over to the Fireplace. Erryk was there already, holding a small basket of young dandelion leaves which he'd gathered as a salad garnish. He was looking a bit dazed. Next to him stood Ashley, who had his arm round the waist of an unknown woman.

With his free hand Ash punched Erryk in the ribs. 'Beat you to it, Romeo.' He turned to us and gestured grandly towards the woman. 'Meet Barbara. She'll be staying here for a while.'

Once we'd all got over the surprise it became clear that Barbara was probably a good thing. She had a wide mouth which made her look as if she was smiling even when she wasn't, though in fact she smiled a lot of the time – or rather laughed, as she seemed to find Ash endlessly amusing. She was about the same size, age, and general shape as him, with a round face and cropped blonde hair and slightly coarse, reddish skin: she was a landscape gardener. She told us that evening that she was divorced, with a son away in the navy, and had been living rather unsatisfactorily with a cousin in Chandleford, where Ash had met her at the hardware store some months before and got chatting over the wheelbarrows. Her work frequently took her out of the area for several weeks at a time, so she wasn't going to be a full-time resident in Lothlorien. We knew that this arrangement would suit Ash very well; I doubt if he could have handled a sudden transition from his solitary state to permanent coupledom. Best of all, Barbara liked Chip. She liked the tree house too, and didn't seem fazed by the idea of having a rather distant downstairs lavatory.

And we liked her. Not an obvious hippie, she nonetheless shared many of the Lothlorien values, especially when it came to vegetarianism and organic fruit and veg. She formed an instant bond with Gogo and Marjoram.

'Such a wonderfully *down to earth* person,' whispered Ginnie to Stella, at a moment when Barbara had gone off to the shower block. 'Not *spiritual*, of course, but then Ash couldn't cope with someone on a higher level of psychic evolution. This is the perfect partner for him.' She must have been extremely pissed off that Ash hadn't consulted her about bringing Barbara in, and was trying to make out that it was only because of her own wise judgement that the latter's presence could continue to be tolerated.

She turned to Erryk. 'So now she and Gail can be new girls together – isn't that nice? She'll be here any day now, won't she?'

Erryk dropped his potato. 'Er... no. She's gone to Wales – to stay with – someone.'

'Really? She didn't say anything about that last time she was in the shop.'

'No – it was a bit sudden. She needed... She has to learn to – to breathe again.'

'Has she got something wrong with her lungs?' asked Jelly Bean.

'Darling, do try to think *metaphorically* sometimes,' said Ginnie. 'Oh Erryk, I do understand. After all she's been through.'

Erryk nodded unhappily.

Ginnie smiled her sweetest smile. 'She'll be back soon – I can feel it. Then we can *all* help her to breathe.'

'Yes... I just hope she'll have enough – space here.'

'Oh, we'll leave you both in peace. We won't crowd you.'

'She'll be fine,' said Marjoram. Like Zoë and Stella, she knew Gail slightly from her visits to the shop. 'I think you're the one who's afraid of feeling crowded, Erryk. After all, you and Curly have had that caravan to yourselves for an awfully long time.'

'I suppose I could move out if you want,' I said truculently. I didn't want to move out in the least – on the other hand I knew it would be mean to spoil Erryk's new shot at domestic bliss. 'I could sleep in your caravan, couldn't I Stella?'

'No! No!' Erryk was truly shocked. 'I only…'

'How about putting her in there for a while?' said Marjoram suddenly, indicating Pete's old caravan. 'Until she gets acclimatised, at any rate. It'll be an opportunity to freshen it up and change things round, so it'll be quite different from when –' She still found it hard to say Pete's name.

This sensible idea went down well with everybody. After a few days' communal effort of repainting and partial refitting, the caravan seemed almost like a new place; we all felt a lot cheerier towards it, even though its potential occupant still showed no signs of turning up.

'You can't hurry females,' said Ashley. 'That's right, isn't it Barbs? Give 'em time and they'll come running.'

Barbara laughed, as she always did at Ash's sexist remarks. 'Let's put some flowers round the door,' she said. So we uprooted some daffodils from the woods and replanted them on each side of the steps, and Ginnie sprinkled water from Galadriel's Pool around the caravan as part of a little spell to bring Gail closer. I no longer put much faith in Ginnie's spells, but at least Erryk's twitchiness subsided, which was a relief. We settled down to wait.

In the meantime, talk among the women had turned once again to Greenham Common, where another big protest was supposedly imminent.

'Oh, we must *all* go this time,' said Stella.

'Yes!' shouted Rain.

'Not you, stupid,' said Shine. 'It's women only, remember?'

'We've only got two tents,' Marjoram pointed out. 'We'll need to get at least one more.'

'Layla and I can sleep in one of the cars,' said Shine.

'I'm not sleeping in a car *or* a tent,' said Layla. 'Aren't there hotels?'

'Actually, I'd rather avoid tents myself this time,' said Jack. 'My hip-bones aren't what they used to be. I'm pretty sure there'll be room for me and Layla in my friends' caravan. The ones we saw there in December. They said they weren't planning to leave until the missiles did.'

So in what seemed a matter of days all the necessary preparations were made – and then, before we had time to fully take in what was happening, they were off. Even Barbara joined the exodus, much to Ashley's chagrin. Ginnie put a notice in the window of the shop to the effect that it was closed until further notice in order to save the children of the world from destruction. It all took place so fast that us Lothlorien males scarcely had time to realise that for the first time ever we were abandoned in a woman-free world.

No-one was worried about the management side of it; daily chores were something we were all used to, and as our number was now reduced by half there wasn't going to be much more to do than usual, apart from in the Garden. Gogo and Bill quickly set up a rota of gardening and meal-making teams: Bill and Rick, Gogo and Sean, Erryk and Rain, Ash and myself. Rick and Sean obviously couldn't be paired; it was clear from the first evening that they would be bingeing on grass and mushrooms, now that Stella and Zoë weren't there to nag them into keeping their consumption within reasonable limits.

Very noticeable were the changes in the pattern of sounds and movement. We all talked more loudly, as if to compensate for the lack of female voices, and filled the silences with stupid jokes. I kept looking around expecting to see Marjoram striding over to the garden, Ginnie gliding between the caravans, Loose and Jelly Bean having some kind of game up a tree... 'It's not the same, is it?' said Gogo, and it certainly wasn't. I think we all felt a bit lost.

It was into this weirdly depleted Lothlorien that Gail finally made her appearance.

Spring had more or less arrived; Sean and I were down in the clearing by Galadriel's Pool for an afternoon session of exercises. Although by no means a weakling, I felt that bulkier biceps could be a useful aid for pulling women, and Sean was only too happy to help me expand them.

We were using a convenient horizontal branch to do pull-ups, and were suspended a few feet off the ground when we caught sight of Erryk and an unknown woman walking slowly down the path in our direction. They didn't spot us immediately, as they had their heads down in quiet but intense conversation.

'At last! The Lady cometh!' Sean called out. He did a double somersault round the branch and then hung with his legs stretched horizontally towards them.

They stopped and looked up.

'WOW!' exclaimed Sean. 'Gollum!' He dropped down, and I did the same.

Erryk's cheek twitched violently, but Gail – for it was indeed she – just looked mildly bemused. Either she hadn't properly heard what Sean had said, or else she was one of those Outsiders who had no inkling of the existence of Middle Earth. (This was long before the movies came out).

It was true that she did have a waxen look about her, and light eyes which looked unnaturally large behind big round glasses; she was also rather skinny. In all other respects, however, she was entirely un-Gollum-like. But then Sean was very stoned, and may in any case have had a mental picture of Gollum very different from my own. 'She's a stretched-out Betty Boop in specs,' said Rick later, which was a much more accurate description.

She was about as tall as Erryk, with short dark hair curling outwards in slightly spiky clumps from a widow's peak, which made her face look like a pale heart. I couldn't take my eyes off her mouth, a Cupid's bow shiny with plum-coloured lipstick.

Erryk was frowning very pointedly at Sean, who by now had probably realised that he'd been a touch tactless. To make up for this he fell to his knees and swept one arm towards the Pool. 'My Lady Gail, let me present you to our Lady Galadriel. Your name tells me you were once related. May she nourish your dreams as she nourishes ours.'

Gail's expression grew a little more surprised.

Erryk coughed. 'Don't mind Sean. He's our kind of, er, court jester. And this is Curly, my...'

'Caravan companion,' Gail finished for him. 'Very pleased to meet you.' She gave a small smile and held out her hand. I thought it might be limp and cold but it was in fact quite warm and firmish. She looked younger than Erryk; that would do him good, I thought. Sometimes he seemed a bit like an old man.

'And now go on your way in peace,' said Sean.

'See you at dinner,' said Erryk. 'Beetroot soufflé.'

Gail's mouth quivered – whether with amusement or foreboding I couldn't tell.

We didn't see all that much of either her or Erryk for the next few days, except at mealtimes. They spent much of the time in what was now her caravan, so I had ours largely to myself. When Gail did appear she was always perfectly pleasant, though she hadn't yet lost the slightly dazed look she'd had at our first meeting.

'That's because of All She's Been Through,' I said to Rain. Whatever that was – and it remained forever a mystery – she didn't seem as traumatised as we'd expected. 'All that breathing in Wales,' said Rain. 'It must have cleared things out.'

In front of Gail all the men were terribly polite: the jokes and banter were replaced by a gallantry almost as great as Sean's.

'It's because they're missing the women,' I said.

'They just enjoy the chance to show off to a new one when the others aren't here,' said Rain. 'It's spooky seeing them like that. Even Ash and Rick.'

'Well, the women would normally be doing most of the welcoming bit, wouldn't they? Showing her around and explaining stuff. So the guys have had to take over.'

In fact, I think they were making a special effort for Erryk's sake.

Bill and Gogo made a point of outlining to Gail all the philosophy and history (abridged) of Lothlorien. She listened patiently.

'You're not *really* drop-outs though, are you?' she said. 'You all depend on Outside for lots of stuff. And most of you earn money.'

'Of course we *interact* with Outside,' said Gogo, 'some of us more than others. But when Outside begins seriously to crumble, as it must do sooner or later, we'll be able to remain autonomous, because we grow our own food. What we don't grow we can do without, if necessary.'

'What about clothes? And soap and things?'

'Fabric can be made from plants such as flax, which we'd begin to cultivate. Certain tree barks could be useful as well. To make soap you need seed oils and a substance called lye, which is easy enough to produce from wood ash.'

Good old Gogo. He had an answer for everything.

'But for the time being,' Bill interjected, 'as I have always said, we choose to be *in* the world but not *of* it.'

It was some time since I'd heard him come out with that. I found it rather comforting, because recently the atmosphere had seemed to me to be doubly dislocated: no women except this new one, and the men acting almost like strangers. It no longer felt like the Lothlorien I knew.

So I was much relieved about a week later when with a whoop and a cheer and a scream of tyres Loose skidded into the gravel parking space. With her was Layla. Rain and I rushed to greet them.

'Oh, oh, oh!' cried Loose. 'So long away from you, I couldn't bear it. Too much time with too many women, all being *English* together.'

'They're English in here, apart from you.'

'But not so concentrated. And there's only six – and Stella is Scottish, anyway. Over there, there were thousands and *thousands*, terribly English. We made a chain! That was fun, it was so long it could have gone to the moon. I took wonderful photos.'

'I think you mean eight,' said Layla. 'Women. In here. You can't count Jelly Bean.'

'There's more now,' said Rain. 'Gail's arrived.'

'Hoorah!' said Loose. 'Is she beautiful? Does she love Erryk?'

'You can judge for yourself,' I said.

'Where are the others?' asked Rain.

'They are staying there. At least one more week. Because of *so-li-dar-ity*. Oh, I am so *bored* by that word. I don't want to be solid!'

'Neither do I,' said Layla. She was looking unusually bedraggled. 'Mud!' she said, stamping her feet. 'And no proper showers. I'd never have gone if I'd known.' She pulled her case from the boot of the car. 'Now I'm going to spend two hours getting clean and then I'm going to do my hair and then please, *please* Loose, take me to Middington. I can't live without Giovanni for one single moment longer.'

Loose laughed. 'She has had terrible – how did you say it Layla?'

'Withdrawal symptoms.'

21. *DEPARTURES*

'CURLY, YOU ARE very *boring* these days.'

Thus spake Loose. She had just burst into the caravan without knocking, and found me slouched listlessly on the settee, staring into space and fiddling idly with my hair.

Her remark stung, and I frowned.

'You have stopped moving. You are in a *rut*.' She grabbed my hands and hauled me to my feet. 'Come with me. We will go to pick up some *crottes de mouton*.'

Sheep droppings. Gogo and Marjoram dug them into the Garden as fertiliser.

'Why can't Gogo get them?'

'Because Marjoram isn't here and he must work twice more than usually.'

'It's raining.'

'So? You can wear a bag, like me.'

Loose always dressed like no-one else; it was only now that I registered that beneath her bright Peruvian woolly hat, the long ear-flaps pulled well down, she was wearing a huge black plastic rubbish bag with holes cut for her head and arms. It almost swamped her. 'Look! I have one for you. Here -' Before I could protest she had pulled it over my head. 'Woo hoo! Now you look *sexy*!'

I wasn't very flattered. If it took a rubbish bag to make me look sexy I reckoned there wasn't much hope for me.

She dragged me outside. 'And now we will race to the top of the Sheepfield! We will collect the *crottes* on the way down.'

She started running – out of the woods, over the stile, and diagonally up across the field, stopping for a moment by the big oak tree to pat a few of the sheep, clustered there for shelter. That gave me a chance to shorten her lead: suddenly I was desperate to catch up with her. My legs were longer than hers, for God's sake. But she was lighter and more agile, and I only just managed it. We stopped at the top of the field, laughing and out of breath. The rain was falling harder now – big warm drops sploshing and bouncing on our improvised rainwear.

'The barn!' said Loose, and darted into the next field towards its gaping entrance.

The barn was very old, and smelled of mice and abandonment. But most of it was dry, apart from a spot where rain dripped through a large hole in the roof on to ancient shreds of straw and a few pieces of rusting farm equipment. I'd played here as a child, but had shunned it completely ever since Tiger Lily had confessed to me what she and Sean had used it for.

'Up there!' Loose pointed to a wooden ladder which leaned against a high platform of planks laid across the beams. She scampered up the ladder and vanished. Then her head, now hatless, reappeared out of the gloom. 'Come on Curly! There is more soft stuff here.'

I followed. Close to the top a rung gave way and I almost fell. I clutched on to the planks above and heaved myself over the top, glad of my expanded biceps. I could make out a layer of straw partly covered by what seemed to be a duvet with a purple cover. Loose was sitting on it, pulling off her black plastic bag. Beneath it she was naked. Her pubic hair was trimmed to a neat triangle; even in the half-light I could see it was dyed electric blue. My erection was instantaneous.

I didn't stop to think – I ripped off my clothes and just let her hands guide me, and collapsed in a shuddering heap barely thirty seconds later. Loose lay completely still.

Eventually I lifted my head, rolled off her and stared – utterly thankful but in a daze of bewilderment. 'Why...?'

She leaned over and pulled my ears gently. 'Because it is the right time and I think you are very nice, Curly.'

'But – Jack...'

'Is not here. And anyway will not mind. She knows that I am a little bit bi.' She giggled and began to sing. '*Sometimes I – am a little bit bi, et des fois chui – juste un petit peu bi...* And now, when you have had a rest, we will get down to some serious business.'

*

What a week. An ecstatic, hilarious, dream-like week. I couldn't have hoped for a better teacher. It was impossible to be shy with Loose: she was so straightforward, and yet so very, very kind. And acrobatic. I've never since had a lover who could twist herself into so many fascinating positions. Each day she astounded and enchanted me.

Back in Lothlorien I was in a state of complete euphoria – but nobody seemed to notice. They were all too busy being nice to Gail. Rain, deep in Outer Space, didn't suspect a thing. Loose was well aware that our trysts had to be kept secret, so every day we would head out of the woods at slightly different times and in opposite directions. Everyone was used to me wandering off on my own. When we were both far enough away to be out of sight we looped round towards the barn, where we would shin gleefully up the ladder to the glorious purple duvet – which, I realised with awe, had been pre-prepared by Loose in readiness for that first miraculous afternoon.

Afterwards, I sometimes wondered what Tiger Lily would have said about all this.

Most likely she would have laughed and laughed, and congratulated me. But she never crossed my mind while I was making love with Loose, who was so extraordinary, so funny – and sometimes so intense – that she swept everything and everyone else out of my head.

Now and then I was gripped by a terrible claw of guilt when I thought of Jack. 'You won't tell her, will you?' I begged. I couldn't bear the idea of hurting her, or of her hating me.

'Curly, this is *our* time,' said Loose. 'It has nothing do with Jack.'

Then my guilty feelings would be burnt up in the volcano of my lust. An unfortunately over-the-top metaphor – but the only one that seems aptly to describe that explosive time. I didn't mind in the least being a temporary bisexual episode in Loose's sex life; she'd made it clear that she'd seduced me out of real desire, not pity or curiosity.

'I want you to remember this always,' she said. As if I could forget. I'm still lost in grateful wonder when I think of all she did for me.

Naturally we knew that as soon as the others came back our erotic interlude would come to an end. Now I wanted them to stay at Greenham Common for weeks, months... But of course they didn't.

We were dozing on the duvet when we heard the cars – luckily at the end, rather than the beginning, of a particularly energetic and fulfilling afternoon. I started up in alarm. Loose pushed me back down again. 'Don't worry. We will just go to meet them as if we are coming back from a walk. No-one will think anything about it.' She gave me a long kiss. 'Thank you, Curly.'

I was very moved. 'Thank *you*,' I whispered.

*

Lothlorien was back to normal. The women were overflowing with stories of their 'holiday', as Rick termed it (much to their annoyance); I can't say I took much of them in. I had other things on my mind. I was feeling magnificent, as if I could take on the world.

Nevertheless, from time to time my guilt towards Jack flamed and itched like a prickly internal rash. I didn't think Loose had told her – Jack was acting completely normally towards me. But I knew she was super-observant, so surely she'd noticed the change in me and put two and two together? If she had, she didn't say anything. She was in high spirits – she'd sold several articles and been approached by a feminist publisher for a book on the Greenham Common women, to be illustrated with Loose's photos. Loose herself occasionally caught my eye or flashed me a quick wink, which was a slight comfort, although it hardly made up for what I was missing.

However, with my new sense of myself as a sexual Colossus, I had no doubt that with a bit of effort I could now score Outside. Housewives weren't currently an option, as Ash and I were once again occupied with work for Our Lord; we were converting his own rather austere ex-nursery into something which Mrs Lord thought would be more suitable for modern-day baby accommodation. I was glad I'd spent my childhood down in Lothlorien rather than in the labyrinthine corridors of the House, their dark lino floors musty with ancient floor polish and faint odours of decay. 'Dry rot and mouldy wallpaper,' said Ashley. 'Toff-stink.'

The next time he had to go into Chandleford I asked him to take me and Rain with him – I thought that it would be a better hunting ground than Middington, which seemed too close to home. It was easy to persuade Ash to spend all afternoon there, once I'd explained that we needed some extended time for what we were hoping to achieve.

Rain was pessimistic about our chances of success – until I had a stroke of inspiration. 'Let's pretend we're French. They'll fall for the accent.'

'They won't believe us. I'll never be able to keep it up, anyway.'

'Of course you will. Just imagine you're in a play.' In our woodland theatrical productions Rain's shyness disappeared when he had a different identity to hide behind.

And so it proved today. To our great delight we succeeded quite easily in chatting up a couple of girls waiting in a cinema queue, from which we extricated them with an invitation to the town's most up-market coffee bar. They must have been a couple of years older than us, but I was sure that Rain and I had a certain suave *je ne sais quoi* lacking in the local boys.

Over cappuchinos we explained in halting English that we were exchange students from Paris. 'Gay Paree!' said the blonde one, and we laughed and nodded encouragingly and murmured lascivious comments to each other in French.

Because we made sure that our grasp of English appeared elementary, the girls weren't afraid to murmur comments of their own, and from these we gathered that the blonde thought I was cute. 'I quite fancy that foreign look,' she said in a stage whisper, while I looked innocently off to one side. 'Well that's handy, cause I like the other one,' said her chestnut-haired and slightly fatter friend. 'He's fucking gorgeous.'

I could see that Rain was having trouble keeping a straight face so I kicked him under the table. 'Excuse me,' I said politely, in an attempt to distract attention away from him, 'What means this word "fucking"?'

The girls dissolved into giggles. 'You tell them,' said the blonde.

'Well now,' said her friend, 'It's a bit complicated, really. Spose we show you?'

I hurriedly paid the bill.

It was a weekday afternoon at the beginning of the school holidays: the girls' parents were at work, leaving two empty houses at our disposal. In one of these we both, as Ash would have said, got our end away – I really can't glorify that occasion with a less prosaic description. Luckily Rain's conquest was the more outgoing and probably more experienced of the two girls, which must have made things easier for him. Mine was boringly passive, almost blasé, but it was still a triumph of a kind: if I could make it here, then I could make it anywhere.

'I've done it! I've done it!' Rain kept repeating afterwards, once we'd got away from the girls. He was in a trance of joy and astonishment. I knew how he felt.

'Mission accomplished, if I'm not mistaken,' said Ash, when we met up with him in the car park.

We grinned and nodded vigorously.

'Good for you. Always best to start early if you can.'

On the way home we all sang loudly and bawdily, until as we were turning into the drive Ashley suddenly broke off. 'Bugger. Should've slipped you a few condoms. Don't want you getting half of Chandleford up the duff.'

'It's OK,' said Rain nonchalantly, 'they were both on the Pill.'

*

Back in Lothlorien we found Ginnie pouring libations round the Fireplace.

'Wonderful news!' she said. 'The baby's arrived.'

We couldn't think what she was talking about.

'The new saviour of the world,' said Rick. 'The Lordling.'

'Oh, that,' said Rain.

'Not *that*!' said Ginnie. '*Him*. His name is Julian Charles Timothy.'

'That's his problem,' said Ashley, but he went up to the House next day all the same, to offer his congratulations and a dozen home-brewed beers. 'Momma Lord got stuck into those right away,' he told us.

Rain and I weren't remotely interested in the new baby, but like everyone else we enjoyed Sean's accounts of Mrs Lord's post-natal fitness classes.

'She still needs to shed some body fat, but she's got this totally amazing anterior core. Glutes like fucking iron. And shit man, you should see her abs. Unreal. I told her, lady, you've got the funkiest abs I ever saw on a chick, and she's like, wow man, awesome, let's get down.'

'She can't have said that,' said Stella.

'Might have been different words, but that was the vibe.'

'You have a psycho-muscular connection,' said Bill, with a rare spark of humour.

'Too right, man.' Sean stretched comfortably.

Stella sighed. 'So long as you're happy.'

'She's going to need a nanny soon,' said Zoë. 'She told me she wants to get back into athletics.'

'Doesn't get anough sport at home.'

'Shut it, Ash.'

'I could do that,' said Gail suddenly. 'Be her nanny, I mean. I'm good with babies.' She gave a sideways glance at Erryk, who looked away rather nervously. This gave me pause for thought. Erryk as daddy? It wasn't beyond the bounds of possibility. He'd been fatherly enough to me.

So Gail was partially adopted into the Lordly circle, as was Barbara too, invited to do some landscaping in the Grounds. The symbiotic relationship between House and Elfland had never been so solidly entrenched.

'It's feudal,' said Ash. 'They keep us here as a pool of sodding hippie serfs. Temporary labour when required.'

'That seems to me a perfectly fair arrangement by which both sides benefit,' said Bill. 'You in particular. And bear in mind that not all of us have a work relationship with the House.'

'Oh yes, I was forgetting. You're just his very best buddy.'

But funnily enough, quite soon after this Bill found himself working up at the House after all. Fearing for the safety of his son and future heir, Our Lord asked him to replace all the House's antiquated wiring. It was a long and complicated job involving dimmer switches, new floor lights from nursery to bathroom, heated towel rails and so on, and we could tell that Bill didn't want to do it – especially as it meant he would have to refuse some far more prestigious work for at least two rock festivals, which would have been more interesting and no doubt considerably better paid.

'But we can't have the baby getting electrocuted, now can we?' said Ginnie brightly. So for several weeks Bill was fully occupied preventing this potential disaster, while Mr Lodge and a mate of his took care of the attached masonry work and redecorating. I thought I could have done a far better job than these two, but I wasn't asked.

I turned fourteen that summer – though I felt, and looked, a good deal older. Being tall helped. I'd shot up recently and hoped I didn't have too much further to go – I didn't want to be a freak. I was several inches taller than Rain by now, and towered above Blue. 'Anybody up there?' he shouted, when we loped into the fairground that season, on the prowl as usual but above all eager to boast to him of our sexual accomplishments in Chandleford. Our first success had been followed by another, again thanks to our assumed Gallic charm and sophistication. On one occasion we'd tried being ourselves, but that didn't get us nearly so far. I wondered how much longer I was going to have to fuck with a French accent.

'Touch of the old oo-la-las, eh?' said Blue. 'I'll have to try that. Maybe I can get that Loose to teach me a bit more of the lingo.'

Or maybe not – because Loose, quite suddenly and unexpectedly, had gone to Carcassonne for her brother's wedding. She'd travelled by train because she hated flying, and crossed the Channel by hovercraft, 'because it's like riding on a beetle which floats.' I missed her hugely. Although I knew quite well that our enchanted week could never be repeated, the complicity implied in her occasional little looks and winks assured me that it really had happened – that I'd known the glories of top quality, high voltage love-making rather than simply casual sex with strangers.

I knew she had relations somewhere in south-west France, but she'd never talked about them much. 'She's a lot more *famille* than you think,' said Jack, 'even if she cut herself off for a while. They may not approve of her relationship with me, but they'd never turn against her the way my parents did.'

'We're your family!' said Shine.

Jack smiled rather sadly. 'Yes. I'm lucky. Sometimes the family you choose is better than the one you get born into.'

I tried to imagine Loose in France. Carcassonne: the name had a romantically brutal ring to it. How I longed to be there too, making violent yet poetic love to her on the hot ramparts under the blazing southern sun. I wrote a few atrocious poems on the subject.

*

'Look! a letter from France!' It was among the Lothlorien mail which Shine had brought down from the Lodge, on a day when Loose had already been away for what felt like far too long. I looked at the envelope. The stamp had a picture of a castle on it, and on the back Loose had written her full name: Lucette Civel. Shine said it out loud, and it sounded as if it belonged to a stranger. The two of us hurried to the campervan, and Shine presented the envelope to Jack with a flourish.

'Goodness, what a treat,' said Jack. 'She's not much of a letter writer, Mademoiselle Loose. Must have been an interesting wedding.' She pushed her typewriter to one side and slit the letter open. But as she read, her face slowly turned to a mask of stone. We watched with dismay – was Loose ill?

Jack put the letter down slowly and stared straight ahead without moving. We didn't dare to speak.

'She's not coming back,' she said at last. Her voice was leaden.

We were aghast, unbelieving.

Jack gave herself a little shake and attempted a hollow chuckle. 'Must be catching, this marriage business. She's decided to get hitched as well, can you believe it. Some friend of her brother's she knew as a child.'

'But – but -' I stammered. 'She can't – she can't. Why would Loose want to get *married*?'

'Who can tell? It might be just a whim – she feels like a new experience. I know she wants to have a child.'

'She could have done that here!' exclaimed Shine. 'What about the sperm banks?'

'Yes, we had talked about that kind of thing. I suppose I wasn't sufficiently – enthusiastic.' She closed her eyes. 'I wanted her all to myself, you see.'

At that moment I was struck by an utterly terrifying thought. *What if Loose had already been pregnant when she left*? I realised now that during my week of rapture this possibility had never even crossed my mind. Surely, surely she'd taken the necessary precautions – the Pill, a coil? I knew all about these things... But no, they took time, you had to go to a doctor, she couldn't have planned that far ahead. She hadn't known she was going to get tired of Greenham Common and come back before the others... In that case, she must have picked a time when she knew it was safe. On the other hand, was it *ever* completely safe? My head reeled.

I tried to calculate – we'd been together in the spring, probably around the middle of April; she'd left soon before my birthday, so that made it a little over three months... No. A second woman leaving Lothlorien because she'd become pregnant by the wrong person would just be too much of a coincidence. It couldn't happen.

Or perhaps it could.

'She might – change her mind -' ventured Shine.

'She won't.' Jack dropped her head in her hands and we crept away.

By evening the news had spread to all the inhabitants of Lothlorien. The woods were awash with shock and sadness. Even Gail and Barbara seemed devastated; although they hadn't known Jack and Loose for very long they still understood that a seismic fracture had taken place in our community. It wasn't of course on the same plane of awfulness as Pete's suicide, but we were nevertheless in mourning of a kind. Jack's despair percolated into all of us. Her loss was by far the greatest, but we'd all loved Loose.

And I seethed with egocentric guilt: impregnator or not, it was all my fault, because it must have been my adventure with Loose which had persuaded her to return to the world of heterosexuality. I'd betrayed Jack – I should have resisted. But how could I have done?

*

For days after this Jack was either drunk or asleep. She waved away the meals we brought her, surviving on the store of alcohol she kept under the campervan settee and a few packets of crisps. She threw away her French cigarettes and started chain-smoking a vile-smelling American brand which she got Ashley to buy for her in Middington. Her skin became grey: she looked old. We were horrified to see her brought so low.

'She has to grieve – this is her way of doing it,' said Marjoram.

We tried to do our best for her on a practical level; we couldn't force her to eat, but at least we could clear Loose's remaining clothes and personal belongings out of the campervan. That was a particularly bad moment.

'What do you want us to do with all this?' asked Stella. There wasn't all that much stuff to dispose of. Loose had taken her most precious possessions with her: her two cameras, folding tripod, extra lenses, all of which she'd wrapped carefully in clothes inside the big new red suitcase she'd bought before she left – she'd said she was going to be the official photographer at the wedding. She had also taken most of her photographs, we discovered, apart from those for the Greenham Common book.

'Oh, give it to the Oxfam shop,' said Jack, kicking over her bottle of sherry. She was sprawled in one of the folding chairs, flicking ash on to the grass.

'Do you have her address?'

'Address, oh yes. A-*dress*.... A *wedding* dress...' She swung round in my direction, and I felt she was speaking only to me. 'Anyway – what's one more broken heart in the life of the Universe? Absolutely sweet fuck all *nothing*.'

No-one dared ask her what we should do with the darkroom and its contents. 'Let's give all the equipment to the photographer's shop in Middington,' suggested Shine sensibly. The structure itself, a constant reminder of Loose, we dismantled.

Erryk looked at the remains sadly. 'Remember, Curly, when we...?' Of course I did.

After about a week Jack roused herself from her torpor, threw away her empty bottles and pulled the cover off her typewriter. We felt hopeful, and plied her with good food. She had obviously resolved to try and return to some kind of normality – but when she sat writing at her table outside the campervan she often stopped and just stared ahead for minutes at a time, expressionless and unmoving.

It was at one of these moments, as I walked quietly past on my way to see Rain, that she suddenly stirred and called me over. 'Fancy a game of chess, Curly?'

I confess I didn't want to go – I hadn't been alone with Jack since the arrival of the letter. But I didn't see how I could refuse.

'Let's go inside – it looks as if it's going to rain,' she said.

While she brought her writing things into the campervan I fetched the chessboard and laid out the pieces. Jack switched on the kettle. 'I think it's teatime, don't you?'

The false cheeriness in her voice made me extremely uneasy. Had she guessed? I couldn't bring myself to speak. She opened the biscuit tin and set it on the table. I couldn't stop myself looking inside: I saw a mixture of custard creams and chocolate fingers. 'Comfort food,' said Jack, and brought our mugs of tea.

She sat down heavily but ignored the chessboard. 'Curly – there's something I need to ask you.'

Dread poured over me. I plunged my hand into the biscuit tin.

'You probably all realise – I can't go on like this.'

'You're not –'

'Don't panic, I'm not going to do a Pete. I mean I can't stay in Lothlorien.'

I let go of my custard cream.

'While Loose and I were together here it seemed like a little Paradise – where we were welcome, and safe. Even if we had to go Outside, I knew we'd always be coming back. But now I just feel trapped inside a cage of memories. The only way I can get on with my life is start again somewhere else.'

I still couldn't bring myself to say anything.

'So I think I'll go to London.'

'London?'

'I've got a house there, you know.' I didn't know. She might as well have said 'I've got a plot of land on the moon.'

'It's near Kew Gardens,' she went on, as I continued to gaze at her in astonishment. 'It's not very big – my mother moved there after my father died. Then when *she* died a few years back she left it to me. As a sort of belated apology, I think. Pity she didn't try conversation.' She laughed rather harshly. 'My aunt and uncle were furious – they thought it should have gone to them. Tough shit.'

'You never talked about all that here.'

'Well I did, up to a point, but not to you lot. You wouldn't have been interested.'

'So that's where you'll go?'

'For the time being. It's been let until now, through an agency – to foreign students. But it's empty in the summer. I'll just tell the agency I don't want new tenants for the autumn term.'

I was having difficulty taking all this in. And I was weighed down by the certainty that I was the root cause of this dreadful double exodus.

'Now – what I wanted to ask you –'

Automatically I reached in the biscuit tin once more, and this time pulled out a chocolate finger.

'– would you care to come and stay with me for a while? The house is sure to need a good deal of work and I'd be glad of some help. And I'd appreciate your company.'

My hand froze in mid-air and I dropped the biscuit again.

'Not having much luck with those, are you? Listen, you don't have to give me an answer today. Just think about it, that's all.'

'But –' I floundered helplessly, trying to find the right words, my burden of guilt now completely unbearable. 'There's something you ought to know,' I blurted.

Jack looked at me with immense compassion. 'I know already, Curly. Loose told me. No – don't try and say anything. I was really, really happy for you, believe me. It was exactly what you needed. And it had bugger all to do with what Loose has done now. She's a totally free agent, she never lets anyone influence her. She just follows her heart.'

I suppose I was still looking anguished, because Jack put a hand on my arm. 'I always knew I was – well, just a phase for her. Even though I still wanted to kid myself that maybe... But how could she have spent the rest of her youth with an ageing dyke?'

'You're not –'

'Face facts, Curly. Oh, for God's sake, don't start crying or you'll set me off as well.'

I sniffed hard.

'And by the way – in case you were wondering, Loose was still having periods before she left.' She smiled. 'Now you can eat your biscuits with a clear conscience.'

When I left the the campervan I ran all the way down to the river and back again. I was weightless, absolved, forgiven. And I was going to London.

*

'You'll have to be really careful while out there,' said Shine gravely.

'What of?'

'Bad influences. Television, people... women.'

'I'm pretty sure I'll be able to handle the women,' I said airily.

'You and Rain think you're so cool, don't you? Just because you *bonk* such a lot in Chandleford.' (We'd wildly exaggerated our exploits, using the most vulgar terminology we knew, just to annoy her). 'In London it'll be quite different. You could get a disease.'

'Yeah, yeah. So my knob'll drop off.'

'Well, it might.' She looked thoughtful. 'How long are you going to be away?'

'Dunno. As long as it takes.'

'I don't suppose you'll be back before the Solstice. By that time I expect I'll have lost my virginity too.'

I was quite surprised. 'I thought you were Miss Pure and Virtuous.'

'I am. I'll do it in a very pure way.'

'So who's the lucky bloke? Or haven't you met anyone pure enough yet?'

'I have, actually. In the reference library. I knew that would be a good place to look. It's got to be someone who understands the importance of education, because I can't let sex get in the way of my O-levels.'

'Wow. Bonk'n'read.'

'It's a pity you don't understand, Curly, that the act of love can be an act of *poetry*.'

If only she knew.

The twins would be taking their O-level exams next year; Gogo had got hold of the relevant syllabus and both were well advanced in their studies. They didn't want to go to school but each intended to go to university, Shine to read law and Rain engineering. I couldn't picture a similar path for myself – I liked reading, writing, drawing and woodwork, but didn't feel the need for some Outside institution to tell me how to pursue any of these activities. Geography interested me too; one day I would travel the world and experience deserts, mountains and tropical islands in the flesh. And exotic women.

Layla saw her future much closer to home – she had given up her fashion ambitions and was now planning with Giovanni to take over his parents' restaurant. 'You – *cooking*?' said Shine. Layla wasn't known for her culinary enthusiasm. 'Of course not,' she said. 'Giovanni'll cook, and I'll be in charge of the ambience. I'll buy lovely tableware and welcome the clients, and we'll be in all the best guidebooks. We're going to change the name to *Casa Layla*.'

Jelly Bean looked at her suspiciously. 'Will you serve meat? And fish?'

'Only Italian things. *Calamari, vongole, scallopini di vitello, pollo ai funghi*... Really pretty and delicate.'

'How about Layla ai funghi? In teeny weeny slices?'

Recently Jelly Bean had managed to make herself useful to the wardens of a large National Trust property on the other side of Middington; she cycled over there every few days and scoured the estate for rare flora and fauna, which she carefully counted and listed. 'I'm their mascot,' she told me. 'They say I'm invaluable.'

'You can take tablets for that,' I said.

'It's better than going to smelly old London.'

'It's not smelly where Jack's house is. You know about Kew Gardens, don't you?'

'That's just a zoo for plants. Not real nature.'

By now I was impatient to leave; I felt more than ready to confront the unknown. Although I was still deeply attached to Lothlorien on many levels, I'd felt lately that some of my ties with it were subtly unravelling. Much of the attention that Erryk and Ash had previously given to me was now redirected to Gail and Barbara – not that I resented this. On the contrary, I was delighted they were both fixed up. Loose's departure had been much more unsettling, and I knew I'd miss Jack enormously when I came back. On the other hand, after London I'd be able to adapt much better to the altered Lothlorien; my new experiences would have turned me into a well-rounded, fully-fledged adult. I really did believe that.

Jack bought a second-hand Austin Minivan from the florist in Middington. She didn't want to take the campervan, even if it could be persuaded to function after being stuck for so long in one spot. We all understood why. Ash reckoned he could get it going, so she was only too pleased to donate it to him. 'Holiday home for me and Barbs,' he said. Better than the pick-up. Barbara thought so too, and started making plans for a trip to the Lake District.

'Females,' sighed Ashley. 'Watch out, Curly – they always want to organise you.' But I guessed that he didn't mind too much being organised by Barbara.

*

'Oh Curly – *both* of you!' Ginnie's eyes sparkled with tears. 'Of course, I do understand about Jack, and I know you'll be in good hands... but there's going to be such a *void*. We must have a great Communal Gathering to send you safely on your way.' Although I had never been able to take Ginnie entirely seriously, I was very touched.

Marjoram and Gogo were concerned for my diet. 'I hope you'll be able to find plenty of organic food,' said Marjoram.

'You can find anything you want in London,' I said. 'And Jack says they like that sort of thing in Kew. In Richmond too – that's next to it.'

'It's not just a question of food,' said Gogo. 'There's all the general contamination you'll have to watch out for.'

'Air pollution?'

'Yes, that of course, but I'm really talking about pollution of the mind. You're going to be surrounded by false values of all kinds. Materialistic greed. Selfishness. Violence Dishonesty. Exploitation.' It was almost as if he were listing the Seven Deadly Sins – though he left out Sloth and Vanity, perhaps out of deference to Sean.

'I'll be OK.'

I felt that I was amply prepared for London, having been well briefed not only by Jack but also Stella, Rick and Zoë. 'It's a den of vice,' said Rick. 'You'll have a blast.'

The Gathering was held on the day before we left. It was an afternoon towards the end of October; the woods were calm and thin sunshine filtered through the leaves, which were just beginning to turn and fall. The fire was lit at midday so the cooking could get going early – Gogo and Marjoram had insisted that everything should be cooked in the Fireplace, in the true spirit of Lothlorien. Everyone was there, even El, who made a special trip from Brighton. I began to see just how much our departure meant to the citizens of Elfland, at least for the hard core I'd known all my life.

'Oh Curly, we'll miss you so much,' said Stella. 'Jack too, of course, but you most of all.'

'It's not as if I'm going away for ever.'

'No – but when you come back I think you'll be sort of different.' She was echoing my own thoughts. She sighed. 'Though really you're different already, in some ways. You all are.'

'Of course we are. We've grown up, we've changed.'

'Yes...' Her voice sounded so wistful that I turned and gave her an enormous hug. Dear Stella – she missed the children she'd sometimes been able to pretend were her own.

'Come over to the caravan,' she said. 'I've got something to give you.'

She sat me at the table and got me to lay my head sideways on a cork mat. Then she fetched a needle and some alcohol and wiggled the needle until it pierced my ear lobe. It took longer than I'd expected for it to reach the far side and its passage wasn't entirely painless.

'Tough lobes, like me,' said Sean. 'But it's worth it, man.' He stroked his own ears, heavily decorated with rings, studs and dangling charms.

'I don't want all that!' I said, alarmed.

Stella laughed. 'Don't worry, this is all you're getting.' She inserted one of her silver five-pointed stars. I managed to keep it in there for years. I wish I hadn't lost it.

The evening started to draw in; Rick and Erryk brought their guitars out to the Fireplace, and Sean his bongos. Foil-wrapped parcels of food glinted and fizzed in the glowing embers of the fire. Blackberry wine and grass began to circulate and I had some of each – I'd never indulged very much in either substance, but this was an exceptional occasion. All of a sudden I had a vision of Galadriel's Pool – the place of my entry into Lothlorien – and knew I had to go there. There was only one person left of the three present at my birth: Marjoram. I wanted her to come with me.

We strolled down the path in the deepening twilight. The Pool glimmered eerily, still bright among the dark trees. A tiny fish jumped with a soft splash. Marjoram took my hand and led me to the far bank. 'This is where I bit off your umbilical cord. Just here.'

'And then you threw it in the water for the fish.'

She laughed softly. 'It was an offering to the Earth Mother.' She touched the trunks of the two crab-apple trees planted at the time of the twins' birth, and smiled. 'They're doing well, aren't they?'

We were silent for a moment. Then she said: 'Do you realise that you're the only real Elf in Lothlorien? Everyone else was born Outside.'

I pondered this. 'I may have been born here, but I wasn't *made* here. I mean conceived. All the others were.'

'True... but I don't think that makes much difference. Besides, you've got the ears. Like Wing.'

I thought about the others, all born in hospital. I knew that the twins' birth had been complicated, and that the Bean had been alarmingly premature, but what about Layla?

'Why wasn't Layla born here too?' I asked.

'I don't think Zoë had your mother's courage.'

'Was it really courage? Wasn't it just because she was stoned out of her mind all the time?'

'Maybe that too... I still wonder about Wing, you know. Don't you?'

'Not really.'

'But you must remember her.'

'Of course – but she was always in a kind of mist. Even when she was here she wasn't really... *here*, if you see what I mean.'

'No, I suppose not.' Marjoram sighed. 'We were all very fond of her, though...' After a pause she said unexpectedly: 'You know, I reckon your biological father must have been a pretty good guy.'

'Why? He didn't stay with Wing.'

'More likely she didn't stay with *him*. Or it could have been – oh, just one of those sixties flings. Perhaps they met at some festival and spent a couple of nights together and were too out of it to get any useful information about each other. Like phone numbers. They probably didn't even *have* phone numbers.'

A light gust of wind flittered over the surface of the Pool. Arm in arm we walked slowly back to join the party. A golden glow was brightening behind the trees. 'Full moon tomorrow,' said Marjoram. 'That's auspicious.'

The food, the music... all was as it should be. Jelly Bean had gathered a fabulous variety of mushrooms that afternoon, Erryk and Zoë cooked some of my favourite dishes, Barbara delighted us with her sweet potato fritters. She could sing, too, and belted out folk songs while Stella's soaring harmonies spun crystals in the air... I could see the notes dancing in the trees, because I was fairly stoned by then. It was almost impossible to imagine that tomorrow evening I wouldn't be here. I took a good few swigs from Erryk's bottle of dandelion liqueur, while he and Rick played an updated version of his old song: *The Ballad of Curly Oswald*. Normally I would have been embarrassed by that throw-back to my childhood past, but tonight I enjoyed it.

At the end of the evening, at a signal from Ginnie, everyone stood up. 'Stay there by the fire,' she said to me and Jack. She'd brought over one of the slender flasks of dark blue glass which she used for her rituals, and now she dripped water from it over our heads – water from the Pool, of course. Everyone else joined hands and began to circle round the Fireplace. 'May the magic of the Elves be with you always,' Ginnie intoned. 'May they guide you safely on your journey through the wilderness. Go with Galadriel's blessing.'

'Right on,' murmured Sean.

Wilderness? I was only going to London for a few weeks, perhaps a month or two...

Still, I'd imbibed enough of the Elfland spirit during my lifetime to feel a heartening eldritch frisson. Jack smiled politely, with only the faintest ironic twitch of her eyebrows.

It was time for the Ceremonial Hugs. By this time I was pretty far gone, and wasn't always sure whose arms I was falling into – until I came to the last hugger, who was Bill. Electricity Bill: the highest peak of Lothlorien, the Mount Everest of our community – not always visible, but ever present, even when hidden behind the clouds. Now I was practically as tall as he was.

He released me and put his hands on my shoulders. 'Well, Curly. I hope you'll be able to infuse your life Outside with all that you've learned in here. Remember: be in the world –'

'But not of it.'

At that moment the only place I wanted to be in was bed.

A little later I lay in a pleasantly fuzzy state while the moonlight streamed through my window and threw shadows on to my new rucksack on the floor, packed and ready for the morning. It hadn't seemed necessary to take much gear with me – certainly not my Laurie Anderson poster, ghostly on the ceiling above my head, an outgrown fantasy. I shut my eyes on her and fell asleep.

*

Next day the woods were veiled in a fine drizzle and leaves had begun to fall in earnest, damply and silently. Jack wanted to get going early; everyone was looking a little worse for wear as they assembled for the send-off, most of them under umbrellas or rain hoods. I'd drunk too much the night before and was discovering for the first time what a hangover felt like.

Jelly Bean, umbrella-free and with rain dripping from her nose and the ends of her hair, came forward with a folded plastic bag. 'It's a card we all made. Everybody's written something. Don't open it till you're in the car or it'll get wet.'

As I took it from her I could feel my throat constrict. I had an urge to run back to the caravan and bury myself under the covers until Erryk brought me a cup of tea and some muesli with a blob of hawthorn jelly. My head was bursting with things I could have said but hadn't: I wanted to go back and say an individual goodbye and thank you to each one of these people. My family.

Instead I mumbled 'See you soon,' and got into the Minivan. I turned round for a final look at the tableau standing quietly on the gravel beneath the patchy canopy of umbrellas. Behind them most of my home was concealed by the yellowing autumn trees.

It really was a final look, because I never went back to Lothlorien.

AFTERWORD

TWO MORE DAYS and I'll be out of here. The medical staff are delighted with me – but not half as delighted as I am with them. They've done a near-perfect remodelling job: apart from a few scars, various pieces of hardware in one leg, and the trace of a limp, I appear much as before.

The psychological remodelling has been more drastic – accumulated layers of Outsider stripped away so that Curly Oswald can live again. I'd been under the impression that I'd been skimming cheerfully over the surface of Outside like a water boatman, never getting even my feet wet – perhaps it was the fact that I was always on the move, always busy, that nourished that illusion. In fact I'd gradually sunk up to the waist. I hadn't become a complete Outsider – much of the world has always seemed to me like a bad sci-fi movie, and I could never have adopted all of its values. But I was certainly helping to prop them up. No point feeling bad about that – regret, as Gogo used to say, is not a viable option. Just take responsibilty for your actions, repair any damage as best you can, and change course. How? I'm not sure yet. I'm a skilled carpenter and joiner – I can always make a living. Somewhere else. Finland, perhaps? That would make a change... I've always wanted to see the Northern Lights – and there must be plenty of wood up there...

This fanciful reverie is interrupted by the nice nurse who comes to take a little more of my blood for testing. *'Vous allez nous manquer, Monsieur l'Ecrivain.'* We'll miss you, Mister Writer. *'C'est votre amie qui va venir vous chercher?'* She twinkles at me.

Ah. That's a point – who's going to fetch me? Certainly not a non-existent 'girlfriend', as the nurse seems to think. All my 'friends', in fact, girl or otherwise, now seem pretty much non-existent; their visits have been steadily dropping off. I've been too long out of circulation, I've faded into oblivion. Fortunately. Even Jeannette Evans seems to have given up on me recently – I confess I've missed the gastronomic treats she used to bring. And the faithful Marco is away working in Italy at the moment and I don't want to ring and ask him to come all this way just to take me – where? That's another point. The studio flat in Villefranche still has a few weeks left on the lease, and the one in San Remo a bit more – but the thought of going to either is repellent. Soon I'll have to deal with the cancellation of the leases and go and collect my junk, though I don't need much of it apart from a few clothes and some tools. But all that can wait for the moment.

To help me reflect on all this I go out into the garden for one of my regular walks. A couple of months ago I tottered on the arm of an orderly: now I stride around alone. As I walk the voices of Elfland still clamour in my head. This morning I read through my chronicle; there's so much I've left hanging in the air, unwritten. Why didn't I go back? What happened to Lothlorien? My false identity – how did that come about? But those are subjects which don't concern this story – that's to say the one I needed to set down in order to unearth what feels like the real Curly Oswald. It's as if I've rediscovered the poncho which Wing made for me all those years back, my name embroidered on it in woolly letters. So I prefer to leave Lothlorien and its inhabitants in their bubble, 'beyond time' in Ginnie's words, the surface now wiped clean of the moss which I'd allowed to grow over it, and from now on always accessible.

Re-entering that bubble now, a plan for my immediate future forms effortlessly in my mind. On the morning of my departure I'll charge my phone, switch it on, and order a taxi to the nearest village, as there's no public transport round here. After a leisurely meal in a simple restaurant I'll catch a bus to the nearest town and draw out some money from my much depleted bank account. From there: a train, another bus, and a walk of a few kilometres to a campsite in a pleasant valley – where I shall rent a caravan! What a brilliant idea.

*

An idea that was destined to undergo a certain degree of modification.

The day dawned; my phone was charging; I'd bagged up my exercise books and other belongings. I was feeling buoyant, almost light-headed.

Then in marched Jeannette.

'What in God's name are you doing here?' I was confused and angry.

'Great welcome – thanks. I've come to collect you.'

'How the hell did you know what day...?'

'This place has a phone, in case you hadn't noticed.'

'I don't need collecting.'

She sat down on the bed and looked at me thoughtfully. 'People who've nearly died are supposed to see life differently, aren't they? Like they've had a reprieve and everything looks wonderful. Isn't it like that for you?'

I was taken aback. 'Yes – I suppose it is, in a way.'

'So isn't it time you started acting a bit nicer?'

In spite of myself I laughed. 'Ok. Just for a few minutes.'

'Right. Where do you want me to take you?'

It seemed churlish not to take advantage of her offer, at least up to a point. 'Well – if you could drop me off at a station on the coast, that would be fine.'

'And then where are you going to go?'

'I'd rather keep that to myself, if you don't mind.'

'I do mind. Want to come and stay with me? I've still got the house. And the daughter. And the dog.'

'Thanks – '

'But no thanks. All right then – how about dinner one night? A good old Aussie barbie in the garden.'

'I'm a vegetarian.'

'I might have known. I'll grill you a couple of zucchini then.'

'I'll think about it.'

'You can help me celebrate my birthday. Thirty-eight next week.' She eyed me carefully. 'How old are you?'

'Forty-six.'

'You look younger than that.'

'When I was a teenager everyone thought I looked older than I really was. It came in very useful, as a matter of fact.'

'When's your birthday?'

'August, I think.'

'What do you mean, you think? You must know when your birthday is.'

'The date of my birth wasn't recorded.' A reckless giving-away of information, but I was surprised to find that I didn't really care.

'How come? Were you born up a mountain in Bhutan or something?'

'Not quite.'

'But you must have a birth certificate.'

'No, I haven't.'

She frowned. 'You can't get a passport without a birth certificate.'

'You can – with a little help from your friends. My passport isn't in my real name.'

'You mean you're not really Jack Robertson?'

'No.'

'Who are you then? And don't tell me you don't know that either.'

I stared at her for a second or two, and then took a deep breath. 'My name is Curly Oswald.' I looked down at the plastic bag bulging with exercise books. 'And by the way – you wouldn't like a typing job by any chance, would you?'

More from IndieBooks...

White Panther

Janez Janša

203BC: For the Karnian people, in the idyllic mountain passes of the Eastern Alps, the Roman Empire is no longer a distant menace: the legions are massing on their borders. It is a time for leaders to step forward - to try through diplomacy to save their independence, and to ready the weapons of war should they fail. Lan is the son of one of those leaders - eager to ride in battle to defend his country. But he must also learn from his father and from the elders of his tribe that courage must be tempered with judgement, and that power alone is not enough. In doing so, he witnesses the forging of a new nation - the Kingdom of Noric. A powerful yet lyrical tale that combines the sweep of history with the human impact of empire and war.

Janez Janša was the Prime Minister of Slovenia from 2004-2008 and 2012-2013, and held the post of Minister of Defence during the Slovenian war of Independence. He is currently leader of the Slovenian Democratic Party.

Quintember

Richard Major

When there are high crimes to be covered up, mysteries to be wrapped up in enigmas, or a murderer to be liquidated – literally – there is only one man in England who can be trusted with the task: Felix Culpepper, tutor in Classics at St Wygfortis College, Cambridge, and assassin-at-large for the British Establishment. From the eerie deserts of New Mexico to the high-rolling hotels of the Adriatic, Culpepper moves with consummate ease and an unexpected penchant for guns, drugs and esoteric methods of murder – all to save himself from the drudgery of cramming Latin into the privileged yet empty skulls of the dregs of Britain's aristocracy. With an intellectual vanity that rivals Holmes, more self-esteem than Bond and a blood-steeped amorality that out-Ripleys Hannibal Lector, Culpepper is the ideal hero for our debased days. And only in his student, side-kick (and pending Nemesis) Margot ffontaines, does he meet his match.

Why Willows Weep

Tracy Chevalier

A charming collection of stories and fables inspired by Britain's nineteen species of native trees, written by nineteen of Britain's leading authors. Why Willows Weep is edited by Tracy Chevalier, bestselling author of Girl with a Pearl Earring, and contains beautiful colour illustrations by Canadian artist Leanne Shapton. With sales in hardback of 10,000 this collection has already helped the Woodland Trust plant nearly 50,000 trees across the United Kingdom, and it is now available in paperback for the first time.

Contributors: Tahmima Anam, Rachel Billington, Terence Blacker, Tracy Chevalier, Amanda Craig, Susan Elderkin, William Fiennes, Philippa Gregory, Joanne Harris, Philip Hensher, Richard Mabey, Maria McCann, Blake Morrison, Kate Mosse, Maggie O'Farrell, Catherine O'Flynn, James Robertson, Ali Smith and Salley Vickers.

Latitude North

Charles Moseley

In this captivating work part travelogue, part history, part memoir of a life-long affair with the northern lands and seas traveller and scholar Charles Moseley describes a haunting world, where the voices of the past are never quiet. From his account of the last days of the Viking settlements in Greenland to his own experiences on the melting glaciers of Spitsbergen, he reminds us how deceptive are human ideas of permanence, and how fragile are the systems of these starkly beautiful lands.

"A love-affair for a region and a realm. Astonishing." *Robert Macfarlane*